Ad Majorem Dei Gloriam!

Jerry

3-4-18

VIGIL

Everyone is waiting.

Vigil

Book One of the Michael series

First published November 17, 2017 by Shalamar.
www.shalamarmedia.com

Cover art by Twila Dickinson of Twilight Designs.

ISBN 978-0-9978019-5-8 (paperback)
ISBN 978-0-9978019-4-1 (hardcover)
ISBN 978-0-9978019-6-5 (ebook)

Visit themichaelseries.com for more information.

In loving memory of Fr. Raymond Fitzgerald, S.J. ’76

Author's Foreword

Where did you go to school?

No, we mean high school. Nobody cares where you went to college. Only your high school matters.

Look, we've been patient. Lord knows we've been patient. We asked you how you met our friend, and we asked you about your job. We even nodded and pretended to listen. But now we need to know your brand. So what is it? Shaw? Franklin? Curtis? Karr? Lusher? Newman? Cabrini? Cross?

Which school is seared into your skin?

Please don't roll your eyes. We get that you don't get it. But families around here rarely break rank, so we've had a few generations to figure this thing out. We kind of know what we're doing. Trust us. Where you went is who you are.

Welcome to New Orleans!

Besides, we have this little ritual. We trade good-natured insults, and we recite the years our ancestors graduated ('23, '61, '87). We recall how we beat you or you beat us in whatever, and we act like it still bothers us (which it does). Then we assure each other that we're only joking, say something nice about the other school, and agree "the whole high school thing" is ridiculous.

Takes about fifteen minutes.

Of course, if you had the misfortune of growing up outside Louisiana, the ritual is much shorter. You tell us which state you're from, and we get you another drink.

Yes, we know it sounds silly.

But live here for a few years, and you'll learn to love our secret handshake. "Where did you go to school?" we'll ask. "Sorry, I didn't go to high school here," you'll reply with a knowing smile. "That's too bad," we'll joke. "Hey, isn't the whole high school thing ridiculous?"

Fun, right?

Well, we think so, but not everyone agrees.

Take Michael Broussard. Michael hated the question, which was particularly strange because Michael was a senior at Jesuit High School, and the Blue Jays are notoriously proud of their school. The Jesuit Mafia is everywhere, and the only thing Blue Jays love more than asking the question is *being asked* the question.

Except for Michael.

Most of the time, Michael fielded the question while working at Rock 'n' Bowl. The bowling alley was only a few blocks away from Jesuit and was always filled with Catholic League rivals. During any given shift, Blue Jays, Tigers, Raiders, and Saders just *had* to know whether Michael was friend or foe.

On good days, Michael abstained from the ritual. On bad days, Michael abruptly ended the conversation by announcing that his father was from Mississippi and he only went to Jesuit because his mother taught there "until she died a horrible death."

Now please don't get the wrong idea.

Michael didn't hate Jesuit. Far from it. He just couldn't shake the feeling that he didn't *belong* to the school and the school didn't *define* him.

Which is ridiculous. But, hey, that's how the kid felt.

The question had become an occupational hazard, but one Michael tolerated because he loved working at the bowling alley. The owners were his mom's closest friends. And when she died, they insisted on Michael's going to work for them.

Four years later, the bowling alley was home.

* * *

Prologue

It was almost midnight in Vatican City.

Pope Simon Peter II was staring seventy in the face, and he was doing it in red pajamas. It was the end of a very long day of formal birthday celebrations and private audiences in the Holy See.

So many well-wishers, he sighed. *Impossible to thank everyone.*

The Pope removed his Piscatory Ring and slowly rubbed his thumb over the bas-relief of a man in a boat. His first act as Pope had been to take the fisherman's name, and he was properly skewered for that decision. Critics called it "hubris." The devout found it wildly inappropriate, and sedevacantists howled with delight. But Simon Peter had been his mother's favorite, and he had promised to take his name if elected Pope. That he was only eleven when he made the promise mattered not.

Sometimes we must follow our heart, the Pope thought with a smile. *And tomorrow I will follow mine to Tivoli.*

Tomorrow, the Commander of the Pontifical Swiss Guard would smuggle the Holy Father out of the Apostolic Palace and drive him to the home of the Pope's brother in Tivoli. Nothing was better than sitting in front of Anna's red velvet birthday cake, flanked by the other November birthdays, and listening to the family sing "Happy Birthday."

But will they sing my name first? the Pope wondered. *Little Meredith complained last year when they started with the oldest, and she rules that roost. God bless her manipulative little heart.*

Church bells interrupted his thought and marked his birthday.

The Pope immediately placed the Fisherman's Ring in its ornate box and looked up at the simple oval mirror that once hung in his mother's bedroom. The gilded gesso wood had seen better days, but it was the only object in the Papal Apartment that actually belonged to him. They arrived together and would someday leave together.

"Seventy years ago," Pope Simon Peter II reminded the mirror, "you watched an extraordinary woman give birth to this ordinary little boy. Do you miss her as much as I do?"

Sadly, no pictures of his mother survived, but the Pope could always picture her reflection in the oval mirror, and tonight was no exception.

"Happy Birthday, Mother," he whispered, honoring a tradition he started the year after she passed. "Thank you for my life."

The Pope smiled as he felt the familiar rush of emotion.

After all these years, marveled the Pope, *I still feel the sting of your loss.*

The Holy Father wiped his eyes and headed for bed. When he reached the four-post behemoth, he grabbed the gold key hanging around his neck and tucked it under his pajamas top. Then he knelt and prayed the same prayer he prayed the night before. But, this time, he ended with a personal request.

Lord, I know they will someday come for the key, the Pope prayed, *but do not let them come tonight. I would like to see my family one more time.*

*   *   *

Chapter 1: Michael Broussard

And God said, Let there be light; and there was light
Genesis 1:3

Saturday, November 2

A storm was bearing down on the Big Easy, and nobody was tracking it. Certainly not the zealots inside Rock 'n' Bowl, who were busy worshipping the gods of strikes and spares. For them, the Mid-City institution was a well-lit oasis on a dreary afternoon. College football was on every screen, and the place was filled with the sound of truly mediocre bowling.

But not for long.

Saturday night would bring hordes of beer-chugging fraternities, bachelorette parties, band groupies, catty debutantes, hopeful divorcees, and high school reunions. Not to mention the most dangerous of all New Orleans night-life: stir-crazy first-time parents.

Michael glanced down at his watch. His shift was almost over, but he was already getting nervous. So he grabbed the nearest duster, waved to the owners' perpetually upbeat daughter, and pointed toward Lane One.

Emma smiled and sarcastically flashed her signature thumbs-up.

Lane dusting was Michael's favorite form of escape. Arguments with his father. Problems at school. Mother's Day. He could always lose himself in this one particularly mindless task. And, as usual, it worked.

Michael soon forgot about his rapidly-approaching blind date. Hypnotized by the tedium, he even failed to notice the end of his shift.

Emma did not.

"Michael Broussard!" the voice of Emma Landry announced over the intercom. "You have a date tonight. You have to go home now. Put the duster down, Michael. Put the duster down... and nobody gets hurt."

Bowling stopped.

Michael shook his head. Emma looked so normal. It was easy to forget she was an evil genius. But she was, and she had patiently waited until Michael was midway between the pin deck and foul line on Lane

Nine. Standing in the middle of eighteen lanes was like standing in the center of an empty dance floor.

All eyes were on broom-boy.

Michael sighed. He had adopted an "always play along with Emma" policy about two weeks after meeting her, and it had served him well.

And maybe it had been two hours.

Michael tightened his grip on the handle, raised the forty-two inch duster head, and started swinging it around as if to say: "Stay back!"

He also started frantically looking around the bowling alley for an escape route. Michael was a terrible actor, but Emma demanded total skit commitment.

Go big or go home.

"We have all the exits covered, Michael," the intercom assured him. "It's over, son. Put the duster down."

Michael could tell Emma was pleased.

He melodramatically lowered the duster head, stared at it for a moment, and dropped the handle with disgust. He was rewarded with a splattering of applause from Lanes Two and Three.

Regular customers, he figured. *Grading for effort.*

"You made the right decision, Michael," the intercom assured him. "Now go home. Go home and comb your hair."

* * *

Michael liked his chances.

Homecoming was only a week away, and Jesuit was an all-boy high school, but Michael's best friend had done his job and done it well.

Leon Rivet Charbonnet, III or "Trey" as his family mercifully called him, had somehow convinced Adele to arrange a blind date for Michael with her very attractive neighbor. Barring a total disaster, tonight was going to end with the group agreeing to double-date to the Homecoming dance.

Michael closed his Rock 'n' Bowl locker and gave the combination lock a spin. He was walking toward the door when Emma stormed into the employee break room and raced past him to the refrigerator.

"Are you okay?" he asked.

Emma turned around and pointed at her face.

"Do I look okay?"

Trick question.

"Gavin promised to drive back so we could go out tonight," Emma reminded him. "Instead, he texted. Would you like me to read it?"

Rhetorical question.

"No can do. Storm. B4N." Emma read aloud.

Michael cringed. He was never a fan of the way Gavin treated Emma, and things had only gotten worse since Gavin left for college.

"No can do..." Emma repeated very slowly.

Two years ago, Gavin Driscoll was a highly recruited quarterback on Jesuit's football team, and Emma was the only girl in the Greater New Orleans area who did not care.

"Storm ..." she repeated more loudly.

Gavin had been genuinely surprised each time the cute sophomore put him in his place, and Emma had been equally surprised each time the popular senior called her. At some point, Gavin realized Emma was hysterical, and Emma convinced herself Gavin was really a nice guy trapped inside an insecure jerk.

And, of course, that she could change him.

"B4N ... Bye For Now!" Emma yelled.

Gavin had become a rising star in the Southeastern Conference, and everyone expected the redshirt freshman to start next fall. He had new friends, new opportunities, and new priorities.

Emma was not among them.

"This is ridiculous!" Emma declared. "It's a storm. It's not even a *named* storm! The roads are open, and Gavin drives a truck the size of a Sherman tank."

All true.

"Don't blame the storm," Emma warned Michael, who would apparently be playing the part of Gavin during this practice confrontation. "Don't blame the roads. Just tell me why you don't want to come home. Just tell me why you don't want to spend time with me."

Emma shook her head in exasperation.

"Tell me what I did wrong!"

"Nothing," Michael assured her.

Wrong answer.

Emma took a step closer with a serious look on her face.

"Then why is he acting like this?" she demanded, poking Michael in the chest to emphasize the last word. Michael grimaced and looked away--which, let's be honest, was a rookie mistake.

"You know something, don't you?" Emma gasped. "Michael Jeremy Broussard, you tell me right now what you're thinking!"

I hate seeing you like this, thought Michael. *I should've told you weeks ago. If the situation was reversed, you would've told me—probably as you were having the thought.*

"Michael!"

"He's tapering!" Michael blurted out.

"He's what?"

"Tapering. Gavin doesn't have the guts to end it with you. He's going to act like a jerk until you dump him."

Emma was actually speechless.

"Look, I'm sorry," Michael added quickly. "But, come on, you're amazing and you deserve to be happy, Em."

Neither Michael's compliment nor his apology registered any reaction. He was pretty sure Emma was thinking of her rebuttal.

Which, of course, Emma was.

"Well, Michael, that's your opinion," Emma eventually replied and her tone was way too polite. "I can see why you might think that about Gavin, but you couldn't be more wrong."

She hesitated before adding: "Maybe if you dated someone for more than a month, your opinion might actually mean something."

And, with that, Emma Landry exited the break room.

Michael stared at the door. He decided to count to one hundred before leaving—just in case Emma was waiting on the other side.

He got to "three."

Emma threw open the door. "I forgot to wish you good luck tonight," she said as if nothing happened. "Where did you decide to take the blind girl?"

"It's a blind date, not a blind girl," Michael corrected her matter-of-factly. He knew Emma hated puns, and that this was her bizarre way of apologizing. "And I'm bringing her here tonight."

"Why would you do that?"

Good question.

"Trey's sister dates a guy in tonight's band," Michael explained, before reluctantly telling Emma the real reason. "And Trey says I need the home field advantage with this particular girl."

Emma smiled at him the way he imagined an older sister might and slowly walked back into the break room.

"Michael, I know you and Trey have been friends for a long time," she said. "And I know you have issues. But sweetie, you don't need the home field advantage with anybody."

Strange pause.

"You've got a good heart, and you're built like an Olympic swimmer," she added with surprising sincerity—and not at all like an older sister.

"Just flash the baby blues and be yourself," Emma suggested before winking and walking out the room again.

This time, Michael counted to two hundred.

* * *

Michael hurried out of the second floor bowling alley. As custom dictated, he slid down the railing and used his momentum to pop open the front door. Only a clap of thunder directly overhead stopped Michael in his tracks. The sky was getting dark, and a heavy rain was about to fall on the Crescent City.

His mother had loved storms, and Michael decided to wait for her favorite moment. He did not have to wait long.

One by one, the street lamps sprang to life.

"Clever storm," Michael said, imitating her voice. "It tricked the lights."

Michael smiled as he remembered her and the way her auburn hair danced in the wind. It was some time before he noticed that the closest lamp had not been fooled.

Probably no light in there, Michael thought.

But he didn't like that explanation, so he considered another.

Maybe it's not dark enough.

Maybe it's the light from the other lamps guarding the street.
Maybe it will never be dark enough.

* * *

Trey blamed himself.

The blind date was a total disaster, and the whole thing had been his idea. Sheri Stevens had nothing in common with Michael, and she was obviously not interested in his buddy.

Truth be told, Trey was a little relieved. Sheri was beautiful, but she was also narcissistic and borderline delusional. Most of her sentences started with the same pronoun, and all of them were designed to make her sound good or someone else sound bad.

Trey stepped in deeper puddles.

As a result, things were pretty quiet on Lane Fourteen where the group was bowling. Trey was stewing next to Adele. Michael and Sheri were sitting at the scorer's table. Trey's older sister, Laura, was preparing to bowl.

Nobody was talking.

"Tough loss last night," Trey told Michael, hoping to jumpstart a conversation. "How bad was the locker room?"

"Pretty bad," Michael reported. "Losing to Cross killed any chance we had of making the playoffs."

Sheri turned and looked at Michael like he was a total stranger.

"I didn't know you were on the football team, Michael."

"Well, I'm on the team, but I'm not a starter."

"Oh, that's okay," Sheri replied as if Michael had just spilled a glass of milk. Then she took out her phone and started texting someone.

"Yes, we all forgive you for not being a starter," Trey announced sarcastically.

"Well, you can still end the season on a good note," Adele suggested enthusiastically. "By winning Homecoming!"

"Absolutely," Trey agreed, toasting the idea with his plastic cup and flashing Adele a grateful smile. She was obviously trying to cheer up Michael, and he appreciated her optimism.

No need to tell her the truth, Trey decided. *Next week, the team is going to get beat like they stole something.*

The live music stopped, and Laura's boyfriend, Blake, rejoined the group. This time, Blake brought the drummer.

"Nice set, Blake," Trey said.

"Thanks," Blake replied before giving Laura a kiss.

"Brought the horn," Trey added, patting the trumpet case under his chair. "Any chance I can play a set?"

Laura rolled her eyes. "He's determined to embarrass himself again."

"Come on. What do you say, Blake?"

"Maybe later. Let me check with the guys," Blake promised with no real conviction whatsoever.

"Tony," the drummer said, introducing himself to Sheri and ignoring the rest of the group.

"Sheri," she replied, perking up instantly. "Want to bowl?"

"No," Tony deadpanned, shamelessly checking out Sheri's curves. "But I'd love to watch you bowl."

"Then pull up a seat." Sheri blushed. "You came to the right place."

Trey almost choked on his drink. Sheri had stubbornly refused to bowl all night. Her litany of reasons included—and this is in no particular order—that she did not like "the look or feel" of bowling shoes. That there was "no way" she was breaking a nail. And Trey's personal favorite: because "Sheri does not sweat."

Trey decided to call her bluff.

"You sure did," he assured Tony. "Sheri was going to bowl the next game. Isn't that right, Sheri?"

Sheri smiled evilly at Trey. "That's exactly right."

Michael slid his chair back from the scorer's table and stood up with a look of resignation on his face.

"I'll go get you some shoes."

"Thank you, Michael," Sheri replied sweetly. "Size sevens please."

Michael flashed Trey a "just shoot me now" look, turned, and headed toward the front counter.

Trey watched his buddy leave and admired his stoicism. Michael never once looked back at the group, which was probably for the best.

Tony had already taken his seat.

* * *

Michael was not angry.

Sheri had not shattered his dreams or dashed his hopes. He never expected or wanted her to fall in love with him. Blaming Sheri for wanting the drummer was like blaming a compass for pointing north.

Michael walked over to the counter. As he approached, he saw the familiar red hair and athletic figure of Emma Landry.

Emma was standing with her back to him and was working her usual magic with the customers. Michael waited patiently as she finished helping a couple who obviously found her amusing. When Emma turned around and saw the pathetic look on Michael's face, she smiled and started walking toward him.

In slow motion.

It was Michael's favorite routine and a real crowd pleaser. Unfortunately, sightings of "slow motion counter girl" were increasingly rare. Regular customers knew better than to be impatient or rude when Emma was working.

Michael would never forget one lawyer who threw a twenty on the counter and barked "elevens." Slow motion Emma took fifteen minutes to retrieve his shoes. She walked past the shoes. She grabbed the wrong shoes. She grabbed one shoe, realized her mistake and went back for the other. She forgot where the lawyer was standing, scratched her head and retraced her steps. Bowlers from as far away as Lane Eighteen reached the counter in time to catch the end of the show, and even the lawyer eventually laughed.

But tonight, Emma was performing for Michael, and he knew exactly how to respond to her charity.

"What are you doing?" he demanded loudly.

Emma responded with her standard "be right there" slow motion gesture.

Nicely done. As always.

"What is wrong with you?" Michael asked gruffly. "Have you lost your mind?"

Right on cue, Emma's eyes widened, and a look of terror spread across her face. It was the fear of realizing she had, in fact, lost her mind. Naturally, she started looking for it behind the counter.

Because it had to be somewhere.

Any other night, Michael would have jumped the counter and helped Emma look. But right now, he needed to get back before his date left with Tony the drummer. And that clock was ticking.

"Uh, my date is going to leave, Em."

Emma stopped immediately and wheeled around.

"How may I help you, sir?"

"Size seven shoes, please."

"Mmmmh," Emma moaned enthusiastically while pretending to write down his order. "Sounds good!"

Emma slid the invisible pencil behind her ear and tucked the invisible book in her invisible apron. She looked to the left and to the right. Then she pretended to walk down a flight of stairs behind the counter.

Emma's firing on all cylinders tonight, realized Michael.

A few moments later, Emma resurfaced on an invisible elevator and holding a pair of shoes. When she reached his floor, Emma placed the shoes on the counter with the number "7" on the heels facing Michael.

Quite professional, actually.

"So, how's it going?" she asked.

"Well, my date is hitting on the drummer, and Trey is threatening to play his trumpet during the next set."

Emma stopped smiling.

"Okay. The important thing is to remain calm," Emma insisted. "What are Trey's demands?"

Michael gave her a courtesy smile, grabbed the shoes, and headed back. By the time he reached Lane Fourteen, Tony was showing Sheri his tattoos, and one thing was perfectly clear:

Sheri liked her chances.

*   *   *

Emma wanted closure.

She marched into the bathroom, threw her phone in the toilet, and slammed the toilet lid closed. Then she slammed the stall door closed.

Closure? Check!

While the phone sank, Emma walked to the bathroom mirror and took a long, hard look at herself.

Not good.

She looked like she had been crying for an hour, which was exactly how long she had been pacing in the parking lot and talking on the phone with Gavin.

Get it together, girl.

Emma decided to skip denial and go straight to anger.

You deserve better.

She was angry with Gavin for being a self-obsessed idiot. She was angry with herself for being surprised when Gavin told her—from Baton Rouge—that he needed "some space."

How could I have wasted two years on him! Emma fumed. *And how could Michael, that social hermit, have seen this coming before I did?*

Suddenly, the bathroom door swung open. In the mirror, Emma caught a glimpse of the two girls who had been bowling with Michael and Trey on Lane Fourteen. They were in the middle of an argument, and neither noticed Emma as they stepped into stalls.

"I don't care, Sheri!" declared Stall One.

"Listen, Addie," replied Stall Two. "I like Michael. He's sweet. And he's very cute. But let's face it. Tony's more my speed."

Suddenly, Emma forgot about her own problems.

"But you're supposed to be on a date with Michael," Stall One pleaded. "And I promised Trey we'd double to Homecoming."

"Relax, Addie. I'll go to Homecoming with Michael. And if he plays his cards right, I may even give those puffy lips of his a little test drive. But tonight, I need some face time with Tony."

By the time the witch stopped talking, Emma had a plan.

* * *

Emma was in the zone.

She waited patiently for "Addie" and "Sheri" to leave the bathroom and return to Lane Fourteen. Then she walked over to the kitchen, grabbed a tray of standard bowling alley fare, and headed straight toward the group.

When Emma arrived at Michael's lane, she immediately slammed the tray down on the scorer's table. Fries flew everywhere.

"I can't believe you!" Emma screamed at Michael. "Here? You had to bring your date here?"

"Uh, Em. What are you--"

"No!" Emma screamed, pointing her finger sharply at Michael. "You don't get to talk!" Then Emma turned and walked right up to Sheri.

"Is this your date?" Emma demanded, looking Sheri up and down.

Michael hesitated.

"Oh, she is beautiful, Michael," Emma announced to the entire bowling alley. "I'll give you that. But I can tell you right now she's not your type. She can't make you happy. She wouldn't know how."

"Okay. That's enough," Michael insisted.

Before Michael could say another word, Emma turned around, grabbed his face, and kissed him like it was the end of the world. Her fingers desperately explored his hair, and her body practically coiled around his.

Wow, Emma thought, shocked by the softness of Michael's lips and the way they seemed to hunger for hers.

Michael is really playing along. It feels so natural and...

Something stirred inside her.

Emma let go of Michael's head but allowed her teeth to playfully tug his bottom lip before releasing it. It was something she had seen in a movie once but had never actually tried. She lowered her head, sighed dramatically, and gently pushed his chest away like it was the hardest thing she had ever done. Then Emma slowly looked up into Michael's big, beautiful eyes...

And slapped the piss out of him.

"Whoa!" Trey exclaimed, as Adele and Sheri gasped.

"Think about that during your date," Emma chuckled before marching out of the building.

* * *

Sheri's heart was racing.

Everyone in the bowling alley had heard the slap, and everyone was looking at her.

Sheri focused on Michael, who was still watching the psycho walk away. She reached up and gently turned Michael's face toward her.

"Are you okay?" she asked sweetly.

Michael paused. He looked like he was trying to remember something. Then his eyes narrowed slightly.

"I'm sorry you had to see that."

In the background, maybe to Sheri's right or maybe several lanes away, she heard Trey chuckling and Addie threatening to call the police.

Sheri's heart was racing again.

That girl had some nerve, she thought while quickly replaying the scene. *Telling Michael I'm not his type. Maybe Michael needs a change. Maybe I'm exactly what Michael needs.*

At some point, Sheri realized Michael was still waiting for her to say something. So, as usual, Sheri said the first thing that came to her mind:

"What did you do to that girl?"

* * *

Emma was thrilled with her performance.

Her hand was still stinging, and her soggy cell phone was blurping with the first of a dozen calls she would receive from friends who saw or heard about the slap.

She didn't care.

Emma now knew two things with absolute certainty: Michael Broussard owed her big time, and Michael Broussard knew how to kiss a girl. Really kiss a girl. The way a girl was supposed to be kissed.

The way she had not been kissed for a very long time.

A curious smile appeared on Emma's face the same time as a curious thought.

Nobody should judge that book by its cover.

*   *   *

It makes a distinctive sound.

Fingernails gently tapping against glass makes a sound unlike any made by branch or bird. It is an unusual sound for an unusual event, and it immediately woke up Michael, who got out of bed and stumbled over to the window.

And there she was.

The raven-haired beauty was standing outside his window in a black Armageddon-style silk cloak. The hood framed her royal blue eyes, scarlet lips, and porcelain skin, but could not conceal her smile.

Michael forced up the large window sash, and she magically appeared inside his room. The graceful creature slowly removed her hood and took a step closer.

Michael smiled. He slipped his right hand between her neck and hair and slid his left hand around her waist. He gently pulled her into him, kissed her soft moist lips, and inhaled her heavenly fragrance—an unforgettable mixture of roses, spring, and incense.

Michael deftly disengaged his right hand and unclasped her cloak, letting it fall to the ground around her perfect legs. The embrace and the kiss grew more and more passionate, and Michael lost himself in the moment. But not for long.

The sound of clicking in the hallway demanded his immediate attention.

"Wake up, Michael," Emma Landry said as she walked past his door in high heels. "You're dreaming again, sweetie."

Michael bolted upright in bed and saw that it was three o'clock in the morning. It was the first time anything had interrupted a dream-kiss with Raven-Hair, and the first time Michael had dreamt of Emma Landry.

He was more than a little confused as he stumbled over to the window and peeked between the shades.

Just in case.

*   *   *

Pope Simon Peter II held many titles but cherished only one.

"Uncle Lorenzo!" little Meredith called as she caught up with him, delightfully oblivious to his position. "Do you know Santa Claus?"

"I do," the Pope told the eight-year-old who had somehow cornered him in his brother's living room. "Are you already thinking about Christmas, Meredith?"

"Yes!" she screamed, clutching the straps of her lavender knapsack and merrily spinning in a circle. "I wrote my letter!"

Is it the sugar from the cake or the thrill of hearing her name sung first? the amused Pope wondered before responding with all the amazement he could muster at seventy years old.

"Have you *really*, Meredith?"

"Yes!" she cried, stopping abruptly and letting her curly brown hair obscure her face rather than let go of the knapsack. "Want to see?"

"I do," the Pope assured the back of Meredith's head as she rifled through the contents of the knapsack.

"Here!" Meredith exclaimed when she found the carefully-folded piece of paper and handed it to her great-uncle. "Read it!"

Pope Simon Peter II smiled and obeyed his great-niece.

"Dear Santa," the Pope read aloud. "Thank you for last year. Now I want a bike and a doll with brown hair. How old are you? How cold is the North Pole? When is the world gonna end? Love, Meredith."

"How cold is the North Pole," Pope Simon Peter II repeated more slowly. "And when is the world gonna end?"

The Pope crouched down and lowered his voice so only Meredith could hear.

"This is a good letter," he assured the proud girl. "But, my dear child, please don't worry about the end of the world."

"That's what Mommy said."

"Your mommy is very wise."

"She also said to ask you."

"Did she?"

"She said you would tell me."

The Pope scanned the house and spotted Meredith's mother and father still cleaning dishes in the kitchen.

"Yes, I would tell you," the Pope assured Meredith as his right hand subconsciously located the gold key under his shirt. "But I do not know when the world is going to end."

I only know how the end will begin.

*　　*　　*

Chapter 2: Awakening

And at that time shall Michael stand up,
the great prince which standeth for the children of thy people;
and there shall be a time of trouble, such as never was...
Daniel 12:1

Friday, November 8

Tad Gormley Stadium is a mecca for high school football. Every Friday night, thousands of true believers descend on City Park with visions of State Championships dancing in their head. Most use the sidewalk, but some cut across the mud, carefully negotiating fire ants and Live Oak roots.

Inside, the irresistible sound of a high school drum corps draws the devout up concrete ramps toward the well-lit night. At the top, only the uninitiated hesitate. The rest dive into a human river that bisects the stadium and eternally flows toward the fifty yard line, toward some mysterious point where parents instinctively climb to safety and students plunge into a standing, swirling mass of spirit and angst.

Nothing changes at Gormley. Not the colors or the cheers. Not the age of the student body. Not the words to the Alma Mater. It is a familiar world, and it is easy for the Gormley faithful to lose themselves in the moment. To forget who they are. To forget that games end and the real world waits outside the stadium walls. To forget they are surrounded by thousands of noisy cicadas.

Whether they hear them or not.

* * *

Jacob could not bear to watch.

As a Guardian, he had always been there for Michael. For his birth and his first steps. For his first day of school and his first kiss. He had literally stood by Michael's side during his mother's heart-breaking funeral. Jacob's love and devotion were absolute.

But this was asking too much.

Jacob shuddered as he watched Michael and the rest of the football team jog onto the field at Gormley. The team would spend the next ten minutes on the ground stretching, and Michael would spend that time desperately trying to get as dirty as possible.

Worst ten minutes of Jacob's week.

Tonight was going to be particularly challenging. Record rainfall had turned the natural grass field at Gormley into a swamp, but Michael had somehow plopped down on the only pristine patch of grass in City Park. No matter what Michael did, his jersey would remain lily-white.

Jacob could feel Michael's anxiety. Jesuit was the home team, and he was going to stick out like a sore thumb on the sidelines. Michael's Homecoming date knew Michael wasn't a starter, but that type of visual had a way of sticking with a girl, especially a girl like Sheri Stevens.

Suddenly, Jacob felt the need to stretch.

He slowly unfurled his wings and flew across the field. Once in position, he scanned the stadium for the Fallen, as unlikely as that threat was during a game.

The Prince of Darkness never attacked large gatherings. Like any predator, he preferred to wait until his prey was alone, and that was certainly not the case tonight. Ten thousand people in the stands meant ten thousand angels were standing the watch. The stadium and the sky were filled with Guardians, who remained vigilant but unseen by their *protelos,* the mortals they protected.

The Blue Jay Marching Band erupted with "Eye of the Tiger," and Jacob watched Michael's best friend struggle to keep up on his trumpet. A moment later, he spotted Trey's Guardian, Ryan, on the Jesuit sideline.

Jacob and Ryan were both Novices and had become friends in lockstep with Michael and Trey. They had stood the watch together for more than a decade and genuinely liked each other. Jacob tried to catch Ryan's attention, but he was too focused on Trey's performance.

Suddenly, raucous laughter erupted in the north end zone, where more than a hundred of the Old Guard had gathered. They were among the most ancient and battle-hardened of the Heavenly Host. Some were veterans of the Great War and had driven the Fallen from the City of God. All had been created before mortals fought the Trojan War.

Jacob could name every one of them. He studied their battles during Orientation and made a hobby out of learning their routines and tendencies.

Just in case one should Fall.

But the relative safety of the stadium eventually put Jacob at ease, and his mind started to wander. He pictured himself fighting alongside the Old Guard and being hailed to join them on a night like this.

Jacob's eyes eventually settled on a grizzled old angel called Agrippa. Other than the Seven Who Stand Before God, no angel was more admired than Agrippa the Great. The legendary warrior had earned a reputation for being fearless in battle.

And half-mad during peace.

Like Jacob, Agrippa was serving as a Guardian for someone in the stadium, and Jacob couldn't help wondering which lucky mortal was Agrippa's *protelos*.

Almost immediately, Agrippa sensed Jacob's stare and turned to meet his gaze. Agrippa's eyes were heavy and dark with unfamiliar savagery. He had the intensity of a sailor in the eye of a storm. Glad for the respite, but wary of what must come.

Somehow, Jacob resisted the powerful impulse to look away. Instead, he locked eyes with Agrippa just long enough to nod respectfully before pretending to resume his scan of the stadium. No small accomplishment, really.

Jacob was quite proud of himself.

* * *

The game was surprisingly good.

The Purple Knights needed a win to reach the state playoffs, and the Blue Jays were only playing for pride. Normally, that was a recipe for disaster in high school football, but this was Jesuit's Homecoming game, and the boys were playing their hearts out. The stands were filled with blue and white banners, flags, hats, and pins. A parade brought the student body to the stadium, and the Homecoming court had been presented during half time.

The fourth quarter had just started, and the score was knotted at fourteen. The entire stadium seemed to live and die with each play.

Jacob knew he was going to miss these games. It was impossible to explain the feeling a Guardian developed for a *protelos*, but the love and pride was on full display after each play. Jacob had become addicted to the sound of the student body cheering and to the sight of Guardians celebrating.

He envied them all.

Michael never played, and his father never attended a game. Just once, Jacob wanted Michael to hear the entire student body cheering for him. Truth be told, Jacob also wanted to know what it was like to feel the admiring eyes of a thousand Guardians come to bear on him.

Urgent whistles snapped Jacob out of his trance.

Jacob looked over and saw trainers running out to help an injured Blue Jay limp off the field. It looked like the player had blown a hamstring.

It looked like the player who started ahead of Michael.

* * *

Michael's eyes were the size of salad plates.

Jacob saw Coach Will turn to Michael and point at the field. Before the coach could say anything, Jacob was already standing behind his *protelos*.

"We can do this," Jacob said confidently into Michael's ear. "We can do this."

"You're up, Michael!" Coach Taylor barked. "Get in the game!"

"We can do this," Jacob repeated and he could hear the excitement in his voice. "We are strong. We can do this!"

Michael sprinted onto the field, and Jacob watched with mixed emotions. He was thrilled Michael was going to play in his final game, but terrified Michael would injure or embarrass himself.

Michael played free safety in the Jays' secondary, which meant he played on an island. Everyone would see every mistake he made, and Jacob fully expected Michael to make more than his fair share.

It took all of Jacob's discipline and training to remain on the Jesuit sideline, but Guardians were strictly prohibited from interfering or encouraging during competition. Players won and lost games on their own.

"Go get 'em, Michael!" Ryan yelled, and a roar went up from all of the Guardians who knew Jacob.

The reaction from the student section was less enthusiastic. Jacob did not turn around to count but it sounded like a half dozen people.

Give or take.

Jacob watched Michael reach the huddle, buckle his chin strap, and bite down on his half-chewed mouthpiece as the Jesuit linebacker barked the defense:

"Fifty Base. Cover Three. Blue…"

"Jays!" The huddle clapped.

A moment later, the Purple Knights broke their huddle and jogged to the line of scrimmage. Two wide receivers lined up to Michael's right.

"Twins right!" yelled the linebackers. "Twins right! Roger! Roger! Roger!"

Michael hesitated for a second and cheated to his right--which even Jacob knew was a mistake.

A really big mistake.

The quarterback surveyed the secondary, spotted Michael, and smiled like it was Christmas morning—which it probably was for the Purple Knights.

"Kill. Kill. Blue twenty-eight rascal. Blue twenty-eight rascal. Hut! Hut!"

The ball snapped and the two receivers launched out of their stances like they were shot out of cannons.

Michael did not move.

The quarterback faked a hand-off to the running back, dropped back two steps, and planted his back foot.

"Pass!" the entire Jesuit sideline yelled.

Then it happened.

Before the quarterback released the ball, Michael's body was moving forward. Moving like a freight train toward a patch of grass ten yards down the track.

Only it wasn't Michael. At least, it wasn't the Michael that Jacob knew. Michael's body did not move like that. Nobody moved like that. And Jacob suddenly realized that one of the receivers was sprinting toward the same patch of grass.

"No!" Jacob gasped.

The disciplined receiver kept his eyes on the ball and, just as his fingers touched the pigskin, Michael slammed into his unprepared body at an unimaginable speed. Both bodies landed with a thud.

Neither moved.

"Michael!" Jacob screamed, already flying to his side.

The brutality of the collision shocked the crowd and silenced the stadium.

Michael was lying on his back. He struggled to roll over, but his body was not responding. His torso moved a little to the left. A little to the right. And stopped.

"We're okay. We're okay," Jacob repeated, trying to sound calm and confident, though he was panicking inside. "We are strong. We have faith. We are strong. We have faith."

Michael slowly turned his head toward Jacob.

"Enough, Brother," Michael said with a kind smile. "You worry too much."

Then he lost consciousness.

* * *

Jacob was a deer in headlights.

That didn't happen, Jacob told himself. *Michael can't see me. And he can't consciously hear me. Not since he was a child. Something is wrong.*

While doctors and coaches ran on the field to care for both players, Jacob stood and slowly backed away from Michael's motionless body.

Something is very wrong.

Jacob looked over at the Jesuit end zone. None other than Agrippa the Great was barking orders, and members of the Old Guard were swarming into battle positions around the stadium.

Like someone had just declared war.

* * *

Five thousand miles from Tad Gormley Stadium, beneath the streets of Rome, the Fallen Angel called "Dante" dragged his bloody prisoner, by the arm, down the rough-hewn tunnel. When the tunnel forked, Dante paused but did not release the dislocated arm.

"Left," Marcellus said from behind him.

Dante immediately started down the left tunnel, jerking the half-conscious carcass forward. Minutes later, the tunnel ended in a large chamber.

"Wait," Marcellus said.

Dante stopped just inside the entrance while Marcellus lit torches along the wall. Flames soon illuminated the crypt, casting shadows on its vaulted ceiling. In the center of the room appeared a row of six ancient coffins under a modern pulley system.

"The first," Marcellus said.

Dante hauled the prisoner across the floor until his battered and bruised body lay parallel with the first Attic sarcophagus. Suddenly, muffled cries and feint pounding could be heard from the row of interred.

"Please," the prisoner groaned. "Don't."

"Yes!" Dante replied with delight, dropping the arm. "Beg me for mercy!"

"No," Marcellus snapped, and his order echoed inside the tomb. "Do not give our Brother false hope."

Dante, despised even among the Fallen, snickered and began binding the prisoner's hands and feet.

"You are called 'Paul,'" Marcellus said. "Are you not?"

"Aye, Brother," the prisoner replied weakly, before summoning the last of his courage. "And I will *never* deny Him."

Marcellus flashed a sad smile.

"We're not going to ask you to deny Him," Marcellus said while Dante positioned the pulleys above the sarcophagus. "Not today. We wouldn't believe you if you did."

Paul watched with despair as Dante started connecting the pulleys to the lid.

"Help me, Brother," Paul whispered desperately. "I *know* who you are!"

"No," Marcellus corrected him, matter-of-factly. "You've heard stories of who I used to be."

Marcellus nodded to Dante, who grinned and grabbed the steel cables.

"Kill him!" Paul pleaded with Marcellus, as Dante pulled the cables and unsealed the sarcophagus. "Kill Dante. Save me. Redeem yourself!"

Dante snorted derisively and continued pulling at exactly the same pace. When the five-ton lid was suspended six feet above the ornately-carved base, Dante triggered the locking mechanism and produced a piece of cloth from his pocket.

"Yes," Marcellus said. "Gag him."

Before the prisoner could object, Dante shoved the cloth into his mouth and expertly tied a knot behind his head. Then Dante found a good hold under the prisoner's shoulders, and Marcellus grabbed the prisoner's legs.

Together, they lifted and dropped Paul inside the marble coffin.

* * *

Marcellus looked down at the bound and gagged prisoner inside the sarcophagus. As the only member of the Old Guard to Fall since the Great War, Marcellus knew all too well the sentence he was enforcing.

"I know you are hurting, Brother," Marcellus said, "And I know you are scared. But you must listen to what I say next."

Paul locked eyes with Marcellus.

"Soon you will be in darkness," Marcellus told him, reciting words spoken to him long ago and repeated by him all too often. "Remember that God knows you are trapped inside this coffin. He feels your suffering. He hears your prayers. And He does nothing. He does not help you. He does not save you. He does not show you mercy. It is a hard truth, but He *has* abandoned you."

Paul slowly shook his head, pitying Marcellus for speaking such words.

"Only our Prince will show you mercy," Marcellus said, ignoring the prisoner's contempt and glancing up at the suspended lid. "Only our Prince will deliver you from the darkness."

Dante grunted his agreement.

"We will return in one hundred years," Marcellus warned. "We will give you one chance to deny the Creator and join the ranks of the Fallen. Prepare yourself for that day, Brother. Be ready for the question. Know your answer. Do not hesitate or you will be lost for another century."

Marcellus paused, recalling how many times he had been asked the question.

"Everyone Falls," Marcellus assured him, with a trace of empathy. "Be they loyal for a hundred years or a thousand. Every. Angel. Falls."

On cue, Dante started lowering the lid from its perch six feet above the sarcophagus, slowly sealing the prisoner's fate.

"You chose to serve Him," Marcellus continued.

Five feet.

"This is a consequence of that choice."

Four feet.

"Curse your choice," Marcellus counseled.

Three feet.

"But do not curse the Prince of Darkness."

Two feet.

"This was the only way..."

One.

"To free you."

* * *

Now that was a great nap.

Michael could not remember the last time he had slept so well. He also could not remember falling asleep, but he must have been really tired because he was lying on his back and he never slept on his back.

It must be late, Michael thought. *Everything is so quiet.*

Suddenly, and to his own surprise, Michael's left eye opened.

His bedroom was pitch-black, but the light from a street lamp was shining through a window and directly into his open eye, which promptly closed.

I can't fall back asleep, Michael immediately realized. *I'm lying on something hard... and cold. I'm lying on something hard and cold... and really damp.*

Michael opened both eyes. He was looking up at stars and smelling something pungent. So pungent it was starting to burn his nose.

"Blue dah wight, Eye-kuhl. Blue dah wight."

Michael tried to focus on the strange-colored oval that was now blocking his view of the stars and holding something under his nose.

The oval is trying to talk to me, Michael thought. *It's definitely trying to talk to me.*

"Michael, due blue no ware blue dar?"

Michael? The flesh-colored oval called me "Michael," and that name sounds familiar.

"Dap duz sum hip."

Why does that name sound so familiar?

"Due were out colb, Sun."

Because my name is Michael and I'm lying on a football field.

"Eeezy now. Tehkit low. Tehkit slow."

Michael started to sit up but stopped abruptly when he felt something.

Like a rush of adrenaline, thought Michael. *But maybe not adrenaline. Maybe pain. Nope. Not adrenaline. Definitely pain!*

A wave of pain ripped through Michael's entire body but stopped almost as quickly as it started.

"You rehdy to tan nup?"

The oval is wearing Doctor Lagarde's glasses, Michael observed. *No, wait. The oval* is *Doctor Lagarde, and he's waiting for me to say something.*

"Fider."

Michael could tell by Doctor Lagarde's face he should try again. And for whatever reason, Michael's brain chose that moment to finish rebooting. Suddenly, he remembered everything:

The game. The pass. The hit.

Michael closed his eyes, took a deep breath, and looked right at Doctor Lagarde.

"Is he okay?" Michael asked.

Doctor Lagarde gave a sigh of relief.

"He's gonna be fine, Michael," Doctor Lagarde replied with amazing clarity. "He's got a concussion, same as you. And a dislocated shoulder. They've already helped him off the field."

"Then give me a hand," Michael said impatiently.

Doctor Lagarde chuckled, grabbed Michael's right hand and helped him to his feet. When Michael stood up, he was facing an empty end zone. Doctor Lagarde gently took his arm and turned him toward the Jays' sideline. Which is when Michael saw thousands of people standing and cheering.

Cheering for him.

* * *

Trey was screaming like a banshee, and he was not alone.

Both sides of the stadium got louder as Michael and Doctor Lagarde walked off the field. Now ten thousand strong. All on their feet.

Some were cheering the collision. Some were cheering Michael's reckless disregard for his body. Some were just relieved Michael was alive.

Almost all of them were applauding a total stranger.

Few actually knew Michael, and many were flipping through the pages of their programs, trying to put a name with the number.

What just happened?

Trey knew Michael Broussard. Same carpool since kindergarten. Best friends since the second grade. Lunches together. Movies once a month. Vacations to Pensacola Beach with Trey's family. Mardi Gras Days pulling "Super-Fun" wagon down Saint Charles Avenue. And a standing agreement to double date to all school dances and proms.

But who was that guy?

Trey watched Michael from the huddle to the hit, and Michael looked like a guided missile. Hardest hit anyone had ever seen at the high school level. Probably at the college level. Maybe in the pros. Maybe ever. And the hit was delivered by Michael.

By Michael?

Trey looked to his left and saw Adele and Sheri in the next section. Adele was cheering loudly for Michael. Sheri was turned completely around, talking to the people behind her and pointing toward the field.

Probably telling everyone she's Michael's Homecoming date, Trey thought. *Possibly taking credit for teaching Michael how to tackle. Nothing would surprise me.*

Trey looked to his right and saw Emma Landry two sections over. Emma was neither standing nor cheering. She was seated, and her hands were pressed against her chest like she was having trouble breathing.

She does not look well.

A swell in crowd noise whipped Trey's head around in time to see Michael emerge from a wall of teammates. Michael stopped in front of the ecstatic cheerleaders and removed his helmet. When the crowd erupted again, Michael grabbed the facemask and raised his helmet high into the night sky. Then he winked at someone to Trey's right.

And projectile vomited.

* * *

Chapter 3: The Seven

And I saw the seven angels which stood before God…
Revelations 8:2

Metairie Cemetery is Naturally N'awlins. Every day, visitors travel there to stand on the site of an 1838 race track, somewhere inside an 1861 Confederate camp, and behold a miniature Greek temple bearing the name of a Charleston-born philanthropist who loved New Orleans and died in New York. Of course, the tourists don't wrestle with trifold maps to admire the Ionic columns of the Hyams Family Tomb. They come to catch a glimpse of the sublime marble statue inside. Surrounded by stain glass windows, and bathed in gentle shades of palatinate blue, she is hauntingly beautiful.

And spiritually unsettling.

The sight of a distraught angel kneeling in perpetual exhaustion and prayer is unnatural and illogical. Sure, visitors can tell themselves her grief is not real. That angels do not know the pain of separation. That they have no cause to weep and no need of chapels. That they are never reduced to prayer. But here's the thing:

It happens all the time.

* * *

Rachel had fallen asleep.

She was still kneeling on the prie-dieu where she had been praying. Her forehead was resting uncomfortably on the top of her right hand, and her left arm hung lifelessly over the front of the kneeler.

Her idle wings were angled forward and stretched from two feet above her shoulders to the cool marble floor. Her long, raven-black hair was still pinned into a knot at the nape of her head, but it was unlikely the chignon would hold much longer.

It was beginning to unravel.

Rachel slowly looked up. It was so peaceful and beautiful inside the Chapel. Stone mullions circled the room. Warm and colorful light streamed through stained glass windows and illuminated honey marble floors.

She was tired of praying. Praying for her husband. Praying his mission as a mortal would succeed. Praying for his return. But mainly, Rachel was tired of praying for the damn Chapel bells to ring. The sound of those bells would mark the moment her husband's eternal spirit finally awoke inside his mortal body. One chime for each year he had lived before his awakening.

It would be the only time during her Vigil that Rachel would know with absolute certainty how many years had passed on earth. The selfish part of her hoped to count sixty chimes, but she knew the strength of her husband's spirit.

And the stronger the spirit, the younger the awakening.

Centuries had passed since God had last called her husband to serve in-theatre. Rachel knew he was eager to put his last tour behind him and prove he could serve without bloodshed.

What Rachel could not picture was her husband *after* his deployment. She could not imagine his being born and raised by the parents he would resemble. She tried but could not picture him with a different face and smile.

And she would not picture him as a man.

Men fall in love.

Rachel needed to get up and do something. She decided to treat herself to a very slow stroll around the small chamber. It always helped to clear her mind.

"The Vigil is a blessing," Rachel reminded herself out loud. Her voice sliced through the silence and echoed off the Chapel walls.

As long as she honored her vow, and remained inside the Chapel, time would pass more quickly on earth. An hour in the Chapel could be years on earth. Had she refused the Vigil, she would have sentenced herself to an even longer period of watching human events unfold without knowing which mortal body contained her husband's spirit, knowing only that God saved His worst missions for His most trusted servants.

Now that would be hard time.

Rachel shook her head. She did not understand why her husband had been called to serve in-theatre. Most of the world was at peace. Why would God deploy His Archistrategos, the Supreme Commander of the Heavenly Host?

What need could be so great?

Rachel's husband was the only Archangel whose orders were followed without question by the Old Guard. His name had even been a rallying cry during the Great War. Without him, the City of God was susceptible to doubt and attack.

Rachel tried to take comfort in the Fourth Great Rule:

Everyone serves.

There were no exceptions and, like the Creator, her husband led by example. But she couldn't help wondering:

What turning point in human history had arrived?

Rachel thought of one terrifying possibility and panicked. She ran to the front door of the Chapel and grabbed the door knob.

But did not turn it.

Rachel knew the rules of her Vigil. She had vowed to remain inside the Chapel until her husband's service in-theatre ended. Leaving meant breaking that vow, and Rachel knew the Second Great Rule.

Choices have consequences.

Evil and misfortune had befallen angels who abandoned their Vigil, which is why no angel had broken that particular vow for a millennium.

"I do not know God's Will," she insisted aloud. "I am His servant and I will not despair. Not this day!"

Rachel slowly released the door knob, turned around, and walked over to the nearest stained glass window. She sighed and decided to repeat the exercise, a mental discipline and time-killing routine she had invented soon after starting her Vigil.

Rachel touched the bottom right corner of the stained glass window and let her eyes follow the strip of lead around the first pane of colored glass, saying a prayer at each soldered joint. When she was tempted to speed up or quit, she told herself the same thing:

Before I reach the top of this window, my Vigil bells will chime.

But they did not.

Rachel sighed. She re-pinned her hair, fixed her sleeveless white chiton, and walked back to the kneeler. Her steps were slow and deliberate.

I will pray God forgives my weakness and grants my husband the strength he needs to fulfill His mission. Whatever it may be.

She started reciting an ancient prayer, one written and forgotten by mortals many centuries ago. Before she finished, she was rudely interrupted.

By the chiming of her Chapel bells.

* * *

Some people should never be summoned.

Agrippa marched down the hallway toward the Great Chamber. He couldn't help thinking about the last two times he had been summoned by the Seven Who Stand Before God.

He grinned. The first time, the Seven had ordered him to destroy Jerusalem. The second time, the Seven had interrogated him about his decision to ignore their orders and spare the ancient city.

Not all of them.

Four of them had respected Agrippa's judgment, especially his Captain, who coincidentally loved Jerusalem and considered himself its protector. Those were the four whose opinions mattered to Agrippa.

The other three were insufferable.

As Agrippa approached the Great Chamber, the angels guarding the entrance recognized the warrior and snapped to attention.

Agrippa nodded and paused while they opened the massive stone doors. Then he sighed and stepped across the threshold.

The Guards rapped the butt of their spears on the marble twice.

"Enters Agrippa!" they proclaimed loudly and a bit too eagerly. They ended up yelling at the back of Agrippa's head.

Agrippa stopped and allowed the ringing in his ears to abate before shooting both Guards a look of disdain.

Novices. God bless them.

"Agrippa the Great!" the Archangel Raphael welcomed him. Raphael's good nature was irresistible. His bearing and his warm greeting instantly put Agrippa at ease.

Agrippa walked forward and embraced his old friend. It had been a long time since they fought together, but Agrippa had not forgotten. Raphael was a skilled fighter and a loyal servant of God.

Agrippa looked past Raphael and saw the crescent-shaped stone table that dominated the room. Three of the Seven Archangels were already seated.

Raguel, Uriel, and Saraquel.

"Let us begin," Raphael announced taking his seat at the table, which meant three seats would remain empty.

Agrippa's head started spinning.

The rumors are true. Michael, Gabriel, and Ramiel are all serving in-theatre!

Agrippa caught Raphael's gaze. He very deliberately glanced over at his beloved Captain's empty place at the Crescent and back at Raphael.

Raphael seemed to understand Agrippa's question and nodded almost imperceptibly.

The Commander of the Armies of God is serving in-theatre!

Agrippa struggled to remain calm. God had never put those three Archangels in the human theatre at the same time. And he could think of only one reason they all needed to be on the board.

The End of Days!

* * *

The meeting was literally driving Agrippa crazy.

Agrippa had taken the Guardian's vow, and Raphael knew every second Agrippa spent away from his mortal would cause him greater anxiety. Eventually, the separation from his *protelos* would drive Agrippa mad—or more mad.

Raphael wanted to avoid that.

"We convene now to discuss an unusual report," Raphael began formally. "We have a report that a *protelos* saw and spoke to his Guardian before thousands of mortals and *malachim*. A Novice who has chosen the name Jacob."

"Thank you for coming, Agrippa," Raphael continued. "It is our understanding you were in the stadium."

"Aye, Brother," Agrippa confirmed. "I was there."

"Forgive me," Saraquel said, interrupting. "How old is the boy?"

"The boy is eighteen."

"That would be awfully young for a modern awakening," Uriel scoffed.

"Aye, it was awfully young," Agrippa replied emphatically, certain he had witnessed a very special awakening.

"The age does not concern me," Archangel Raguel announced. "The gray matter in a mortal's frontal lobe thickens until it peaks. Age eleven for girls. Age twelve for boys. Then it starts to thin as connections are pruned..."

"Yes, Rags, but we are here—" Raphael said, trying to interrupt Raguel's professorial discourse before the meeting got sidetracked and Agrippa started taking prisoners.

"Which means an awakening could occur in a twelve-year-old boy," Raguel continued, undaunted. "I would compare the mortal mind to a radio. When the last connection is made, it can finally receive a signal that has existed since birth—"

"Yes, thank you—"

"Of course, it is not an external signal but an internal signal," Raguel explained. "And by signal, I mean an immortal or divine spirit. The stronger that spirit, the earlier the awakening. As I recall, a certain Nazarean boy was only twelve when he—"

"Aye, it was awfully young, Rags," Agrippa barked.

Raphael could tell the meeting was not going to last much longer. The Seven needed to find out what they could while they could.

"Brother Agrippa," Raphael said. "Please tell us what you saw."

Agrippa nodded gratefully. "I saw the boy enter the football game. It was his first play, and his reaction was... not natural."

"What does that mean?"

"The hit was fearless," Agrippa reported. "Vicious. Perfect. Unnatural."

"Unnatural?" repeated Uriel.

"It was."

"Understood," Raphael said. "Please continue, Brother."

Agrippa paused, picturing the scene again.

"The boy was lying on the ground. He was not moving. The boy's Guardian—this Jacob—reacted quickly. Without thought. He flew to the boy's side. I was impressed by the Novice and the bond he has forged with his *protelos*."

The Great Chamber fell silent. Like Raphael, the others were waiting to hear for themselves what happened next. It was the real reason for this meeting.

"Guardian Jacob was speaking to the boy," Agrippa continued. "He was encouraging him. Inspiring him. Then the boy looked right at Jacob."

Agrippa paused again.

"The boy saw him."

"Not possible!" Uriel exclaimed.

"I know what I saw," Agrippa insisted. "And what I heard."

"What you heard?" Raphael repeated, genuinely surprised. Other Guardians had reported seeing the boy speak to Jacob, but none had heard what the boy said. "What did the boy say?"

Agrippa looked right at Raphael.

"'Enough, Brother. You worry too much.'"

Raphael tried not to betray anything by reacting, but Agrippa's stare tested his resolve. He looked away and saw Saraquel trying to suppress a smile.

Which means she knows, Raphael realized. *Which means others will know.*

"Ridiculous!" Uriel declared.

Agrippa's face contorted. "Are you calling me a liar, Uri?"

Raphael cleared his throat. "What happened next, Brother?"

"I ordered the Old Guard to reinforce the perimeter," Agrippa replied. "And I prepared to repel the Fallen when they attacked."

"But there was no attack," Uriel chided. "You succeeded only in terrifying thousands of Novices."

"Good!" Raphael declared, trying to change the tone of the meeting. "Nothing wrong with a good drill!"

Raguel ignored both comments. "I am more interested in why you established a perimeter," he said with genuine curiosity. "Was it because you witnessed an awakening and realized what the boy was?"

"No, Brother," Agrippa replied sincerely. "I did not sound the alarm because of *what* the boy is."

Agrippa hesitated. He knew certain bells could not be un-rung but he quickly decided the Seven needed to hear the truth.

"I did it because of *who* the boy is."

* * *

Saraquel knew what she was doing was wrong.

She paused outside the Chapel with her hands on the ornate door handles. Before the meeting with Agrippa, she would never have violated the sanctity of Rachel's Vigil. Now, all of the Fallen could not stop her from opening the Chapel door and getting the answers the Seven needed.

Saraquel took a deep breath and forced herself to think of the Great War.

And pulled hard.

* * *

The Chapel doors creaked open, and Rachel bolted awake.

My Vigil is over!

Rachel jumped up and turned around so quickly that she sent her kneeler crashing forward. By the time it slammed into the marble floor, Rachel was already standing at the end of the center aisle, waiting to receive her husband.

What happened next almost broke her.

"Sara?" Rachel gasped. "Why have you done this?"

Saraquel seemed to falter as she saw the pain and fear in Rachel's eyes.

"Your Vigil is not over," Saraquel told Rachel quickly. "He still serves."

Rachel dropped to her knees and grabbed the railing of the nearest pew.

"Forgive me, Sister," Saraquel continued. "There are two questions only you can answer, and the Seven need those answers."

Rachel started sobbing uncontrollably.

"Have you heard your Vigil bells?" Saraquel asked, and the simplicity of the question snapped Rachel out of her despair.

Rachel looked up angrily.

"Yes."

"How many times did the bells chime?"

Rachel was about to answer Saraquel's second question when she realized something about her first.

Sara was not surprised. Which means Sara already knows my husband has awakened. But how can that be? Only those keeping a Vigil hear the bells.

God told nobody, not even the Seven, when or where His angels served in the human theatre. No Guardian knew whether their *protelos* had a mortal or angelic spirit. It had always been that way, and it had always been for the best.

Rachel pulled herself to her feet and straightened her chiton.

"Eighteen," she said. "I counted eighteen chimes, but you already know that, don't you?"

Saraquel nodded.

"Agrippa is certain he has found your… husband," Saraquel said, diplomatically choosing to use Rachel's term of endearment for the Archistrategos, even though she personally found the term distasteful. "And I believe him."

Rachel quickly tried to figure out the implications.

If the Seven know, who else knows? And how much danger is my husband in?

Rachel felt the panic coming again and did not know whether she could control it this time.

"Sara, what can you tell me?"

* * *

Saraquel had to choose.

What was said in the Great Chamber was sacrosanct. The Seven never repeated what they discussed there. It was a vow Saraquel had taken before man discovered fire, and it was a vow she had never broken. Never even considered breaking until now.

Every angel is unique, and Rachel was one of God's most beautiful creations.

How could I bring such pain to those eyes? Saraquel wondered as she beheld Rachel's tormented face. *How can I make this right?*

"Your husband is well," she volunteered.

Rachel exhaled. She walked forward and hugged her. The display of affection and gratitude took Saraquel by surprise.

The Vigil is taking a toll on her. Rachel is not herself.

Saraquel knew it was time for her to leave the Chapel. She also knew Rachel would face a terrible decision after she left.

Whether Rachel stayed and honored her vow would be Rachel's choice. But Saraquel had violated the Vigil and she felt compelled to tell Rachel one more thing before she left.

"La Nouvelle-Orleans."

* * *

Sound!

Sealed inside the sarcophagus, bound and gagged, the prisoner waited.

Another sound!

The prisoner had lost all track of time. He had no idea how long he had spent in darkness.

Closer!

"Please," the prisoner muttered through his gag. "I can't do this."

Nothing.

"Please!" he yelled, unable to comprehend spending another day, let alone a hundred more years, in the darkness.

Nothing.

The prisoner panicked. He started thrashing and screaming, but his muffled cries did not escape—and his futile pounding did not disturb—the massive stone coffin.

Marcellus spoke the truth, the prisoner realized. *God does not love me enough to save me. Only the Prince of Darkness will show me mercy.*

Suddenly, the grating sound of stone sliding over stone exploded around him. Light and fresh air flooded the sarcophagus as the lid was slowly pushed open, from the prisoner's right to his left.

Inch by inch.

This time, I will deny Him, the prisoner resolved, eager to answer the Fallen's question and rejoin the world. *And I do deny Him… for He has forsaken me.*

The prisoner's eyes needed no time to adjust to the light. But, instead of Marcellus, the prisoner found himself looking up at a disheveled priest.

"We're here to save you," the priest said as four of his comrades—straining together—pushed the stone lid past midline and allowed its weight to do the rest.

Save me?

As the side of the lid crashed to the floor, strong hands and muscular arms lifted the prisoner out of the stone coffin. Stood him up. Removed his gag. And cut loose the ropes that bound his hands and his feet.

You cannot save me.

A wave of profound shame and sorrow overcame the prisoner.

I've already denied Him.

Bloody and battered priests in black cassocks filled the tiny chamber and surrounded the open sarcophagus at its center. Two were stationed, swords drawn, by the entrance. Two were retrieving weapons. Two were tending to him, and one was standing directly in front of the prisoner.

All of them looked dangerous and determined.

How can I ever be in His presence again?

The priest standing in front of the prisoner waited patiently for his full attention.

How can I return to the City of God?

"Let it go," the priest said when the prisoner's eyes finally settled on him. "Whatever you were thinking inside that damn box. Whatever you were prepared to say this time. Let. It. Go."

I have Fallen.

"Whatever you were becoming in that accursed cocoon," the priest continued, seeing the prisoner's tortured expression. "Let. It. Die."

I am Fallen.

"Solomon," the priest said, trying desperately to reach the traumatized prisoner. "My name is Dean … Dean Cawley. Please, look at me, Solomon."

Yes, I was called Solomon.

"We know who you are," Cawley insisted. "Captured in England as a Novice and interred by Marcellus. Here in Istanbul."

Yes, I was only a Novice.

"Four times you were asked the question, and four times you refused to deny Him," Cawley said with great respect. "Four hundred years of darkness. Four hundred years of fidelity and faith. That's who you are."

No, that's who I was.

"Solomon, we lost three men fighting our way into these tunnels, and we need your help fighting our way out."

Fighting priests. On a rescue mission. Can it be?

Solomon remembered the legend.

A secret order of priests. Led by a vigilante angel. Executing the Will of God.

"Show me your wrist, priest."

Cawley hesitated—but only for a second—before pulling up the sleeve of his black cassock and exposing his right wrist.

And there it was. The telltale brand of the Order of the Judged.

Crossed keys set in a pair of wings.

"Kill, capture, or protect?" Solomon asked gravely, remembering the Order's controversial history. "Which is your mission, priest?"

"To save you from being asked a fifth time," Cawley answered without hesitation. "To remind you that you are loved."

Solomon believed the priest and was overcome with emotion.

"Now, are you with us, Solomon?"

"Aye, Brother." Solomon grinned. "Let's get the hell out of here."

"On me!" Cawley ordered, leading the warrior-priests back into the tunnel.

* * *

Chapter 4: The Order

... and at that time thy people shall be delivered,
every one that shall be found written in the book
Daniel 12:1

Liam MacLaren quietly prayed for strength.

The Great Hall of the Order of the Judged was located deep inside Castle Stalcair in Alpin, Scotland. As the Steward of the Order, Liam was standing in his appointed place behind the ancient stone altar at the end of the Hall.

Waiting to receive the catechumen.

A moment later, the doors swung open and Liam watched a single hooded figure walk toward him, passing slowly between two rows of Brothers. Eventually, the young man stopped on the other side of the sacred altar.

And stood at parade rest.

Liam looked down at the dagger and the red-hot branding iron on the altar. He could feel the tension in the room. After the sacred rite of Gennisi, members of the Order feared nothing, except this night.

"On this altar, God has placed yer fate," Liam announced. His mixed Scottish brogue echoed down the Great Hall.

"But th' choice is yers. It's not too late tae turn back."

Liam intentionally paused because the next part must be clear.

"Th' rite will not start 'til ya choose."

The young man responded by removing his hood and looking across the altar directly at Liam. It was an impressive act of confidence and faith.

He's choosin' tae face his death.

Liam nodded his approval and looked into the determined eyes of Joshua Jackson Reid. He knew this young man. He personally trained him for the past five years. And "Jax"—as he insisted on being called—had earned his respect and trust.

"But once ya choose, th' rite must be finished," Liam reminded him. "An' th' rite ends in death or brotherhood."

Jax had spent two unspeakable years with a foster couple in Detroit before the Order found him. Then, he had been a boy of ten. Now, Jax was twenty-six years old and a candidate to join the Order that had rescued him.

"Do ya understan' th' choice yer makin' here?

"I do."

Jax was a fighter. He lived for combat. To hit and be hit. To push himself to the breaking point. To release the anger and hate inside him. He fought only the instructors, and he fought every day. Bloody and bruised, he looked more like a biker than a priest. He was disciplined and fearless.

A lethal combination.

"Then it's time for ya tae choose."

Jax stood in silence, and Liam remembered the night he stood before the same altar. Heard the same edict. Faced the same decision.

He wondered how long Jax would stand there before speaking. Some catechumen stood there for hours.

"I choose to be judged," Jax said almost immediately.

"Then ya will be judged," Liam replied formally. "Th' rite of *Gennisi* has begun. May God have mercy on yer soul."

Liam stepped aside and watched helplessly as an angel of the Lord stepped out of the shadows and strode toward the altar.

Toward his young catechumen.

* * *

Jax called on the rage.

He quickly forced himself to think of them. Both of them. Bound and gagged. Being tortured to death in front of their eight year-old son.

In front of him.

The rage came, as it always did, and gave him the fortitude he needed as he watched the beautiful and terrifying creature walking toward him.

The angel known only as "the Founder" was wearing a Centurion helmet that could not conceal his commanding chin. A gold cuirass protected his torso, and a blood-red Roman cloak swirled behind him as he walked. His amazing ivory wings were shaped like a peregrine falcon's.

Like a bird of prey.

Jax stood his ground, but it took all of his self-control. Brother Liam had warned him countless times of what would happen after he chose, but he was not prepared for this moment.

Nothing could have prepared him for this moment.

The angel stopped when he reached the altar and snapped his wings out. The sudden movement displaced the air inside the Great Hall, and Jax felt it pass across his face.

The Founder looked down and considered the two pieces of iron on the altar.

"Choices have consequences," he said.

Jax tried to control his breathing. He knew the angel would not delay and the rite would be over soon.

One way or the other.

"You have chosen to have God judge your soul," the Founder continued. "I am His messenger. I will deliver His message and enforce His Will."

Jax watched as the Founder picked-up the dagger.

"The Damned may not join this Order. The Damned must be sent to their master to start serving their eternal sentence."

The Founder paused.

If I'm damned, kill me now, Jax thought, preparing himself. *Let me spend eternity searching the fires of Hell for the monster who killed my parents. Let me hunt the beast. Let me find and torture him for his sins. Eternity might just be long enough to do the job right.*

The Founder smiled and put down the dagger.

"Your name is written in the Book of Life," the Founder announced. "You may serve in the Order of the Judged."

Adrenaline rushed through Jax's body. He was so excited he forgot, albeit only for only a moment, that the ceremony was not finished.

The Founder nodded at Liam.

"Place yer right wrist on th' altar," Liam instructed Jax.

Jax regained his composure and laid his right arm on the cold stone. The moment had finally arrived.

The Founder picked-up the glowing branding iron in his right hand and stared deeply into Jax's eyes. Then, in one fluid motion, the

Founder's left hand grabbed and pinned Jax's right arm as he slammed the brand into Jax's wrist.

Searing an ancient symbol into his skin.

Crossed keys set in a pair of wings.

"Serve well. Die well," the Founder told him when the striking was finished.

The Founder's words completed the sacred rite of passage. The angel stepped back from the altar and disappeared.

"Th' *Gennisi* has ended," Liam declared as the other members of the Order erupted in applause. "Welcome Brother Reid!"

*　　*　　*

Jax was three sheets to the wind.

It had been five hours since the *Gennisi* ended, and Jax had not stopped celebrating with his brethren, which was saying something because the Order always feasted before the *Gennisi* started.

Every Brother knew from personal experience that the imbibing served a purpose. Jax's brain needed time to decompress. Time to process everything it saw and heard during the sacred rite.

Tonight, the Brothers had taken their mission to get him drunk very seriously. Two hours ago, the burn on Jax's right wrist stopped hurting. One hour ago, he lost all sensation in his face. And, about ten minutes before, he had walked into a wall—while talking to it.

Mission accomplished.

Jax was hammered, but certain doubts lingered. He trusted the Messenger, but he could not wrap his head around the message.

It was hard to believe God had weighed his soul. That he had been judged, and his name written in the Book of Life. That no matter what happened while he served in the Order, he would join his Brothers in Heaven when he died.

That eternal salvation was his.

"So I got that goin' for me!" Jax declared in a drunken stupor. "Which is nice!"

Jax chuckled at his own joke, but nobody else did. There were few American-born members of the Order, and none of them were film buffs.

"Yer drunk," a familiar voice declared behind him.

Jax drained his mug of beer. He turned around slowly on the bench and found his mentor standing behind him and grinning like a Cheshire cat.

"Brother MacLaren!" Jax exclaimed. "Steward of the Order! Where the hell have you been? And why aren't you drinking with me?"

"Seen th' Founder," Liam MacLaren replied with good humor. "An' I will have that drink before I tell ya th' news."

Jax wiped his mouth on his sleeve and watched his mentor pour.

What news could he bring from the Founder?

The answer hit him like a sack of bricks.

"Founder's got a mission for me?" Jax asked incredulously.

"Aye," MacLaren replied, raising his mug to toast his pupil. "Serve well, Brother Reid!"

"Die well, Brother MacLaren!" Jax replied, honoring the very old custom.

MacLaren drained his mug, leaned forward, and lowered his voice.

"Look aroun' th' room," he told Jax. "These are good men. Many fooght well aginst th' Fallen. Many waited years fer their first assignment. Many have received their last."

Jax quickly scanned the room and almost fell off the bench in the process.

"Yer drunk," MacLaren continued sternly. "But ya must accept th' mission with humility, Brother."

Jax nodded respectfully but only because of MacLaren's tone. All he actually heard was: "Blah blah blah. Mission. Blah blah blah."

Jax knew one thing. The mission must require him to leave immediately. Otherwise, MacLaren would have waited until morning and would have spoken with him in private. Only one mission required immediate deployment.

"An awakening?" Jax gasped, barely able to control his excitement.

MacLaren smiled.

"Not just an awakenin'... an *American* awakenin'!"

Total silence.

"Damn straight!" Jax yelled, slamming his hand on the table and turning the head of every Brother in the room. "The Founder knows talent. Damn straight!"

"So much fer humility," the Steward muttered to himself.

"Where? Tell me *where* in America, Brother."

"New Orleans," MacLaren answered, again lowering his voice. Not everyone in the room needed to know his destination.

"Oh, this just keeps getting better!"

It had been more than five years since Jax set foot in America, and he was more than a little homesick. For the food. For the music. For the people.

"Kill, capture, or protect?" Jax asked, trying to sound more professional and pretending not to care about the answer, though he cared very much.

"Don't know," MacLaren told him. "Founder said he'd give ya specific orders when ya get there."

Jax sobered instantly at the thought of standing face-to-face with the Founder again, and his next lucid thought was disturbing:

That makes no sense. No sense at all.

"I thought the Founder delivered all messages to the Steward of the Order… I mean… to you."

"Aye," MacLaren admitted. "It's unusual."

"Then why wouldn't the Founder deliver His orders now?" Jax wondered aloud. "How could His orders change during a plane flight?"

"Don't know," MacLaren repeated, shaking his head. "Ask th' Founder tae explain when ya see him again."

"I'll do that," Jax sarcastically promised, knowing he would be lucky not to soil himself next time he stood before the Founder.

While Jax pictured the streets of the French Quarter, Old Brother Vogel walked behind him and gave him a surprisingly strong pat on the back, causing Jax to spill his beer and think of his next question.

"Who's the Founder sending with me?"

"Brother Cawley will be yer Elder., MacLaren said. "Just finished a mission in Istanbul. He'll meet ya there."

Jax could live with that. Dean Cawley was from Brooklyn. Mid-fifties. A veteran of some pretty horrific missions. Only an average fighter but excellent with a blade and arguably the smartest guy in the room.

In any room.

"Not a bad wingman," Jax said, yanking his mentor's chain.

"No, I said Brother Cawley will be yer Elder," MacLaren laughed. "But don't worry yerself. Founder said tae put ya in charge of a large crew of yoong men."

Jax was too drunk to decipher the Steward's comment.

"Alright, let's have it," Jax said, pouring them both another drink. "What do you mean by that?"

MacLaren shrugged and Jax waited.

"Awakenin' happened yoong," MacLaren finally replied. "Lad's still in school."

MacLaren drank deeply from his mug and smirked.

"No, no, no..." Jax pleaded, realizing where this was going.

"Order will see yer placed inside th' school," MacLaren continued more loudly and clearly enjoying Jax's distress.

"Don't say it!" Jax warned him.

"Aye, Brother!" MacLaren roared. "Yer a teacher!"

* * *

Chapter 5: Homecoming

And the LORD opened the eyes of the young man; and he saw...
2 Kings 6:17

Saturday, November 9

Ed Broussard was alone.

The retired boxer had just turned fifty, but he still looked like he could handle himself in a fight. He was almost as tall as his six-foot-two son, and his body was still lean and mean. He had muscular arms and strong, calloused hands.

The respected mechanic's fingers and nails were discolored from a lifetime of working with grease and oil, but he had kind eyes and a deep raspy voice.

Ed wasn't much for talking, but he never broke his word, which is why he rarely lost a customer and his Mid-City garage was always full.

On this Saturday morning, in the rear of his shotgun home, Ed was sitting at the kitchen table pushed up against the wall. He was staring at two empty chairs, drinking his coffee, and remembering better times.

Like every other morning.

Ed loved his son, but he did not consider himself a good father. He was better with machines. When they broke, Ed knew how to fix them.

People were harder.

It had been a long night. Doctor Lagarde had told him to wake Michael every three hours, and Ed had done exactly that, even though he didn't understand what all the fuss was about. When Ed was still fighting, they called it getting your bell rung. As long as you could count the trainer's fingers, you'd be fine in a couple of days.

Give or take a year.

But that was a long time ago. Before he met Kathy Evans. Before he hung up his gloves. Before his life really started.

The sun was up when Ed finally heard noise coming from Michael's bedroom. A few minutes later, Michael stumbled into the hallway. Ed could tell by the way Michael was walking that his son was still hurting.

Worse than he's hurt in a long time.

"Good morning," Michael mumbled as he opened the refrigerator.

"Morning. How you feelin', Mikey?"

"Like I got hit by a truck."

"Figured you would." Ed said with an understanding grin. "Course, the way I heard it. You were the truck."

"Yes, sir. I guess so."

Ed watched Michael grab the jug of milk and fill his favorite cup. He gulped it down, filled the cup again, and put the jug back in the refrigerator.

Like every other morning.

Michael was a creature of habit, and Ed was relieved to see his son acting normal until his son sat down.

In Kathy's chair.

* * *

Ed Broussard could not believe his eyes.

Every morning for the past four years, he waited for Michael to wake up. Every morning, he hoped Michael would finally sit in Kathy's chair at the end of the table. Every morning, Michael pulled out the chair next to him instead.

It was a daily reminder of their loss and a crappy way to start his day.

But the day had finally arrived, and Ed decided to let it pass without calling attention to it.

It's a good thing, Ed told himself. *Time should heal all wounds... except mine.*

"I wish I could remember more," Michael said, dragging Ed back to the present.

"Give it some time," Ed replied, handing him the newspaper he still had delivered to the house.

Michael pulled out the Sports section. He flipped to the prep page but soon folded it and started rubbing his eyes.

Not a good sign.

"What did it say?" Michael asked.

"You lost and it was a hard-hitting game."

"Well, that's all I remember," Michael chuckled.

Ed got up and poured himself another cup of coffee. He inhaled deeply and took another sip.

"Doc says you've gotta take it easy," Ed announced. "So we're gonna skip the gym today."

"But we've sparred every weekend since…" Michael started to object, without really knowing why.

"Tradition or not, we cool it for a couple of weeks."

"Yes, sir."

"How about we go to church instead," Ed proposed. "Catch the vigil mass at four o'clock. Give thanks for you walking away from that hit."

"No, thank you," Michael replied automatically, having denied similar requests for the past four years. "I don't believe in God."

"God didn't kill your mother," came Ed's familiar refrain.

"God didn't save her," came Michael's familiar reply, which usually ended the exchange. But this Saturday morning, there was more Ed wanted to say. So he sat back down at the table.

"Well, I should've been there last night, Mikey."

Michael looked a little uncomfortable, and Ed realized he had never apologized to his son for anything.

Technically, he still hadn't.

"You had no way of knowing I'd get in the game," Michael said without looking up at him. "And it was only one play."

"Still, I..."

"By the way, how did you find out?" Michael asked, interrupting Ed's apology and obviously trying to change the topic.

Something he learned from his mother.

"Trey called me from the stadium, a few minutes before the Landry girl. Said it was pretty bad."

"Emma called you?"

"She did," Ed confirmed. "You takin' her to the dance tonight?"

"No, sir," Michael said. "I'm taking another girl."

Ed got up, walked to the screen door and looked at the overgrown gardens in the backyard.

"This other girl have a name?"

"Yes, sir. Sheri Stevens."

Ed shoved his left hand into his jeans and leaned against the door frame.

"How you gettin' there?"

"Trey's driving."

Ed took another sip of coffee and stared at the tangled mess in the northwest corner of the garden. He wondered if Kathy's rose bush was still under there.

Somewhere.

"No, that won't do," Ed said a few minutes later. He pulled the keys to his 1964 Pontiac GTO out of his pocket and put them on the table.

"Man should drive his date to a dance. Take the Goat."

Ed turned back around.

"Uh, thanks ... I mean ... Thank you, sir."

Ed smiled as he heard the surprise in his son's voice. Then he opened the screen door and stepped outside. It was a cool November day in the Crescent City. He had a garage full of cars and deadlines.

Good day to spend working in the garden, Ed decided.

He paused on the top step, but only long enough to give his son a little sentimental advice.

"And son ..."

"Yes, sir?"

"Right girl will love the Goat."

*　　*　　*

This was not in the brochure.

Michael Broussard was sitting alone, and the white circular table seemed larger than it had when the group arrived at the Homecoming dance.

Much larger.

Michael looked at his watch. It had been almost twenty-four hours since the hit and about twenty-four minutes since he had seen his date.

Sheri was missing in action, and nothing was going as planned. When he picked her up, Sheri took one look at the classic muscle car and asked if it was a loaner. Then, when they arrived at the dance, the DJ stopped the music to introduce him.

As Jesuit High School's "One-Hit Wonder."

The next hour at the dance wasn't much better. Everyone stopped to congratulate him on the hit, and every conversation was the same. The only thing that changed was the verb used to describe how Michael had "leveled," "crushed," or "destroyed" that wide receiver.

Sheri seemed to love the attention, but Michael quickly tired of answering the same three questions:

"How ya feeling?"

"What do you remember about the hit?"

"How many cheerleaders did you puke on?"

Michael always gave the same three answers:

"Better. Nothing. Not sure."

At one point, Michael and Sheri were like newlyweds standing at the end of a reception line, receiving plenty of handshakes and slaps on the back from familiar-looking strangers. Eventually, the line disappeared.

And so did Sheri.

Michael did not miss the social butterfly. He was tired of hearing her describe for everyone what it was like for her to watch him lying on the field, and how she felt so helpless: "Like the wind had been knocked out of her."

None of it rang true.

Michael was glad to see that Trey and Adele were finally dancing. Adele had insisted on sitting with him until Sheri returned, and Michael literally had to pull her out of her chair before she would dance with his buddy.

Adele is a keeper.

Michael was also glad to be alone. He had not felt right all day and needed some time to regroup. It wasn't that he felt sick.

Just different.

He felt more aware. Of music. Of movement. Of laughter and bickering. Of body language. Of everything.

It was more than sensitivity to light and sound. For the first time in his life, Michael was starting to think he could read people. He could tell whether laughter was sincere. And he knew, without knowing, whether hand-holding was welcomed or forced. He figured it was all a result of the concussion. And whatever it was, he wanted to turn it off. As soon as possible.

Michael looked down at the white table cloth. He tried to stare at it and block out everything else, but that only heightened his other senses, which were telling him that a man wearing familiar after-shave was approaching.

"May I join you?"

Michael looked up and saw his position coach.

Coach Will Taylor struck an imposing figure. He was thirty-five years-old, north of six feet tall, and could still run every route in the passing tree. He was born on d'Hemecourt Street, just a stone's throw from Jesuit High School, and his caramel skin was a true New Orleans blend. Far and away Michael's favorite teacher. And the best-dressed chaperone in New Orleans.

The guy should run for mayor, Michael thought. *I'd vote for him.*

"Yes, sir."

Coach Will had been a highly-recruited wide receiver before he injured his knee during his junior year at Jesuit. Surgery and rehabilitation went well, but he never got his speed back, and it cost him a college scholarship. Instead of reporting to Tiger Stadium for spring training, Coach Will reported to Parris Island for basic training.

"I'm afraid I've got some bad news."

"My date left with someone else?"

"Well, yes, but that's old news," Will replied, hopefully joking. "I said bad news. I went down to the school this afternoon, and there's no video of your play."

"How's that, Coach?"

"I'm sorry to say that the camera was broken."

"That's too bad," Michael said half-heartedly, having seen the hit replayed on national sports shows all weekend.

"It was pretty special."

"The hit?"

"Negative. The way you read that play."

"Sir?"

"Twins right. Play action pass. Our linebackers bite, leaving a giant hole about ten yards in front of you."

Michael was riveted.

"Here's the thing," Will continued. "I watched film of every snap Saint Aug took this year. Their receivers always ran the same two routes out of that formation—just like I told you at practice. But on that play, both receivers ran routes they'd never run before."

"Really?"

"Really. And let me tell you what I remember seeing," Will added, with a slightly accusatory tone. "I remember seeing you move to the ball before it was thrown and before the receiver started his break."

That's not possible, Michael thought.

"So, here's my question, Broussard. How could you know what route the outside receiver was going to run when I didn't?"

Good question.

"I'm sorry, Coach, but I don't remember anything," Michael replied truthfully. "Maybe I was just lucky."

Coach Will smiled.

"Maybe it was luck," he said. "Maybe I owe you an apology."

Will leaned forward in his chair and clasped his hands together like he was in a confessional.

"I was your coach. It was my job to figure out if you could play, and I had no idea you had that kind of killer instinct inside of you."

Michael thought about it for a second.

"Neither did I."

* * *

"Well, you clean up pretty."

Emma Landry was standing at the other end of the table and looking fantastic. Her black dress made her red hair and green eyes pop. Against all odds, she was wearing a pair of black high heels that showed off her cross-country calves. Her toes were painted crimson, and she was wearing a diamond drop necklace.

"My eyes are up here, Broussard."

Michael smiled.

"Coach, this is my friend, Emma Landry."

"It's a pleasure to see you, Miss Landry," Coach Will said. "And against my better judgment, I'm going to leave you alone with Mr. Broussard. Call me if he gives you any trouble."

"Thanks, Coach," Emma said. "I think I can handle him."

"I know you can," Will said.

Michael stood up as Coach Will offered his hand.

"Good luck, Broussard."

* * *

Michael could not take his eyes off Emma.

Word on the street was that Emma received a flood of offers after her breakup, mainly from seniors who coveted her since they first saw her on a date with Gavin. The last person to ask her was none other than Jesuit's current quarterback, Brad Shipley, who played behind Gavin for two years.

"Where's your date?" Michael heard himself ask.

"Brad went outside for a smoke."

"You can't stand smoking."

"Yes, I'm aware of that, Michael."

"Well, my date has flown the coop," Michael added, just in case she was planning on staging another scene for her benefit. "So no slapping or kissing, okay?"

Michael could tell by Emma's face that his joke did not have the desired effect. Instead of making Emma laugh, it seemed to really annoy her.

Emma put her hands on her hips.

"Get up and dance with me."

* * *

The jitterbug was the only club in Michael's bag.

Michael was not comfortable dancing to hip hop, rock, or rap music. He could foxtrot and waltz, but jitterbugging was his only option for a fast song and good jitterbug songs were pretty rare at high school dances.

Best he could hope for was a slow song.

Michael and Emma reached the dance floor as a popular line dance ended. Out of the corner of his eye, he saw Emma wave at—or possibly signal—the DJ, who smiled and started playing one of Emma's favorites:

Otis Redding's "These Arms of Mine."

Michael's wish had been granted. The first few notes of the classic slow song were enough to spook the line dancers and start a stampede off the dance floor.

Emma took Michael's hand, and Michael led her through the crowd. When they reached the center of the floor, Emma let go.

Then Emma took a step back and performed a Victorian curtsey.

Michael knew what Emma wanted and refused to disappoint her. While the remaining line dancers paired off like Noah's ark, Michael straightened up, paused, and bowed.

Slowly and deeply.

* * *

Emma was in her own world.

She was quite pleased by Michael's execution of the deep bow. Initially, she gave him a "B+," which she considered more than fair. She couldn't give an "A" for anything less than a true bow-and-scrape. But, after a few seconds of slow dancing, Emma considered the possibility Michael had never seen a proper scrape. She decided to give him an "A."

And to put her head on his shoulder.

Emma was surprised by how well Michael negotiated the dance floor and by how good he smelled, like leather and fresh mint. She thought about telling him, but stopped herself. She did not want to send any mixed signals.

"You're a good dancer," Emma said instead.

"Thank you," Michael replied with a degree of confidence she did not expect. "You're a surprisingly good follow."

"What does that mean?" she asked sweetly.

"We move well together," Michael explained.

Emma knew he was right. Gavin had a tendency to treat slow songs like a timeout. On those rare occasions when they did slow dance, Gavin either rocked in place or sprained her hand spinning her around him.

This is the way people were meant to dance, thought Emma.

Michael knew how to telegraph each move by applying the slightest pressure to her hand or lower back. It was so effortless Emma forgot they were dancing, which allowed her to focus on other things.

Like Michael's body.

Emma found herself playing with Michael's hair and letting her nails slide up and down the nape of his neck. Michael responded by lowering his head until they were dancing cheek to cheek. Just like in the movies.

Just like Emma wanted.

Emma rewarded him by sighing softly. Her warm breath caressed the back of his neck and, on the next pass through, her nails gently raked goose bumps.

Oh well, Emma thought. *A few mixed signals won't kill him.*

Emma sighed again and a little closer to his neck. This time, Michael responded by slowing down their dancing… and by forgetting to breathe.

Decision time.

Emma wasn't quite ready to take the next step, which would have involved Michael's ear lobe. So she decided to get him talking.

"Where did you learn to dance so well, my dapper friend?"

On hearing the last word, Michael straightened up and resumed his original tempo, like he had been snapped out of a trance.

"In the living room. To Motown. With my mom."

Crap.

"I'm sorry, Michael," Emma said, lifting her head and leaning back far enough to make eye contact. "I should have known."

"It's alright," Michael insisted with a smile that assured her it really was. "Times like this… I enjoy remembering her."

Emma kept staring at Michael. He was so confident and relaxed. It suited him.

And it attracted her.

"Put your head back on my shoulder," Michael whispered and Emma did exactly what she was told.

Quite possibly for the first time in her life.

* * *

Sheri Stevens was looking like a million and moving like a cat.

The song was almost over when Michael spotted her stunning figure heading toward the dance floor.

"Heads up!" Trey warned Michael as he spun Adele out of the line of fire.

The music stopped, and Sheri crossed the dance floor during the silence. Even her heels sounded angry.

"Michael, thank you for accepting my apology," Emma said loud enough for Sheri to hear. "And thank you for sharing one last dance."

Emma turned to Sheri.

"He's all yours," Emma said preemptively. "Take good care of him, okay? Michael's one of the good guys."

Emma smiled sadly and walked off the dance floor.

* * *

Emma was mad as a hornet.

Take good care of him? Who talks like that? Emma wondered, chastising herself. *One of the good guys? How corny is that?*

Emma decided to make it official.

"Worst performance ever!" she announced to the empty parking lot.

Now she could focus on figuring out why.

Maybe I didn't want to stop dancing, thought Emma, but she did not dwell on that possibility. *Maybe I felt guilty about what I was doing to Michael's chances with Sheri... well, no, that definitely wasn't it.*

It was Emma's fault Sheri was interested in Michael, and it was her responsibility to save him from that man-eater.

I did what I had to do.

Unless Emma was sorely mistaken, Sheri was the type of girl who wanted what she could not have. The type who craved excitement and attention, not the responsibility of a long-term relationship.

Poor Michael, Emma thought. *He probably thinks my performance guaranteed him a second date with Little Miss Thing. Little does he know.*

* * *

Sheri was a gone pecan.

Michael did not need to rely on his newly-discovered powers of observation to know how this date was going to end.

"You don't have to walk me to my door," Sheri said as they pulled up to her house. "You can leave the car running."

Of course I can.

"Well, thank you for going to the dance with me," Michael said politely.

Sheri took a quick look out the passenger window at her front porch and then sat still, staring out the front windshield.

"I know I was a little loopy tonight from the hit," Michael continued. "I hope I wasn't bad company."

Sheri smiled a peculiar smile. She carefully adjusted her dress, turned completely sideways in her seat, and adjusted her dress again. She performed the maneuver with a workman-like economy of motion.

She's done this before.

Michael could see the "let him down easy" look on Sheri's face, but he felt completely detached from the situation. He was more curious about how she was going to go about it.

"I hope you had a nice time," Michael added.

Sheri's hand shot out like a whaling harpoon, snagged him behind the head, and pulled him in for a kiss.

Her lips tasted like strawberry and the smell of expensive perfume engulfed Michael. She alternated long, hard kisses with short, soft kisses. She did it passionately, but it struck Michael as rehearsed.

Almost mechanical.

Michael gave as good as he got, and it was some time before Sheri stopped, disengaged, and gave him a final soft peck on the lips.

"Thank you for a wonderful evening, Michael," Sheri said. "And a very nice kiss good night."

"But..." Michael said, encouraging her to finish her thought.

"But we both know this isn't going anywhere," Sheri said matter-of-factly. "Listen, I like you, and I'd be happy to go out with you again if you ever need a date, but we have nothing in common."

"You may be right."

"Of course I am," Sheri assured him kindly.

"So we are one-and-done?"

"We are."

"Okay," Michael said. "Let me get your door."

Michael got out and walked around to Sheri's side. He opened her door and offered his hand. Sheri took it and stepped out of the Goat.

Michael headed back to the driver's side. When he glanced back, Sheri was still standing there. Something told him she was a little surprised at how well Michael was handling the bad news.

And maybe it isn't surprise, Michael realized as he sat down and started the engine. *Maybe it's disappointment.*

"One more thing," Sheri said, leaning through the open passenger window. "Tell your little friend, Emma, this had nothing to do with that line she fed me earlier. She didn't fool anybody with that performance."

Michael laughed.

"In her defense, it wasn't her best performance. She was just trying to help me get a second date."

Michael's comment seemed to amuse her.

"Help you?" Sheri snickered. "Is that what you think Emma was trying to do? Help you get another date?"

Michael's mysterious new powers told him Sheri knew what she was talking about, and he was missing something.

Something obvious.

"Wasn't she?"

Sheri started to say something but stopped herself. Michael got the impression it took quite a bit of effort.

"Of course she was," Sheri deadpanned. "Emma was trying to *help* you. You're lucky to have a *friend* like her. Good night, Michael."

As Sheri stepped back and turned around, Michael thought he heard her say:

"Good luck with that."

* * *

Chapter 6: Questions

Prove all things; hold fast that which is good.
1 Thessalonians 5:21

(12:15 a.m.) Sunday, November 10

Lance Corporal Will Taylor needed a medic.

He was pinned down. The grenade had detonated directly in front of him. He could not move, but he could hear moaning.

Whoever it was needed help.

Will tried to work the problem. It was too dark for him to see anything, but the heat on the back of his neck told him there was a fire behind him, and the fire was getting closer.

On your feet, Marine!

He needed to grab the moaner and move. He heard the popping and crackling of small-arms fire behind him. It sounded random and unfamiliar, and it did not concern him, but the smell of gasoline did.

Let's go, Marine, move!

Will tried to stand up, but his body did not respond. Only then did he start to panic. Something was really wrong.

Glass exploded to his left and cooler air rushed toward him. He was either inside a building or trapped in a confined space.

Don't you quit on us!

Somebody grabbed him under his arms. The man was desperately trying to lift him up and pull him through the hole.

Will was dead weight, but that didn't matter to the determined marine trying to save his life.

Damn shame, Will thought as he felt the heat overtaking them. *Both of us will burn.*

Suddenly, Will regained consciousness.

He opened his eyes and saw that he was not in a war zone. He was being pulled out the window of his burning car.

By Michael Broussard!

* * *

Jacob knew they were out of time.

Michael had Coach Will's torso almost completely out of the driver-side window, but his legs were still inside the car. The fire had reached the front passenger seat, and smoke was now billowing out of every broken window.

The car was going to blow.

"Get him out!" Jacob screamed at Michael. "Don't stop! Get him out now! No time! No time! Now! Now! Now!"

Michael ducked his head under Will's arm, braced his right foot against the car door, and pushed with everything he had. He succeeded in pulling Will free of the window, and the momentum sent both men crashing to the ground. Michael's back slammed into the concrete, and Will landed on top of his chest as flames consumed the rest of the car.

Michael and Will lay side by side. Michael was trying to catch his breath and Will was trying to clear the cobwebs.

Jacob knew Michael was still too close to the car, which could explode at any moment. And that it was way too quiet.

Will's Guardian, Adrian, had been berating his *protelos* like Will's old gunny sergeant in a desperate attempt to wake and motivate him.

"No!" Jacob yelled when he saw Adrian dressed like a truck driver and walking toward Will with grim determination. "Don't intervene!"

Something in Jacob's voice reached Adrian, who stopped and disappeared from mortal sight. But not quickly enough.

Will Taylor was staring at the spot where Adrian had been standing.

* * *

The Concussion Club's first meeting sucked.

Will and Michael were sitting next to each other on the back of the ambulance. They were wrapped in blankets and watching firefighters extinguish the last of the flames that engulfed all three vehicles. Thankfully, they had been able to crawl to safety seconds before the explosion.

Will's paramedic was calculating his Glasgow Coma Scale score. Michael's paramedic was checking for burns and cuts.

"I don't know what to say," Will sighed. "You saved my life. Thank you."

"You're welcome, Coach."

"I don't know what kind of medals they pin on civilians, but I'm going make sure they pin one on you."

"I wish you wouldn't, Coach. I've had enough attention lately."

Will stared at him for a moment.

"Just a feeling I have," Michael said. "And I didn't do this..."

"For the medals," Will muttered like he was remembering something he heard someone say a long time ago. "I understand. I'll keep it quiet."

"Thanks, Coach."

"Were you driving home from the dance?" Will asked, changing the topic.

"Yes, sir."

"Did you see the accident?"

Michael shook his head. "No, sir. I was two cars back. I just pulled over to see if I could help."

"I'm glad you did."

Will looked around at the first responders and the line of cars being allowed to drive around the accident. The line moved slowly because of the rubber-necking.

"When did you realize I was in the car?"

"When I unbuckled you."

The paramedics finished their evaluations and insisted on taking Will to the emergency room, but Will asked Michael to drive him home instead.

"You sure, Coach?"

"I'm good to go," Will replied, even though his head felt like it was going to explode. "Any tips on dealing with a concussion?"

"Don't puke on a cheerleader."

* * *

The Goat speaks to some guys.

Michael had witnessed it countless times. Sometimes, it was because the guy worked on a similar car with his father. Sometimes, it was because the guy owned one or lost touch with a friend who did. There was always a story, and it was always told with a big smile and a tinge of regret.

Coach Will's response to the Goat was more emotional than most.

"Pop the hood," Will told Michael.

"Shouldn't we..."

"Boy hush," Will commanded. "And pop the hood."

Michael walked over and lifted the hood. Then he stepped out the way. Having seen this type of reunion before, he knew what was going to happen next.

Coach Will walked right past him and took a long look under the hood.

"Pontiac 326 high output V8 engine with a four-barrel carburetor." He whistled. "Did your dad restore it himself?"

"Yes, sir."

Will shook his head with admiration. "Well, the man knew what he was doing."

Michael could tell Coach Will genuinely appreciated the car, but it felt wrong to hang out at the scene of a car accident. When Will did not launch into his car story, Michael was certain there was another reason for the delay.

"Are you sure you're okay?"

Will did not answer right away. He just kept staring at the engine. Eventually, he looked up at Michael with a serious expression.

"Did you see anything strange after your concussion?"

Michael hesitated.

Something told him not to say anything. But Coach Will was obviously disturbed by what he saw, and maybe he would feel better when he heard about Michael's bizarre vision.

"Yes," Michael confessed. "I saw an angel kneeling next to me."

Silence.

"But that's not the weird thing," Michael continued, surprised at how good it felt to finally tell someone. "When I saw the angel's face... I'm telling you, Coach. It was like..."

"You knew him."

"Exactly," Michael said, surprised. "How'd you know that, Coach?"

*　　*　　*

Michael's long night was about to get longer.

He was headed home on Carrollton Avenue after dropping off Coach Will. As he drove past Rock 'n' Bowl, he saw lights were on outside the bowling alley. It was two o'clock in the morning, and there were no cars in the parking lot, which meant something was wrong.

Michael parked in front of the entrance. He grabbed his keys, let himself in, and slowly walked up the stairs to the second floor. When he reached the top, Michael saw something that scared him more than the sight of a burning car.

Emma Landry was dusting Lane Seven in bare feet and a Homecoming dress.

*　　*　　*

Emma hated being alone.

She thought a silent table was an unhappy table, and people who were alone were always lonely. Right now, she was both.

Emma was quietly cursing Michael Broussard. Lane dusting always seemed to cheer him up, which is why she decided to give it a try. But it was not helping her figure out her life, get over Gavin, or forget her date with Brad Shipley.

It was only giving her blisters.

"Ladies and gentlemen!" the intercom announced loudly, scaring Emma to death.

"Let me direct your attention to the tightrope high above us," the voice of Michael Broussard continued. "Where Emma the, uh, the… where Emma the Amazing, uh…"

Worst ringmaster ever, Emma thought. *But I love him for trying.*

"Where she prepares to… to… uh, to amaze us!"

Like, she corrected herself. *I like him for trying.*

Emma picked up the lane duster and held it out like a balancing pole. She cautiously took a single step forward on the wire and toward the foul line on Lane Seven. Then two more steps forward. Two back. One forward.

The last step was a mistake.

Emma desperately struggled to regain her balance. The pole helped but her panic was palpable. She was about to fall a hundred feet to the floor of the circus.

How many children will watch Emma the Amazing die tonight?

"No more, uh, wait, what do they call it? Flash photography! Please!" the intercom yelled at the crowd below her. "Emma the Amazing's life depends on it!"

Emma regained her composure and finished walking the tightrope to the foul line. With a flourish, she turned around and waved enthusiastically to the star-struck crowd below.

Total skit commit.

* * *

Michael turned off the intercom.

He watched Emma collect her things and grab her high heels. She took about three steps toward him, stopped, and slipped them on.

Which was odd.

"How did your date go?" Emma asked when she got within hearing range. It was a perfectly-timed preemptive strike.

Such an evil genius.

"We had a nice time."

"Did she take your lips for a test drive?"

Michael grimaced. "Where did you learn to talk like that?"

"In the girl's bathroom," Emma replied as she reached the counter. "And you haven't answered my question."

"Gentlemen do not kiss and tell."

"Yeah, right," Emma scoffed. "Well, did we get a second date?"

"No," Michael informed her. "*We* will not be going out with her again because *we* got dumped before *we* got out the car."

Emma looked at him like he was a child with a boo-boo.

"I'm sorry to hear that," Emma said, without sounding the least bit sorry. "I did what I could."

Emma broke eye contact, and Michael waited patiently for her to look back at him before asking her pointedly:

"Did what you could to what?"

Emma looked offended for a split second but dropped the pretense almost immediately.

"To save you from Look-At-Me Barbie," she admitted. "And I'm a little impressed you figured it out on your own."

"I didn't," Michael confessed. "Sheri figured it out. She was not impressed by your performance tonight."

"It wasn't my best performance."

"That's what I told her."

"Thank you, Michael," Emma replied, apparently relieved that Michael had set the record straight about her acting ability.

Such a strange bird.

"Now let's do you," Michael said quickly, convinced by Emma's levity that whatever ended her date wasn't too serious. "How long have you been here?"

"Since the dance ended."

"What happened?"

"Nothing really," Emma shrugged. "We were driving past here on the way to a party, and I asked him to drop me off."

"And he did it?"

"I told him my father was still closing up inside," she explained. "And there was a car parked in the parking lot."

"The abandoned car?" Michael asked, wondering how that could have fooled Brad. "At the far end of the parking lot?"

"Yes."

"Did somebody leave the bowling alley lights on?"

"No. He's not the sharpest knife in the drawer."

Michael smiled.

"Let me drive you home, Em. Your parents must be going crazy."

"I already called home, and Dad will be here in about five minutes." Emma looked down at her watch. "Actually, you should probably get going unless you want to be here for his meltdown."

"I do not."

Together, they shut off the lights and walked down the stairs to the front door where Emma would wait for her dad.

"No way!" she cried. "He gave you the Goat!"

"He did."

Emma whistled in admiration. "Wow. I can't imagine how awful a date you must be to get dumped in a car like that."

"Neither can I," Michael assured her as he walked around to the driver's side. "But at least my date let me drive her home."

Michael expected at least a courtesy laugh. When he heard none, he looked back and saw that Emma was not smiling.

"I started dating Gavin as a sophomore," Emma reminded him and the change in her tone was a warning to listen carefully. "This was my first date in years with somebody else. I had Brad drop me off because everything was different."

"Different good or different bad?"

"Doesn't matter when you're not ready for different."

Emma's honesty blind-sided Michael.

She's right. She's not ready to date anyone.

"Maybe next time it'll be easier for you," he told her.

Emma smiled.

"Maybe next time you'll invite the right girl."

Michael opened the car door and looked back at her.

"Maybe I'll do just that, Emma Landry," he told her with a devilish little grin.

Then Michael winked for the second time in his life and ducked inside the car. As he drove off, Michael turned to the empty front passenger seat of the Goat and asked aloud the question he had been asking himself for hours.

"What's happening to me?"

* * *

Michael's question was not lost to the night.

Jacob looked back at his *protelos* from the front passenger seat. He had seen enough during the last forty hours to know, with absolute certainty, the answer to Michael's question.

"You're becoming what you are, Brother," Jacob told him calmly and confidently. "Just becoming what you are."

* * *

Brother Dean Cawley was a hard sell.

He was a good man, but he could never trust people the way he trusted mathematical certainty and method. Cawley was enamored with numerology. He believed everything in the world was made of numbers and could be described in terms of numbers and proportions. Not just the physical properties of every object and every living organism, not just concepts like time and space, but every discovery from harmony to philosophy. He believed that even human emotions would someday be deciphered and reduced to a numerical value. He looked forward to that day, because numbers do not lie.

People lie.

Cawley trusted nothing he heard. He timed the length of pauses and answers because statistics proved liars paused longer and gave shorter answers. He tracked eye movement because statistics proved liars looked up and to the side when visualizing a new response.

Cawley constantly looked for facial tells. He measured the angle and duration of every facial expression, searching for micro-expressions of concealed emotion because concealed emotions were more reliable than expressed emotions.

After a lifetime of scrutinizing the messenger, Cawley was incapable of simply listening to the message. He needed the numbers to add up.

Interesting guy.

Before his last mission in Istanbul, Cawley had been studying the history of the Order and analyzing its known missions. He had spent six months interviewing the oldest members of the Order and translating the earliest documents in the archives.

The sample size was too small for Cawley to draw any conclusions, but he was growing more and more frustrated with his inability to discern the logic behind many of the Founder's orders.

It was starting to weigh on his mind and affect his disposition. During his last interview, he had to apologize profusely for upsetting Old Brother Vogel, who did not care for his questions or observations. Which is why, when the Steward asked him the next day to lead a rescue mission, Brother Cawley had welcomed the chance to get back in the field.

But now, the Founder was asking him to serve on back-to-back missions, which was an intriguing statistical anomaly. Under the circumstances, Cawley had to consider the possibility that the Founder did not want him to return to his research.

Or return at all.

* * *

Cawley was sitting in a French Quarter courtyard with a serious case of jet lag, watching the sun rise. He was reconsidering his long-standing objection to Einstein's theory of relativity while waiting for Brother Reid to wake up.

"Good morning," Jax said an hour later, interrupting Cawley's train of thought.

"Morning, Brother."

"Got a minute?" Jax asked, gesturing indoors.

"Of course," Cawley said.

"The Founder visited me this morning," Jax said as soon as Cawley walked inside and closed the doors.

"What are our orders?"

"I've got to call the President of the Jesuit High School," Jax replied without any hesitation. "Name is... Finnegan. Father Finnegan. He'll put me in the classroom with my target."

"And then?"

Cawley saw Jax's lips thin and the corners of his mouth angle downwards for a fraction of a second. The young priest was not happy about something.

"Look, I don't know how to say this," Jax said plainly. "The Founder told me not to share those orders, even with my... I mean... even with you."

He's telling the truth, thought Cawley. *The self-correction was necessary because he was repeating what the Founder said.*

"What can I do to help you, Brother?" Cawley asked as casually as possible.

“Nothing. The Founder wants you to stay here. If I return tonight, the Founder will visit me again. If I don’t, he’ll visit you.”

Cawley nodded, but he thought Jax’s conversation with the Founder was illogical. After researching hundreds of orders delivered by the Founder, Cawley knew the Elder was always trusted with the specifics of a mission. There was no logical reason for the Founder to deviate from tradition or to hide Jax’s mission from another member of the Order. But now was not the time to voice that particular concern.

“Good enough. I’ll wait for you here,” Cawley said, trying to sound disinterested. He considered the illusion necessary. Any reluctance to follow the Founder’s orders could endanger them both.

“Serve well, Brother Reid.”

* * *

Chapter 7: School

But if our unrighteousness commend the righteousness of God, what shall we say?
Romans 3:5

Monday, November 11

The Jesuits know how to teach young men. Since 1847, they have been producing men-for-others at Jesuit High School, and only the school's address has changed. The "new" campus is located at the corner of Carrollton and Banks, where hopeful moms have been surrendering their sons since 1926.

"Today is Christmas," the Reverend Harry Tompson, S.J. '54 famously told mothers of pre-freshman at the start of every school year back in the 80s. "Because today you give me your sons. I promise to give them back. And, when I do, they *will* be fine young men." Small wonder moms would chew through walls for the man and his beloved school.

But to passers-by, it's just another high school. Brick and mortar around which students sometimes swarm like a kicked ant pile. Where lives are changed every day.

And nothing ever *really* happens.

*　　*　　*

Father Daniel Finnegan, S.J., was going to enjoy this.

His secretary, Liddy, pressed the intercom key on her phone and coughed loudly, which was the signal that Father Unger was coming down the hallway.

A second later, his phone rang.

Finnegan picked it up and heard Liddy, per his plan, tell Unger:

"Finn is stuck on an important call, but you can go right in."

Finn held the phone to his ear as he watched Unger walk into the President's Office, and enthusiastically waived him closer.

"I understand your concerns," Finn said into the phone.

"I don't think you do," Liddy replied softly from her desk in the adjacent room. "Are we really going to do this every time you have to break bad news to Unger?"

"Not every time," Finn replied. "Just this time."

With his peripheral vision, Finn saw Unger walk over and stand behind a leather wing-back chair. It was the first time the Head of the Theology Department had been inside his office since the much younger Finnegan had gotten the nod for President.

Instead of Unger.

Naturally, Unger had made no attempt to disguise his indignation. He was "livid" and felt "betrayed" by the Society, which is exactly what he told Father Finnegan.

Instead of "congratulations."

Unger was looking around the redecorated office and openly coveting Finn's mahogany bookshelves.

"Well, why don't you tell me in your own words," Finn told Liddy, who thankfully recognized the cue and started reading the newspaper aloud on the other end of the line.

Father Finnegan melodramatically rolled his eyes and covered the mouthpiece.

"I'm sorry, but this is going to take a while, Father Unger."

"Do you want me to come back later, Daniel?" Unger asked, clearly annoyed and still staring at the bookshelves.

"No, that's not necessary," Finn assured him. "Just wanted to let you know a young priest will be taking over your Theology class for seniors starting today."

Unger's jaw hit the ground.

"What! Why on earth ... ?"

Finn held up his index finger politely and turned his attention back to the phone call. "If that's true, then we have a much bigger problem, don't we?"

He covered the mouthpiece again.

"Not my call," he told Unger. "The Father Provincial called me this morning and told me to assign your class to this young priest."

"Were there complaints?"

"Of course not," Finn replied, before succumbing to temptation and adding: "At least, I don't think so."

"Well, why did he insist on giving the priest *my* class?"

Finn uncovered the mouthpiece.

"Go on, then. Get it off your chest," Finn told Liddy on the phone, who ignored him and continued to read the paper.

Finn covered the mouthpiece again.

"I asked the Father Provincial the same question," Finn assured him, which was true. "He said the order came from the top, whatever that means."

"From the top," Unger muttered skeptically.

Finn did not care for Unger's tone.

"Call him yourself, Donald," Finn told him sharply. "But why would you look a gift horse in the mouth? You just got a free period every day."

"But..."

"We'll talk more about this later," Finn told Unger with finality. "Please close the door behind you. This call is about to get ugly."

Finn uncovered the mouthpiece.

"Now it is my turn to talk," he said sternly into the phone for Father Unger's benefit. "Last time I checked, I'm the President of Jesuit High School. This is exactly the kind of decision I'm going to make. Now, I appreciate everything you've done for this school and for these boys, but I'm not going to go ten rounds with you every time we disagree."

"Unger is gone," Liddy reported. "And you are a sad little man."

Father Daniel Finnegan hung up the phone and smiled.

Best Monday morning. Ever.

* * *

Jax was late.

He had about two minutes before the bell, but he refused to run. He opened the door, passed the switchboard, entered the first floor hallway, and stopped to get his bearings.

Eighty seconds.

"Use the Banks Street entrance," Jax said, repeating aloud the instructions the President had given him. "Take a right. Lime green stairwell. Third Floor. Room 314."

Seventy-five seconds.

The absence of any students in the hallway was unnerving. When Jax reached the stairwell, he started taking two steps at a time. His shoes echoed on the tiled steps, but were muffled by the gray carpet on the second floor.

Forty-five seconds.

The rattle of glass shelves confirmed Jax ventured too close to the trophy cabinets as he negotiated the turn and reached the longer flight of stairs to the third floor. He picked up the pace.

Forty seconds.

Jax had received his orders directly from the Founder. He didn't have to like them. He didn't have to understand them. He just had to follow them, which was exactly what he was going to do when he reached the classroom.

Thirty-five seconds.

Jax reached the third floor and started down the Hall of Champions. He unconsciously shifted from a march to the quick-step as the last of the khaki uniforms disappeared into classrooms.

Thirty seconds.

Jax had tunnel vision. Doors and framed team photographs passed in a blur, with the years increasing and the classroom numbers decreasing.

1941. Room 334. 1979. Room 324. 1991. Room 320.

The second bell rang as the door to Room 314 slammed shut behind Jax, sounding like a bomb. Every head whipped around and beheld Jax's stern face and unforgiving eyes.

He had their full attention.

Jax did not hesitate. He walked to the board with purpose and wrote his name.

"I'm Brother Reid," he said with his back to the class. He finished writing the words and turned around.

"I'm your new teacher," he announced, scanning the room for his target. "Turn to Genesis, Chapter 1."

Five hands.

"In the beginning, God created the heavens and the earth," Jax recited from memory.

Three hands.

"The earth was formless and void and darkness was over the surface of the deep. And the Spirit of God was moving over the surface of the waters."

One hand.

"Then God said, 'Let there be light,' and there was light."

No hands.

Jax stopped, not for dramatic effect, but because he had already spotted the aberration. While other students dug for Bibles, wrote in notebooks, raised a hand, or looked around the room confused, one student remained perfectly still.

Front row. Two seats from the window. Directly in front of Jax.

Unnaturally still.

Jax looked at the white letters etched into the black nametag above the student's right shirt pocket. Letters that formed two words:

"Michael Broussard."

Jax was not surprised. Everything was exactly as the Founder said it would be. He stared into Michael's eyes.

Fight or flight? Jax wondered. *What will it be?*

"God saw that the light was good," Jax said slowly, mentally preparing to do what needed to be done and to do it properly.

"God separated the light from the darkness ..."

Jax lunged at Michael. As his hands closed on their target, Michael simultaneously stabbed his pencil upward at Jax's throat.

As the pencil point pierced his skin, Jax had only one thought:

Outstanding.

* * *

Doctor C.J. Lagarde loved medicine and Texas Hold'em poker.

He had spent his life studying and practicing both, and his instincts told him something was wrong.

Michael's cranial nerve exam was normal. His mental status exam revealed no evidence of cognitive dysfunction. He did not have the benefit of CT or MRI scans, but Lagarde was certain of two things: Michael's brain was normal and Michael was different.

Very different.

"Tell me again what happened, Brother Reid," Lagarde asked the stoic young man with an old bandage on his right wrist and a fresh bandage on his left forearm.

"Mr. Broussard was sitting at his desk," Jax replied. "His eyes rolled up in the back of his head like a shark. He started to fall forward. I lunged to stop his fall. I grabbed his shirt, and I popped him back up. He immediately regained consciousness."

Same exact words, thought Lagarde cynically. *Which only happens when a patient is sticking with a script.*

"And your left forearm?"

"I lost my balance when I grabbed his shirt, and my forearm came down on the tip of Mr. Broussard's pencil."

Lagarde nodded as if that made sense, but he was convinced Reid was lying.

But why is he lying? Lagarde wondered. *Who is Brother Reid protecting?*

He took his penlight and pretended to check Michael's optic nerve.

"Michael, tell me again what you remember."

Michael continued to stare forward as the light swung between his pupils.

"I definitely remember his lunging at me," Michael said. "But I don't remember losing consciousness."

Lagarde heard the sound of the door opening behind him and the familiar voice of a baby he delivered thirty-five years ago.

"I don't either!" declared Coach Will Taylor. "How are you feeling, Michael?"

"I'm good to go," Michael said, smiling for the first time.

"What's up, Doc?" Coach Will said, slapping Doctor Lagarde's shoulder.

"Hello, William."

"If he was a horse, would you shoot him?" Will asked, closing the door.

"He'll live," Lagarde replied. He smiled, patted Michael's shoulder, and turned around to introduce him properly. "Coach Will Taylor, this is Brother Jax Reid."

Lagarde watched the two men step toward each other and shake hands. Will was completely at ease, but Brother Reid's body language was odd. It was like Jax had been dreading this specific moment.

Like he was shaking hands with another fighter inside the ring.

Lagarde and Michael looked at each other at the same time. By the look on Michael's face, Lagarde could have sworn his patient was thinking the same thing.

"That's some grip," Will said, and his tone had changed. "You've got some serious callouses. Reminds me of Gunny Higgins."

Jax said nothing in reply. The handshake and the eye contact continued. It was Michael who interrupted the awkward silence.

"Why are you here, Coach?"

"I'm here to get checked out," Will said, releasing Jax's hand and looking at Michael. "Had a little car accident this weekend. Maybe you heard."

Michael nodded and smiled.

"But you seem to have cut in line," Will continued. "With that little stunt of yours in Brother Reid's class."

Lagarde did not welcome Will's levity. He knew something was wrong, and he needed time to figure out what it was.

"Uh, Doc, my next class is going to start soon," Michael said. "It's not my best class, and we have a test tomorrow."

"Then you'd better get going," Lagarde agreed. "Brother Reid, would you please walk Michael to his next class? I want someone with him when he takes the steps for the first time."

Jax nodded affirmatively while Michael shot Lagarde a quick look of surprise.

Not alarm, noted Lagarde. *Just surprise.*

"No exercise for the rest of the week, Michael." Lagarde added. "Definitely no boxing with your dad on Saturday. I want you to take it easy."

"Yes, sir," Michael promised, before turning to Coach Will. "See you in class this afternoon."

"Count on it," Will replied. "Nice to meet you, Jax."

Jax nodded but said nothing before walking out the room and down the hallway.

"William, I don't know what happened," Lagarde stated when Reid and Michael were gone. "But I don't believe Brother Reid."

"Why not?"

"Michael was conscious when he stabbed Brother Reid," Lagarde said bluntly. "And I want you to keep your eye on him."

"I'm on it," Will promised. "I'll watch Brother Reid like a hawk."

"Not Reid," Lagarde said, shaking his head emphatically. "Michael."

* * *

Michael was in uncharted waters.

He was certain Brother Reid was lying, but he had no idea what to do about it. His newly acquired instincts told him not to say anything and to go along with Brother Reid's story for now.

Michael watched the way Brother Reid walked down the gym corridor.

He walks like a gladiator entering a Coliseum, Michael thought. *He's a killer.*

Brother Reid stopped at the glass exit doors. He didn't rest his hands on the push-bar. Instead, he grabbed the push-bar like he wanted to prevent the door from being opened from the outside. Then he looked outside at Banks Street and up at the overcast sky.

"Do you see something?" Michael asked.

"No," Brother Reid replied, opening the door for Michael.

"Were you looking for something?"

"Yes."

When Brother Reid was finished, they crossed the street and entered the main building. Reid walked slightly behind Michael and followed him up the stairs to the second floor. They reached the classroom before the end of the period.

"We need to talk," Reid told Michael, breaking the silence. "We both know I lied to Doctor Lagarde."

"Yes, sir."

"I've got a job to do, Broussard," Reid said. His tone was deadly serious. "The instincts you've discovered since your Awakening should tell you I'm speaking the truth."

"Since my what?"

The school bell rang.

"Now is not the time," Reid said. "I'll deal with you later."

Michael got the feeling Brother Reid knew exactly what was going on, and he didn't want to wait for answers.

"What is happening to me?" Michael asked quickly, as the first wave of students entered the hallway. "Tell me something!"

"Strangers are coming for you," Reid replied, unfazed by the students starting to swarm around him. "Trust your instincts, but trust nobody."

Reid took a step closer.

"And I mean nobody."

Brother Reid turned abruptly and disappeared into a sea of students.

Michael was suddenly aware of how fast his heart was beating. *Something* told him Brother Reid was right. Strangers were coming for him, and he couldn't trust anyone.

Especially not Brother Reid.

* * *

Agrippa was expecting the worst.

He had been summoned again to the Great Chamber. Twice in the same century was a bad century. Twice in the same week meant the Seven had a job for him.

A job nobody else could do.

Agrippa watched the same two Guards open the doors to the Great Chamber. This time, he gave them both a look of admonition before entering, and they waited until he was halfway in the room before announcing him.

"Enters Agrippa," they practically whispered.

Again it was Raphael who greeted him, but his tone was all business.

"Thank you for returning, Brother Agrippa. We want you to hear the report of a Guardian we've summoned."

Agrippa looked over at the crescent-shaped table. Three seats still remained empty.

Michael, Gabriel, and Ramiel still serve in-theatre.

"It will be the Guardian's first time in the Great Chamber and the most important report the Seven have heard in many years," added Raphael. "Please join us at the Crescent, and let us present a united front."

Raphael's not exaggerating, Agrippa realized when he saw the faces of Uriel, Raguel, and Saraquel. *Time to close ranks.*

Agrippa walked over and stood behind his Captain's empty place at the table. Moments later, the doors of the Great Chamber opened, and Agrippa heard the sound of two spears rapping against the marble floor.

"Enters Phillip!" the Guards barked loudly.

"Welcome, Guardian," Raphael declared. "Is this your first time in the Great Chamber?" he asked, pretending not to know the answer.

"Aye, Elder Raphael," Phillip replied, his voice filled with respect and awe.

Raphael gave him a reassuring smile. "We summoned you because we need to know how and why your *protelos* left Scotland."

"Report, Guardian," Uriel commanded.

"Aye, Elder Uriel," the Guardian said, snapping to attention. "My *protelos* is Joshua Jackson Reid. Born in Detroit to the late Doug and Michelle Reid. Witnessed his parents' torture and death. Adopted by the Order of the Judged during his tenth year."

Agrippa turned to Raphael.

"What in the hell is he talking about?"

"Please, Agrippa," Raphael replied. "Let the Guardian give his report, and we will talk in private."

When the Guardian heard Agrippa's name, he immediately looked over at Agrippa and nodded so respectfully at the legend that he practically bowed.

"Continue, Guardian!" an annoyed Uriel ordered.

"Aye, Elder Uriel," the Guardian replied. "Jax was chosen for Initiation into the Order. He faced the dagger and the brand. Stood before the Founder and was judged worthy. The Founder branded him on the right wrist."

"I already know the answer, but I will ask anyway," said Raguel. "Did you witness the *Gennisi*? Did you see the Founder?"

"No, Elder Raguel," the Guardian reported with regret. "According to tradition, the *Gennisi* was held inside Castle Stalcaire. I could not enter."

"When were you reunited with your *protelos*?" Saraquel asked.

"The Founder gave him a mission late that night," the Guardian replied. "It was an unusual honor. Jax left before dawn for New Orleans."

Madness seized Agrippa.

He jumped over the table and landed inches from the face of the Guardian. To his credit, the Guardian did not flinch.

"Who were they sent for?" Agrippa demanded. "Tell me now!"

"You forget yourself, Agrip—" Uriel started.

"Silence!" Agrippa yelled, pointing at Uriel, but never taking his eyes off the Guardian. "Derrick Hill is in New Orleans, and I will know right now if my *protelos* is in danger."

Both Guards charged into the Great Chamber, but hesitated when they saw an enraged Agrippa the Great. Raphael quickly waved off the Guards, who visibly sighed before turning and exiting the Great Chamber.

Raphael nodded to Phillip to answer Agrippa's question.

"I don't know their target," Phillip reported. "Jax and Brother Cawley were trained by the Order. They would never discuss their mission in the open."

"Derrick is safe," Raphael told Agrippa in a calm and reassuring voice. "I would not have called you away from your *protelos* if he was in danger. Tell me you know that, Brother."

Agrippa had to get control of his rage. He took a deep breath and exhaled.

"Aye, Brother," Agrippa said before patting the Guardian on the back twice and returning to where he had been standing. "I know that."

"That is good to hear," Raphael said sincerely. "Please continue, Guardian."

Phillip snapped back to attention and proceeded.

"Jax arrived late in New Orleans and met with Brother Dean Cawley. They established a base camp in a Colonial-era building in the French Quarter, not far from the Cathedral. The next morning, Jax went to the high school run by the *Societas Iesu*. He seemed to be in a hurry."

"Did you see the incident?"

"Aye, Elder Saraquel. The windows of Jax's classroom face Carrollton Avenue, and Jax made no attempt to obscure our view, which I cannot explain."

"What does that mean?" Raguel asked.

"Jax was trained to conceal himself from our kind," the Guardian replied. "If he left the shades open, it was for a reason. Either Jax wanted me to see what happened or he wanted the other Guardians to see."

"Well, what did you see?"

The Guardian hesitated before replying.

"I saw Jax *appear* to attack a student."

"Which student?"

"A boy named Michael Broussard."

Agrippa looked at Raphael again, but Raphael's demeanor suggested he already knew this fact.

"Why do you say *appeared* to attack?" Saraquel asked.

"Because the student was not injured," the Guardian responded. "If Jax's intention was to injure an unarmed student, he would have succeeded."

"Then what was his intention?"

"It was a test," Agrippa replied, guessing Jax's true purpose and answering for the Guardian. "He was evaluating Michael."

"Aye, Brother," Phillip agreed. "Jax was testing the boy's instincts."

"Well, how did he respond?" Raphael asked.

The Guardian cleared his throat before answering.

"The boy stabbed Jax with a pencil."

Agrippa looked over at Raphael and chuckled.

"Sounds like he passed."

* * *

Will was working the chalk and watching the clock.

"There are three branches of government," Will told the class, quickly labeling the three boxes he drew on the board. "The legislative, the executive, and the judicial branches. These three branches create a system of what, Mr. Crane?"

"Checks and balances," the future valedictorian replied, sounding bored.

"Correct. The President has the power to veto Congress," Will explained while drawing an arrow from the executive box to the legislative box. "Congress has the power to override the President with a two-thirds majority vote, and the Supreme Court has the power to rule on the constitutionality of law."

Will added the additional arrows.

"We don't give all of the power to one branch because power corrupts, and absolute power corrupts ... ?"

"Absolutely," Crane yawned.

"Hey Coach, what does that mean?" big Gary Hotard asked.

Will checked the clock. Two minutes before the final bell of the day.

Perfect time for the annual Gyges Ring lesson.

"Plato tells the story of Gyges the Lydian to prove the point," Will said, putting down the chalk and sitting on the corner of his desk. "Gyges is a shepherd. He gets his hands on a gold ring that makes him invisible. So what does the good shepherd do? He seduces the Queen and kills the King. Absolute power corrupted Gyges, absolutely."

The entire class murmured either their understanding or their sincere admiration for the shepherd.

Ninety seconds.

"What would you do if you were invisible, Coach?"

"I'm a high school teacher, Mr. Hotard. I am invisible."

"It's a fair question," Crane observed. "What would you do if you were totally invisible, even to God?"

"You're forgetting something, Mr. Crane," Will replied.

Will surreptitiously reached into his desk drawer and palmed one of the yellow plastic rings he saved for this occasion.

"One person would still see and remember my choices."

Will scanned the class, wondering who would earn the plastic ring this year.

"You would."

"Correct, Mr. Broussard," Will said, surprised he had beat Crane and the rest of the class to the punch. "I would always remember my choices."

Thirty seconds.

"A truly just man always acts justly," Will continued. "A just man does not care about appearing just. A just man would act justly even if it would appear to the world he was acting unjustly."

Will tossed Michael the plastic yellow ring.

"To a just man, that plastic ring is as valuable and as worthless as Gyges' ring."

The ringing of the bell added an exclamation point.

Perfect timing.

"Mr. Broussard, Mr. Charbonnet, and Mr. Hill," Will yelled over the din of packing and leaving. "Let me see you up here for a second."

Will watched the three students make their way to the front of the class.

"Gentlemen, I've got to run, but I want to introduce you to our new student, Derrick Hill," Will said, gesturing to the broad-shouldered, muscular African-American student wearing a brand-new school uniform. "Mr. Hill is a junior who just transferred from Saint Aug."

Michael immediately recognized Derrick's last name.

"Hill? Did you play football at Saint Aug?" he asked. Given Derrick's impressive size and build, Michael pegged him for either a defensive end or a tight end.

"No, I was on the chess team."

Pause.

"You were on..."

"The chess team," Derrick repeated truthfully. "I had no choice. We ran out of smart kids."

Trey snorted.

"Hey, I didn't..." Michael started to say.

"What? Think I was smart?" Derrick quipped.

"No..."

"No?"

Something told Michael that Derrick was only teasing and to let Derrick have his fun. Hopefully, that *something* was correct.

"No, I mean... I'm sorry if I...."

Derrick finally let loose with a contagious laugh and gave Michael a friendly slap on the back.

"Relax, I'm kidding!"

Michael gave an exaggerated sigh of relief for Derrick's benefit.

"Actually, he's not kidding," Will assured them. "Mr. Hill *was* on the chess team, and he *is* smarter than both of you. Combined."

"But I didn't play football," Derrick admitted. "You're probably thinking of my cousin, Keith Hill. I'm into track and field. Discus. Javelin. And two-hundred meter dash."

"Well, that settles it," Trey announced. "Derrick's the wingman I've been looking for. No offense, Michael."

"None taken."

Will closed his satchel. "Derrick needs someone to show him around. Something told me to volunteer you two."

Will paused at the door and looked back at the unusual trio.

"Welcome aboard, Mr. Hill."

* * *

Raphael was getting an earful.

"I do not agree with this," Saraquel said passionately. "What we did was wrong, and Agrippa is a loose cannon."

"Perhaps," Raphael replied. "But he's *our* loose cannon."

"Which makes him *our* responsibility," Saraquel added. "Cannons have started more wars than they have ended."

Silence filled the Great Chamber.

"We are already at war," Uriel reminded her. "And Agrippa was already on the board. We just voted to move Agrippa to a position where he could support and protect Broussard."

"We did not vote to move Agrippa," insisted Saraquel, who had been the lone dissenter. "We voted to move Agrippa's *protelos,* Derrick Hill. For the sake of protecting one mortal, we endangered another."

"That is exactly what we've done," Uriel snapped. "Did you really think this war could be won without risking and losing mortal lives?"

"I agreed with the decision," Raguel declared. "The needs of the many outweigh the needs of the few or the needs of the one. But I share Sara's concern. What happens if Agrippa must someday choose between saving Broussard and saving Derrick? Would he break the Guardian's vow, Raphael?"

Raphael knew the answer, as did the others. As soon as Agrippa agreed to their plan, they all knew what Agrippa would do. Raguel just wanted to hear Raphael say it out loud.

So Raphael did.

"If we allow the Fallen to take Broussard, we may be sacrificing all mortals," Raphael declared with conviction. "If this is the End of Days, we do what must be done."

"And the mortals we have sworn to protect become means to an end?" Saraquel asked in total disbelief.

"They become exactly what they are," Raphael said. "Casualties of war."

"You don't really believe that, Brother!" Saraquel gasped. "That path leads—"

"That path leads wherever it leads, Sister."

*   *   *

Saraquel grabbed the ornate door knocker.

She banged four times and paused. She banged once more, paused, and banged a final time. It was the bizarre signal Rachel had requested if, for any reason, Saraquel had to re-enter the Chapel before her Vigil ended.

Saraquel took a deep breath, opened the door, and entered the rear of the Chapel. This time, Rachel was not standing at the end of the aisle to greet her. This time, Rachel remained kneeling and did not turn around.

Saraquel did not delay. She had come to tell Rachel one thing and one thing only.

"The Fallen have found him."

*   *   *

Chapter 8: Skirmishes

For he shall give his angels charge over thee, to keep thee in all thy ways....
Psalm 91:11

Thursday, November 14

Father Unger wanted answers.

He had been teaching for more than forty years, and had never heard of a teacher losing a class in the middle of a semester unless they were being fired.

Father Unger pressed the phone to his ear and patiently waited for the Father Provincial to get on the line.

"This is Father Moore."

"Randall, it is Donald Unger in New Orleans."

Pain-filled pause.

"What can I do for you, Father Unger?"

"I don't know if you are aware of this, Randall, but Father Finnegan gave my senior elective class to a Brother Reid."

"Of course I'm aware of it," Moore said. "I told him to do it. Now what can I do for you, Donald?"

The Father Provincial's tone threw Father Unger, but only for a moment.

"I need to know why."

"No, you don't need to know why," Moore replied. "You just want to know why, which is somewhat understandable under the circumstances."

"Did you say *somewhat*?"

"This has nothing to do with you," Moore assured him. "And I'll tell you exactly what I told Father Finnegan. This order came from the top."

Unger grimaced. He did not dare reveal that he already knew that little tidbit. Father Moore thought very highly of Father Finnegan and would be furious with Unger for not trusting him.

"What does that mean?"

"You wouldn't believe me if I told you."

"It would mean a lot to me if you would, Randall."

Unger heard the Father Provincial groan on the other end of the phone.

"The Superior General called me," the Father Provincial reluctantly told him. "And I'm not at liberty to tell you anything more than that."

Unger was stunned.

"Now, is there a problem with Brother Reid?"

Unger could not bring himself to say "no." He knew that particular answer would mean the end of the call, so he repeated exactly what he heard earlier that day.

"I heard he attacked a student on Monday."

"Did he kill the student?"

"No."

"Have a great day, Donald."

Click.

* * *

Emma was loaded for bear, and the damn bear strolled right into Rock 'n' Bowl.

It had been twelve days since Gavin dumped her, which was twelve days longer than Emma Landry needed to think of a dozen really hurtful things to tell him. Things that Gavin would remember for the rest of his life.

Truths that would bring him to his knees.

Emma laughed out loud when she saw that Gavin had brought most of his offensive line with him. Even in a loud and crowded bowling alley, Gavin was too much of a coward to face her alone. Too afraid of what she might say or do to him.

With good reason.

Emma was filled with excitement as she watched Gavin saunter toward her counter. She couldn't wait for him to flash his "are you okay" face, and to hear whatever lame apology he had been practicing.

I wonder if he'll give me the "it's not you, it's me" line, Emma mused. *Or is he dumb enough to blame the break-up on our "drifting apart"?*

Emma had prepared devastating responses to both, but she personally hoped Gavin would go with the "drifted apart" line. Of course, it didn't really matter.

I'm ready for anything, she thought as Gavin reached the counter.

"Emmy-licious!"

Well, maybe not anything.

"What did you just call me?"

"Emmy-licious," Gavin repeated, before turning around and making certain his friends could hear him. "But what's in a name, right, guys? That which we call a rose by any other name would smell as sweet."

"Wait... what did you just say?"

"From *Romeo and Juliet*," Gavin replied, obviously forgetting Emma had explained the quote to him while writing his paper on Shakespeare.

"Yes, I uh..." Emma started to say.

"Hey, listen," Gavin interrupted, lowering his voice and flashing his most charming smile. "I hope this is cool with you. My buddies wanted to bowl, and I told them this was the best place in town. You okay with our bowling here?"

"Uh, no, I mean... yes, it's okay with... but what I don't..."

"Great!" Gavin said. "I'm glad this isn't going to be awkward for us."

And, just like that, Round One went to Gavin.

"Me too," Emma said, forcing a smile. She quickly grabbed a pair of size twelve bowling shoes for Gavin and found out what sizes the other players needed. Then she mindlessly turned on the monitor for the last available lane.

"All set," she told Gavin. "Lane Six."

Emma watched Gavin's friends head toward Lane Six and noticed that Gavin was intentionally hanging back.

Here it comes, thought Emma. *Here comes the apology he owes me and the excuse he can't wait to give me.*

"Hey, Emma. I gotta tell you something."

"What?"

"These guys are starving," Gavin said. "Will you grab us some dogs, a few nachos, and a pitcher?"

Emma nodded, too stunned to object.

"Thanks, Babe."

Emma watched Gavin traipse over to Lane Six, where the mastodons were waiting for their alpha male. When he arrived, the herd parted and Emma caught a glimpse of Lane Seven. Only then did she realize Gavin would be bowling in the lane next to Michael, Trey, and their new friend.

Which is fine, Emma told herself. *Gavin doesn't know about Michael and me.*

She thought about that for a second.

Because there is no "Michael and me," Emma reminded herself as she placed Gavin's order with the kitchen, marking the official end of Round Two, which also went to Gavin. On all cards.

Emma needed to regroup.

By the time Gavin's food was ready, she had decided on a new strategy for handling the situation. Instead of attacking Gavin, she was going to kill him with kindness, and she was going to start by personally delivering their food.

"Thanks, Babe!" Gavin said enthusiastically, while Emma set down the tray of food. "What'd I say, guys? Emma's the best!"

"You're welcome, Gavin," Emma said graciously, still trying to remember when he started calling her "Babe," and silently swearing to kill the next boy who did.

"You're all set," she added. "Enjoy your game!"

"Hey, Emma," Gavin said before she could leave. "Wasn't this the first lane we bowled together?"

"No," she replied. "It was Lane Eight."

"That's right," Gavin agreed, eager to recite the jingle he invented that night. "Lane Eight was great for our first date!"

"Yes, Lane Eight was great," Emma reluctantly admitted, remembering how nervous Gavin had been and how special he made her feel that night.

Suddenly, Emma's smile disappeared.

"Hey, but I do remember the lane where I gave you my letter sweater," Gavin announced proudly. "Lane One. I took your picture against that wall."

Emma felt her throat tighten as she recalled how good his sweater had felt and smelled the first time she put it on.

"You still have it, right?" he joked. "You didn't burn it?"

Emma nodded, now struggling with unexpected emotion.

"Good times," Gavin said, dipping another chip into the vanishing nacho cheese. "Celebrating all those wins. Good times, huh Babe?"

"I don't want you here," Emma said softly, almost to herself.

"What's that, Babe?" Gavin asked, dipping another chip. "What'd you say?"

"I don't want you here," she repeated only a little more loudly. "Please leave."

Gavin heard the last word and looked up.

Eye contact was more than Emma wanted. She turned around and started to walk away.

"Wait!" Gavin said, jumping up and grabbing Emma's wrist firmly enough that it kind of jerked her back toward him. "Don't leave like that."

Emma stopped dead in her tracks and looked down at the gigantic paw now gripping her wrist.

It was exactly the wake-up call Emma needed, but before she could give Gavin a piece of her mind, she heard a familiar voice say:

"Let go of her wrist."

*　　*　　*

Michael was cool as a fan.

"Let go of her wrist... and grab mine."

That got Gavin's attention. He released Emma's hand and squared off on Michael. Simultaneously, four of the largest men in the State of Louisiana stood up behind Gavin. Out the corner of his eye, Michael saw Emma take off running.

Hopefully for help.

Michael knew Gavin's posse. Giant slabs of beef who spent months in the weight room and on the practice field training to make certain nobody touched Gavin. They had sweat equity in their quarterback, and they looked eager to protect their investment. And prove their loyalty.

This is going to get ugly.

By all accounts, Michael should have been panicking, but he wasn't. *Something* was already sending his brain information.

Important information.

It told him that Gavin was a lover not a fighter and would never swing first. And that the baby-faced lineman, who was the last to stand up, was breathing a little faster than the others. Michael was certain

Baby-Face had never been in a bar fight and was much braver in shoulder pads and a helmet.

Which was good to know.

Unfortunately, that same *something* told Michael the other three linemen were veterans of countless fights and knew the drill.

Even if I drop Gavin and Baby-Face, those guys are going to kill me.

"Is there a problem here, gentlemen?" Trey asked as he walked up and stood shoulder-to-shoulder with Michael.

Make that kill me… and my best friend.

"No Trey. There's no problem, here," Derrick said matter-of-factly as he too walked up and stood shoulder-to-shoulder with Michael. "Way I see it. This is just between Michael and the prima donna."

Derrick's arrival and his bold proposal wiped the smile off Gavin's face and caused Baby-Face to start puffing-up like a blowfish. The other three linemen said nothing. They just put their cups down.

Go time!

"Take Baby-Face," Michael said quickly to Trey, hoping it would improve his buddy's chances of survival.

"Ladies and gentlemen!" Emma's voice rang out over the intercom. "Please turn your attention to Lane Six, where Rock 'n' Bowl is honored to have five—count 'em five—members of our very own L-S-U Fighting Tigers football team, including former Jesuit great, quarterback Gavin Driscoll. Gavin and the guys have to leave *right now* for a charity event, but let's give them a big hand as they go!"

The packed bowling alley erupted in applause.

Michael locked eyes with Gavin. The entire bowling alley now knew exactly who they were and where they played ball.

They're not invisible anymore.

If Gavin and his gang started a fight now, there would be plenty of witnesses, an article in the morning paper, and a formal investigation by the school. And if they stayed to bowl another frame, everyone would think they had skipped a charity event.

"Geaux!" the intercom cried.

"Tigers!" the bowling alley replied.

"Next time, Broussard," Gavin told Michael before heading toward the exit.

"Geaux!"

"Tigers!"

Michael watched as Gavin and his engorged entourage waived to the crowd and walked out. Michael expected to feel relief, but he didn't. Instead, he felt a mixture of frustration and sadness.

Like disappointment, Michael thought. *Exactly like disappointment.*

"Geaux!" Emma cried one last time.

"Tigers!"

"L-S-U!" Everyone chanted together.

When the clapping ended, it was Derrick who broke the silence.

"Late for a charity event." He chuckled. "That girl is crazy."

* * *

Agrippa the Great loved drama.

It was the worst-kept secret in the City of God. Nothing entertained Agrippa more than human confrontation. He considered himself a student of the game, and he tirelessly studied the fine line between love and hate.

Strange but true.

Agrippa did more than just watch Emma Landry run out of Rock 'n' Bowl with Michael Broussard in hot pursuit. He mentally dissected and savored everything from the look on her face to the length of her stride. He could see Emma was upset. Her clenched fists indicated she was more angry than sad.

But what most interested Agrippa was the way Emma slowed her pace as soon as she heard the bowling alley door open and slam behind her. At least subconsciously, Emma wanted Michael to catch her before she reached her car.

Agrippa couldn't wait for Michael to do exactly that.

Suddenly, Emma stopped running, wheeled around, and fired for effect.

"You had no right!" she told Michael. "That was none of your business. That was private. It was between me and Gavin. It was not your place!"

"What are you talking about?" Michael fired back. "He grabbed your wrist!"

"He wasn't hurting me!"

"Hurting you?" Michael declared in disbelief. "He doesn't touch you!"

The parking lot fell silent.

"He doesn't touch me?" Emma repeated slowly. "Well, no wonder you were angry, Michael. Gavin was touching me without your permission!"

"Get in there, Brother Jacob," Agrippa chuckled. "Our boy's in trouble."

"Enough, Emma!" Michael snapped. "You're mad. I get it. But we both know I'm not that guy."

"Well, I'm not that girl," Emma assured him. "I didn't need you to rescue me. I didn't *want* you to rescue me. I'm stronger than you think, and you made me look weak in front of Gavin. Weak and—"

"I know you're strong," Michael interrupted. "You know you're strong. Why do you care how Gavin sees you?"

Agrippa heard Emma's Guardian second that emotion, but Emma looked angrier than she did before the compliment.

"Don't you lecture me, Michael Broussard!" Emma screamed. "Don't you dare! You've been a zombie for the past four years. Now you want to tell me something? Okay, tell me why I should care how *you* see me!"

Jacob quickly whispered something in Michael's ear. For Michael's sake, Agrippa hoped it was good advice.

Michael did not hesitate. He walked right up to Emma, cupped her face in his hands, and kissed her as passionately as Agrippa had seen for centuries.

When Michael stopped, he looked Emma in the eyes and smiled.

Agrippa watched with bated breath as Emma took a step back, steadied herself, and threw a set of keys at Michael's chest.

"Close up!" Emma told him.

Agrippa chuckled as Emma walked away, angrily mumbling something that sounded a lot like "idiot."

"You told him to kiss her?" an astonished Agrippa asked Jacob a moment later.

"Of course not," Jacob replied. "I told him to run."

* * *

"The ambush is tonight."

Brother Cawley nodded but said nothing. Taking his time, he closed the book he was reading and returned it to the bookshelf. His experience told him Brother Reid was seventy percent more likely to volunteer additional information if he remained quiet. As usual, his calculation was correct.

"I've got my orders from the Founder," Reid continued. "In a few hours, Michael will be alone in the bowling alley parking lot."

Cawley knew he was out of time, but there was something he needed to do.

"Good," he replied. "I'm tired of waiting. We are going to need weapons. Follow me."

Brother Cawley led Reid down the hallway toward the courtyard. He let Reid go outside first and closed the French doors behind them.

"We don't have much time," Cawley said with urgency while making certain to keep his back to the windows facing the courtyard. "Where did he visit you?"

"In the kitchen," a stunned Reid replied. Discussing the Founder and his mission in the open was strictly prohibited.

"That's interesting," Cawley told him. "He's never visited anyone in a kitchen, even the kitchen of Castle Stalcaire. Why would he appear in a kitchen?"

"Because I was in the kitchen."

"No, it doesn't add up," Cawley insisted. "For the past hundred years, the Founder has always visited the Steward, and the Elder has always known the mission."

"We need to get going," Reid stated in a tone that made it clear Cawley had crossed a line.

"Come on, Brother. Think!" Cawley demanded. "I can accept one or two deviations from the norm, but why would everything about this mission be different? What are the odds of that being random?"

"Brother, I have no idea," Reid replied impatiently. "May we discuss this later?"

"Of course," Cawley said, walking alongside him and lowering his voice. "But you'd better start thinking for yourself, and you can start by figuring out why this mission is being kept a secret from the rest of the Order."

Brother Reid stepped back and removed a dagger from his black robe. His grip tightened as he lowered it to his side.

"I have no doubt about my mission," Jax said, sounding calm and certain. "But I need to know right now. Are you with us or against us?"

"I'm with you, Brother," Cawley said, sounding exhausted and sincere. "Forgive me. I was wrong to question the Founder."

"Good," Reid said, sighing almost imperceptibly before sheathing the blade.

"We must always follow orders," Cawley added, carefully watching Reid's face.

What Cawley saw gave him hope. The corners of the young priest's smiling mouth had betrayed him.

With a micro-expression of disapproval.

* * *

Michael could feel *something* coming.

It was past midnight, and he was alone in the empty bowling alley. Trey and Derrick had left around ten o'clock because it was a school night. And Emma had not returned.

Michael walked around the bowling alley, turning off lights and making sure all the rooms were empty. When he was finished, he slowly walked down the steps and stopped at the front door.

Something is definitely wrong.

Michael peeked out the front door half expecting to see Gavin waiting for him, but the parking lot was empty, except for his father's car. The sight of the Goat reminded Michael that his dad was out of town and nobody was waiting at home.

Why does that concern me? Michael wondered. *It never has in the past.*

Michael pulled out the keys Emma had melodramatically and unnecessarily thrown at him earlier that evening. He had no idea which key on the ring was the front door key. He shook his head, crammed Emma's keys back into his pocket, and pulled out his own set. He entered the alarm code, stepped outside, and locked the door.

It was unusually cold and windy for November. Michael pulled the hood of his sweatshirt over his head and headed for the Goat. When he got about halfway, he looked up and stopped dead in his tracks.

Two priests were standing at the far end of the parking lot about a hundred yards from Michael. They were standing unnaturally still, and the bottoms of their long black robes were whipping in the wind.

The one on the right was Brother Reid.

Both priests pulled strangely shaped knives from their sleeves, looked at each other, and started sprinting toward Michael.

Michael spun around and saw that he was trapped. Two more strangers were now standing between him and the bowling alley entrance, blocking his retreat. They were not priests, but they were also dressed in black. The pale man to his left was tall and thin. The man to his right was much larger and looked African. Michael could tell they were evil by their eyes.

Eyes filled with pain and hate.

* * *

Michael was a statue.

Before either stranger could attack, Brother Reid raced past Michael and engaged the pale man, slashing his dagger with barely controlled fury. The pale man dodged Reid's blade effortlessly before striking the young priest's head with his hilt of his sword. The force of the blow knocked Reid unconscious, and Michael watched Reid's limp body slam into the concrete.

Motionless.

A moment later, Reid's comrade ran past Michael and attacked the African. This priest seemed to be more skilled, and the tenacity of his left-handed attack forced the African to take several steps back.

But only for a moment.

The African was quicker and stronger. He methodically slashed the priest's torso and arms, until the priest made a desperate lunge for his chest. The African parried the thrust and drove his sword through the priest's heart and out the priest's back. The light from a street lamp reflected off the exposed tip of the bloody sword before the African withdrew the blade, and the dead priest fell to the concrete.

Michael looked at the two motionless priests and back at his attackers, who did not wipe or sheathe their swords.

"What do you want?" Michael heard himself ask.

"It's not what we want. It is what we have been ordered to do," the pale man replied with what sounded like regret.

"We've been ordered to kill you, Mikha El."

Michael watched as both men started walking toward him, but he did not watch for long. His view was suddenly obstructed by the appearance of a third man who appeared out of nowhere and stood between Michael and the killers.

It was the angel he had seen kneeling beside him at the game.

"You will not harm this mortal," the man said while drawing a sword. "Not on my watch. Not ever."

"Welcome, Guardian," the pale man sighed, as if this meant more work for him. "You are called 'Jacob,' are you not?"

Yes, that's his name, thought Michael.

"I am."

How do I know that?

"Well, I am Marcellus, and this is Dante," the pale man replied, and Michael heard his Guardian swear under his breath.

Probably not a good sign.

"Then you are counted among the Fallen," the Guardian said. "And my duty is clear."

"We have no quarrel with you, Jacob," Marcellus said calmly. "Leave us now to our unpleasant task."

"No," Jacob replied. "You will not harm him."

Marcellus looked disappointed, but Dante looked amused.

"Yes, we will," Dante jeered. "But first we will tear your body to pieces and—"

"So be it," Marcellus said, interrupting Dante's threat. "We admire your loyalty, but choices have consequences. Please remember we offered to spare you, Brother."

Just then, a black-haired beauty appeared behind Michael and walked past him to stand beside Jacob, wielding a short sword.

"You heard what the Guardian said," the woman declared in a melodic but menacing tone. "Return to your master. It is not Michael's time."

"Rachel!" Marcellus declared. "You beautiful creature! It has been too long, Sister."

"Yes, what a pleasant surprise," Dante said wryly and without sounding the least bit surprised by her arrival. "Welcome, Rachel of Judah."

"Dear God," Jacob gasped. "You're *that* Rachel."

"She is indeed," Marcellus confirmed.

Rachel looked back at Michael.

"This won't take long," she promised with a mischievous smile before letting loose a guttural battle cry and attacking Marcellus.

She moved quickly, but Michael recognized her at once.

Raven-Hair!

* * *

Michael's brain was fried.

Ten minutes ago, he was locking up a bowling alley. Now, he was standing near two motionless priests and watching a sword fight. And he was pretty sure he knew two of the combatants.

Really well.

Some part of Michael's brain watched Jacob react to Rachel's charge by simultaneously attacking Dante. Another part of his brain catalogued the arrival of a third protector beside him, but Michael could not take his eyes off Rachel. For some reason, her presence was the most difficult to accept.

"Spectacular, isn't she?" the newest arrival declared.

"Help her!" Michael pleaded.

"I cannot," the iron-jawed man replied calmly, never taking his eyes off the fight. "Once single combat begins, I cannot interfere."

"Then give me your sword," Michael demanded.

Iron Jaw smiled but did not turn his head.

"Do you know how to use it?"

"No."

"Then be patient," Iron Jaw told Michael. "This is only a skirmish, and I am only here to make certain these assassins do not harm you."

Marcellus slammed his sword into Rachel's, and the force knocked her off balance. She recovered, but barely in time to block the next blow. To her left, Dante and Jacob were circling each other. Dante was smiling and Jacob looked frustrated. The reality of the situation came crashing down on Michael.

"They can't win."

"No," Iron Jaw agreed matter-of-factly. "Rachel is weaker and less skilled. Jacob is surprisingly good, but Dante is stronger and more patient. It is only a matter of time."

He's right, thought Michael. *I have to do something.*

"They fight like they are possessed," the man observed with admiration. "They must love you, Mikha El."

Michael stole a second look at the man standing beside him. He was older than Dante and Marcellus, but strikingly good-looking. His eyes were tracking the fight like a hawk, but his body was completely at ease. Something told Michael he was deadly. Whoever sent him had chosen well.

The sound of fighting stopped abruptly.

All four combatants were staring at the darkness on the edge of the parking lot, where a dozen figures were emerging from the darkness.

"No!" Dante bellowed. "We must not fail!"

"No choice," Marcellus replied sternly. "Another time, Rachel!"

Marcellus and Dante started running north and disappeared in the middle of the empty parking lot. Six of the new arrivals immediately took off in the same direction and disappeared into the night.

"What the hell!" Michael exclaimed. "Did you see that?"

But Iron Jaw was already gone.

*   *   *

Guardian Jacob's head was spinning.

The ambush had been planned, and he could not imagine why the Prince of Darkness would send his most trusted servants to kill Michael Broussard.

Who are these armed priests who attack without hesitation? Jacob wondered.

Where are their Guardians?

Why am I standing next to Rachel of Judah?

Jacob watched as Elder Saraquel, one of the Seven who stand before God, approached from the edge of the parking lot. Just then, the young priest moaned and tried to sit up. When he did, Jacob caught a glimpse of a bandage on his right wrist.

No!

Jacob rushed over to the dead priest and lifted his right arm out of the pool of blood. He whispered a quick prayer, wiped the blood from the priest's right wrist, and saw the brand.

Suddenly, the pieces of the puzzle fit.

"Mother of Pearl!" Jacob exclaimed, looking at Rachel. "Tell me this is not what it looks like. Tell me my first assignment wasn't..."

"You fought well, Guardian," Rachel said, flashing an irresistible smile. "We will never forget your loyalty and courage."

"Merciful God," Jacob gasped, turning to Michael. "How can I protect you now?"

*   *   *

Rachel was smiling.

"Good timing, Sara!" Rachel called as Saraquel approached. "This time, I am very glad to see you."

"Save it, Rachel," Saraquel replied angrily. "I will deal with you later."

Saraquel turned to the closest member of the Old Guard.

"You know where Agrippa is," Sara said. "Find him quickly, Kadmus. Tell him what happened and that I need him to get Michael home."

Kadmus nodded and disappeared as Sara faced Jacob.

"Report, Guardian," Saraquel ordered.

"Aye, Elder Saraquel," Jacob replied, snapping to attention. "My *protelos* is Michael Broussard. He was attacked by Marcellus and Dante. Two priests with tattooed right wrists attacked the Fallen. Neither priest was protected by a Guardian. One priest is dead. The other is wounded. When they failed, I intervened, as did... uh, Sister Rachel."

"Wait. I'm your... what?" a stunned Michael asked.

"Good report," Saraquel said, ignoring Michael. "Take the boy and the priest to the Broussard home. They will be safe there. The Old Guard will go with you, but I doubt there will be another attack tonight. The Fallen were not expecting us, and they do not attack without numbers."

"Aye, Elder Saraquel," Jacob replied. "Michael, get in the Goat."

Michael remained where he was.

"Who are you?"

"Your friends," Jacob replied, lifting the unconscious priest off the ground and putting him in the backseat of the Goat. Then Jacob picked up both daggers and walked around to the driver's door.

"But... those men... vanished," Michael stuttered.

"Michael, get in the Goat," Jacob repeated, pointing at the front passenger seat. "I'll drive."

Michael looked over at Rachel.

"And... I... I dream of you."

"You dream of me, Michael?" Rachel repeated, more than a little amused. She fully intended to tease the warrior about this for centuries.

"Why do I—" Michael continued.

"No!" Saraquel insisted. "Rachel, I forbid it."

Rachel gave a mischievous smile.

"What is the month and day, Michael?

"There's no time!" Jacob pleaded as sirens could now be heard in the distance.

"November," Michael replied. "Fourteenth... no, uh, fifteenth."

"Really?" Rachel beamed. "November fifteenth."

"Oh, for goodness sake!" Saraquel declared. "It's a coincidence, Rachel. Nothing more. We have to get him out of here."

"Agreed."

Rachel went to Michael, reached up, and gently tucked some of his hair behind his right ear. She thought of how long it had been since they were together, and how much longer it could be.

"Now!" Saraquel ordered as the sirens got closer.

Rachel slid her hand behind Michael's neck, kissed him on the cheek, and whispered in his ear:

"Happy anniversary."

* * *

Jacob was driving like a madman.

The radio had been blaring "Blitzkrieg Bop" since Jacob started the car and peeled out the parking lot. Michael was in the front passenger seat and a groggy Brother Reid was sandwiched between two members of the Old Guard in the back.

"Hold on!" Jacob yelled.

Members of the Old Guard kept appearing on street corners just ahead of the Goat and pointing out the detours they wanted him to take.

Which is smart, Jacob thought. *The Fallen will expect us to take the most direct route.*

Jacob turned onto a stretch of straight road and hit the gas. Houses and parked cars flew past on his left and right, contributing to his tunnel vision. Nothing was going to stop or distract him.

Except this.

Jacob slammed on the brakes, and the car screeched to a stop three feet from the outstretched hand of Agrippa the Great, who was standing in the center of the road like a traffic cop.

"Wait here," Agrippa told Jacob. "You may be driving into an ambush."

Jacob nodded in agreement, but then said exactly what he was thinking:

"Act quickly. We are sitting ducks."

"Enough, Brother!" Agrippa chuckled. "You worry too much!"

As Jacob watched through the front windshield, four more members of the Old Guard appeared in the middle of the street and positioned themselves around the car like Secret Service agents.

"Who are you?" the shaken voice of Michael asked Jacob.

"I'm your Guardian Angel, Michael," Jacob said as unfamiliar Guardians started appearing on nearby porches and balconies.

Probably guarding the residents, but there is no way of knowing for certain.

"And right now I have my hands full, buddy."

"But I… I don't believe in God," Michael stammered.

"Yes, I know," Jacob replied as a group of local Guardians started approaching the vehicle. "You may want to re-think that."

"Hold, Brothers!" Agrippa yelled, drawing his sword and prompting the rest of the Old Guard to do the same. "I cannot allow you to approach those in our care."

Uncertain silence.

"Who do you guard tonight, Brother Agrippa?" the oldest of the neighborhood Guardians replied a moment later, gesturing to the others to stay where they were.

Agrippa turned around and looked back at the Broussard vehicle.

Don't say it, Brother, Jacob pleaded with his eyes. *Please don't say it.*

A little smile formed on Agrippa's face before he replied.

"Who is like God?"

*　　*　　*

Hopelessly outnumbered is a state of mind.

Agrippa and thirty hastily-recruited Guardians crashed into a wall of Fallen, determined to clear a path for the car and its precious cargo. At the point of the spear, Agrippa was the first to breach and was instantly surrounded by screams and slashing steel.

Yes! the tortured warrior thought as he felt the familiar surge of adrenaline. *It has been too long!*

Agrippa sliced an unprotected gut to his right, ducked a wild swing, stabbed a thigh, grabbed a wrist, dodged a thrust, severed a hand, and cut a throat. Then instinct and muscle memory took over, and Agrippa really found his groove. He began attacking in short, controlled bursts.

And laughing maniacally.

Agrippa plowed forward, and the car followed in his wake. Nothing else mattered. Not the odds. Not the slashes he felt. Not even the Guardians falling around him. He had focus and purpose again. Singular purpose.

And it was exhilarating.

The servant of God lost himself in the battle until the squeal of crunching steel erupted behind him. Agrippa wheeled around and found himself looking up at a dark angel on a caved-in hood.

"Here!" Agrippa yelled as the Fallen smashed the windshield. "Here is your fight, Brother!"

The dark angel hesitated but answered the challenge. He spun around, planted his right foot, and leapt at Agrippa, swinging his blade downward with all of his force and momentum.

Agrippa waited until the last second before shifting to allow the committed blade to pass inches from his nose, and the foolish attacker landed a split second before Agrippa's sword severed his lumbar spine.

Two more Fallen fought through the ring of Guardians and reached the stalled car. Agrippa tackled the closest, savagely head-butted him, and then crushed his larynx with the butt of his sword. In his peripheral vision, Agrippa saw the Fallen dragging the innocent boy out of the car.

He could not reach the boy in time.

"Now, Kadmus!" Agrippa ordered.

Kadmus obeyed, instantly transforming from an eighteen year-old boy to a battle-hardened member of the Old Guard. The surprised assailant lost his grip, and Kadmus buried his blade in the angel's kidney.

"Stay!" Agrippa barked as the rest of the Fallen realized Michael was not in the car and fled. "Stay and fight, Brothers!"

Kadmus and a handful of surviving Guardians quickly regrouped around Agrippa, but none of the Fallen remained behind.

"Come back!" Agrippa the Great chuckled, knowing they had bought Michael and Jacob the time they needed. "We're outnumbered!"

* * *

Chapter 9: Investigation

Then shalt thou enquire, and make search, and ask diligently...
Deuteronomy 13:14

(2:23 a.m.) Friday, November 15

This was the fun part.

No matter how many cases Detective Thomas Cavet worked, he always got the same thrill out of trying to solve a homicide. It was better than working on a jigsaw puzzle because the crime scene only gave him the borders.

He had to earn the center pieces.

Cavet was old school. He took out his pocket notebook and removed the tiny pencil he stored inside the metal rings. One notebook for each homicide, and Cavet always burned the notebook after typing his final report.

It was his little tradition, and it was one of the reasons defense attorneys called him "Detective Caveman." They meant it as an insult, but he kind of liked it.

Cavet walked across the Rock 'n' Bowl parking lot to the victim and immediately started scribbling.

Male. White. Face-down. 6', 170 lbs. Clothes = black + clerical.

The clothing was unusual. It looked old-fashioned, but it was made out of lightweight and modern material. Like it was designed to resemble clothing from another century, but to be more functional. No tags or markings of any sort on the inside of the collar. Hand-made and very expensive.

Not local.

Cavet looked around. The congealed blood around the victim was the only blood they found in the parking lot. There was no evidence anybody else had been injured, but he never trusted his eyes.

"Delery, grid the entire parking lot and check every inch for blood and hair."

"That could take all morning, Tom."

"Then it takes all morning."

The sight and sound of a large white pickup truck meant the rather colorful coroner had arrived.

Tom never understood why the Great State of Louisiana thought the position of coroner should be an elected position, and an office for which literally anyone could run. Personally, Cavet believed coroners should be appointed by a blue ribbon panel, but what did he know? He just had to solve murders with them.

At least Cavet had it better than detectives in other parishes. The Orleans Parish coroner was a real character, but he was also a damn fine forensic pathologist and the only genius Cavet had ever met.

Doctor Claude Villere had been the coroner for thirty years, and Cavet had learned to respect and trust his opinion. Not just Villere's medical opinion regarding the cause and time of death, but his opinion on everything from the type of weapon to the position of a shooter.

Like Cavet, Villere was an anachronism. He was the only coroner who still insisted on examining the body at the scene, and his instincts were uncanny.

Cavet watched the coroner get out his pickup truck. Against all odds, he appeared to be totally sober.

"Hi neighbor, hi neighbor, what are ya doing? What do ya say!" Villere sang as he walked toward Cavet and slipped on latex gloves.

Okay, relatively sober, thought Cavet.

"Sorry to drag you out of... uh, bed. But we have a dead priest and no suspects. I wanted you to see the crime scene before we touched anything."

"Yes, yes, my good man. Now, let's move this crime scene indoors!" Villere declared loudly. "This night air is doing nothing for my singing, *right, right, okay, right?*"

Cavet gave a courtesy chuckle and waved Delery over with his camera. You never knew what the mad scientist would find.

Villere walked over to the priest. He paused over the body for several minutes, then crouched down and started examining the body.

Suddenly, Villere was all business. He took out a Dictaphone and started recording his observations:

"Male. Caucasian. Found face-down. Wearing an unfamiliar black ryassa, possibly Russian. Time of death between midnight and 1:00 a.m."

While Villere talked, Cavet wrote:

Wearing black ree-ah-suh (phon). Russian? TOD 12-1.

Villere stared at the right arm for a moment, turned off the Dictaphone, and looked up with a very serious face.

"Did one of your guys move this arm?"

"No," Cavet replied. "Techs shot the scene, but nobody disturbed the body. Why do you ask, Doc?"

"The entire right arm is above the victim's shoulders, and the pool of blood starts at mid-chest and stretches down to the knees. So why is the victim's right hand and forearm covered in blood?"

Good question.

Villere carefully lifted and rotated the right forearm and hand before stopping abruptly.

I've seen that look before. Something is bothering him.

"Tom, take a look at this," Villere said. "Do you see this brand on the right wrist?"

"Looks like crossed keys set inside a heart... or maybe wings. Have you seen it before?"

"No, but I'm not interested in the symbol. I'm interested in why we can see the symbol when the rest of the hand and forearm are covered in blood."

"Because somebody wiped the blood off?" Cavet guessed.

"Probably."

"So whoever did it was probably checking for that symbol, which means the symbol is important."

"I'm not so sure about that. The wrist was pulled out of a pool of blood and checked after the victim was dead," Villere reminded him, while holding the arm up long enough for Delery to photograph the wrist. "If the symbol was important, I think the killer checks the wrist before he kills the guy, *right, right, okay*?"

Cavet nodded and wrote:

Crossed keys + heart/wings. Rt wrist. Checked post-mortem.

Then he flipped to a fresh page and quickly sketched the symbol. When Cavet looked up again, Villere was examining the wound on the priest's back.

"Grab a pair of gloves and help me roll the body on its side," Villere instructed.

Cavet complied without hesitation.

“Good, now hold it right there,” Villere instructed when the body was in the right position. He inspected the bloody front of the priest’s clothing and whistled.

“Well, you don’t see that every day,” Villere announced. “The wound in the back is an exit wound, not an entry wound. The victim was stabbed with a sword that entered his chest here and with an impressive amount of force.”

“Did you say sword?”

“Yes. When I measure the width of the entry and exit wounds, I may be able to tell you more about the blade,” Villere replied, examining the hole in the clothing and taking care not to enlarge it. “You can let go now, Tom.”

Cavet gently allowed the body to return to its original position, flipped back to the first page of his notebook, and wrote:

Sword, front entry, rear exit.

This time, when Cavet looked up, Villere was standing over the body and concentrating.

He’s probably reviewing everything he’s ever read about swords. Which, given the size of his private library, could take some time.

A minute later, Villere smiled like he had remembered something important. Then he walked over and started examining the priest’s hands.

“I can tell you two more things,” Villere announced proudly. “The victim was left handed, and he was an expert swordsman.”

“How could you possibly—”

“Callouses,” Villere replied, interrupting Cavet. “The victim has callouses on his left hand, and I’ll bet you Saints tickets, *okay,* they’re consistent with sword training. Based on the size of these callouses, this guy was Miyamoto Musashi, *right, right, okay, right?*”

Tom smiled, even though he had no idea who Mimosa Mitsubishi was, and told Delery to photograph the left hand while Villere held it.

“Now take a look at the right hand,” Villere continued. “It’s bloody, but you can see there are no callouses like that, *okay*? Manual labor and weight lifting are going to cause callouses on both hands, not just the left hand.”

Tom nodded in agreement.

"Maybe rowing," Villere mused. "If he was a sweep rower and only rowed port, his left hand could develop different callouses from pulling than his right hand would from feathering and squaring the blade. But both sets of callouses would heal, *okay, right?*"

"Right," Cavet said, not entirely following him.

"I mean. Call me crazy, but I'm thinking a swordsman is more likely to die of this particular wound than a rower, *okay*? Live by the sword, die by the sword, *right?*"

"So you think the victim was armed?"

"I certainly hope so," Villere chuckled. "Imagine how embarrassing it would be to train your whole life and forget to bring a sword to a sword fight."

The pieces were starting to fit together, and Cavet started writing again.

No callouses on R hand. Callouses on L hand = sword?

"So the killer and the victim are swordsmen, and they meet here," Cavet proposed. "Empty parking lot. Closed bowling alley. Some sort of a duel?"

"Well, duels are rare nowadays, *okay,*" Villere quipped. "But they're more common than rower-priests being robbed at sword-point, *right, right, okay, right?*"

"Let's go with a duel for now," Cavet agreed and added to his notebook:

Check suspects for callouses on dominant hand.

"What are you thinking, Tom?" Villere asked.

"I need to find out whether the victim was really a priest. Any advice?"

"Yes, don't look directly at the sun!" Villere replied, taking his plastic gloves off. "What? That's good advice, *okay, right?*"

Cavet walked Villere back to his truck. He knew Villere would perform the autopsy later that day and would call him if he found anything interesting.

"Thanks, Doc," he said as they reached the truck. "I don't know what I would do without you. You spoil me."

The coroner opened his car door and turned around.

"Just a kiss, just a hug, then we're necking on the rug," Villere sang with renewed enthusiasm. *"You're getting to be a rabbit with me!"*

*   *   *

Fences make good neighbors. Homicide detectives do not.

"Detective Cavet, the owner would like a word."

Cavet sighed. This was going to be awkward. Russell Landry had been his friend since they wrestled together at Archbishop Rummel High School. They had also been neighbors for the past twelve years, and Emma was his go-to babysitter.

His daughters absolutely loved her.

Detective Cavet ducked under the police tape and made his way over to where Russell was standing.

"Hey Russell, thanks for turning on the lights," Cavet said, shaking his hand. "And thanks for waiting while I spoke with the coroner."

"No problem, Tommy," Russell said. "Any idea what happened?"

"We're working on it," Cavet promised. "I don't think the victim was one of your regulars, but we'll show you a photo after we clean him up."

"No problem. Anything else I can do, or should I head home?"

"Do you have time for a few quick questions?"

"Sure."

"Do any clubs meet in your parking lot? Maybe a martial arts club or some of those renaissance people?"

"I don't think so."

"Any groups who like to use your parking lot to sit and sip?"

"Not that I've heard of," Russell told him. "Sorry."

"That's alright," Cavet assured him, taking out his notebook. "What time did you close the place up last night?"

"Well, Carol and I didn't work tonight, but the alley was supposed to close up around midnight."

Cavet nodded and wrote: *Alley closed at 12 per Russ.*

"Who closed up?"

"Emma. Well, Emma was supposed to close up, but I don't know if she did. Carol and I went to bed before she got home and she's still asleep."

"Alright," Cavet said after writing down Russell's answer. "We'll knock on some doors and find out if anybody saw or heard anything. When Emma wakes up, would it be alright if I come by your house and find out if she saw anything unusual?"

"Sure, Tommy," Russell assured him. "And you don't have to wait for her to wake up. Swing by whenever you want. You've got a job to do."

"Thanks, Russ. I appreciate that."

* * *

Damn it hurts.

Jax woke up lying on a sofa. He knew he was in the front room of the Broussard house because of the framed photograph of Michael and his mom on the end table. A moment later, he heard two voices coming from the back of the house, but he only recognized Michael's.

Time to get up, Jax.

Jax sat up slowly and quickly realized he wasn't ready to stand. He turned his head and looked down the hallway, where he saw Michael and presumably Michael's Guardian sitting at the kitchen table.

Bet that Guardian is happy, thought Jax. *How many mornings has he dreamt of sitting at the kitchen table and talking with Michael?*

"No, I don't understand," Michael told the Guardian in response to a question Jax had not heard. "Why couldn't her Guardian save her?"

Good question, Jax thought without needing to know the context.

"We can't intervene in mortal affairs," the Guardian explained. "It is forbidden. We are only permitted to protect mortals from the Fallen."

"So if Brother Reid attacked me?"

"I would have watched you die."

That should rattle the kid a little.

"Got it. You're really a Watcher until these Fallen show up. And then you become a Guardian."

Smart kid. That's why the Founder started the Order. To get things done.

Jax watched from the sofa as the Guardian walked to the refrigerator and carefully removed a drawing secured to the door by alphabet magnets. The Guardian treated the drawing with reverence and carefully handed it to Michael.

"Remember this?" Jacob asked.

Michael looked down at the drawing of two stick figures.

"I drew that when I was three. Mom said it was a drawing of me and my invisible friend."

"Read what you wrote."

"Me and C-cup."

"That is a backward 'J.'"

"J-cup," Michael read aloud. "Me and ... Jacob."

Jacob nodded.

"I've done more than watch you these eighteen years."

Brother Reid interrupted their conversation by walking into the kitchen, grabbing a beer out of the refrigerator, and taking a swig.

"How do you feel?" Michael asked.

"Like crap."

Jax took another sip of beer before asking the one question he wanted answered.

"Is Brother Cawley dead?"

"He is."

"Did he die well?"

"He did," Jacob assured him. "He bought us the time we needed and paid for it with his life."

"And you saved my life," Michael said. "Thank you."

"I was only following orders," Jax replied, finishing the first beer and opening a second. "As your friend here will explain."

"I can't explain everything," Jacob said. "Like how you knew when and where the ambush was going to happen."

It was the kind of question Brother Cawley would have asked, and it reminded Jax that he would likely be dead before dawn.

"Just be glad we did," Jax suggested before pointing to the front room. "May I use the phone?"

"Yes, sir."

Jax walked down the hallway, still weighing the risk and the reward. Dialing the number would set in motion a course of events he could not control. Jax shook his achy head and picked up the phone.

When the deck is stacked against you, re-shuffle the deck.

Jax listened intently as the phone rang three times.

"Aye," answered the familiar voice of Brother MacLaren.

"Michael Broussard," Jax said, hanging up the phone and hoping the Steward would know what to do if he disappeared or did not live to see morning.

Jax walked back into the kitchen and locked eyes with the Guardian.

"May I go?" Jax asked.

"You may, and these are yours," Jacob said, walking over and handing him the two daggers he had picked up in the parking lot. "Will we see you again?"

"That seems unlikely," Jax said, first tucking away his blade and then staring for a moment at Brother Cawley's.

"What is that?" Michael asked.

"An uncommon weapon," Jax replied, securing it as well. "Like you, I suspect."

Jacob nodded somberly. "Give me some time and I'll arrange for as many of the Old Guard as we can spare to take you wherever you need to go."

"I don't rate that kind of protection," Jax told him, finishing his beer. "And it would only delay the inevitable."

"What does that mean?" Michael asked.

"The Fallen know who he is now," Jacob said. "They will make certain Brother Reid does not help you again."

The kitchen fell silent but only for a moment.

"Where can we take you that you will be safe?" Michael asked.

"I have no idea," Jax chuckled.

Jax put his empty bottle down and opened the refrigerator again.

"What's your plan?"

"I'm taking your last beer, Michael," Jax replied. "And I'm leaving."

"You know what is at stake and what we are facing," Jacob piped up while Jax headed to the front door and unlocked it. "Can you tell us anything? Anything at all?"

Jax paused with his hand on the door knob.

"It's gonna get worse before it gets better."

*   *   *

Heroic acts can be ordinary acts.

Michael watched Brother Reid walk out the front door. He was stunned by how casually the man faced certain death, and he wondered how far Brother Reid would get before the Fallen got him.

Michael looked across the kitchen table at Jacob, wondering what would happen when it was his turn to walk out that door.

"Why did you bring me here?"

"We're safe here, as long as we remain inside," Jacob explained. "Only the Guardian of a mortal who calls a dwelling home can enter without invitation."

"Let me get this straight. Dante can't open my screen door, but he can kill me in a parking lot?" Michael said in disbelief. "What kind of god forbids entry but not murder?"

"One who respects the privacy of mortals and the free will of angels," Jacob replied with absolute conviction. "The Fallen have choices, and those choices have consequences."

"I don't understand any of this," Michael sighed, walking over to a window and peeking out the blinds. "Why is this happening?"

"You have been targeted by the Fallen. They consider you a threat, and they will not stop until you are dead."

"I got that part. But why?"

"Because you are one of us, Brother." Jacob told him without hesitation. "You are an angel, an angel who chose to serve in-theatre."

Michael did not need convincing. He had seen enough to know Jacob was telling him the truth.

"What does that mean? To serve in-theatre?"

"Angels can serve mortals in two ways," Jacob explained. "We can take the Guardian's vow, as I did for you, and serve as a Guardian for as long as our *protelos* lives."

Jacob smiled uneasily.

"Some of us are also given the honor of serving in the human theatre. Of being born and raised as a mortal child until our spirit awakens, as yours did during the Homecoming game."

"But I don't remember being an angel."

"You never will," Jacob confirmed, shaking his head. "Only your spirit awakens in-theatre. Only what makes you who you are returns. Your dyed-in-the-wool character. Your instincts and traits."

"Good and bad?"

"Aye, Brother," Jacob said ominously. "Courage and cowardice. Kindness and cruelty. Humility and vanity. No two angels are alike. And, while serving in-theatre, you will become what you are, Michael. We all do."

"Have you ever served in-theatre?"

"No," Jacob admitted. "But I would. As mortals, we can change the world. Fight the wars. Heal the sick. Teach the young. Consider the possibility Mother Teresa was an angel serving in-theatre. What if she had chosen not to serve and had never been born?"

"Wait. Saint Teresa of Calcutta was an angel?"

"I have no idea," Jacob admitted. "God never reveals whether a human's spirit is mortal or angelic. But every child is born with one or the other."

Jacob looked right at Michael.

"It has always been that way, and it has always been for the best," Jacob advised Michael. "When the Fallen think they've identified an angel serving in-theatre, they hunt the mortal down and send a message."

"What kind of message?"

"The kind that tests even God's resolve."

Michael remembered the faces that had stared at him through the car window. The faces of angels who were determined to save him from that fate.

"Who am I?"

The kitchen grew quiet and the night still, like the world was waiting for Jacob to answer Michael's question.

"An angel with a mission," Jacob replied, remembering Saraquel's orders and refusing to say more.

"What mission?"

"Your mission is your life," Jacob said, reciting the mantra taught during Orientation instead of disclosing the prophecy. "Your life may give you one chance to change the world or a thousand. Save a life. Save a marriage. The only thing we know for certain is that your Spirit was needed here. In this family. In this city. And at precisely this time in history."

"So you have no clue?"

"None."

"Well, at least you're honest," Michael said, shaking his head. "Okay. Tell me what I need to know about the Fallen."

Jacob nodded.

"We *malachim* choose or will our appearance in this world. We can appear human and in any attire simply by willing it. It allows us to serve you better."

Or kill us more easily, thought Michael.

"We can manifest with or without our wings. We can appear to be any age. That's important to remember, Michael. A monster like Dante can approach you as a fifty year-old man or a five year-old boy."

"Can Dante make himself look like you?"

"No. God insists on accountability. Picture Dante as a hundred-year-old man holding a photo album of his life. He can appear as he appeared in any picture in that album, but he will always appear as himself."

Jacob stole a glance at the kitchen clock.

"I know you have a thousand questions," Jacob said. "But I need to find out whether we are moving you tonight. Try to get some sleep. I may be gone a while."

"One more question," Michael insisted. "Why did Rachel tell me—"

"Oh no," Jacob said, shaking his head. "You need to ask Sister Rachel that question yourself."

Michael thought of the passion in Rachel's eyes, her sweet smell, and her voluptuous lips.

You got that right, Jacob.

* * *

Chapter 10: Reactions

And it came to pass that night, that the angel of the LORD went out, and smote in the camp of the Assyrians an hundred fourscore and five thousand...
2 Kings 19:35

(3:46 a.m.) Friday, November 15
Raphael hated the sight of it.

A circular stone table had been added to the center of the Great Chamber, directly in front of the crescent-shaped bench. In the City of God, it was called the "Crescent and Moon," and it was a sign of war.

A sign of the times, Raphael realized.

Uriel and Raguel were both standing before the Moon, staring intently at a map of New Orleans. Strategy was not Raphael's forte. Fortunately, Uriel and Raguel were brilliant tacticians and were doing an excellent job of breaking down their options. Raphael had forgotten how well they worked together at the War Table.

War brings out the best in them.

The Seven needed to decide quickly whether to move Broussard. Assuming, of course, Agrippa was able to get him home safely.

"We could divide their forces," Raguel proposed. "Three units of the Old Guard leave the Broussard house in three different directions."

"I like it," Uriel agreed. "We could set up three ambushes and have three units lead the Fallen into the ambushes."

"Yes, yes, that is good," Raguel said. "But where in the city should we plan the three ambushes and how far away from the Broussard house?"

"That is the real question. How far can each unit go before they are overtaken?" Uriel wondered. "There is no way for us to know for certain."

Raphael hated to interrupt their brainstorming, but there was a decision to be made before they evacuated Broussard out of New Orleans.

"Brothers, where are we going to take Michael?"

"Enter Saraquel and Rachel!" the Guards announced loudly as the doors of the Great Chamber swung open.

That's too bad, thought Raphael. *We were just starting to get some work done.*

"Hello, boys!" Rachel declared, grinning ear-to-ear.

"What is that harpy doing here?" Uriel declared, pointing at Rachel.

Here we go again.

* * *

Kadmus marched into the Great Chamber with a sense of urgency, but stopped on a dime when he saw Elder Uriel and Rachel of Judah squaring off.

"You fool!" Uriel scoffed at Rachel of Judah. "You should never have broken your Vigil. You've betrayed him with your selfishness and your stupidity!"

Rachel shrieked and lunged over the War table at Elder Uriel, her hands held out like claws in front of her.

Uriel was ready for the attack and impossibly quick. He deftly grabbed her wrists and threw her across the room.

Kadmus watched Rachel slam into the marble floor of the Chamber and slide about seven feet into the Crescent. Out of the corner of his eye, he saw Elder Raphael grab Uriel's sword hand and Sara move with surprising quickness to reach Rachel, almost before Rachel stopped sliding.

Uriel taunted Rachel for being slow and weak, while Rachel struggled to break free from Sara's restraint.

"Don't just stand there!" Raphael yelled to the Guards who had scurried into the chamber. "Help her!"

While both Guards moved to restrain Rachel, Uriel stopped insulting her and stormed out the Great Chamber. Raguel was hot on his heels, insisting he return to the War table.

Raphael ignored the mayhem around him and walked over to Kadmus.

"Report, Brother Kadmus."

"Aye, Elder Raphael," Kadmus replied, continuing to watch the brawl. "We got the boy home, but not without a fight."

Kadmus' report was interrupted by the sight and sound of Rachel front-kicking the first guard and punching the second guard in the face.

"What happened?" Raphael asked, also watching the melee.

"The Fallen were waiting in ambush along our route to the boy's house—"

"No, Rachel!" Raphael yelled, as Rachel straddled a prone Guard's body, removed his helmet, and prepared to beat the guard with it. "For goodness sake, Uriel is gone. Stand down!"

Rachel stopped. She nodded, dropped the helmet, and started helping the rather embarrassed guard off the floor.

"Thank you, Sister," Raphael sighed. "Go ahead, Brother Kadmus."

"We got the boy home," Kadmus reported. "But twenty local Guardians were lost, and another five injured."

"Where's Agrippa now?"

"Establishing a perimeter around the Broussard home and waiting for his orders," Kadmus replied before clearing his throat. "And…"

"And?" Sara repeated impatiently.

"And he insists on those orders being clear."

"The unmitigated gall," Sara gasped, shaking her head in disapproval.

"Tell Agrippa to hold until relieved," Raphael declared. "He should understand that order."

"Aye, Elder Raphael," Kadmus sounded off before turning smartly and marching out of the Great Chamber and past the disheveled Guards.

All too well.

* * *

Michael heard the familiar tapping against his window.

Again, he got out of bed and walked to the window. Again, he pulled up the shades and saw the beautiful Rachel standing outside in a hooded, Armageddon-style silk cloak. Again, he lifted the sash and offered the angel his hand.

This time, she did not take it.

"You're dreaming, Michael," Rachel scoffed with an amused look on her face. "I'm not climbing through your window."

"You're not?"

“Of course not,” Rachel assured him. “Now get dressed and meet me on the front porch. We do not have much time.”

Rachel disappeared while a confused Michael closed the window.

Michael stood there, staring out the window, for a moment. Then he quickly put on a pair of jeans and headed to the front door.

“You forgot your shoes,” Rachel observed from a chair on the front porch when Michael finally emerged.

Michael scanned the deserted street and sat down. Something told him they were alone, but that seemed impossible under the circumstances.

“Where’s Jacob?”

“Reporting to the Seven,” Rachel said with a lovely smile. “And the Old Guard has expanded their perimeter to give us some privacy.”

Rachel held the answers to all his questions, and Michael wanted one answered before they could be interrupted.

“Why did you tell me--”

“Just look at you,” Rachel interrupted with a mysterious smile. “It has been so long since I’ve seen you this young. Since I’ve seen your eyes unburdened by centuries of war and ...”

Rachel trailed off and sighed.

“I forgot how attractive innocence can be.”

Michael sat in the chair next to her and forced himself to look at the moon. They sat in silence until Michael found the courage to say something.

“We were taught ... I mean, I thought angels don’t marry.”

“We don’t,” Rachel agreed. “We share the same Creator. We are akin to brothers and sisters. But you and I were mortals when we married.”

“When?”

“701 BC. In Judah. We were both serving in-theatre. It was my first tour, and neither of us had awakened. We didn’t know whether angels existed, let alone suspect that we were angels. I believe we were about the age you are now.”

Rachel was smiling, but a far-off look appeared in her eyes. Something told Michael her mood had shifted from playful to sentimental.

“So young. So in love.”

And a little sad.

"I'm sorry I don't remember," he said.

Rachel looked at him with surprise.

"I accept your apology," Rachel replied. "But only because this is the first time you have apologized for anything."

Rachel leaned over and kissed him softly on the lips.

"Don't let the Old Guard hear you talk like that, my love. They might lose respect for you."

Michael's head was swimming when he heard himself ask the next question.

"How long were we... married?"

"Not long enough. Sennacherib laid siege to Jerusalem. To our Jerusalem. It caused you to awaken. The next day, you rode out and challenged their champion."

"Did I win?"

"Yes, Michael, you won."

Rachel's tone changed.

"But instead of striking their tents and leaving, the cowards killed you."

Michael saw a strange look come over Rachel's face. Something told him there was more to the story.

"And then?"

"And then... you showed the world how much you loved me," Rachel replied, looking a little uncomfortable.

"How?"

"By intervening, Michael," Rachel replied, lowering her voice and becoming very serious. "Like no angel has ever intervened."

Michael waited while Rachel decided whether to tell him the whole story.

"You were not going to let those barbarians take Jerusalem," she added a few moments later. "You were not going to let them get their filthy hands on me. So you chose to remember your time in-theatre."

"I chose to what?"

"After you died, God gave you the same choice He gives all angels after their service in the human theatre ends," Rachel explained. "He allowed you to choose whether you would remember or forget your life as a mortal."

Rachel smiled.

"You chose to remember your time in-theatre," Rachel continued. "You chose to remember our marriage. You chose to remember me."

Rachel sighed.

"And then you returned that night as the Angel of Death."

Rachel leaned over again and tucked a tuft of hair behind his ear, exactly like she had in the parking lot.

"You slaughtered a hundred and eighty-five thousand Assyrians that night," Rachel told him with a coldness that betrayed her lingering hate for the enemy. "While a hundred and eighty-five thousand stunned Guardians, all loyal to you, watched in silence. You butchered every last one of them."

She paused.

"It was really quite sweet."

* * *

Emma had a rough night.

She could not sleep because she could not stop thinking about the way Michael kissed her. She was practically comatose when her father knocked on her door.

"Sweetie?" her dad said, cracking the door open. "Tom Cavet is here."

Something's wrong, thought Emma.

"He needs to speak with you downstairs."

Something must be wrong with one of my girls!

Emma jumped out of bed, threw on a robe, and hurried downstairs. When she entered the kitchen, Emma saw Detective Cavet sitting at the table with her mom and dad.

"Good morning, Emma," Cavet said, looking serious and gesturing for her to sit down.

Oh no!

"What's wrong? Emma asked bluntly. "Are the girls okay?"

“The girls are fine,” Cavet assured her, suddenly realizing it had been weeks since Emma last baby-sat. “We'll have you over soon.”

“Okay… then what's going on?”

“Did you close up the bowling alley last night?” Cavet asked.

“No, Michael did,” Emma reported. “Why?”

Did something happen to Michael?

“Detective Cavet is here because he's investigating a murder,” Russell Landry explained to his daughter. “Sweetie, it happened last night in the parking lot of Rock ‘n’ Bowl, right after closing—”

Darkness.

* * *

Carol Finnegan Landry knew this was bad.

Yes, she liked Michael Broussard. Yes, Kathy Broussard had been her best friend since the first grade. But none of that really matters when your daughter is lying unconscious on the kitchen floor.

No mother welcomes that kind of attachment to a boy.

“Do you want me to call for an ambulance?” Tom asked nervously, while Russell paced back and forth with his hands on his head.

“No, give her a second,” Carol said, kneeling next to Emma and trying to sound calm and confident. “Her head hit the floor, but I don't feel a hickey.”

Emma opened her eyes, and everyone in the kitchen gave a sigh of relief.

“You're okay,” Carol assured her. “You just fainted.”

“Why did I… wait, is Michael… *is Michael…*”

“It's okay, it's okay…” Russell assured her quickly.

“No, it's not! It's my fault. It's my fault. I… I… I made him lock up,” Emma interrupted, almost hysterically. “He kissed me, and it was so… but I didn't…. I never told him!”

Jesus, Mary, and Joseph, thought Carol Landry. *It's worse than I thought.*

* * *

Evacuate or shelter in place.

Archangel Raguel had the same choice mortals had when a hurricane threatened New Orleans. He could evacuate Michael or leave him right where he was. Both options were risky.

Leaving Michael in New Orleans was the more logical option.

Come morning, thousands of Guardians would be outside Jesuit High School, and Michael would be safe in the brick fortress. Not to mention the large church at one end of the horseshoe and the small chapel on the second floor at the other end. Both could be used to transport reinforcements and the wounded.

It was so obviously the better plan that Raguel distrusted it.

Lucifer knew how Raguel thought and had repeatedly demonstrated the ability to predict his strategy. By taking the most logical course of action, he was almost certainly playing right into Lucifer's hands.

I cannot choose to shelter Michael in place. Lucifer will expect me to choose the more logical option.

Of course, it was also possible Lucifer would engage in exactly that same line of reasoning and conclude Raguel would avoid the most logical option.

Lucifer will expect me to avoid the more logical option.

Raguel shook his head.

The sun would rise soon in the human theatre, and he was no closer to making a decision. The only thing he knew for certain was that the Seven had two options, and Lucifer knew both of them. Suddenly, Raguel realized his best chance of surprising Lucifer.

"Guards!" Raguel yelled. "Bring me a two-sided coin!"

* * *

Michael opened his eyes and closed his mind.

It was all just a dream, he told himself. *Just a crazy dream.*

Michael got out of bed. He shaved, showered, and got dressed for school. He decided not to iron his khaki uniform or shine his shoes, but he had to fix his broken nametag. The clear tape attaching the metal pin clasp to the back of his nametag was in bad shape. Michael removed the old tape and headed to the kitchen to grab the tape dispenser.

"Good morning, Michael," Jacob said, sitting in his father's chair.

Crap.

Michael grabbed his favorite cup and walked over to the refrigerator. He poured himself a glass of milk, drank it, and poured a second glass.

It really happened.

"How are you doing?" Jacob asked.

"You tell me."

"You're doing fine. This is not the life I wanted for you, but it is the life you are going to live."

"What's the plan?" Michael asked, sitting down in her chair.

"We are not moving you to another city," Jacob reported. "We are going to protect you right here. You are safe in your home and at school. Hand-picked members of the Old Guard are going to escort you safely wherever you need to go."

"Let me get this straight," Michael said, somewhat incredulous. "I'm being hunted by the Devil, and I still have to go to school?"

"The Seven want you to have as normal a life..."

"Seriously?"

"It's not a perfect plan," Jacob admitted.

"Did you vote for it?"

"Nobody asked for my vote. But it is better than spending the rest of your life running. If war is coming, there are certain advantages to fighting it in a large city and on familiar ground."

"Look, I don't know who the Seven are, and I have no idea what you're talking about," Michael reminded him. "But if I'm going to school, I'd better get going."

"Agreed."

"And if my dad gets back from his trip early, wait for me to get home before you bring him up to speed. I gotta see his face when he hears."

"Look, Michael, we cannot tell your dad anything."

"Forget that," Michael scoffed. "I'm telling him everything as soon as I see him. He's in as much danger as I am."

Jacob leaned forward.

"You can't tell *anyone.* Not Trey. Not Emma. Please understand. Mortals are judged by the choices they make *before* they receive proof of God's existence."

"I don't care."

"You should," Jacob warned. "Who are you to decide whether your dad should be judged today? Who are you to decide that Trey or Emma should be judged on a fraction of the choices they would have made during their lifetimes?"

Michael stared at Jacob.

"Are you telling me Hell is real, and the God of Love damns people to hell?"

"I am telling you Judgment is real, and people are most certainly judged." Jacob assured him. "I will not say more. I have already said more than I should."

Michael pushed back his chair and stood up.

"Where are the keys to the Goat?"

"Wait, Michael." Jacob grimaced. "You should sit down."

* * *

Chapter 11: Challenges

We are troubled on every side, yet not distressed;
we are perplexed, but not in despair…
2 Corinthians 4:8

(6:30 a.m.) Friday, November 15

Jax was trapped.

His chest was pinned by the heavy bar. There was no point in trying to bench press the weight again because his arms were worthless. Fortunately, he had not put collars on the bar.

I'll lower the left side. Both plates will slide off that slide and the weights on the other side will...

"Need some help?"

Jax let loose an involuntary groan as Will lifted and racked the bar.

"Thanks," Jax said begrudgingly.

"My pleasure," Will said. "Did your ego write a check your body couldn't cash?"

"No, I was lifting to failure."

"Sure you were," Will replied sarcastically. "Can I grab a set?"

Jax nodded, but the last thing he wanted was to lift weights with a Chatty Cathy like Coach Will. It had been only six hours since Cawley died. Four hours since he walked out of the Broussard home expecting either the Fallen or the Founder to kill him. Two hours since the Founder delivered new orders.

Jax's mission had changed, and he needed time to think.

Will plopped down on the bench, lifted the bar off the rack, and started talking, pausing only long enough to press the weight.

"Jax is short… for Jackson?"

"Yes."

"Why… Jackson?"

"Stonewall Jackson. Dad was a military history professor."

"Middle… name?"

"Jackson is my middle name."

"First… name?" Will groaned while completing the sixth repetition.

"Joshua. For Colonel Joshua Chamberlain."

"Little… Round Top?" Will grunted during his eighth repetition.

"You got it."

Will finished his tenth repetition, racked the weight without help, and switched places with Jax.

"Well, Joshua Jackson Reid. Have you always gone by your middle name?"

"No," Jax said as he plopped down on the bench. "Only since they died."

"Hey, I'm sorry to hear that," Will said.

As Jax adjusted his grip and prepared for his set, he noticed the Coach was staring at the disintegrating bandage on his right wrist.

"They were murdered," Jax continued, trying to distract the man who was still staring at his right wrist. "Murdered in front of me when I was ten."

"Oh my God..."

"My first name," Jax continued before lifting the bar. "Was the last word my mother ever spoke."

It had been a long time since Jax had told anyone about them, and the rush of emotion surprised him. This time, he did almost twice as many repetitions.

In total silence.

*　　*　　*

Derrick Hill paid for his lunch, grabbed his tray, and walked over to the long cafeteria table where Michael and Trey were waiting for him.

"Okay, we're all here," Trey announced as Derrick sat down next to him on the long bench. "Tell us what happened after we left Rock 'n' Bowl last night. Did you see the murder in the parking lot?"

"I can't say," Michael replied, looking very uncomfortable.

"You can't say because you don't know?" Derrick asked, doing his best impersonation of his father cross-examining a witness. "Or you can't say because you are not free to say?"

"Good question," Trey said, obviously amused by the challenge of forcing a confession. "Which is it, Michael?"

"I had a really long night," Michael assured them. "I'm barely keeping it together. Can we please drop this?"

Something did happen last night, Derrick thought, after seeing the look in Michael's eyes and hearing the exhaustion in his voice. *He really can't tell us what happened.*

The awkward silence that followed did not last long.

Derrick saw three football players walking toward Michael, who was unfortunately sitting on the other side of the table and had his back to them. Derrick quickly read their name tags.

Shipley, Perez, and Dodd.

"Look guys, it's big bad Michael Broussard!" the one named Shipley declared as Michael turned around instinctively. "I heard you tried to start a fight last night at the bowling alley. Heard you made a play for Emma right in front of Gavin."

Damn, I'm out of position, thought Derrick. *Wrong side of the table.*

"You heard wrong," Trey told them as Michael stood up, grabbed his tray with his left hand, and calmly placed trash on it with his right.

Michael's acting like he's leaving, Derrick realized. *But that's not going to work with these guys. Too many students are watching.*

"Shut up!" Shipley said, pointing at Trey. "I'm not talking to you."

Derrick turned sideways and tried to casually slide his right leg over the bench, but he could tell Perez and Dodd were watching him. And only him.

If I stand up, this escalates.

"What do you want?" Michael said turning to face Shipley and holding his cafeteria tray of trash in front of him. The tray was all that separated the two.

"You know what I want."

"World peace?" Derrick quipped, hoping to draw attention away from Michael, but only causing Trey to snort like a seal.

Shipley turned to say something, but was distracted by Michael's poking him in the stomach with the edge of his tray.

"Watch it!" Shipley grunted, slapping the tray away with his right hand.

As the slap dislodged the tray from his left hand, Michael's right fist was already headed up and toward Shipley's mid-section, just below his ribs.

The punch knocked the wind out of Shipley and doubled him over at the waist. Michael then hit him with a lightning quick left cross to the kidney and a right to Shipley's face, dropping Shipley like a sack of bricks.

"Enough!" Michael yelled at Shipley while gesturing to Derrick to stay on his side of the table. "Enough!"

The speed with which Michael dispatched Shipley stunned both crews, and his yelling drew the eye of every teacher.

Derrick watched Michael walk out of the cafeteria as a half dozen teachers headed quickly toward their table.

"Who was that masked man?" Trey asked in disbelief.

Derrick shook his head.

"You tell me, Tonto."

* * *

Thank God for Friday.

It had been the worst week of Father Finnegan's brief tenure as President. On Monday and Tuesday, families received acceptance and rejection letters for next year. The acceptance rate was only twenty-five percent, and more than thirty-five percent of the applicants were sons of alumni or had siblings currently at school, which meant ten percent of the families wanted Father Finnegan's head.

Finn had personally taken every angry call and crammed as many sit-downs as possible into his week. He believed it was the least he could do for the families, not that it mattered to most.

"Send Mr. Broussard in and hold my calls," Finn told Liddy, looking forward to speaking with a student for a change, even if it regarded a disciplinary matter.

Finn sighed deeply and watched Michael Broussard walk into his office for the first time in years. He remembered Kathy Broussard well, and he had been Michael's Sacred Scripture teacher when she passed during his freshman year. He knew Michael, and he wanted to get to the bottom of what had happened.

"How are you, Michael?"

"I've been better, Father."

"Doctor Lagarde says you knocked Brad Shipley unconscious, and you did it without breaking any of his facial bones. He'll have a nasty bruise, but that's all."

"Good."

"Lagarde sounded, for lack of a better word, *suspicious* of your fighting ability," Finn continued. "Like it couldn't possibly have been a lucky punch."

"It wasn't, Father," Michael admitted. "My dad was a boxer, and we spar on Saturdays. We both find it helps with... Anyway, I knew what I was doing."

"Apparently," Finn observed. "Look Michael, I'm not going to suspend you for fighting. It sounds like Brad started the fight and you showed some restraint."

"Thank you, Father."

"Besides," Finn continued. "I know you pulled Coach Will out of that burning car, and I have a strict Never-Expel-A-Hero policy. But I am curious. Why were you two fighting?"

"Brad took your niece, Emma Landry, to Homecoming," Michael told him.

"Yes... and?"

"And Brad thinks I'm interested in her."

"Are you?"

"Yes, Father."

"Then good luck, Michael, and may the best man win!" Finn declared with a smile. "Now go to class and, uh, I don't know... say two Our Fathers and a Hail Mary... or something."

Finn watched a confused Michael Broussard nod and walk out of his office.

Break time!

Finn unlocked his bottom drawer and grabbed his lighter and cigarettes.

"I'll be back!" Finn said as he hurried past Liddy like a speed walker.

"Nasty habit!" Liddy practically yelled down the hallway.

To avoid teachers and students, Finn took the less-traveled hallways and staircases until he reached the stairwell that led directly to the roof.

The roof of Jesuit High School was Finn's sanctuary. It was the one place where he could enjoy a cigarette in peace. Even Liddy wouldn't disturb him there.

Finn climbed the last few steps, turned the corner, and pushed the usually unlocked door. As the heavy door swung open, he saw Brother Reid standing on his roof and arguing.

With an angel of the Lord.

* * *

Finn stared at the impossible scene and panicked.

He spun around and flew down the steps as fast as his flamingo legs could carry him. As he hurled himself down the stairs, he heard the door open and slam above him. Heavy footfalls in the stairwell confirmed he was being pursued, and whoever or whatever was closing fast.

"Father!" Brother Reid call down to him. "Father Finne—"

Brother Reid's voice was interrupted by the sound of his body falling down stairs and coming to an abrupt stop.

Finn reached the bottom of the stairwell and a decision. He could go through the door or back up the stairs. Neither option seemed viable, so he pulled out his phone.

"Will!"

* * *

Two concussions are not better than one.

Jax was lying on the sofa in the President's office. He vaguely remembered being half-carried there by two men.

"I'll call an ambulance," Jax heard a woman say.

"No!" both men replied in unison from the other end of the room.

"Why not?"

Jax remained still. He was in too much pain to open his eyes, and he wanted to hear how this played out.

"Just go downstairs and get him some aspirin," he heard the now recognizable voice of Coach Will tell the woman.

"That's a good idea," Father Finnegan agreed.

"I don't think—" the woman started to object.

"Please, Liddy. For once in your *blessed* life just do what I ask!"

"Alright, alright," she relented. "But you watch your tone, Daniel Finnegan. I swear. You are both acting very strange."

Jax heard the door close.

"Why didn't you want to call 9-1-1?" Will asked.

"Why didn't you?" Finnegan countered.

No response.

"To hell with it," the priest eventually said. "This is going to sound crazy, but I have to tell you something."

"So tell me."

"Will, we've been friends since we were freshmen. Same homeroom. Remember?"

"Yes," Will said, wondering where this was going. "Room 310. You liked my impression of Scooby-Doo."

"Have I ever lied to you?"

"No..."

Finn braced his hands on his hips and sighed.

"Brother Reid was chasing me down those stairs because I caught him on the roof and..."

"And..." Will urged.

"And he was arguing with an angel," Finn reported, and his voice was deadly serious. "Wings and all. I give you my word, Will."

Will stared at Finn for a moment. "Do you have any scissors?"

"Did you hear what I just--"

"Every word," Will assured him. "Now grab a pair of scissors and quickly."

"Why do you need—"

Just then, Jax sat up slowly, silencing both of them.

"To cut *this* off," Jax replied, pointing at the bandage on his right wrist. "Go ahead and get 'em, Father. Then lock the door and sit down. I've got some really bad news."

Will looked at Finn.

"Ruh-roh."

* * *

Michael was staring at a dead man.

Brother Jackson Reid was sitting behind his desk at the front of the classroom. There was a half-full glass of water on his desk and two ripped-open packets of headache powder. He looked worse than he had the night before, if that was possible, but at least he was alive.

"Take your seat, Broussard," Brother Reid said preemptively. He clearly did not want to discuss anything before the class started.

"Yes, please sit down," Trey added as the bell rang.

The class settled down and Brother Reid stood up gingerly.

"Today, we are going to talk about, uh, angelology," Reid announced, staring right at Michael. "Listen up if you want to survive."

Brother Reid walked to the board while Derrick and Trey looked at Michael for some explanation.

"Survive what, Brother?" Gillen asked while raising his hand.

"The End of Days," Reid replied matter-of-factly. He drew a vertical line on the board and wrote "Good" on one side. He stared at the word for a moment. Then he erased it, wrote "Michael" on that side and "Lucifer" on the other.

"Two armies. Two Archangels. Lucifer commands the Fallen. Michael commands the Heavenly Host."

"Why doesn't God command the Heavenly Host?" Crane asked.

"God does not intervene," Reid said, taking another gulp of the headache powder water and shutting his eyes until *whatever it was* passed.

"Why not?"

"How the hell should I know?" Reid snapped.

Stunned silence.

"I only know the rules," Reid continued, again looking at Michael. "Learn them. First Rule: God does not create slaves. Angels have choices, and they must choose to serve. Second Rule: choices have consequences."

"Do we have to know this for a test?" asked Hotard.

"Third Rule: serving God means serving man."

"Brother Reid?"

"Fourth Rule: everyone serves," Brother Reid continued, ignoring Hotard. "Fifth rule: Guardians must not intervene."

"Where are these rules written, Brother--" Crane began to ask.

"You!" Reid barked, pointing at Crane. "You *don't* speak again."

Crane did not.

"Sixth Rule: their homes are their castles. No angel may enter a mortal dwelling uninvited, except for the Guardians of those who call that dwelling home."

"What about public places like the mall?" Michael asked to the general surprise of the entire class.

"My guess is no."

"Churches?"

"Churches are Houses of God. Only those angels who serve God may enter. The Fallen may not."

"Synagogues?"

"Yes, and mosques and temples," Reid said impatiently. "Any house of worship."

"If they can't enter a house, can they burn it down?" Michael asked.

"No," Reid said emphatically, while sitting down to rest. "The Sixth Rule comes with a nasty penalty. Whatever angels do to a house, they do to themselves. Setting fire to a house would be the same as setting yourself on fire."

"Thank God," Michael said, obviously relieved.

Brother Reid nodded in agreement while the rest of the class looked around the room in total confusion.

"Let me ask you this," Michael continued. "I understand why Guardians don't reveal themselves, but why don't the Fallen?"

"Lucifer forbids it," Reid replied. "Anyone who sees an angel finds faith. One photograph could convert the entire world."

"Got it."

"The Fallen are only allowed to reveal themselves to victims," Reid said, half-grinning at Michael. "Lucifer's orders."

"What can you tell me about him?" Michael asked very seriously.

Brother Reid thought for a moment.

"Not much. Before the creation of man, Lucifer walked with God. He was loved above all others. The smartest and most talented of His creations."

"I thought Michael cast him out of Heaven?" Trey asked.

"That's what your Bible says," Reid replied, but Michael's heightened *whatever* told him Reid had doubts.

"Do you believe that?" Michael asked.

"I couldn't care less," Brother Reid said plainly. "And you, your friends, this school, *your* Church, and *your* Pope had better forget the past and start worrying about the future."

Brother Reid stood up and addressed the entire class.

"War is coming," Reid warned the bewildered students. "The Final Battle. Everything hangs in the balance. Everything you know and love. And none of you are ready. Not for the fight. Not for judgment."

During the silence that followed, Brother Reid sat back down, produced a third packet of headache powder from his pants pocket, ripped it open, poured it into a half-empty glass of water, and drained it with one gulp.

"Help us," Michael eventually said. "Tell us how to kill the Fallen."

Brother Reid sighed like the answer was onerous.

"Angels are immortal," Reid explained. "The Fallen are immortal. Brother Cawley compared them to energy. They can't be created or destroyed, but their spirits can be... driven off."

"With what?"

"Hate," Reid replied. "Angels were brought into Being by God's Love, so hatred can drive an angelic spirit back into... uh, Non-Being. But it takes a very specific act of hatred. Only murder can banish *malachim*."

"I'm good with that," Michael assured him, trying to sound confident. "What type of weapons are we going to need?"

"We?" Trey repeated incredulously.

"The weapon doesn't really matter," Reid replied, ignoring Trey. "But the weapon must be physically connected to the hate... I mean, to the hater."

"Somebody has to be holding the sword?"

"Yes, but not just swords," Reid corrected Michael. "Any object can serve as an extension of the hatred. Axes, knives, spears..."

"Forget that," Hotard bravely interjected. "Give me an AK-47 assault rifle with a thousand rounds, and I'll take care of your Fallen Angel problem."

The class erupted in nervous laughter, but Brother Reid shook his head and waited for them to stop.

"Bullets and arrows don't work, do they?" Michael asked a moment later, ignoring the rest of the class and understanding the reason behind the rule.

"No, they don't."

"Well that sucks," Hotard chuckled as Michael asked his next question.

"Why?"

"The dose is the poison," Reid replied. "It takes true hatred to stab someone face-to-face. Anyone can pull a trigger from a hundred feet away."

"How long before the angel's *whatever* returns?"

"Spirit returns... and it depends," Reid said. "The hatred of a Novice could never compare to Lucifer's."

"Well, what chance does Michael have if Lucifer is smarter and quicker?" Derrick asked to everyone's surprise.

"Don't underestimate the Archistrategos," Reid warned. "Michael leads from the front. He's loved by legions. He's tougher and he's stronger."

"Will that be enough?" Michael heard himself ask.

Brother Reid looked right at Michael and smiled.

"You bet your—"

The slamming of the classroom door interrupted him.

"Good morning, Brother Reid," Father Unger said with a disingenuous smile. "I'll be observing your class today."

"No, you won't," Brother Reid said calmly but firmly. "But thank you for visiting. You need to leave now."

Pin-drop silence.

"See here, Brother Reid, you can't talk to me that way," Unger said. "I'm the Head of the Theology Department, and I evaluate all of my teachers."

"Not this one," Reid corrected him. "But I could be wrong. You should go speak with Father Finnegan."

"This is outrageous!" Father Unger declared.

"Look, I'm not a patient man, Father," Brother Reid said. "You're disturbing my class. You should leave now."

"I, uh… yes, I will… go now," Unger stammered, as he fumbled to open the door. "I will go see the… Daniel and… uh, I *will* have your job!"

Brother Reid waited until the door was completely closed.

"Now, where were we, class?"

* * *

The only constant is change.

Father Finnegan was standing before the largest window in his office. This morning, he would have seen and thought only of the students congregated in the Mary Courtyard. Now, looking out the same window, he thought only of the hundreds of unseen angels circling overhead.

Finn was still in shock when he heard Liddy depress the intercom button and cough loudly. He knew it was a warning, but he didn't care.

"Daniel, I demand satisfaction!" Father Unger decreed as he stormed into the President's office. "Brother Reid just threatened me and threw me out of his classroom. I told him I was there to evaluate him, like any other teacher in my department, and he threw me out! He said he doesn't get evaluated!"

"That's correct."

"What's correct?"

"Everything. You don't evaluate Brother Reid."

"With all due respect, Daniel—"

"I'm not done," Finn interrupted. "You don't evaluate Brother Reid. You don't go into his classroom. You don't bother that man again."

"Why is that?" Unger demanded, flabbergasted.

"Because I said so," Finn replied. "Now get out of my office, Donald. And the next time you want to speak with me, make an appointment with my secretary. I won't have you barging in here to discuss your petty complaints again. You might interrupt something important."

"Petty complaints? Who do you think you are?"

"I know exactly who I am," Finn assured him. "I'm the one responsible for all of these young men. Today, I was given a glimpse of what's coming our way, and I'm going to make certain we're ready. Come hell or high water."

"What's coming our way?"

Finn looked out the window again.

"That's the first good question you've asked," Finn replied.

Without another word, Father Finnegan walked out of his office and past a euphoric Liddy Daigle. He was headed to the roof.

To get some answers.

* * *

Some messages should be delivered in person.

Emma's hands held the wrought-iron gate to the Broussards' front yard. She was not aware of the hundreds of angels patrolling the streets and skies of the neighborhood. She was only aware of how hard it was for her to swing the gate open and walk the last five yards to Michael's front porch.

Impossibly hard.

Emma forced herself to remember how she felt when she thought Michael was killed in the parking lot. Lying on the kitchen floor, she swore to tell Michael how she felt about him, and she was determined to do just that.

Only a hastily-made promise to her mother had kept her in class all day, and only her vanity had kept her from driving straight to Michael's house. She was not going to share her feelings and redefine their relationship while wearing her drab school uniform.

Emma opened the creaky gate and walked up the steps to the front porch wearing jeans and her favorite sweater. Almost immediately, she heard the sound of two male voices inside the Broussard house.

She took a deep breath and knocked on the door. She knew what she wanted to say, and she was pretty sure what was going to happen next.

The voices inside the house stopped abruptly and were replaced by the sound of footsteps on a wood floor. When the footsteps reached the other side of the door, she heard a muffled conversation that ended with "her sake" before the lock turned.

Emma waited almost giddily as the door opened. It was the moment she had been picturing and waiting for all day.

Michael opened the door but did not step outside. He actually looked past her and scanned the neighborhood like they were being watched. When Michael finally made eye contact, Emma felt none of the love or the passion she remembered from the parking lot kiss.

She got the feeling she was the last person Michael wanted to see on his porch.

Something's wrong.

"Why are you here, Emma?"

Not what he's supposed to say, Emma thought. *Not the way he's supposed to look at me. Not at all.*

"Emma?"

"Yes, well, I have to, uh, close up tonight," she said, remembering the excuse she rehearsed in the event Michael's father answered the door. "I need my keys back."

"Okay," Michael said. "Wait here and I'll get them."

Michael closed the door.

Something's really wrong.

Emma heard Michael's footsteps and what sounded like yelling in the back of the house. This time, the argument may have ended with the word "married."

He's arguing with someone. Someone he doesn't want me to see.

The door eventually opened and Michael handed her the keys.

"Here's your set."

Emma flashed her cutest smile.

"Thanks for not throwing them at me," she said, trying a little levity.

"Why would I... oh, right, because you did."

Okay, this is ridiculous, thought Emma. *What could make him forget last night?*

"Who's inside, Michael?"

"Nobody," Michael lied. "I was talking to myself."

"What is that plastic yellow ring on your right hand?" Emma asked, noticing it for the first time.

"It's, uh… well, it's kind of a reminder," Michael told her.

"A reminder that…?"

"It's better to be just," Michael mumbled barely loud enough for her to hear. "Than…"

"Than *what,* Confucius?" Emma quipped.

Michael sighed.

"It means you should go," he said. "And I don't want you getting… I mean, I don't want you coming back here, Emma."

"You don't want me getting what?"

Emma's question was interrupted by the sound of an approaching motorcycle, and all of the color drained from Michael's face.

"Michael, what on earth is wrong? Last night, you were so…"

"Emma, that's my dad coming down the street," he said, almost frantically. "I need to talk with him, and I'm begging you to leave without asking any more questions."

Emma hesitated.

Nothing had gone according to script. Normally, that would have driven Emma insane, but something was going on here. Emma was more curious than hurt and more interested than insulted. Michael was many things, but he was not fickle.

He didn't fall out of love with me overnight, Emma told herself. *He's obviously trying to protect me from something or someone.*

"Get out of here," Michael repeated more loudly, as if he was talking to someone standing in the front yard. "And don't come back!"

Just like that, Emma shifted into detective mode.

"Fine!" Emma screamed, matching his tone. Then she lowered her voice to a whisper.

"I'll play along."

"This is not a game!" Michael said in an unfamiliar tone. "Life is not one of your romantic comedies. Everything doesn't always end well. Sometimes it just ends, and this—whatever this was—is over. I'm tired of spending every minute trying to figure out what you want me to do or say. And hoping I get it right."

Michael turned his attention to whoever he thought may be watching and listening in the neighborhood.

"No wonder Gavin dumped you!" Michael screamed. "You're a whiny, deranged, pathetic—"

This time, the slap sprained Emma's wrist.

*   *   *

Emma Landry was part bloodhound.

She was walking away from the Broussards' porch and rubbing her wrist when she realized the parking lot murder was the only thing that happened between Michael's kissing her and his pitiful attempt to brush her off.

By the time she reached the gate, Emma was certain Michael had seen something that was putting him in danger. By the time she reached her Jeep, she had caught the scent.

Someone is coming for him, and he doesn't want me in the line of fire, Emma thought. *Bless his heart. He needs my help.*

Emma waved to Mr. Broussard as he got off his motorcycle.

They both need me.

Emma started her Jeep and pulled away from the curb. Given Michael's desperate behavior, there was no time to go home. She was going to have to start her investigation in her favorite sweater, and she was going to need help.

Someone who loves Michael enough to do whatever it takes.

There was only one person who fit that description. Emma turned on her blinker and made a left turn.

*   *   *

Tensions were high.

Detective Cavet looked across the kitchen table at Ed and Michael Broussard. Ed looked furious, and Michael had a bag of ice on the side of his face.

"What happened to your face, Michael?"

"Emma Landry slapped me," he replied without hesitation.

His honesty surprised Cavet.

"Did you deserve it?"

"Yes, sir."

"Okay, Michael. I don't know if you saw on the news today, but a man was murdered in the parking lot of Rock 'n' Bowl last night." Cavet informed him. "Were you at the bowling alley last night?"

"Yes, sir."

"Were you there until closing?"

"Yes, sir."

"Did you close up?"

"Yes, sir."

"What time did you leave?"

"Between midnight and one o'clock."

"Anybody help you when you closed up?"

"No, sir."

"Well, as I've told your dad, the murder happened not long after you closed up," Cavet said. "Did you see anybody in the parking lot?"

Michael hesitated before shaking his head.

"No, I, uh... I closed up, got in my dad's car, and went straight home."

"Was anybody else in the car with you?"

"Well, my friends went home earlier that night," Michael replied. "So I would have been alone."

"Oh well," Cavet said, smiling broadly. "Guess I'll have to earn my salary."

Cavet looked down and wrote in his notebook:

Broussard, Michael. Closed up between 12 & 1. Drove Dad's car. Hesitated before saying he drove "straight" home & nobody in car. Answered yes or no to all but 2 ?s - See anyone? & Alone in car?

Cavet was acutely aware of how quiet it had been while he was scribbling. He waited to see if Michael was nervous enough to volunteer any more information.

Michael did not.

"Hey, what kind of car does your Dad drive?" Cavet asked, deliberately closing his notebook and putting it back in his pocket.

"I've got a 1964 Pontiac GTO," Ed said, answering for his son. "I went out of town and told Mikey he could drive it while I was gone."

"You're a lucky young man," Cavet told Michael. "My father wouldn't trust me with the keys to our tool shed."

"He's a good kid."

Something told Cavet that Ed Broussard spoke the truth. That same something told him Michael had already lied twice.

"That's exactly what Russell and Carol told me," Cavet assured him, intentionally using their first names. "And I'm done here, Ed. Now don't punch me or anything, but you look exhausted. When did you get back in town?"

"About thirty minutes ago."

"Punch… Broussard." Cavet repeated. "Are you Hurricane Broussard?"

"That was a long time ago, Detective."

"Not that long ago." Cavet chuckled, hoping to ease the tension in the room. "I saw you fight Golden Gloves. You were good. Did you go pro?"

"Never did," Ed said. "Met Mikey's mom and hung 'em up."

Cavet nodded.

"How about you, Michael? Are you a boxer like your dad or do you like martial arts?"

"No, sir. Just football."

Back to the truth.

"Probably for the best," Cavet said, watching closely to see how Michael reacted to his next comment. "Live by the sword, die by the sword."

Michael's eyes betrayed him.

He knows the murder weapon was a sword.

"Listen, Ed, I sure would love to see that car," Cavet said with feigned envy, primarily to see Ed's response. "I've never seen a restored original Goat."

"Another time," Ed Broussard promised Cavet. "You have my word."

"Fair enough," Cavet said, trusting his instincts and offering his hand to Ed. "Thank you for your time."

"Yep," Ed said, without any real emotion but returning a very firm handshake.

"Michael, here's my card. If you remember anything—anything at all—give me a call, alright?"

"Yes, sir," Michael replied, visibly relieved Cavet was leaving.

Cavet turned, took a step toward the front door, and stopped. As always, he saved the most important question for last.

"One more thing I've got to know, Michael," Cavet said, remembering that neighbors heard the sound of a car peeling out of the parking lot after midnight.

"How did the Goat handle?"

"Uh, fine, I guess," Michael said.

"What?" Cavet asked with exaggerated disbelief. "You had a muscle car in an empty parking lot. You didn't try a few donuts or peel out or anything?"

"No, sir."

"If he did, it's probably best I don't know about it," Ed Broussard interjected. "Now let me get that door for you, Tom."

Cavet nodded and walked out the door. The good news was that he had a suspect. The bad news was that Emma was not going to babysit for him again.

Ever.

* * *

Ed Broussard was going to be sick.

He was standing inside his garage and looking at what was left of his beautiful car. Every panel was crushed or dented. Most of the tail lights were smashed and the hood was caved in. Michael had described the damage for him, but he still wasn't prepared to see her in this condition.

"I took your mother on our first date in this car, Mikey."

"Yes, sir."

Ed walked around the Goat in complete silence. He looked at every dent and every scratch. When he got to the hood, he ran his hand as far as he could down the bowl-shaped depression and back up again.

"This wasn't a car accident," Ed said, sounding like a heartbroken and confused accident reconstructionist.

"No, sir."

"Vandalism?"

"Uh, sort of. Yes, sir."

"Something landed to the right of center," he said, feeling the damage to the hood. "The paint is not scratched, so it wasn't a sledgehammer or a tool. If I had to guess, I'd say somebody landed feet-first."

"I don't know, sir."

"You don't know because you weren't there," Ed said, prying. "Because you gave the Goat to somebody, and he gave it back like this. Was it Trey?"

"No, sir."

"Would you tell me if it was?"

"Yes, sir. I mean … I think so."

Ed stopped when he saw the red smears on the front windshield.

"Is that blood?"

"Yes, sir, but it's not what you think," Michael assured him.

"Well, I think it's blood, Mikey."

"Yes, sir. I mean … it's blood, but it's not human blood."

Ed stared at his son.

"I don't know what to say. You've never lied to me, Mikey. Not once. I want to trust you, but you've got no idea what this is doing to me."

"Dad, I'm in trouble," Michael told him plainly. "Detective Cavet wants to see this car, and I can't explain this."

Ed walked to the corner and punched the speed bag hanging there as hard as he could. The punch would have shattered a jaw, and the sound echoed inside the garage like a gunshot.

"Did you kill the priest?"

"No, sir."

"Do you know who did?"

"Yes, sir."

"Thank God," Ed said, feeling a wave of relief. "Now listen carefully. You're going to tell me …"

"No, sir," Michael replied firmly. "I can't."

"The hell you say!" Ed erupted in anger. "You're going to tell me and you're going to tell that detective. No matter who it is, Mikey. You hear me? No matter what you saw or what you think they'll do to you. No matter what the consequences. I lost your mother, and I'm not going to lose you. Do you understand me?"

"I can't do that."

"You can and you will!" Ed yelled, slamming his fist on the car roof.

This is the turning point in his life, Ed suddenly realized. *I have to save Mikey from himself, and the only way to do that is to find out what he knows. Right here. Right now.*

"Defend yourself!" Ed warned as he always did when they started to box.

Hurricane Ed Broussard headed toward Michael with his fists up and absolutely resolved to beat the answers out of him.

No matter how long it took. No matter what the price.

The sound of a fist banging on corrugated metal stopped Ed before he reached Michael, who never raised his fists.

"Cavet?"

They waited in silence for the next bang. When it came, even louder than before, Ed had the gut-wrenching feeling he had just missed his chance to save Michael.

I'm so sorry, Kathy. I failed you.

* * *

Chapter 12: Prosecution

But the LORD is with me as a mighty terrible one; therefore my persecutors shall stumble, and they shall not prevail...
Jeremiah 20:11

(5:12 p.m.) Friday, November 15

The grandeur of Orleans Parish Criminal District Court is easily overlooked. Since 1931, friends and family with tunnel vision have been hustling up her steps looking for justice or hoping for mercy. Nobody cares about the twelve fluted Corinthian columns or the 418-foot facade of the courthouse known as "Tulane and Broad." Nobody stops to appreciate Angela Gregory's stone carvings. Nobody notices the cast iron bronze bas-reliefs. Everyone is too focused on getting inside.

Most head to the second floor, where their anxious eyes dart from one set of brass letters to the next, oblivious to the cathedral ceilings and art-deco chandeliers. They always find the right courtroom, and they always miss the beautiful pediment and green marble columns marking its entrance. Their haste is understandable and probably for the best.

The hallway is heavy with forgotten despair. Somehow, the walls absorb every wretched cry and the windows every despondent stare. The benches remember every hopeless vigil, and the marble floors every dejected step. Outside, carved letters may promise "the rule of law not men," but the hallway knows better.

Behind every door, fates are decided by flawed strangers and the skill of ambitious advocates.

*　　*　　*

Coach Will Taylor was waiting outside of Section D. When Will poked his head into the courtroom, closing arguments were already over and the judge was starting to read his standard jury instructions. Deliberations would follow, and that meant he had only a few more minutes to make the biggest decision of his life.

Am I rushing this? Will wondered. *Is this a reckless, knee-jerk reaction?*

Will knew the answer. A few hours ago, Brother Reid had shown him a tattoo and convinced him the End of Days had arrived. The news had hit the Marine harder than it had Father Finnegan. Of course, Finn had never been in a war, and his soul was better prepared.

Will had tried hard to forget his tours of duty, but he still remembered the carnage. Will had a better idea of what was coming their way, which was why he had drained a glass of Finn's best Scotch and driven straight to Adler's Jewelry Store.

Reckless and romantic, Will decided as people started filing out of Section D.

A crowd soon formed outside the courtroom. Some were sharing sad hugs. Others were discussing the trial or deciding whether to wait for the verdict. Nobody was smiling, and everybody was speaking in hushed voices. It felt like the end of a long funeral. And perhaps it was.

Suddenly, Coach Will heard Joy's confident footsteps striking the marble and carving a path through the crowd.

Assistant District Attorney Joy Glapion was five-foot-nothing, but her trademark high heels made her legs look much longer than they were. She had beautiful brown eyes and cocoa-colored skin. She was arguably more cute than beautiful, but she was always elegant and poised. Public Defenders called her the "ice queen."

Bailiffs called her "short and sweet."

Will tried to play it cool as he watched her approach, but he was pretty sure she could tell how much he was digging her.

Joy stopped a few feet away, and Will knew better than to hug or kiss her inside the courthouse. She had just finished a murder trial, not a piano recital. He could congratulate her later.

"Ready?" Joy asked like he was her chauffeur.

"Ready."

They walked in silence down the marble stairs to the first floor and stopped in front of the massive doors facing Tulane Avenue. Joy exited first and was immediately surrounded by reporters and cameras. Will counted to twenty before exiting and passed unnoticed behind the throng.

She won't be long, Will thought. *She never talks to the press before the verdict.*

Will waited at the corner of South White Street, halfway between the courthouse and the District Attorney's office. Reporters were creatures of habit. Even if they needed film of Joy walking on the sidewalk, they would get what they needed before she reached South White Street.

"How are you?" Will asked when she arrived a few minutes later.

"Better now," she said as they started walking together. "What do you think?"

"Guilty as charged," Will predicted. "And these jurors aren't going to play around. It's after six o'clock on a Friday night. You'll have a verdict before eight."

"I hope you're right. I have a hot date tonight."

"Yes, you do," Will agreed, smiling for the first time since Brother Reid opened his eyes. Even in the middle of a murder trial, Joy Glapion knew exactly what to say to make him feel special.

They walked across South White Street and up the ramp to the concrete monstrosity that was the District Attorney's Office. Joy let them both inside and her cell phone starting ringing before they reached the elevator.

Too soon for a jury question or a verdict, Will figured.

"Detective Cavet, how are you?" she said, pressing the phone firmly against her ear. "I'm good. Just waiting on a verdict. How's the dead priest investigation?"

Yep. That would explain why Joy took the call.

The whole city was talking about the priest found murdered in the parking lot of Rock 'n' Bowl. When Will saw it on the morning news, he immediately called Finn to make sure it wasn't one of theirs. According to Finn, the deceased wasn't a Jesuit, and probably wasn't local.

"Doctor Villere believes the murder weapon was a what?" Joy asked in disbelief. "What is a gladius and why does he think... Seriously? Okay, but why would a priest… Well, that is interesting, I guess."

Joy looked up at Will for a moment. She smiled and looked down again. "Okay, do we have any suspects? Good, tell me why we think that."

Uh oh. She said "we." She's hooked.

Will had seen that particular look on Joy's face before. It meant she already thought of the homicide as "her" case. It meant she would probably spend more time this weekend with Detective Caveman than with him. From this moment on, she would be obsessed with solving the priest murder.

"Where are you now?" Joy asked. "Okay. Why are you at the dad's garage?"

And there goes our date, Will thought as he watched Joy's face cringe every time the detective said something wrong.

"Let me see if I've got this straight. You followed them to the garage. You waited for them to go inside. You heard yelling and knocked on the side of the shed. They took forever to come out. When they did, you asked to see the car. Dad refused and you insisted. Then Dad told you to 'stop barking up the wrong tree', and he put a padlock on the door?"

"Smart move," Will said, chuckling.

"Baby, hush," Joy said, momentarily covering the phone. "Then they hopped on two motorcycles and took off. Okay, we're on the same page. What's your question?"

Will watched Joy listen intently.

"Probably, if you go to the right judge," Joy said. "Do you have your silly little notebook and pencil ready? Good. Here's what you say to get the search warrant. Victim stabbed with sword. Time of death between midnight and one. Suspect was last person in the parking lot between midnight and one. Neighbors heard swordplay and saw black sports car leaving lot. Suspect admits he left parking lot driving a black sports car."

"Garages have tools," Will reminded her.

"Oooh, that's good, Will!" she said, forgetting to cover the phone. "Be certain to mention the garage is a professional repair shop that is, uh, likely to have tools that can be used to repair or hide any incriminating damage."

Joy rewarded Will with a little wink while Cavet was almost certainly reading back his notes.

"Hey, how about Mandina's for dinner?" she said, covering the phone. "Soon as the verdict comes back."

"You read my mind."

"You're welcome," Joy told Detective Cavet a few seconds later. "By the way, where does the suspect go to school?"

Joy stopped smiling.

Crap.

"What's the boy's name?" Joy asked, and she grimaced when she heard the response. "No, I don't... uh, okay... thank you, Detective. Good night."

Will watched Joy put the phone back in her purse and waited for her to look up at him before asking the question he needed answered.

"One of mine?"

Joy stared at Will with a pained expression. She couldn't answer that question without violating her oath as a prosecutor, so she asked her own.

"What is the name of the student who saved your life?"

* * *

Lamar Joseph Hill hated losing.

About an hour ago, he stood next to his client in a packed courtroom and heard the Judge read the jury's verdict. No matter how many cases he tried, Lamar would never get used to the sound of parents wailing after a conviction.

Even when their child is a tattooed monster.

The verdict hit Jimmy Foster's parents harder than most. Maybe they could still picture the three-hundred-pound, forty-year-old killer as a child. Maybe they blamed themselves. Whatever the reason, it was always a gut-wrenching moment.

Tonight was no exception.

The Foster family was devastated, and there was nothing Lamar could say to make them feel better. The ice queen tried the case cleanly. There was no chance the second-degree murder conviction would be reversed on appeal.

Lamar walked through the door. He found his wife sitting on one couch and his old chocolate lab on the other.

"Uh-oh," he said. "What happened?"

"That dog of yours," his wife said with a sneer. "Does not listen to a thing I say."

"The dog is deaf, Luv," Lamar reminded her.

"I know that, LJ," Doctor Alysha Hill snapped. "But I'm telling you, that dog knows what I want, and he refuses to do it. Just to spite me!"

Lamar looked at his dog.

"Is that true, Hershey?"

Silence.

"Hershey is invoking his right to remain silent," Lamar informed his wife with his courtroom voice. "And no matter what I tell jurors, that's a sure sign of guilt."

"You bet your butt it is."

Lamar chuckled and gave his wife a kiss. Then he plopped down on the sofa next to Hershey and started scratching him behind the ears.

"Where's my other son?"

"On the phone with one of his new friends," she replied closing the book she was reading and putting it on the end table. "I think it's the Broussard boy."

"The one that knocked my nephew out at Gormley?"

"The same."

"I don't know how I feel about that. I was at that game. I thought he killed Keith."

"Keith is fine, and you'll get over it," she said. "Just like you did when Derrick decided to transfer to Jesui--"

"Don't mention that school in this house!" Lamar declared loudly and only half-joking. "Don't you say it in this house!"

Alysha shook her head. "I'll never understand this high school thing."

"It's not a high school thing. It's a Catholic League thing."

"It's a stupid thing."

Derrick walked into the room, holding a phone.

"Hey, buddy," Lamar said before noticing the very serious look on his son's face. "What's wrong?"

"I need your help, Dad," Derrick said. "My friend's in trouble."

Lamar sighed and took the phone.

"Where are you and who is with you?" Lamar asked.

He listened very carefully for several seconds. When he spoke again, his tone was authoritative and grim.

"Say nothing. Tell him you've retained me as your defense attorney."

Lamar sighed.

"Tell Detective Caveman I'm on my way."

*   *   *

Ed Broussard was on the ropes.

"I think we both know why I'm back in your kitchen, Ed."

Damn it, thought Ed. *He's seen the car.*

"I obtained a search warrant for your garage," the detective continued. "I cut the padlock about an hour ago, and we both know what I found inside."

Fight back, Ed!

"I don't think you do," Ed muttered as he poured himself a cup of coffee and sat down at the table next to Cavet.

"What's that, Ed?"

"I don't think you know what you found," Ed repeated. "My wife was the brains of this operation, but I'm guessin' the priest wasn't hit by a car. If he was, you'd be arresting my son instead of talking to me."

"Well, you got me there," Cavet admitted. "But that boy wrecked your car and got somebody's blood all over it. That can't sit well with you."

Steady, Ed told himself. *This is just Round One.*

"Unless I've misjudged you, I figure you got to the bottom of it," Cavet explained, staring right at him.

Ed took another sip of coffee rather than respond.

"So why don't you tell me the truth," Cavet suggested. "Tell me what happened, and we'll figure out how to help Michael. I owe Russell and Carol that much."

Ed stopped drinking coffee and seriously considered Cavet's proposal. He still didn't know what happened, but he knew Mikey was not the killer. Together, they probably could get the story out of the boy.

Before Ed could say anything, Michael walked back from the bathroom and stopped at the entrance to the kitchen. Ed did not like the look on Michael's face.

"Michael, I want you to do something for me," Cavet said as soon as Michael entered the kitchen.

Cavet paused and opened the manila envelope he was carrying. He pulled out a piece of paper, and Ed could see it had rows of phone numbers on it. Only one row was highlighted yellow.

"I want you to tell your Dad why you called Scotland when you got home the night of the murder."

Ed looked at Michael like he was looking at a total stranger. Ed was no expert, but his son looked confused.

Not scared or guilty, thought Ed. *Legitimately confused.*

"Tell him why, not long after the priest was murdered, you needed to call an unregistered number somewhere in Scotland," Cavet continued.

The word "priest" seemed to ring a bell with Michael, who glanced down the hallway at the phone in the front room.

"Detective Cavet, I've hired Lamar Hill as my attorney," Michael announced. "He's on his way over now, and I'm not answering any more questions."

"You did what?" Ed asked, unable to stop himself.

"You don't have to leave," Michael added, ignoring his father's surprise. "But I would appreciate it if you would please get out of my mom's chair."

"That's too bad, Michael," the shocked Cavet said. "You're making a big—"

"No, sir." Michael interrupted impatiently. "I'm not. Now will you please get out of her chair."

Michael's tone and request were exactly the smelling salts Ed Broussard needed.

Cavet is not our friend. And Mikey's in the fight of his life.

It was time to let Mikey know Dad was in his corner.

"Okay, Michael," Cavet said, standing up and looking over at Ed like he expected Ed's support. "I sure hope you know what you're doing, son."

"He's not your son," Ed said. "He's mine. And I should have said something about the chair when you sat down. Now I'm askin' you to leave our house."

"Now hold on, Ed—"

"No, sir. I will not," replied Hurricane Ed Broussard. "And I won't be asking you again."

*   *   *

The ring was burning a hole in Will's pocket.

Will looked across the table at Joy, who was still enjoying her bowl of gumbo. He knew in his heart there was no way Michael Broussard killed a priest. He also knew tonight was the wrong night to discuss Michael's innocence.

But is it the right night to propose?

"What?" Joy chuckled. "Why are you looking at me like that?"

Will smiled and thought quickly. "Well, I'm waiting."

"Waiting for what?"

"Look around," Will encouraged her. "Mandina's. November 15th. . . ."

Joy stared at him for a moment.

"Oh no!" she shrieked. "I forgot our anniversary!"

Will nodded. "Two years ago tonight. Our first date."

Joy looked genuinely contrite. She threw her napkin on the table, stood up, and gave him a heartfelt kiss.

"Baby, I'm sorry. Happy anniversary."

"Happy anniversary," Will said with a reassuring smile. "Thank you for two wonderful years."

"You're welcome," she replied, giving him an even nicer kiss. "And I'll be right back. I've got to use the little prosecutor's room."

Will nodded and watched her weave her way through the hungry tables.

That does it, Will decided. *I'm asking her as soon as she comes back.*

A few minutes later, Joy returned. She was talking on the phone and had a very serious look on her face.

She was staring right at Will.

"I don't care, Detective!" Joy insisted as she sat down without breaking eye contact with Will. "He's not going anywhere, and you can't arrest him yet. You need to know if the blood on the hood matches the priest's."

Joy waited for a second.

"Not a problem," she told Cavet. "Call me when you hear from the crime lab."

Joy scanned the room, dropped her phone into her purse, and sat down.

"Cavet wants to get an arrest warrant," she whispered across the table. "I bought Michael a day. Maybe less." Joy scanned the room again. "I owed him that for saving your life," she added. "But I can't do anything… uh, I mean… now, I have to wash my…"

Will stood up and gave her a kiss on the cheek.

"Happy anniversary, my love. And thank you."

Will walked outside of the restaurant and pulled out his phone.

"Finn, it's me," Will said. "Michael's in trouble."

* * *

Chapter 13: Friendship

Now when Job's three friends heard of all this evil that was come upon him, they came every one from his own place…
Job 2:11

Saturday, November 16

Sheri Stevens was primping.

The process was taking longer than usual because she was out of practice. Sheri had dedicated the past week to caring for her little sister, Brandi, who had Down syndrome and a particularly nasty stomach virus. With their mother out of town on business again, it fell to Sheri to nurse the seven-year-old back to health.

Which was just fine with Sheri.

Sheri adored her sister and was more than happy to give Brandi the constant care and love she deserved. For the past seven days, Sheri had not left Brandi's side, even though it meant Sheri missed a week of school, her senior picture, and a second date with Tony.

None of that mattered.

Brandi was the only person who loved Sheri unconditionally, and Sheri could not bear to see her sick or sad. Fortunately, Doctor Lagarde lived down the street, and the antibiotics he prescribed eventually did the trick. Brandi's fever broke and her appetite returned. Now, Brandi was more tired than sick, which was why Sheri was allowing Adele to come over.

Adele's visit meant Sheri could take a long hot shower, shave her legs, and do her hair and make-up. It was exactly the kind of "me time" Sheri cherished but rarely enjoyed since her mom's business had grown.

Wherever Sheri's dad was, and whatever he was doing, Sheri prayed he was failing miserably and suffering greatly. She would never forgive him for walking out on them after Brandi's birth. The man was going to burn in hell someday, but at least his leaving taught Sheri a valuable lesson:

Men cannot be trusted.

No matter how sweet. No matter how many times they said they loved you. They were always one decision away from leaving you and never looking back.

Sheri skipped about seven fairly important steps in her primping routine because she did not want Adele to think she was dallying. She threw on some clothes and hurried down the stairs, where Sheri found Adele and Brandi sitting on the sofa and watching television. Brandi had the blanket up to her nose, and Adele was gently combing her hair.

"Hey, Boo," Sheri said. "How are you feeling?"

"Better," Brandi yawned, enjoying Adele's attention.

"I bet you are," Sheri said. "Addie knows what she's doing. You're going to look even prettier when she's done. I'm so jealous!"

"You're always jealous," Brandi announced, while pulling down the blanket. "But you're pretty too."

"Aw, thanks Boo," Sheri said, smiling. "And thanks, Addie. I really appreciate your coming over. Brandi missed you."

"Well I've missed Brandi," Adele replied, and Sheri knew she meant it. They had been the "Three Musketeers" since Brandi was old enough to walk.

"Hey, Brandi, I've got an idea," Adele said, stopping mid-stroke. "Let's hang out tonight. We could watch a movie!"

"Yes!" Brandi squealed in delight.

"Addie, you don't have to..." Sheri started to object.

"Great! It's a date!" Adele announced, ignoring Sheri. "Your sister has been hogging you all week. It's about time she shared you. Can you find something else to do tonight, Sheri?"

"Addie, that's very sweet, but I'm fine. I want to make sure Boo's fever doesn't come back, and I don't want you to break your date with Trey."

"You don't want me to break my date with Trey because Trey is my what?"

"I'm not going to say it."

"Come on!" Adele teased. "I've been dating Trey for a year, which means that Trey is..."

"Not welcomed in my house?"

"Try again," Adele suggested. "Trey is..."

"A troll who lives under a bridge?"

"Sheri Stevens!" Adele protested. "That's not true. Tell Brandi that's not true."

"Oh, but it is true, Boo," Sheri said, rather sadly. "Addie thinks by kissing him she can turn him into a prince, but she can't. She's wasting her kisses!"

"Really?" Brandi asked, looking concerned.

"No, not really," Adele said, feigning indignation. "Trey's a good boy and—"

The ringing of the phone interrupted Adele and sent Sheri hurrying to the kitchen. Sheri grabbed the phone without seeing who was calling.

"Stevens' residence," Sheri answered formally, just in case it was somebody calling for her mom.

"Hello, this is Emma Landry. May I please speak with Sheri Stevens?"

Oh, you've got to be kidding me.

"You are."

"Oh, uh… hi, Sheri. I didn't recognize your voice."

"I'm not surprised. This is the first time you've called me."

"Yes, well, about that," Emma said. "I was calling because, well, I think we got off on the wrong foot, and I'd like for us to double date tonight."

"Double date?"

"Brad Shipley and I would like to grab dinner with you and Michael Broussard."

Silence.

"Are you kidding?"

"I know, it would be so great, right?" Emma said with such over-the-top giddiness that Sheri could not possibly mistake her enthusiasm for sincerity. Because this was not a double-date invitation.

It was a double-dog dare.

* * *

Adele knew the real Sheri Stevens.

Sheri just didn't want to get hurt. That was the real reason she avoided nice guys like the plague and preferred a steady diet of casual dates with guys she could dump without remorse. Unfortunately, Sheri usually erred on the side of caution and dated guys nobody could ever fall in love with.

Ever.

An eternal optimist, Adele was certain Sheri would eventually grow out of it, which is why she set her up with Michael Broussard. Those two had more in common than either suspected.

But when Sheri saw Michael dancing with that lunatic, Emma, at Homecoming, she had felt a twinge of jealousy. It was something Sheri had not felt in a long time, and it spooked her. She instantly decided to dump Michael at the end of the date, and even a "remarkable" kiss good night could not change her mind.

At least, that was what Sheri told Adele later that night.

Adele was still surprised by Sheri's candor. Maybe Sheri felt she owed Adele an explanation for dumping Michael. Maybe Sheri secretly hoped Adele would leak the information to Trey. Either way, Michael was on Sheri's radar, and that could be a good thing.

A very good thing.

Adele kept combing. With each stroke, Brandi drifted closer to sleep.

Poor Brandi. She doesn't have a fever, but she's so tired and weak. She needs to get her strength back.

Adele could hear Sheri talking on the phone but could not hear her conversation. Adele gently slipped a pillow under Brandi's head, stood up, and stretched her arms. As she placed a blanket over Brandi, she heard Sheri hang up the phone.

Adele wished Trey could see this side of Sheri.

She only craves the spotlight because it's never on her at home, thought Adele. *She's one of the most unselfish, loving...*

"Addie, get your bony butt in here!"

Adele chuckled and walked into the kitchen.

"Sheri, you're the worst insulter of all time," Adele informed her. "I absolutely love it when you call my butt bony."

"Was this your idea?" Sheri interrupted. "Tell me the truth."

"Was what my idea?"

"The double date!" Sheri snapped.

"I don't know anything about a double date," Adele replied truthfully. "What are you talking about?"

Sheri stared at her for a moment, apparently trying to decide if Adele was lying to her for the first time in her life.

"What double date?" Adele demanded impatiently.

Sheri smiled.

"Michael and I are going to double date tonight."

"That's great—" Adele started to say.

"With Emma Landry."

"You're joking."

"I don't joke about Emma Landry," Sheri assured her. "And another dose of Michael Broussard may be exactly what the doctor ordered."

Adele did not like Sheri's devilish grin.

"What the doctor ordered… for whom?"

*　　*　　*

Not all surprises are welcomed.

Detective Cavet returned to his office at 1030 hours on Saturday, November 16th and almost fainted when he found the coroner sitting behind his desk. Doctor Villere was drinking a cup of the Homicide Division's coffee and looking cold sober.

To Cavet's knowledge, it was the first time for both.

"Good morning, Detective," Villere said, as if they were meeting for the first time. He sounded worse than he looked, and Cavet was certain the mad scientist had worked through the night. "May I speak with you for a moment?"

"May you speak with me?" Cavet repeated mortified.

"About your investigation, Detective," Villere explained, standing up and moving to one of the vinyl guest chairs.

"This can't be good," Cavet muttered as he sat down.

"I completed the test you requested," Villere said, ignoring the detective's tone. "The test on the blood specimen taken from the hood of the suspect's car."

"Already?"

"I tested it personally," Villere continued like he was testifying in open court. "In fact, I tested it twelve times."

"You did what?"

"I tested it personally, and I tested it twelve times," he repeated. "The result was the same every time."

"Okay, Doc. You have my full attention."

"The blood specimen does not match," Villere reported with a gravitas in his voice that suggested there was far more to the story.

"Does not match ... the priest?"

Villere was staring right at Cavet, and the coroner's eyes were filled with emotion. Villere was many things, but he was not an alarmist. Something was wrong, and Villere seemed to be deciding whether to trust Cavet.

Villere took a deep, steadying breath.

"Does not match ... anyone or anything," Villere eventually replied.

"Doc, is that your way of saying it's not blood?"

Villere leaned forward.

"It's my way of saying the sample is like nothing I've ever seen before," Villere explained, lowering his voice. "It's like nothing *anyone* has ever seen before."

Villere pointed to the little notebook in Cavet's pocket.

"May I see that for a second?"

Something in Villere's voice conveyed the need for his unprecedented request. Cavet trusted his instincts and handed the coroner his notebook.

Villere opened the book to the first blank page and grabbed a pencil from Cavet's desk. He scribbled "Red Blood Cells" at the top of the page and quickly drew a vertical line down the center of the notebook. He labeled the left column "mammalian" and the right column "avian." Then he drew three horizontal lines and labeled the three rows: size, shape, and nuclei.

"Exactly nine microns in diameter," Villere told Cavet. "Most avian RBCs are 6.0 to 8.0 microns in diameter. Most mammalian RBCs are 5.5 to 7.5 microns."

"RBCs?"

"Red Blood Cells," Villere said while writing a "no" in the "size" row for the mammalian and avian columns.

"Not a round shape like in mammals," Villere continued. "More of an oval shape like in birds."

Villere wrote another "no" in the "shape" row for the mammalian column before suddenly remembering an exception to the rule. "And in Arabian camels. But I hardly think the kid hit an Arabian camel in the Rock 'n' Bowl parking lot, okay?"

"Okay," Cavet muttered, still not knowing where this was going.

"And the cells were a-nucleated," Villere announced, shaking his head in disbelief. "Avian red blood cells have nuclei. Mature mammalian RBCs do not."

Villere wrote a final "no" in the "nuclei" row for the avian column and stared at Cavet, waiting for some sign Cavet recognized the significance of his findings.

Which, of course, Cavet did not.

"Doc, what in the hell are you trying—"

"If this is blood," Villere interrupted him, "and I believe it is, it's the blood of a creature that doesn't belong."

Villere stopped himself from saying more.

"In Louisiana?" Cavet guessed.

"No, Tommy," Villere said, regaining his control and his conviction. "To our world."

* * *

The damage was done.

Doctor Villere had left his office an hour ago, but Detective Cavet was still sitting behind his desk, rubbing his eyes and considering his options. One thing was certain: Villere had finally lost his mind.

Unfortunately, he had done so while testing a blood sample in the dead priest investigation. Why Villere performed the test instead of the NOPD crime lab was beyond Cavet, but there was no way to un-ring that bell.

Villere was now of the opinion that the Broussard boy drove his dad's car into a creature that "is not indigenous to Earth."

What do I do now?

Fortunately, Cavet had no trouble convincing Villere to sit on his report for a few days. The mad scientist was lucid enough to realize the political and social repercussions of telling the world he found evidence that an alien life form traveled all the way to the Big Easy to get hit by a classic muscle car.

Now Cavet needed to decide whether to retest the blood, and he needed to decide today. Otherwise, the delay between the taking and the testing of the blood would become a red flag.

Cavet shuddered when he thought of another decision he had to make down the road--whether to include Villere's findings in his final Incident Report. He took out his pocket notebook and considered what to write about his bizarre meeting with Villere. He decided less was more.

Sample from hood of Broussard car does not match victim's blood.

Cavet shook his head, put away his notebook, and started flipping through the photographs of the crime scene. When he came across a photo of the priest's right wrist, he stopped and picked up the phone.

*   *   *

"Go for Matt Frosch!" answered his cocky nephew.

Officer Matthew Frosch had graduated from the Police Academy two years ago, but this was the first time Cavet had allowed him to work a homicide case.

He was already regretting it.

"Good morning, Officer Frosch. What do you have for me?"

"Morning, Uncle… er, Detective," Matt replied. "Last night I checked a dozen tattoo parlors, and nobody's seen the symbol branded on the priest's wrist. I looked at books with thousands of angel wing designs, but none of them had crossed keys. Nobody even heard of that design. What a colossal waste of time!"

Detective Cavet took a deep breath.

"It was not a colossal waste of time, Matty," Cavet replied, testily. "If the symbol is not in any of the books, the branding iron is not local and is probably rare. Both facts are important."

"If you say so."

"I do. Now where are you?"

"I'm on the porch of the big blue house that faces Rock 'n' Bowl. I've interviewed every house that faces the parking lot. Nobody saw crap last night, except for the guy who saw the kid peeling out of the parking lot."

"Did anybody lie to you?"

"How would I know that?"

"How would you know?" Cavet repeated incredulously. "What did your gut tell you? Was anyone defensive? Was anybody impatient?"

"Not really," Matt replied. "I mean, they were all a little pissed they had to tell the story again, but nothing unusual."

"I'm sorry. Did you say *again*, Matthew?"

"Yeah," Matt replied. "Apparently, two students came out here last night and earlier today interviewing people for their school newspaper."

"Please tell me you're joking."

"No, uh, it was a boy and a girl," Matt reported.

"Did you get descriptions of them?"

"Why would I do that?"

Detective Cavet silently counted to ten before answering.

"No reason. Can you tell me anything about the two students?"

"Well, the boy told one neighbor that he also played the trumpet. And everyone said the girl was a spunky redhead."

Detective Cavet gritted his teeth.

Of course they did.

* * *

Emma Landry loved it when a plan came together.

She opened the front door and smiled at the boy holding the plastic-wrapped flowers from Rouses Supermarket.

"Hey, Emma."

"Hello, Brad!" she said enthusiastically, before noticing the giant bruise on his left cheek. "Oh my gosh! What happened to you?"

"Got in a fight at school." Brad shrugged, a little embarrassed. "But I'm fine. Uh, you should see the other guy."

"I bet," Emma said with feigned admiration. She detested violence and anyone who took pride in hurting someone, but this was not the time to lecture Brad.

"I was surprised you called," Brad said as Emma laid the flowers on a table, stepped out the house, and locked the door.

"Why is that, silly?"

"Well, you didn't let me drive you home after Homecoming," Brad reminded her while opening the passenger door for her.

"I'm sorry about that," Emma said. "I wasn't feeling right."

Emma watched as Brad got in the car, turned on the engine, and started driving down the street. He was still chewing on her answer.

"Because I thought you were having a bad time," he said, fishing for more information and possibly a compliment.

"How could I?" Emma replied. "Now take a right turn at the next light."

"But that's not the way to the restaurant."

"No, it's not," Emma agreed, as the first few raindrops appeared on the windshield. "But it's the way to Sheri's house."

"Uh, who's Sheri?"

"We're double dating with Sheri and her boyfriend."

"Uh, okay," Brad said, turning on the wipers. "But you didn't tell me we were—"

"Oh no!" Emma gasped. "I didn't tell you this was a double date? I'm so sorry, Brad. I'm such a ditz! Please don't be mad at me… and turn left at the light."

"I'm not mad," Brad assured her. "I'm just—"

"Yay!" Emma declared. "Because you are going to love Sheri. She is so pretty. I just hope you don't spend the whole night staring at her."

"No, I wouldn't--"

"Take a right at the stop sign," Emma instructed. "Sheri should be the third house on the right."

"Uh, yep, I see it," Brad told her, pulling the car over and turning off the engine. "Should I honk or are we… uh, Emma?"

Emma was already getting out the car. She quickly closed the door and leaned into the open window to answer Brad's question.

"Wait in the car. I'll go get Sheri. Be right back!"

Now comes the hard part.

* * *

Clarity has a price.

Michael ran out of his house like it was on fire. He leapt off the front porch, landed with a splash in the rain-soaked grass, and ran down the side alley to the garage. As he jumped on his motorcycle, a bolt of lightning lit up the neighborhood and rattled the shed.

Michael drove down the alley toward the street. There was no time to explain to anyone that strangers had followed Emma to a restaurant.

"Jacob!" he yelled at the top of his lungs. "Everyone, follow me!"

Michael had no idea what he was going to do when he got to the restaurant, but a host of angels was going to follow him wherever he went, which was why he had told Emma to stay put.

Michael hit the throttle.

Nothing made sense anymore. Not what he was. Not what was happening to him. Not what was expected of him. But the terror in Emma's voice brought everything into focus. Suddenly, Michael knew exactly who he was.

I'm the guy who comes when Emma calls.

* * *

They were closing fast on Agrippa's position.

It was still light out, but the tight formation of angels was flying so low on Veterans Boulevard that Agrippa did not spot them until they turned north onto Severn. They were more than a mile away, but Agrippa's experienced eyes counted at least a dozen.

Agrippa watched with admiration as the left echelon formation smoothly transitioned into a flying-vee formation. The assailants were now half a mile from the perimeter of local Guardians that Agrippa established, and they were hopelessly outnumbered, but they appeared disciplined and determined.

One or two might actually break through the line, Agrippa thought indifferently.

Agrippa was standing in front of twenty Novices whose *protelos* were either working or eating inside the Mexican restaurant. He knew from experience that the closer he stationed them to their *protelos,* the harder they would fight.

"The first to breach is mine!" Agrippa declared, and he was instantly rewarded with the sound of nervous cheering and the clatter of clumsily-drawn swords.

Maybe I should take all of them, Agrippa thought.

Agrippa's eyes continued to track the assault. When the skein was only a block from his perimeter, the defenders quickly shifted to a concave line formation. It was the right tactical counter, and Agrippa was suddenly proud of his decision to place Trey's Guardian in charge of the perimeter. That Ryan knew what he was doing.

Agrippa was still smiling when he heard the bells on the restaurant door jingle.

"No!" Agrippa yelled as Derrick and Trey ran outside holding cameras.

Centuries of discipline trumped Agrippa's Guardian instincts and forced him to turn around and face the attack, even though it meant turning his back on Derrick.

Agrippa spun around just in time to see the entire formation pass through the perimeter.

Intact and unchallenged.

* * *

Michael flew into the parking lot of Taqueria Corona and skidded to a stop. He dropped the kick stand and ran inside the restaurant.

Something told him to be prepared for anything when he got inside, but nothing could have prepared him for what he found.

Emma was sitting with Brad Shipley and Sheri Stevens.

"¡Hola, Miguel!" Emma declared enthusiastically. "¿Comó estás?"

"¿Comó estás?" Michael panted. "You've got to be kidding!"

"She's not," Sheri assured him.

"¡Siéntate, Miguel!" Emma exclaimed with illogical delight and pointing to the empty chair next to Sheri.

Before Michael could scream, Sheri popped out of her chair and gave him a quick kiss on the cheek.

"This was her idea," Sheri whispered in his ear. "She's up to something."

"Ya think?" Michael muttered sarcastically as an astute waiter brought him a menu.

"¿Conoces al Señor Shipley?" Emma asked as Michael reluctantly sat down.

"Yes, I know Brad!" Michael snapped, observing that Brad looked equally surprised to see him.

"¡Muy bien!" Emma practically screamed. "¿Son amigos?"

"No," Michael replied, fairly certain Brad did not speak Spanish.

"¿Quién es más macho?" Emma wondered aloud. "¿Señor Shipley o Señor Broussard?"

"Emma, I swear—"

"I know! I know!" Emma interrupted proudly and dropping out of character. "You didn't think I could make it happen, but here we are. Isn't this great? We even ordered for you!"

A second waiter magically appeared with chips, salsa, and guacamole.

"I've got to go," Michael told Sheri. "I'm sorry she dragged you into this."

"No, stay," Sheri whispered in his ear.

"I want to see what she does next."

* * *

"Detective."

"Good evening, Ed," Cavet said. "I have a warrant to search your home."

"Mikey's not here," Ed Broussard said, tucking a folded newspaper under his arm before accepting the document Cavet was offering him. "Left a little while ago."

"He doesn't have to be," Cavet informed him matter-of-factly. "We just need to take a look around."

"I got any say in this?" Ed asked, while starting to read the warrant.

"No. Not really, Ed."

"Should I call Mikey's lawyer?"

"Well, that's up to you."

Ed Broussard stopped reading the warrant, looked up, and locked eyes with the detective.

"Would you?"

"Yes, I would, Ed," Cavet replied truthfully. "I'd call him right now."

* * *

Agrippa had a bad feeling.

He should have been relieved when he realized that the angelic formation was Michael Broussard's escort and that Michael was meeting the Landry girl for an early dinner. Given the intense look on Michael's face, Agrippa should have been delighted by the prospect of another parking-lot confrontation. But he wasn't.

Something's wrong, Agrippa thought. *I feel it.*

When Michael's escort reached the Mexican restaurant, the three angels that comprised the tip of the flying-vee broke-off and landed in the parking lot. Brothers Jacob and Carson strode toward Agrippa as the wings of the formation split and passed to his left and right. A fraction of a second later, both wings circled the building, re-formed, and headed back down Severn Avenue.

"Report, Brother Jacob," Agrippa ordered.

"Aye, Brother Agrippa," Jacob replied. "We had no notice. Michael ran out of the house, ordered us to follow, and came straight here."

"His route was direct?"

"Aye, Brother. He took Interstate 10."

Agrippa cringed. "Were you followed?"

Jacob looked at Carson, the best tracker on Michael's protection detail, for an answer. Carson nodded.

"Aye, Brother," Jacob replied. "We left a rear guard at the Causeway exit, but only enough to slow the pursuit."

"How long do we have, Brother Carson?"

"It won't take their scouts long to find us."

"How long?"

"We leave now or we circle the wagons."

*   *   *

As instructed, NOPD crime-scene tech George Delery waited patiently in the backseat of the strategically-parked Ford Police Interceptor SUV and captured Ed Broussard's every move with his video recorder.

Through the tinted rear passenger window, Delery saw Ed Broussard step aside and allow Detective Cavet to enter his home, along with two NOPD crime-scene techs, who intentionally left Broussard alone on the porch.

Here we go, thought Delery. *Time to find out what Daddy knows.*

But, to Delery's chagrin, Ed Broussard didn't do anything suspicious. He didn't remove anything from his jacket and throw it in the neighbor's yard. He didn't pace nervously on the front porch. And he didn't glance, not once, to see if anyone was searching under the house or the alley by Michael's bedroom.

He just sat down, made a phone call, and read his paper.

How about that? Delery mused. *Cavet was wrong. Daddy doesn't know crap about his son.*

*   *   *

Brad Shipley was confused, but the guacamole was good.

Really good.

"What am I doing here, Emma?" Michael asked while Brad speared another chip into the tasty green stuff.

This guacamole is chunky, thought Brad. *I like chunky guacamole. And the chips are warm.*

"You're in trouble, Michael," Brad heard Emma say. "The police think you murdered the priest in the parking lot."

What is Emma talking about? Brad wondered.

"Trust me. The police are the least of my concerns."

"I believe you, Michael," Emma assured him. "Trey and I interviewed the neighbors. There were five men in the Goat when it left the parking lot, and you were not driving."

Did she say "goat"? Brad wondered, looking at Sheri to see if she was similarly confused. *You can't drive a goat.*

"Don't say another word, Emma," Michael pleaded. "Not another word."

I mean… I guess you can ride a goat and steer with the horns, but no goat is large enough for five men to ride. And she said "in the goat," not "on the goat." So even if it was a really big goat….

Silence eventually caused Brad to pause mid-chip and look up.

Michael and Emma were engaged in a staring contest, and Sheri looked completely amused by the whole scene.

"Tell the police who they are!" Emma told Michael, breaking the silence. "The men you thought were following me."

"I can't do that, Emma."

"You didn't kill that priest, and you're worried about everyone but yourself," Emma insisted. "I know you!"

"You don't know me," Michael promised her with an unmistakable edge to his voice. "You don't know anything about me."

"Whatever, Michael. I've got Derrick and Trey outside with cameras. They're going to photograph and get the license plate of every car that enters the parking lot while you're here. If you don't tell us who was in the car with you, we're taking the photographs and the license plates to Detective Cavet."

Who's Detective Cavet? Brad wondered, almost forgetting to dip the next chip before eating it. Well, almost.

"This was a trap?" Michael said, sounding angry again. "You used me as bait?"

"I did."

"This is not a game, Emma!" Michael growled. "What about Brad and Sheri? Do you have any idea how much danger you've put them in?"

Danger?

"I'm not an idiot," Emma replied indignantly. "Brad drove me and Sheri here, and I used the restaurant phone to call your house. As long as we pay with cash and leave separately, there's no trail for them to follow."

"Who's them?" Brad finally asked.

"Good question," Emma replied, smiling at her date. "*They* are the guys who killed a priest outside Rock 'n' Bowl, and Michael won't tell anyone who *they* are."

Michael dropped his head into his hands and groaned.

"Uh, I was going to pay with a card . . . ." Brad announced nervously.

"That's okay, Brad. I have plenty of cash," Emma assured him, while pushing the basket of chips closer.

"Enough, Emma," the previously quiet Sheri suddenly declared. "This cloak-and-dagger routine is starting to bore me. Nothing you say is going to convince me Michael is dangerous and mysterious. No offense, Michael."

"None taken," Michael assured her, his head still buried in his hands.

"Sheri, you adorable little egomaniac," Emma scoffed. "I'm not trying to trick you into dating Michael. I don't want Michael to touch you with a ten-foot pole."

Brad stopped with a loaded chip poised inches from his mouth.

Why not?

* * *

Agrippa made a battlefield decision.

He hurried over to the car where Derrick and Trey were waiting with cameras, willed himself visible to mortals, and instantly felt the chill in the air.

Agrippa rapped on the window and waited while his surprised *protelos* lowered it.

"Your friend is in danger," Agrippa told Derrick. "The men you are waiting to photograph are coming and they are going to kill him."

Derrick stared at Agrippa.

"I know you, don't I?"

"Yes, you do," Agrippa said, unable to suppress a smile. "Now go inside. Tell Michael his friends need him to leave this place right now."

Something in his tone or in his eyes convinced Derrick the danger was real.

"How do we know you are—" Trey started to object.

"Derrick, there is no time," Agrippa interrupted.

"Yes, sir," Derrick replied, tossing his camera to Trey and bolting from the car.

"And Derrick," Agrippa added. "Nobody leaves the restaurant except for you and Michael."

Derrick nodded and took off running toward the restaurant, while Agrippa suppressed a grin.

That's my Derrick.

* * *

Sheri enjoyed a good show.

I expect this from Emma, she thought. *But I'm surprised Michael's playing along.*

The sound of a water buffalo charging into Taqueria Corona turned the head of everyone at the table as Michael's gorgeous friend barreled into the room.

"Michael!" Derrick called from across the room. "Your, uh, *friends* say you have to leave *right now*."

Michael was already on his feet. He turned and looked at Brad.

"Sorry about the fight," Michael said. "Please get Emma and Sheri home safely."

"Uh, yeah, okay, me too," a bewildered Brad stammered.

Michael nodded and turned to Emma.

"I was wrong to try and scare you off," Michael told her. "I won't do that again, but I need you to stay away while I take care of this. When things calm down, I will find you. Nothing will stop me from finding you, Em."

Sheri watched as Michael and Derrick rushed off together, and something told her the danger was real, but she was so afraid of being a mark that she could not hold her tongue.

"Not working!" Sheri called out. "Not turning me on!"

Michael ran out of the restaurant as Emma muttered her reply.

"Speak for yourself."

* * *

"Report, Guardian."

"My *protelos* is Tommy Cavet. Born in New Orleans. Raised by Arthur and Leslie Cavet. Homicide detective for the New Orleans Police Department."

"Has he been investigating the stabbing of a priest?" Raphael asked.

"Aye, Brother," the Guardian said. "Earlier today, Tommy executed a search warrant at Ed Broussard house and arrested Michael Broussard."

'What did the police find at the Broussard house?" Saraquel inquired.

"Nothing inside the house," the Guardian reported. "But Tommy ordered the crime-scene technicians to search under the house, and they found a bloody sword under the son's bedroom. Open and shut case."

Saraquel and Raphael exchanged concerned looks.

"That's where I come in," Agrippa interjected. "I left Derrick at the Mexican restaurant and high-tailed Michael home with the Fallen on our heels. As soon as we pulled up to the Broussard house, the detective arrested Michael. On the spot. In front of his father."

"Aye, Brother," the Guardian said, a little confused by Agrippa's tone. "Tommy was just doing his job."

"Of course he was," Saraquel assured the Guardian diplomatically. "But Michael did not kill the priest. Rachel of Judah and Michael's Guardian both witnessed the murder in the parking lot that night."

"Then who—"

"Marcellus and Dante," Raphael replied. "And the Seven could use your help changing Tommy's ... I mean ... Detective Cavet's mind."

"Aye, Brother. I'll do whatever I can," the Guardian promised. "But the case is out of Tommy's hands. The District Attorney will charge Broussard with second-degree murder."

The reality of Michael's facing criminal prosecution silenced the room.

"This is Lucifer's doing," Raguel decided. "Michael cannot command an army or fulfill the prophecy from a prison cell. The Fallen must have planted the murder weapon under his room."

"That would explain why the Fallen didn't catch us or ambush us on the way home," Agrippa added. "They weren't chasing us. They were driving us. Right to Detective Tommy."

"Where is the boy now?" Raphael asked.

"Central Lockup," the Guardian replied. "He'll stay there until his hearing."

"And how bad is Orleans Parish Prison?" Saraquel asked, genuinely concerned.

"The boy won't survive a week," the Guardian reported gravely. "He might not survive a day."

"Brother, you can stop worrying about Michael," Agrippa assured the Guardian as he walked out of the Great Chamber.

Save your prayers for the other inmates.

*　　*　　*

Chapter 14: Incarceration

My God hath sent his angel, and hath shut the lions' mouths,
That they have not hurt me: forasmuch as before him innocency
was found in me...
Daniel 6:22

Monday, November 18

Shackles bind more than they touch.

Michael shuffled into the courtroom with the other prisoners. The room was filled with reporters, but Michael saw a number of friendly faces.

Father Finnegan, Coach Will, Derrick, Trey, and Emma were sitting together in the third row. All of them smiled or waved as he entered, but he could see the concern in their eyes.

And that his dad was not in the room.

"All rise!" the bailiff declared as a black-robed figure entered the courtroom.

"All relax!" the disarming judge responded as he took the bench.

The judge had a mixture of red and gray hair and his face was strangely familiar. He looked like a tough but fair man.

"Next case," the judge said.

"Michael Broussard," the clerk announced.

"Good morning, Your Honor," the prosecutor said. "Joy Glapion for the State of Louisiana. The State is ready to proceed."

"Good morning, Ms. Glapion."

The judge respects her but doesn't like her, Michael's instincts told him.

"Good morning, Your Honor. Lamar Hill appearing for Michael Broussard. The Defense is ready to proceed."

"Good morning, sir," the judge replied more formally.

Interesting. He likes Mr. Hill but doesn't want to show it.

"Your Honor, may my client please join me at the defense table."

"Of course."

The bailiff gestured to Michael to stand up and follow him to defense counsel's table. When they got there, Mr. Hill patted him on the back and pulled out his chair. From his new position, Michael could now read the judge's name plate.

Unbelievable, thought Michael. *No wonder the judge looks familiar.*

"Michael, this is a probable cause hearing," Lamar explained. "The judge wants to make sure there was probable cause for your arrest before he sets your bond. Do you understand?"

"Yes, sir."

"Good. And from now on, please call me 'Lamar.' I fight harder for my friends, understand?"

"Yes, sir."

The clerk handed the judge a light green folder, and everyone waited while the judge read something inside.

"Ms. Glapion, call your first witness."

"State calls Detective Thomas Cavet."

Michael watched Detective Cavet take the witness stand, face the clerk, and raise his right hand.

"Do you swear to tell the truth, the whole truth and nothing but the truth, so help you God?"

"I do."

Michael listened as Joy Glapion examined Detective Cavet, methodically extracting the facts and the evidence in a way that told a story. The climax of that story was the discovery of the sword under Michael's bedroom.

She's really good.

Glapion picked up a plastic-wrapped sword from the State's table and paused while she read the attached evidence tag.

She's pretending to read the tag, thought Michael as he watched her eyes dart up and down instead of left to right. *She's trying to build suspense.*

"May I approach, Your Honor?"

"Ms. Glapion, this is a probable cause hearing, not a trial," the judge politely reminded her. "You may approach whenever you want. Just move this along."

"Yes, Your Honor," Glapion replied, unable to disguise her disappointment. Then she walked to the witness stand and showed the sword to Detective Cavet.

"Is this the sword you seized?"

"It is," Cavet replied before looking at the evidence tag. "And I observed what I believed to be dried blood on the blade."

"Did you have the sword tested?"

"I did," Cavet reported. "I asked the Crime Lab to determine whether it was blood and whether it matched the victim's blood. I received their report this morning."

The entire courtroom watched in silence as Glapion placed the sword on the State's table and grabbed the crime lab report. While Glapion walked back toward the witness, Lamar Hill put his arm around Michael.

"The report is hearsay, but hearsay is admissible at a probable cause hearing." Lamar explained to Michael. "I can't object."

Michael nodded.

"Is this a copy of the Crime Lab report?" Glapion asked.

"It is."

"Please tell the court the results of all blood testing performed by the NOPD Crime Lab in this case."

Detective Cavet hesitated.

He doesn't want to answer the question, Michael thought. *Not the way it was asked.*

"Are you asking me to tell the Court about the testing on the sword found under Mr. Broussard's house?"

Michael caught the momentary look of surprise on the prosecutor's face. The question took her off guard.

"Please, Detective."

She's trying to sound nonchalant. Trying a little too hard.

Cavet nodded.

"Testing of the sword found under Mr. Broussard's house revealed the substance on the sword was blood, and DNA testing confirmed that blood matched the priest's blood. I mean ... the victim's blood."

Glapion picked up the sword.

"So DNA testing conclusively proved this was the murder weapon?"

"Objection to form," Lamar Hill said.

"Overruled. You may answer, Detective."

"DNA testing conclusively proved the sword had the victim's blood on it."

"Thank you, Detective," Glapion replied quickly, appearing a little vexed by the Detective's refusal to identify the sword as the murder weapon.

"I tender the witness."

The judge looked over at Lamar Hill.

"Do you wish to question the witness, Mr. Hill?"

"Yes, Your Honor," Lamar said, standing to address the court. "Detective, is there any video of the murder?"

"No, sir."

"How many witnesses say they saw Michael stab the victim?'

"None."

"How many witnesses say they saw Michael stashing the sword under his house?"

"None."

"How many witnesses say they have ever seen Michael holding a sword?"

"None."

"Were Michael's fingerprints on the sword?"

"No, sir."

"Were there any fingerprints on the sword?"

"No, sir."

"You always prepare a Gist which summarizes your full report, do you not?"

"Yes, sir."

"Did I read in your Gist that that you got the search warrant based on an anonymous tip?"

"Yes, sir."

"Did the mysterious tipster call the Crime Stoppers hotline?"

"No, sir. The caller called me on my cell phone."

Lamar looked at the judge and then the prosecutor, who started rifling through her file looking for something.

That clearly surprised Lamar, Ms. Glapion, and the judge.

"Did the mysterious tipster tell you how he knew you were in charge of the investigation?"

"No, sir."

"Did the mysterious tipster tell you how he got your cell phone number?"

"No, sir."

"Did the mysterious tipster tell you where to find the sword?"

"Yes, sir."

"Did you find the sword exactly where the mysterious tipster said it would be?"

"Yes, sir."

"Did the mysterious tipster tell you why he put the sword there to frame Michael?"

"Objection!" Joy Glapion declared, jumping to her feet and almost falling in the process. "Assumes facts not in evidence."

"Overruled," the judge said, suppressing a smile.

Lamar nodded, obviously pleased with himself and with the judge's reaction, before repeating the question.

"Did the mysterious tipster tell you why he put the sword there to frame Michael?"

"At no time did the caller state or suggest that he killed the priest or planted any evidence to incriminate Michael Broussard."

He!

Lamar caught it as well.

"And what is *his* name?"

"Objection!"

"Sustained."

"Isn't it possible the mysterious tipster knew where the sword was placed because he placed the sword there?

"Objection. Calls for speculation."

"Overruled. Answer the question, Detective."

"Yes, sir. That's possible."

"Isn't it also possible the mysterious tipster knew where the sword was placed because the mysterious tipster is the real murderer?"

"Objection. Calls for speculation."

"Overruled."

"Anything is possible, Mr. Hill."

"No further questions."

"Re-direct, Ms. Glapion?"

"Yes, Your Honor," Glapion replied, trying not to sound flustered.

"Did the coroner determine what time the victim was murdered in the Rock 'n' Bowl parking lot?"

"Yes, ma'am. Between midnight and 1:00 a.m."

"What time did the defendant close Rock 'n' Bowl and leave the parking lot?"

"Michael told me he left between midnight and 1:00 a.m."

Which proves I was at the scene of the crime.

"Did a witness actually see the defendant's car peeling out of the Rock 'n' Bowl parking lot?"

"Yes, ma'am."

Which proves I left in a hurry.

"When you interviewed the defendant, did you ask him if he peeled out of the Rock 'n' Bowl parking lot?"

"Yes, ma'am. He denied it."

Which proves I'm a liar.

"Was the defendant's car damaged?"

"Yes, ma'am."

"I know there was a great deal of damage to the defendant's car, but was some of it consistent with sword marks?"

"Yes, ma'am."

Good grief.

"Did the defendant mention the damage to his vehicle during your first interview?"

"No, ma'am."

"What did the defendant's father do when you arrived at the garage and asked to see the car?"

"Objection. Relevance."

"Overruled."

"He padlocked the door and told me to get a warrant."

And that should do it.

"No further questions," Glapion announced. "State submits."

The judge ruled immediately from the bench.

"I find probable cause for the charge of second-degree murder. Bail is set in the amount of—"

"Wait! Your Honor, may I approach?"

Michael turned and saw two surprised bailiffs moving to intercept a distraught-looking redhead.

Oh Dear God!

*　　*　　*

Judge Ronald Landry did not like surprises, but he loved grandchildren, and Emma was his favorite. The little rascal reminded him of his beloved wife, Rose, who had the same wonderful spirit.

God rest her beautiful soul.

"Emma? I didn't see you out there," Judge Landry announced with a big smile and a voice filled with pride. "Whatcha doin' here, pumpkin?"

"I'm here to stop a grave injustice."

Uh-oh, thought Judge Landry. *Emma's got a bee in her bonnet.*

"Your Honor, the State objects to this—"

Judge Landry flashed the prosecutor the "stop" sign with his right hand, and Emma the "stop" sign with his left.

"Hold it right there, Emma," he said firmly. "What's going on?"

"Michael Broussard is my..." Emma started to say before faltering.

"He's your what?" Judge Landry demanded.

"Side-bar?" Emma croaked, and the courtroom erupted in laughter.

Judge Landry rapped his gavel on the sound block until everyone was silent.

"Do you see that gate you opened, and the railing you just passed?" Judge Landry asked, deciding this was a teachable moment.

"Yes, sir," Emma said.

"Well, that railing is the bar, Emma," he continued. "And you're supposed to pass the bar exam before you pass that bar. Now, have you passed the bar exam?"

"No, sir."

"I didn't think so. My son would've mentioned it, and your mother would've thrown a party. Now, where did you learn to ask for a side-bar?"

"I saw it on television, Paw-Paw."

"Of course you did!" Judge Landry frowned, and Ms. Glapion and Mr. Hill took their seats. They knew what lecture was coming and were getting comfortable.

"Emma, there's no such thing as a side-bar. I don't know who started it, but they should be punished. You're already on my side of the bar, young lady. What you wanted to do was approach the side of my bench, which is a perfectly reasonable request for a lawyer. Unfortunately, asking for a 'side-bench' doesn't sound nearly as cool. So here we are, stuck with this idiotic custom when lawyers should be requesting a bench conference."

"Your Honor, I request a bench conference," Emma said, not missing a beat.

"Denied."

"Check Michael's right hand!" Emma begged Detective Cavet. "Check for callouses on his dominant hand!"

The courtroom full of reporters started mumbling and scribbling. Judge Landry glanced at Detective Cavet for an explanation, but the detective was frantically flipping through his little notebook searching for a specific entry:

"Check suspects for callouses on dominant hand."

"Oh Emma, you didn't!" Cavet gasped when he read the entry and deduced the real reason why Emma surprised his girls with cookies and a quick visit last night. "How could you read my—"

The crack of a prized gavel splitting a wooden base startled Cavet and alerted the local media that they just missed something important.

"Bail is set at five hundred thousand dollars," Judge Landry declared. "Remand the prisoner. The Court stands in recess."

He turned to Emma.

"I'll see you in my chambers, young lady!"

* * *

When it rains, it pours.

Michael was under arrest for second-degree murder. His bail was set at a half million dollars. Detective Cavet and Emma's grandfather were both convinced he killed a priest, thanks in part to callouses collected during four years of weight lifting and unnecessary lane dusting. He was being hunted by the Devil. His father was missing in action. And his handcuffs were too tight.

Hard to say what bothered him the most.

Michael followed Deputy Kinler's instructions and continued down the hallway. He did not know where they were going, nor did he care, as long as Kinler removed the handcuffs when they got there.

"Prisoner, enter your cell," Kinler instructed. "Prisoner, stop."

Michael heard the cell door roll and lock behind him.

"Prisoner, turn around. Place your hands through the cuff hole."

Kinler unlocked the handcuffs, looked over Michael's shoulders, and paused.

"Good luck," Kinler whispered before walking away.

Michael spun around and saw his cellmate getting up from the bottom bunk. The man had at least a hundred pounds on Michael. His right arm was a tattooed sleeve, and prison tats covered his neck. Something in the man's eyes and the way he stood up told Michael the man had already made up his mind.

"This is going to be hard on you," the man said.

Michael raised his fists and heard the sound of his father's voice very clearly in his head:

Defend yourself!

* * *

Detective Cavet was not in a hurry.

He waited patiently in the back of the hospital elevator. When the last person got off, he finally stepped out. He knew Baptist Hospital (or whatever they called it this year) like the back of his hand, but he decided to stop and ask for directions anyway. He needed a little more time to prepare himself.

"I'm looking for Broussard."

The nurse looked it up on her computer.

"He's in ICU," the nurse advised. "Down the hall. Take a right. Last room on your left."

"Thank you, ma'am."

Cavet walked down the hallway deep in thought. He blamed himself for what had happened. After all, it was his investigation that started the chain of events that ended with Broussard lying comatose in a hospital bed.

Cavet stopped outside Broussard's room and braced himself for what was on the other side of the door. He quietly knocked twice and entered the room.

Damn it to hell.

Hurricane Ed Broussard was barely recognizable. The unconscious man's face was a bloody mess, and Cavet's stomach churned with guilt. A woman's jacket on the back of a chair suggested someone was already visiting.

Cavet decided to say what he needed to say before she returned.

"I'm sorry, Ed," Cavet said. "I'm going to find the men who did this, and I'm going to do what I can for Michael. You have my word."

The opening of the door behind him caused Cavet to turn around.

Carol Landry walked into the room and did not flinch when she saw Detective Cavet. Like her unsinkable daughter, Carol did not startle easily.

"Get out!" Carol told him.

Or mince her words.

"Carol, I just came to—"

"I said *get out,* Detective Cavet!" she repeated. "Haven't you done enough?"

"Now hold on—"

"I've known Michael since he was born. There's no way he killed anybody. A boy like Michael doesn't close up a bowling alley and magically turn into a killer by the time he reaches the parking lot. Something I suspect you already know."

"I suspect—"

"I don't care what you suspect! Michael wasn't even supposed to close up that night, or have you conveniently forgotten what Emma said?"

"I haven't—"

"I'm not done!" Carol snapped, taking a step closer. "I don't care if you never speak to me again, neighbor. I'm going to tell you what I think."

So much like Emma.

"This is all your fault," she declared, starting to tear up. "When you arrested Michael, you were beating the grass to startle the snake. Well, take a good look. You startled the snake, and Ed paid the price!"

She's right. This was a message to Michael. You talk to the police and the people you love die.

"Ed and Michael didn't deserve this," she continued. "Not after everything they've been through. They are good and kind. And, instead of helping them, you're going to get them both killed."

Cavet watched Carol return to her chair and gently pat Ed's hand.

"It's okay," she told her unconscious friend. "The idiot is leaving."

* * *

Jimmy Foster was impressed.

It was difficult to see out of his swollen eye, but he watched patiently as his bloody cellmate struggled to pull himself off the floor. When he got to one knee, Foster kicked him in the stomach as hard as he could. The gut-shot dropped the kid, who started coughing up blood.

"Get up!" Foster told him, but the boy was too busy fighting for air.

While he waited for the kid to recover, Foster reached up with his hands and assessed the damage to his own face. His nose was definitely broken. His left cheek was split, and his face was covered in blood. When he turned to reach for a shirt, he felt a searing pain in his midsection and knew from experience he probably had broken a rib. No doubt about it. The kid had held his own against him.

For a lot longer than anybody his size had any right, thought Foster.

Foster had been fighting in prison or on the street for longer than he could remember, and nobody had fought him harder than the bloody lump in front of him. If Foster had fought fair, or if the cell were any larger, he might have lost.

Makes no sense.

Foster had been warned not to underestimate the kid, but he had ignored that warning. Something he would not do again.

"Get up!" Foster repeated. "We've got to get you ready for the yard, and we don't have much time."

The kid rolled over and looked up at him, obviously confused.

"I promised our, uh, mutual friend, I'd take care of you," Foster explained gruffly but low enough that the next cell could not hear. "The beating was necessary."

The kid tried to pull himself up but lacked the strength.

"Your face will send a message," Foster continued. "It may buy us enough time for me to teach you what you need to know."

"To what?" the kid's swollen mouth mumbled before he doubled over in pain and spat up some more blood.

Foster recognized the need to punish the kid for speaking, but decided to answer the question first.

"To survive."

* * *

Guardians do not speak of prison.

The thought terrifies them. Thousands of Guardians standing in a prison yard, waiting for their next chance to be close to their *protelos*. Thousands of prisoners sitting in their cells waiting for their next hour in the yard, mistakenly believing it is sunlight and fresh air that they crave.

The separation is manageable at first, but eventually it severs the bond between a Guardian and a *protelos*, destroying even the prisoner's ability to hear the Guardian's voice. Deaf to the Guardian's love and encouragement, the prisoner loses hope and the Guardian goes mad.

Jacob was standing in the back of the prison yard. It was heartbreaking to observe the various stages of despair among the assembled Host. Some Guardians walked and talked with their *protelos*, even though the prisoner was already deaf to them. Other so-called "Lost Guardians" watched their *protelos* from a distance, resigned to their fate and remembering better times. And some Guardians, whose *protelos* would soon be lost, talked frantically and searched desperately for any sign of being heard. For them, each word could be the last their *protelos* heard.

The thought of losing Michael was enough to panic Jacob, and he unconsciously took a half-step closer to the door through which prisoners entered the yard.

"New to the yard?" asked a spent but sincere Guardian to Jacob's right.

"Aye, Brother."

"Any questions?"

"Why can't we enter the prison building?" Jacob asked without hesitation, eager to rejoin Michael.

"No prisoner ever really calls prison 'home,'" the morose Guardian explained. "No matter what their sentence. They always think of some place they lived, or could have lived, as home."

Jacob shuddered at the thought.

"Want some advice?" the Guardian offered.

"Please, Brother."

"Prepare yourself for the first melee in the yard," the Guardian warned. "Remember your training. Do not intervene."

"Aye, Brother. I understand."

The Guardian turned and faced Jacob.

"I don't think you do," the Guardian said, and his tortured eyes suggested he spoke from experience. "There are Guardians here who have watched their *protelos* stabbed or worse in this yard, and they did not break the Fifth Great Rule. If you intervene, the Lost Guardians will make an example of you both. They will dispatch you, and torture Michael as a warning to others."

"They would destroy me?"

"Aye, Brother," the Guardian sighed. "We would."

* * *

Pain brings perspective.

Michael was still hurting so badly from Foster's beating that he did not mind being handcuffed. And when Deputy Kinler unlocked the door to the attorney conference room and sat him down at the table,

Michael was not the least bit worried about whatever bad legal news Lamar Hill was probably bringing him.

He was just happy to be safe for a few minutes.

A few moments later, the door swung open and Father Finnegan walked into the room.

"Hello, Michael."

"Hello, Father."

"Merciful Lord, what happened to your face?"

"Where's my dad?"

Finn took a deep breath.

"He's in the hospital, Michael. They found him half-dead in your front yard. He must have been jumped while leaving for your hearing."

"Is he going to be alright?"

"We don't know," Finn replied truthfully. "He hasn't regained consciousness. I talked to the neurologist, and they won't know anything until the brain swelling goes down. He took some bad blows to the head."

"It's my fault."

"That's not true, Michael," Finn said, lowering his voice. "We both know the Fallen did this."

Michael stared at Father Finnegan like he never met the man.

"How do you--"

"Brother Reid introduced me to your, uh, friends."

"Does anybody else know?"

"Just Coach Will," Finn said. "Now listen, we don't have much time, and I need to tell you something. You're not getting out of here. Nobody is going to post your bail. Brother Reid's orders."

"Brother Reid's orders?" Michael repeated incredulously. "Did Brother Reid happen to say why I need to stay in this godforsaken place?"

Finn nodded.

"He said it was necessary."

"Did he say anything else?"

"He said it was Jacob's call."

"I seriously doubt that."

"It's true," Finn assured him. "I insisted on hearing it from Jacob myself. Jacob says you should trust him, and he handed me this to give you."

Finn handed Michael the familiar drawing of a cup. Michael looked at it and took a deep breath.

"Then I stay."

"Listen to me, Michael," Finn said very seriously. "You do whatever you have to do to survive in here. Whatever it takes. Do you understand me?"

Michael nodded.

"Please tell my dad that I…" Michael started to say, struggling to control his emotions. "Tell him I..."

"He knows, Michael, but I'll tell him," Finn promised. "Now look, Jacob also told me to bring someone with me. I pulled some strings, but you won't have long."

Finn gave Michael a hug and quickly walked to the door.

"I'll try to get in to see you again tomorrow."

"Thank you, Father."

As soon as Finn knocked, Deputy Kinler opened the door and let Finn out.

"Five minutes," Kinler announced before stepping aside to allow Michael's other visitor to enter. This time, Kinler did not close the door, and Emma Landry walked into the room.

Dressed like a nun.

* * *

"Emma, have you lost your mind?"

"It's Sister Landry, and… oh no!" Emma screeched before cupping her mouth. "What happened to your face, Michael?"

"I'm fine," Michael said, shaking his head at the absurdity of the situation.

"You are not fine!" Emma cried. "You have a split lip, a black eye, and a golf ball sticking out your cheek. It's absolutely—"

"What are you doing here, Emma?"

"Sister Landry," she corrected him while sitting down. "And we don't have much time. I just wanted you to know that I have the con."

"You have the what?"

"I'm taking control of the investigation. Mr. Hill may be an excellent trial lawyer, but he's not much of a detective."

"Please tell me you're joking."

"Don't worry. I've got everyone working, and I'll find the killer, my child."

"'My child'?" Michael repeated. "Look, this is *not* a rom-com. This is my life—"

"I know that!" she snapped. "Don't you think I know that? I can't think about anything else!"

"Okay, take it easy."

"I can't sleep knowing you're in here!" she continued. "I can't breathe when I think of your being convicted for something you didn't do."

"It's okay, Em—"

"And it's not just your life, Michael Jeremy Broussard. It's our life!"

Emma's declaration hung in the air while Michael struggled with his response.

"Maybe it could have been," Michael told her with regret. "But we can't—"

"Why?" Emma demanded, reaching across the table and grabbing Michael's cuffed hands. "Because you're in jail?"

"Uh… no, that's not—"

"Then why?"

"Because…" Michael chuckled deliriously. "I'm married."

"Because you're afraid." Emma insisted, ignoring his silliness. "You're afraid I'll get hurt or—"

"Die," Michael stated emphatically. "Everyone I love dies, and they all die horrible deaths."

Emma stared at Michael in silence.

"Where did you get those clothes?" an exhausted Michael eventually asked, trying to change the subject.

"It's Sister Landry… and my aunt is a Carmelite nun," she replied, getting back into character and remembering her mission. "Now, what haven't you told Mr. Hill?"

"Plenty."

"Good. Tell me everything."

"No."

The door to the attorney room opened, and Deputy Kinler entered.

"I'm sorry, Sister, but that's all the time I can give y'all. I need to take the prisoner back to his cell."

"Of course, I understand."

Emma stood up and pushed her chair back. She winked at Michael, turned around, and headed out.

"Wait."

"Yes, Michael?"

"Please visit me again… Sister."

Emma smiled.

"As you wish, my child."

* * *

Chapter 15: Sacrifice

And the angel of the LORD called unto him out of heaven,
and said, Abraham, Abraham…
Genesis 22:11

He was going to be a legend.

Brother Kirkegaard was certain his name would become synonymous with sacrifice among members of the Order, and his life an anecdote taught to every new class of catechumen. The perfect lesson in patience and faith.

Brother Kirkegaard leaned back and tried to relax. It had been many years since he flew on an airplane.

Remember Brother Kirkegaard, he imagined Stewards saying for centuries to come. *He was ninety years old when he was given his last mission. Too old to fight. Too weak to walk. But with one selfless act, he freed an awakened eighteen-year-old boy.*

Kirkegaard smiled.

And not just any eighteen-year-old boy.

"Michael," he unintentionally said aloud, and immediately paid the price.

Kirkegaard wheezed and coughed violently into his handkerchief. When he looked down at the white silk, the size of the blood stain had doubled.

"Aye… Michael," Brother Liam MacLaren said from the seat to his right. "We're gonna help Michael. Now rest easy, Brother. It's a long flight, an' you'll need yer strength when we land."

Kierkegaard smiled as he watched the High Steward of the Order gently re-insert his nasal cannula and increase the flow of oxygen. As the concentrated air rushed into his fragile lungs, he felt the prick of a needle in his right arm, followed by the warm sensation of hydromorphone.

The potent opioid immediately eased his pain, and he drifted into a deep sleep. His last lucid thought on the plane was a simple three-word prayer:

Let me wake.

* * *

It was a good day to die.

Inmates Broussard and Foster entered the yard side by side. The air was clear and crisp, and Michael felt better as soon as he felt the sun on his face.

Everything is going to be alright, Michael thought. *I'm strong. I have faith.*

Michael smiled as he realized, almost immediately, that his thoughts belonged to Jacob. His Guardian was close and already encouraging him.

"Hello, Jacob," Michael said under his breath. "Good to hear you, buddy."

Good to be heard, Michael thought as Jacob replied.

Michael and Jimmy walked toward the south wall. They stopped when they were close enough to use the wall to protect their rear, but far enough away to give themselves space to fight. Both stood on a diagonal from the wall. Jimmy faced northwest and Michael faced northeast. Each was responsible for a different field of vision.

"Anything?" Jimmy asked a few minutes later.

"No," Michael replied. "Why?"

"Something's going down," Jimmy said. "Too many eyes lookin' this way but not at us. Anything moving behind me?"

"Two inmates coming toward us, talking to each other."

"Do they have a shadow?"

Michael shuffled his feet like Jimmy taught him and glanced down at his shoes before looking up again.

"Yes," Michael reported. "Straight right arm."

"How long do they have?"

"Not long. What do we..."

"Too late to move," Jimmy ordered. "Give me a count."

"Ten."

Michael saw a shank drop from Shadow's right sleeve.

"Five."

One of the targets made eye contact with Michael, who now felt an irresistible impulse to do *something*.

"Watch out!" Michael yelled as he blind-sided Shadow with the second hardest hit of his defunct football career. The blow knocked Shadow off his feet and sent him sprawling on the concrete.

The entire yard reacted. Large groups of inmates mobilized. Some took defensive positions around gang leaders. Others distanced themselves from the fight.

Six headed straight at Michael, and the first two had shanks.

Michael remembered his training. He dropped to a knee, grabbed a handful of dirt with his left hand, and threw it at First Shank's eyes. Then he hit First Shank with a devastating right uppercut. At the exact same time, Foster charged Second Shank and the Recently-Saved attacked two of the other four hostiles.

As soon as First Shank hit the ground, Michael spun around to deal with the unaccounted pair of attackers. The first did him a favor by swinging wildly at his head instead of tackling him. Michael ducked beneath the blow, punched the passing attacker in the kidney, and hit the next attacker with a sharp jab.

Yard sirens sounded as the fight intensified, and reinforcements arrived for both sides. Michael was quickly covered in sweat and blood.

Which is when *something* snapped inside him.

Michael started fighting like a man possessed. He took on all comers, and he wasn't just fending them off. He was punishing them, really punishing them.

And enjoying it.

It was a partially blocked punch to his head that finally knocked Michael to the ground. Michael rolled like Foster taught him and saw Shadow emerging from the fray with a bloody shank.

Michael scrambled to get up, but Shadow kicked Michael in the stomach. The blow knocked Michael on his back again.

Shadow did not hesitate. He jumped on Michael even as Michael yelled:

"Jacob!"

* * *

Jacob was wearing an orange jumpsuit and closing fast.

Michael blocked the first stab by Shadow and glanced over in time to see Jacob leave his feet.

But Jacob did not dislodge Shadow.

Michael watched helplessly as Jacob sailed over them and crashed into Rachel of Judah—a split second before her jumpsuit-clad body would have dislodged Shadow and saved Michael. The collision knocked both *malachim* to the ground. They landed and instantly disappeared from mortal sight.

Jacob's betrayal paralyzed Michael as Shadow raised the shank and stabbed down as hard as he could.

But the shank never touched Michael.

Out of nowhere, Jimmy Foster slammed into the side of Shadow. They rolled twice and Foster ended up on top.

Michael jumped to his feet, barely in time to fend off the next attacker. When he looked back, Shadow was gone and Foster was lying motionless on his back with a shank buried deep in his chest.

"Behind you!" shouted another inmate.

Michael whipped around as Shadow charged, stepped to his right, and landed a crushing right cross that knocked Shadow off his feet.

The inmate who shouted the warning was the inmate whose life Michael had saved at the start of the melee. That inmate jumped on Shadow and stabbed him to death without hesitation.

Guards finally entered the yard and ended the fight. When they reached Michael, he was holding Jimmy's head in his lap.

"You saved my life," Michael said. "I can't believe you did that for me."

"For you?" Jimmy guffawed before speaking his last:

"Fool."

* * *

If Joy Glapion had claws, she would have been stuck to the ceiling like a cartoon cat. Instead, her obnoxious phone was still ringing, and she was still searching her nightstand for the offensive noise.

Too early for anyone to be calling.

"Hello. What? What!" Joy Glapion demanded.

"It's Cavet. I'm sorry to wake you."

"It's four o'clock."

"I know, but this can't wait," Cavet assured her. "I'm at a crime scene in Baton Rouge, and I'm looking down at another dead priest."

Joy sat up in bed and turned on the lamp.

"Cause of death?" she asked.

"Probably the sword through his heart."

Joy gasped.

A serial priest killer? she thought. *That kind of prosecution will make national news. The world is finally going to meet "short and sweet." And they are going to love her!*

"Hello, Joy?"

"Yes, I'm here," she assured Cavet quickly.

"Would you like to know if I checked the priest's right wrist?"

Joy already knew the answer. Cavet would not have called unless the brand was there. Still, she *wanted* to hear him say it out loud.

"Don't tease me."

"Joy, it's the same symbol."

"Yes!" Joy declared, raising her fist in celebration.

A calling-card conviction like this will open doors for me, she realized. *I could run for judge or District Attorney or Attorney General. No more fighting crime one defendant at a time. I could change the entire criminal justice system. Really change the system.*

The thought was intoxicating.

"We've got ourselves a serial killer!"

"We sure do," Cavet said. "And that's not the best part."

What could be better than a serial priest-killer?

"The priest is ancient," Cavet reported.

"Too old to duel?" Joy asked excitedly.

"Too old to eat. He's got to be north of ninety."

Joy practically squealed.

There goes self-defense, she told herself, letting it play out in her mind. *And if it wasn't self-defense in Baton Rouge, it wasn't self-defense in New Orleans.*

"Send a patrolman to pick up Doctor Villere," Joy told Cavet emphatically. "Tell the patrolman to bring a bucket of coffee!"

"Relax," Cavet said, his tone almost fatherly. "My nephew works in the First District. I called him about an hour ago. He and the mad scientist are on the way. They should be outside Prairieville by now."

"Good. Villere needs to perform the autopsy, or at least attend the autopsy. That's important, Tom. He has to personally compare the two wounds for the jury."

"The jury?" Cavet repeated. "Aren't you forgetting something?"

"What?"

"I still have to catch the killer."

"Well, get back to work!" she told him playfully and ended the call.

Joy got out of bed and hurried toward the shower. She was already thinking about her next two phone calls. The first would hopefully get her boyfriend back and the second would definitely result in the release of a wrongfully-accused eighteen-year-old boy—a boy who could not have been in Baton Rouge that night.

And maybe that would be her first call.

* * *

Officer Matt Frosch was westbound and down.

Uncle Tommy told him to drive the Orleans Parish coroner to Baton Rouge as fast as possible. His orders were clear.

Lights on. Siren off. Mouth shut. Just drive.

Matt tried to follow Uncle Tommy's orders to the letter, but Doctor Villere was in a particularly good mood. The mad scientist spent the entire drive talking.

Crazy old coot.

Matt now knew everything about the homicide investigation and the possibility of a serial priest killer. Thanks to a monologue the coroner delivered between the Gramercy exit and the Sorrento exit, he also knew way more about existentialism, which Villere did not consider a humanism.

Whatever the hell that meant.

Matt tucked in his shirt as he escorted Villere past the police tape and across the large parking lot.

"Hello, Doc!" Cavet replied, taking out his notebook and flipping it open, exactly the way other detectives did when impersonating him.

So ridiculous, thought Matt. *The guy's a dinosaur.*

"Tom, what are you doing here?" Villere asked, feigning surprise. "Look, we have to stop meeting like this. People will start to talk, *right, right, okay?"*

Matt chuckled. The guy cracked him up.

"Officer Frosch," his uncle said. "Thank you for getting Doctor Villere here safely and quickly. Now please roll down your sleeves. We don't need to see, uh, Thunder and Lightning."

"No problem," Matt said, surprised and pleased his uncle remembered the correct names for his biceps.

"Thunder and Lightning?" Villere asked, happily taking the bait.

"Yeah. You'll feel the Thunder," Matt explained, shadow jabbing with his left fist before pretending to land a big right cross. "But you'll never see the Lightning!"

Villere waited for him to stop shadow-boxing and looked at Cavet.

"What an interesting lad!" Villere declared. "Tom, double his salary and give him the rest of the week off, *right, right, okay, right?"*

"Whatever you say, Doc," Cavet replied before taking a step closer to the coroner and lowering his voice. "Look, Doctor Shaw has agreed to let you handle the crime scene and perform the autopsy. But he's the coroner for East Baton Rouge Parish, so we can't step on his toes."

"Well, that's awfully nice of Eugene," Villere said, also lowering his voice. "Given the fact he was a gynecologist before he was elected coroner, *right, okay?"*

Matt watched Doctor Villere put on a pair of latex gloves and start examining the body with surprising skill and professionalism. His hands moved quickly and thoroughly over every inch of the victim. Matt had heard about the mad scientist but had never actually seen him in action.

What a freak. Total Jekyll and Hyde.

Villere took out his Dictaphone to record his thoughts and Uncle Tommy simultaneously pulled out his pencil. The tip remained poised inches above the notebook while Villere rewound the tape.

Are these two for real? Matt wondered, shaking his head and listening to the sound of the tape rewinding. *It's like watching a cop show from the 70s.*

"Priest, elderly," Villere said when he finally started recording. "Cause of death. Single stab wound to the front of his chest. Through and through. Manner of death: homicide. No callouses on victim's right hand or on his left hand. Symbol appears burned on the right wrist. Wings and crossed keys. Symbol appears to have been scored a very long time ago."

Villere turned off the Dictaphone.

"You can hire an expert to double-check, but the victim was branded when he was young."

"Got it," Cavet said, writing in his notebook.

Why is that important? Matt wondered.

"Signs of bilateral muscle atrophy in the upper and lower extremities," Villere continued, turning the Dictaphone back on. "Signs of dehydration and recent weight loss. Skin color... appears mottled."

Mottled? That's a funny word.

Villere looked at Cavet. Then he took out a penlight and started examining the inside of the priest's nose.

"The lining of the nose is irritated. Dry and bloody."

Villere stood up. He looked around the parking lot, shook his head and looked right at Matt.

"Officer Frosch, will you excuse us, please?" Villere said very seriously.

"Uncle Tommy and I need to talk."

* * *

Villere needed to nip this in the bud.

"What's on your mind, Doc?" Cavet asked as soon as his nephew was gone.

"The *Pia Mater*, but that's not important right now," Villere said, only half-heartedly delivering his favorite retort. "Listen, this crime scene is so staged it belongs in the Globe Theatre, *okay?*"

"Come again?"

"The victim had end-stage lung cancer," Villere explained. "He's been on oxygen for so long that either the oxygen or the cannula irritated the inside of his nose."

"Okay, he was old and sick," Cavet said. "But what was staged?"

"Everything," Villere insisted. "This victim was driven here and helped out of the car. It probably took whatever strength the man had left to remain standing long enough to be stabbed with a sword."

"Now hold on, Doc," Cavet said, putting his pad back in his pocket. "How can we tell this was suicide?"

"Assisted suicide," Villere corrected him. "And we can tell that because the killer made one crucial mistake. He chose to sacrifice someone he respected."

"How do you—"

"The Devil is in the details," Villere noted. "The victim has only one wound. The killer couldn't bring himself to cut this man before or after the fatal blow. Which makes no sense, *right, okay?* I mean, if staging a homicide is important enough to sacrifice this man's life, do it right."

"Sacrifice this man's life for what, Doc?"

"Not for what. For whom?"

Cavet started to take out his notebook but stopped. He already knew the answer to that particular question, and he was not writing it down.

He had a promise to keep.

* * *

Michael was numb.

He was shackled and waiting to be brought up to the courtroom. Jimmy Foster was dead. Jacob had betrayed him, and his father was dying alone in a hospital bed.

I've got to get out of here. To hell with what Jacob and Brother Reid say.

"Eric LaFell," the prisoner sitting across from him said, introducing himself.

Michael looked up and saw the inmate who Shadow had tried to ambush in the yard. Like Michael, Eric was headed to Judge Landry's court.

"Michael Broussard."

"You saved my life," Eric said with a mixture of gratitude and disbelief. "That hit was ordered by some pretty bad dudes."

Michael nodded but said nothing.

"I owe you."

"Forget about it," Michael shook his head. "You saved me too. We're even."

"Nah, not even close," Eric said rather seriously. "Wasn't your fight."

True.

"So why'd you do it?"

Michael had been wondering the same thing since Jimmy died, but only now did he realize the answer.

"Because I could."

Eric stared at him a second.

"Well, I'm glad you did!" Eric chuckled. "So why are you on the docks today?"

"No idea," Michael replied, not knowing why he was being brought back to court. "You?"

"Motion hearing," Eric replied. "Caught a charge for possession of a firearm."

Two deputies returned from the courtroom with the last group of prisoners. One of them looked at his list and read the names of the next group.

"Broussard, Murray, Geddes, LaFell, Walker. Let's go."

Michael and Eric stood up and followed the Deputies. When they reached the courtroom, they were seated next to each other in the empty jury box.

"Let's take Broussard first," Judge Landry instructed the clerk, and Michael immediately stood up.

"Stay there, Mr. Broussard, until I learn what this is about."

Michael sat down.

"Joy Glapion for the State, Your Honor."

"Lamar Hill for Michael Broussard," said Michael's attorney, who was positively beaming at him.

"Ms. Glapion, you asked my clerk to add this case to the docket," Judge Landry announced. "What's your pleasure?"

"Your Honor, at this time, the State of Louisiana is voluntarily dismissing all charges against Mr. Broussard."

Judge Landry paused, waiting for Ms. Glapion to volunteer more information.

She didn't.

"Well, mine is not to reason why," Judge Landry eventually said. "Mr. Broussard, the charges against you have been dismissed. I'm ordering the Sheriff to release you as soon as possible. Next case."

Michael watched indifferently while Joy Glapion walked toward him. As she got closer, Michael saw a look of horror spread across her face as she assessed his injuries. It was followed by a look of guilt.

"I'm so sorry, Michael," Joy said. "I should've listened to Will. I hope someday you can forgive me."

Michael remained perfectly still.

Maybe someday. But not today.

"Ms. Glapion, when you're done socializing," Judge Landry called from the bench. "Perhaps we could get back to my docket."

Joy turned and walked away

"Hey," Eric whispered. "You're free!"

Michael thought about the war waiting for him outside the prison walls.

No, not really.

*　　*　　*

Emma Landry was perseverating.

"General Robert E. Lee was a gentleman," Sister Lucille Anne told the class.

Michael is a gentleman.

"General Ulysses S. Grant was a thug," the old-school nun continued. "He finished at the bottom of his class at West Point. But he had more soldiers, and he was willing to sacrifice them to get what he wanted."

I want to see Michael.

"Ms. Landry, am I boring you?"

"Yes, Sister," Emma replied matter-of-factly.

The spontaneous combustion of Sister Lucille was fortuitously interrupted by a loud knocking on the door.

"I'm sorry for the interruption, Sister," Russell Landry said. "But I need to take Emma out of your class."

"Michael!"

"He's fine, sweetie!" Russell said quickly, terrified she would pass out again.

Oh, thank God.

"Well, I can't say the same for your daughter," Sister Lucille told Mr. Landry. "I'm giving her detention this afternoon."

Emma flashed her dad a desperate look while she stuffed her book bag.

"She'll serve your detention, Sister," Russell promised. "But she'll have to serve it another day."

"Why is that, Mr. Landry?"

"Well, her boyfriend just got out of jail."

"He did!" Emma gasped with delight in front of the bewildered class.

"He did."

"Yay!"

"It's a special occasion," Russell told a stunned Sister Lucille as Emma hurried past her. "Not every day a young man beats a murder rap."

"For what?" the mortified nun gasped as Emma Landry hurried past her.

Emma paused at the door and shot Sister Lucille a devilish grin.

"Killing a priest."

* * *

Some traditions are better than others.

"Cell-uh-brate good times, come on!" Lamar Hill sang, blaring the song he always played when driving a client home from jail. "Let's celebrate!"

Michael was sitting with Coach Will in the back seat of Lamar Hill's sports utility vehicle and Brother Reid was riding shotgun. Michael had been "free" for about ten minutes, and he was waiting patiently for the song to end.

"Cell-uh-brate good times, come on! Let's celebrate!" Lamar sang a final time before the song ended.

A second of silence.

"Why did you leave me in that godforsaken place, Brother Reid?" Michael asked. "And don't tell me you were following orders."

"You had to stay inside until the killer struck again," Brother Reid said without turning around.

"Did he?"

"So it would seem."

So it would seem.

Michael was exhausted, but he divined Brother Reid's meaning.

So it would seem... because that's the way Brother Reid wanted it to seem. And that's what he arranged. For another priest to die while I was in prison. To free me.

Michael wasn't sure whether he should feel guilty or grateful, but he knew one thing for certain: he didn't deserve to die in jail for a murder he didn't commit.

"Mr. Hill," Michael said. "Please drive me to the hospital."

"I'm supposed to take you straight to that pathetic school of yours," Lamar said playfully. "Father Finnegan said he'd explain when you got there."

"Change of plans. Please take me to the hospital."

"We can't," Brother Reid said, turning around. "They're waiting at the hospital and at your house."

"I don't care."

"Uh, who's waiting?" Lamar inquired.

"The priest-killers," Michael replied. "And I don't care if all of them are waiting for me. I need to see my father."

"We understand, Michael," Reid assured him. "If everything goes smoothly, Finn will take you there after your last class. You have my word."

"Did you say priest-killers?" Lamar asked, looking at Michael in his rearview mirror.

"What has to go smoothly?" Michael asked.

"You've got a meeting," Will said. "And your friends need the extra time to make certain they can get you to the hospital safely."

"Because it sounded like you said priest-killers."

"Who am I meeting?"

"Someone who can help you," Will promised.

"I'm not ready to face Rachel again," Michael warned. "I still have to figure out whether Rachel and I…"

"It's not Rachel," Jax promised.

"Look, if Michael's still in danger—" Lamar started to say very seriously.

"I'm not, Mr. Hill," Michael assured him from the backseat. "Everybody is overreacting. But thank you for asking Foster to watch my back."

Lamar glanced up in the rearview mirror.

"James Foster?"

"Yes, sir. Didn't you represent him?"

"I did, but I haven't spoken to Foster since his trial," Lamar reported somberly. "Were you in the yard when he was killed?"

"Yes, sir. He died saving my life."

"Really?" Lamar said, genuinely surprised. "Why'd he do that?"

"He said we had a mutual friend," Michael replied. "I figured it was you."

"Not me," Lamar assured him. "But I don't doubt Foster did it for somebody or for something. That man never gave a damn about anyone but himself."

Lamar glanced up at Michael in his rearview mirror again.

"But you say Foster…"

"Took me under his wing."

* * *

Detective Cavet decided to beat the grass with a crozier.

It was an idea Carol Landry had given him at the hospital. But this time, he would only endanger himself.

I'm not going to find the priest-killer on my own, Cavet realized. *But if the right people start asking questions, I might flush him into the open.*

"His Excellency will see you now," the young Seminarian announced. "Please remember to stand until the Archbishop invites you to sit. Are you from the Archdiocese of New Orleans?"

"Yes, I'm a parishioner."

"Then you may kiss his ring when you enter and leave the room."

Cavet nodded his understanding. He walked into the room and reverently kissed the ring of a priest he once served as an altar boy.

"It's good to see you, Tommy. Please sit down."

"Thank you, Fath… uh, your Excellency."

"I'll always be Father Hunt to you, Tommy," the Archbishop said with an enigmatic smile. "And you will always be the boy who couldn't find the bells during Christmas Vigil."

"That was you?"

"Yes, of course, Tommy!" the Archbishop announced. "Your, uh, improvisation remains one of my favorite stories. I confess I tell it too often, but it always makes people smile. Of course, I never do it justice, though I remember so well the sight and sound of you. All of nine years old. Leanin' over the microphone…"

Oh Dear God.

"Yellin' ring-a-ling-a-ling!"

How could I forget Father Hunt said that mass!

"With such a serious face. I'll never forget it."

"I wish you would."

"Ring-a-ling-a-ling!" the Archbishop repeated, shaking his head in disbelief. "Did you really think you were foolin' anyone, Tommy?"

"I panicked, your Excellency."

"Forgive me, Detective," the Archbishop said. "I know you came here on serious business. What can I do for you now?"

Cavet nodded his appreciation.

"Two men dressed like priests have been murdered," Cavet told the Archbishop. "I'm in charge of both investigations."

Cavet pulled out the crime scene photographs for both victims. He wanted to bring one of the black cassocks, but both were covered in dried blood and stored in Central Evidence & Property. The photos would have to suffice.

"Their clothing had no tags," Cavet reported. "I was hoping you could point us in the right direction, your Excellency."

Archbishop Hunt looked very closely at the disturbing photographs.

"The black ryassa is not familiar, Tommy," Archbishop Hunt said, sounding genuinely surprised. "It's not Anglican or Roman and it's not Jesuit. But then…"

Archbishop Hunt paused and looked through all the crime scene photographs. He selected four pictures and placed them on the desk facing Cavet.

"Tell me what you see, Tommy."

"Solid black cassocks."

"Exactly. Nothing is distinctive. The cassock has no colored piping around the collar and cuffs, or down the front panel. No colored sashes or cinctures. Nothing that would identify the religion or the order."

"So it's generic?" Cavet asked more than a little surprised and writing furiously in his little notebook.

"No, not generic. The market for black cassocks is small, and a company making a generic cassock would sew a label on their product. It seems more likely this cassock was made for a specific order. But made to be… untraceable."

Cavet decided it was time to give Hunt the biggest piece of the puzzle. He pulled out photographs taken of the right wrist for both victims.

"Can you tell me anything about this symbol?"

Archbishop Hunt picked up the photograph.

"Crossed keys surrounded by wings?" the Archbishop asked, seeking some sort of confirmation.

"Yes your Excellency."

"Interesting. The crossed keys are a symbol of the Holy See," the Archbishop told him. "You will find them on the papal insignia and on the Vatican City flag. They represent the keys to the Kingdom of Heaven."

"And the wings?"

"The wings are, of course, angelic."

Archbishop Hunt looked at the photograph of a dead priest he now held in his left hand and the close-up of the symbol he held in his right.

"What have you stumbled upon, Tommy?"

Silence followed except for the sound of a pendulum wall clock.

"I wish I knew, your Excellency."

"I'll contact the Vatican," Hunt said. "The Camerlengo is a very dear friend. May I send him these two photographs?"

"Yes your Excellency."

"Good. We need to know whether these men were friends or enemies of our Church. These photographs should tell the Vatican what is at stake."

"Thank you, your Excellency."

"Godspeed, Detective."

Cavet kissed Archbishop Hunt's ring and walked out of the office. He had a feeling that word of his investigation would spread and he was hopeful somebody would come looking for him.

Either with an answer or a sword.

*   *   *

Lamar Hill was in enemy territory.

He drove through the Banks Street gate and officially entered the campus of Jesuit High School.

"I can't believe I'm on this campus," Lamar said. "I'm going to have to shower when I get home. You do realize that?"

"Behave yourself," Coach Will said before pointing out a parking spot near the steps of the Chapel of the North American Martyrs.

"Tell Derrick we're going to have dinner as a family tonight," Lamar said as he pulled to a stop. "He needs to be home by six o'clock."

"Yes, sir," Michael said. "And thank you, sir."

Michael, Coach Will, and Brother Reid jumped out the car and hurried up the Chapel steps to where Father Finnegan was waiting.

"Get inside, quickly!" Finn urged as they hurried past them into the narthex of the Chapel.

Finn closed the doors behind them.

"It's good to see you, Michael," Finn said, giving him an earnest hug. "We've set you up with a room in the residence on the fourth floor. You will be safe here until your dad gets better."

"When can I see him?"

"Soon," Father Finnegan promised. "But they're waiting inside for you. And, Michael, this is no ordinary meeting. We're supposed to send you in alone."

"Whatever," Michael said, not giving a damn who was inside the Chapel.

"Will and I will be waiting in my office," Finn said. "When the meeting is over, go to class and see your friends. When class is over, come to my office. Hopefully, we'll be ready to take you to your dad."

"Yes, Father."

Brother Reid cleared his throat.

"Look, Michael, I have to leave. Brother MacLaren and I have a mission, and you're not going to see me for a couple of days."

"Thank you," Michael said sincerely to the man who had already saved his life twice. "And good luck."

"You too," Reid said before turning to Coach Will.

"Take good care of him, Will. I expect to find him alive when I return."

"Count on it," Will replied as Reid walked out of the church.

Michael turned around and pushed open the inner doors to the chapel. As he walked between two imposing men, he heard them yell:

"Enters Michael!"

* * *

"Please hold."

Archbishop Hunt had almost forgotten what it was like to be put "on hold," but this was no ordinary call, and the Camerlengo was a particularly busy man.

"Your Excellency," a voice said with sincere affection. "It has been too long."

"Hello, my friend, and thank you for taking my call."

"How are things in the Big Easy?"

"We are truly blessed, Robert," Hunt said. "But I'm afraid I need your help."

"Name it, Patty."

"Two men dressed like priests have been murdered in as many weeks," Hunt reported, choosing his words carefully. "We can't identify them or their order, but they bear the same symbol seared onto their wrists."

"Describe the symbol."

"Crossed keys set in a pair of wings," Archbishop Hunt replied.

His description was greeted with silence.

"What is it that you are asking of me?" the Camerlengo asked a moment later in a far more formal tone.

He knows the symbol, Hunt realized with absolute certainty.

"I was hoping you could tell me if the symbol is associated with an order."

"I cannot."

Hunt recognized that it was the Camerlengo who was now choosing his words very carefully. He waited to see if his friend would volunteer his resources, but a couple of seconds passed without either saying more.

"I hate to impose," Hunt said very respectfully. "But I promised the Homicide detective that I would leave no stone unturned."

Still, the Camerlengo said nothing.

"Perhaps you could have the Papal Archives searched?" Hunt proposed.

"Yes, I can," the Camerlengo said. The relief in his voice was palpable. "I will put our best and brightest on it."

Something told Archbishop Hunt that the Camerlengo already knew the impossibly large Papal Archives contained no reference to the symbol.

But how could the Camerlengo know that?

"Thank you, my friend," Hunt replied. "Would you like me to send you a photograph of the symbol?"

"No, that's not necessary," the Camerlengo assured him. "Crossed keys and wings on the right wrist, correct?"

"Correct," Hunt confirmed.

"Consider it done," the Camerlengo said. "But I'm afraid I must go now."

"Of course," Hunt replied. "Hopefully, our next conversation will be of more pleasant things."

"I look forward to it, my friend," the Camerlengo said before ending the call.

Archbishop Hunt sat quietly for a few minutes before speaking aloud the question now weighing heavily on his mind.

"How did you know it was the *right* wrist, my friend?"

* * *

The best meetings are meetings of the mind.

"Welcome, Michael Broussard!" Raphael said, being careful to use his guest's mortal name. "My name is Raphael."

Michael nodded respectfully but did not offer his hand.

"Your name is familiar," Michael said, sounding exhausted. "Are you the Archangel Raphael?"

"I am."

"Are you in charge?"

"Yes, I speak for the Seven, Michael."

"What should I call you?"

"That is a very good question," Raphael replied with a smile. "It has been a long time since I have spoken with a mortal. This is a rather historic meeting."

Michael waited patiently.

"I would be honored if you would call me Brother Raphael."

"Okay. Please tell me the bad news, Brother Raphael. I'm late for class."

Raphael stopped smiling.

"Forgive me, Michael," he said. "You are angry and weary. You want your life back, not a historic meeting."

Michael nodded.

"The Seven need you to remain inside this brick fortress until we can figure out how to protect you."

"Not a chance," Michael replied, shaking his head. "I'm not trading one prison for another. Whatever I was sent here to do, I can't do it trapped in this building."

"What do you propose, Michael?"

"Tell me where I can find Lucifer and give me the army I need to kill him."

Raphael smiled.

"You're not ready, Brother," Raphael assured him. "And when you are, I suspect Lucifer will find you."

"Well, can you get me ready?"

Raphael smiled.

"Aye, Brother. We can do that."

* * *

Unions can be tricky, but reunions are always great.

"Excuse me," Russell Landry said as he opened the door to the second classroom in two days. "Are you Father Unger?"

"Yes."

"I'm sorry to interrupt your class, but Father Finnegan needs to see you in his office. He asked me to substitute-teach for you."

"Who are you?"

"I'm..."

"Roger LaBarre," Emma whispered to her father from her hiding place outside the classroom.

"... Roger LaBarre."

"This is most unusual, Mr. LaBarre."

"Uh, Father Finnegan said it was urgent, Father."

Unger nodded. He handed his marked-up copy of St. Augustine's "City of God" to the substitute teacher.

"Read and discuss the highlighted passages from Book XII."

Father Unger started locking a few things in his desk as Russell Landry cleared his throat and focused on pronouncing all of the words correctly.

"That the contrary propensities in good and bad angels have arisen," Russell read aloud. "Not from a difference in their nature and origin because God, the good Author and Creator of all essences, created them both, but from a difference in their wills and desires. It is impossible to doubt."

Russell stopped reading as Unger disappeared down the hallway.

And Emma entered.

* * *

Michael was spent.

He had not slept since Foster's death. Even Father Unger did not say a word when he gently laid his head on the cool desk and closed his eyes. Long before the substitute teacher arrived, Michael was fast asleep.

It was the whistling that woke him.

When Michael opened his eyes and saw Unger was gone, he spun out of his desk and stood up. Standing in the doorway at the back of the class was Emma Landry.

Her eyes were locked on him like Doppler radar.

Michael grinned and headed toward her.

Emma smiled through fresh tears and did the same. When they got within six desks, Emma sped up and half-lunged into a tippy-toe embrace, hugging him like Michael was returning from war.

Which he was.

"Do you have any idea how worried I was?" she mumbled with her face buried in his neck.

"I'm okay, Em," Michael promised, overwhelmed by the smell of her apple shampoo.

"Don't do that to me again, Michael," Emma said without coming up for air.

"Do that to you?"

"Yes, to me," Emma mumbled.

"You know, it's not always about you, Em."

Emma hugged him a little more tightly.

"Of course it is."

Michael felt his heart beating faster and the weight of the world being lifted from his shoulders. Like nothing before this moment mattered.

This is the way my dad felt about my mom, Michael realized.

This is why he never remarried.

This is love.

*   *   *

Deception is the mother of tragedy and comedy.

The ringing of the school bell marked the end of the last period and the start of what would become Liddy Daigle's favorite Father Unger story.

Of all time.

"I'm here," Unger announced unnecessarily when he arrived at the President's office.

"Yes, you are," Liddy said, casually turning off the intercom into which she had just coughed her warning.

"Should I go right in?"

"Right in?"

"It is urgent, Ms. Daigle."

"What is urgent, Father Unger?"

"How should I know?"

They stared at each other.

"Well, you said it was urgent," Liddy reminded him.

"No, I didn't say it was urgent," Unger corrected her. "Roger LaBarre said it was urgent."

"Who is Roger Labarre?"

"The man who's teaching my class right now."

"And why is he doing that, Father?"

"Because Daniel said it was urgent."

"What did Daniel say was urgent?

"My dear lady, how should I know?" Unger snapped impatiently. "Now, are you going to let me in?"

"I'm sorry," Liddy replied. "But Father Finnegan gave me very strict instructions. I'm not to allow anyone to disturb him for any reason this afternoon. I'm afraid I'll have to ask you to wait here until he comes out."

"This is outrageous," Unger decreed. "Daniel summoned me here only to make me wait for him."

"I guess so."

Father Unger sat down, crossed his arms, and harrumphed. Years later, Liddy would forget how long Unger waited, but she always remembered how his wait ended:

With Michael Broussard entering her office.

"In there?" Michael asked, pointing at Finn's door.

"Go right in."

"What!" Unger bellowed.

The door of the President's office swung open before Michael could grab the door knob, and Father Finnegan stepped out.

Finn nodded to Michael and glanced from Unger to Liddy to Michael.

"Follow me, Michael," Finn said, pointing to the hallway.

"Daniel, I insist—" Unger started, jumping up.

"Whatever it is, Father Unger," Finn interrupted as he and Michael walked past the enraged Head of the Theology Department.

"It's not as urgent as you think."

*   *   *

Sometimes, ya gotta put the skunk on the table.

Finn and Michael walked down the hallway to the small chapel on the Banks Street side of Jesuit High School. When they entered, Finn pointed to the front pew where Jacob was kneeling in prayer.

"Why is he here?" Michael asked.

"Because you need to talk," Finn said.

"The only thing I *need* is to see my father," Michael said. "I have nothing to say to Jacob."

"Don't tell me, tell him," Finn suggested, sliding into the back pew. "I'll watch the door."

Michael walked down the aisle and sat in the pew behind Jacob. He looked at the stained glass windows that originally hung in the school when it was located on the corner of Baronne and Common. Students had prayed for answers in the light cast by these windows for more than a hundred years, and Michael wasn't leaving until he got the answers he deserved.

"You were going to let me die in that yard."

"Yes, I was," Jacob said, still kneeling and looking forward.

"I called your name, and you *stopped* Rachel from saving me."

"Yes, I did."

"A convicted murderer saved me when you wouldn't."

"We must not intervene," Jacob replied. "It is the law."

"Then you *break* the law of God."

"Not just the law of God," Jacob corrected him. "The law of the yard."

"Wait... what?"

"Every Guardian of every prisoner in that yard spends every day resisting the temptation to grab their *protelos* and fly to safety," Jacob promised Michael. "If I had allowed Rachel to save you, the Lost Guardians would have killed her and made an example of you."

"How do you—"

"There are fates worse than death," Jacob said. "I saved Rachel, and I gave you a fighting chance at survival."

Michael thought about that for a second. His instincts told him Jacob spoke the truth, and Jacob's intervention had saved his life and Rachel's.

But he still felt betrayed.

"Whatever," Michael eventually said, trying to sound indifferent, but instantly hating the way he sounded. "I guess I owe you an apology."

"Not necessary," Jacob assured him. "I would have been angry as well."

Michael flashed a tired smile but said nothing in reply.

"Come on, Michael," Jacob said glancing at Finn. "Let's go see your father."

* * *

Ed Broussard was gardening again.

He could not remember how long he had been working in her garden, but he was really enjoying it. The sun was shining, and a cool breeze revived him every few seconds with the smell of confederate jasmine.

Ed grabbed his trowel and started digging a hole for the next violet.

"How are you doing, my love?"

"Hey, Kath!" Ed said, wondering how long she had been standing there. "I'm doing great. Take a look at your garden. What do you think?"

"I think… I've missed you," Kathy said slowly and sweetly. "More than you will ever know."

"Then stop going inside," Ed suggested as he stood up and gave his bride a kiss.

"Mmmh," Kathy Broussard sighed approvingly. "You're not going to make this easy for me, are you?"

"Make what easy?"

"I have bad news, my love."

"We're out of your famous lemonade?"

Kathy laughed.

"I forgot how much you hated my lemonade. I guess it was always a little sour."

"Don't be silly," Ed told her. "I love your lemonade."

"You love me," Kathy corrected him. "And I have a favor to ask of you."

"Anything," Ed told her, looking around the yard and wondering what project his clever wife had in mind.

"I need you to go back."

"Go back where, Honey?"

"I need you to go back and help Michael."

"Where is that boy?" Ed wondered, unable to remember the last time he saw their son.

"He's helping someone else right now," Kathy informed him. "And he's going to need your help."

"You want me to go help him?"

"It's not what I want," Kathy assured him. "It's what our boy needs."

"Then I'll go help him," Ed told her, taking off his work gloves and dropping them into her little red wagon. "I'll be back as soon as I can."

Kathy wrapped her arms around him and gave him a long, passionate kiss.

"You take your time, you hear? He needs you more than I do."

"If you say so," Ed replied, giving her a good firm hug. "Hey, when I get back, let's go for a ride in the Goat."

"That sounds wonderful. I'll think of nothing else."

"Good," Ed said. "It's a date."

"Now, when you see Michael, you tell my boy I love him and I'm proud of him," Kathy said, fixing Ed's shirt and combing his hair with her fingers. "You tell him to be strong. You hear me, Ed? You tell my boy he has *got* to be strong."

"I will, Kath," Ed promised, suddenly realizing why everything seemed so perfect. "And I've missed you too. I've missed you so much that—"

Kathy silenced him with a final kiss.

Ed opened his eyes and heard the beeping of the hospital monitor to his left. When he looked to his right, he saw his son reading in a hospital chair.

"Mikey?"

"Dad!" Michael said, dropping his book and reaching for his arm. "You're awake!"

"Unfortunately."

"Are you in pain?" Michael asked, grabbing and pressing the call button.

"I'll live," Ed promised. "How long have I been out?"

"Days," Michael informed him. "And the doctors told me less than an hour ago they didn't think you were coming back."

Ed smiled.

"They don't know your mother."

* * *

Chapter 16: Crossed Keys

And I will give unto thee the keys of the kingdom of heaven…
Matthew 16:19

His heart was beating way too fast.

Pope Simon Peter II tried to slow his breathing, but his heart was filled with terror and excitement.

Are they really here? After all these centuries, is the hour finally upon us?

A thousand images flashed before his eyes. Millions of faces in hundreds of countries. Pages from ancient texts. A statue in his grandfather's garden. His mother's smile on the day of his ordination.

It felt like the room was starting to move. The Pope bent forward slightly, grabbed the top of his desk and took a few short breaths. It was too little too late. He started to falter and had to sit down.

The Pope caught his breath, kissed his gold pectoral cross, and recited the Lord's Prayer to steady himself. As he finished the prayer, a flustered Camerlengo ran into the room.

"They're here, Holy Father!"

The Camerlengo started to say something more but stopped and hurried closer to the Pontiff.

"Two of them," he practically whispered. "I examined their wrists myself. Merciful Lord, is this really happening?"

The Pope nodded.

"It is, my friend."

The Camerlengo sat down next to him, and the Pontiff suddenly remembered the first and only time someone whispered to him about the Order of the Judged.

Ten years ago.

The Pope could still picture his predecessor, sipping cognac in front of a roaring fire. What he was told that night was a story and a promise passed down, circumstances permitting, from Pontiff to Pontiff and from Camerlengo to Camerlengo.

He remembered everything. The words he swore never to forget. Words he had sworn to repeat to his successor.

A familiar voice brought the Pontiff back to the present.

"Your Holiness," the Camerlengo said, staring at his vestments. "How shall you receive these men?"

The Pope felt the watered silk of his white simar and considered the white zucchetto on his balding head.

"Perhaps your gold cope?" the Camerlengo suggested.

The two old friends looked at each other and smiled nervously.

This is the most important audience any Pope has ever granted, thought the Pope. *But these men won't care what I wear.*

Or that I am Pope.

* * *

Genius comes with a price.

It was midnight in New Orleans. A storm was swallowing the city, and Doctor Claude Villere was just starting his research. The reclaimed cypress walls gave his private study the feel of a cave, dimly lit by gilt bronze double-arm wall sconces.

Villere could not forgive himself for initially disregarding the importance of the symbol on the first victim's wrist, but its appearance on the second victim's wrist was *prima facie* evidence of a secret order of priests.

And enough to drive the Orleans Parish coroner quite mad.

After considerable analysis, Villere was convinced the same branding iron seared both symbols, even though a half century likely separated the two events.

Now Villere was obsessed with learning as much as he could about the symbol itself. He knew the crossed keys of St. Peter were symbols of the papacy, and he decided to start at the beginning.

He gently opened his great-grandmother's Bible to the Gospel of Matthew and found the verse where Jesus made Simon Peter a remarkable promise.

"And I will give unto thee the keys of the kingdom of heaven," Villere read aloud as a flash of lightning illuminated the study. "And whatsoever thou shalt bind on earth shall be bound in heaven; and whatsoever thou shalt loose on earth shall be loosed in heaven."

Villere reverently closed the family Bible and roughly grabbed his paperback Interlinear English-Greek New Testament.

He flipped to Chapter 16 verse 19.

The original Greek word was "kleidas." Which does mean "keys."

Villere swiveled in his chair and addressed his computer.

"But when did crossed keys first appear?"

Villere typed and clicked furiously for several minutes. He soon determined that the Vatican City flag bearing crossed keys was adopted in 1929 and was based on an 1803 flag of the Papal States.

"But that's just the flag," Villere said. "Crossed keys showed up before 1803."

It took several hours, but Villere eventually proved his intuition correct. He discovered that, for centuries, crossed keys had appeared as external ornaments on papal heraldic achievements but always behind the coat of arms and never as a heraldic device on the coat of arms.

Except from 1447 to 1455.

Upon his election, Pope Nicholas V had become the first pope to eschew his family's coat of arms and choose a new coat of arms that featured crossed keys on a red field.

"I have a question for you, Pope Nicholas V," Villere announced as rain started pelting the windows.

"Why are your crossed keys connected by a cord?"

* * *

These were not men of his flock.

Two black cassocks entered the Pope's private library and stopped on the other side of his desk. Neither were interested in kissing the Ring of the Fisherman. Neither cared about the Swiss Guards that lined the Papal office.

These are hard men, thought the Pope. *They look more like killers than priests.*

The Pope had seen combat as a military chaplain. He instantly recognized their discipline, and their vestments could not hide their chiseled physiques.

Their eyes are cold and determined.

The moment was exactly as he always pictured. A wave of resignation washed over him. He relaxed his grip on his chair and his heart finally slowed a beat.

"Yer Holiness," the elder priest stated with a thick Scottish accent.

Respect but not admiration, noted the Pontiff.

The Elder did not wait for a response. He immediately stepped forward and raised his right sleeve.

Crossed keys set in a pair of wings.

All at once, the Pope felt the weight of his office. He was the leader of the Roman Catholic Church, and he understood the gravity of the moment.

"Colonel Alberg," he said to the Head of his Papal Swiss Guard. "Please dismiss your men, lock the door, and remain with us."

Neither priest watched the Swiss Guards file out the papal office. Neither admired their pomp and precision.

The Pope got the feeling that the Elder was struggling with a decision. When Alberg closed the door behind the last of his men, the Elder shifted his body ever so slightly and faced the Head of the Schweizergarde.

Colonel Karl Alberg stared right back at him.

The Elder looked back at Pope Simon Peter II, held his gaze, and then looked down at the white fascia tied above the Pope's waist.

He's looking at the crossed keys near the fringed end, the Pontiff realized, and his heart started racing again. *This is the night I've feared, and I must decide whether Colonel Alberg learns the Church's greatest secret.*

The decision to allow Alberg to remain was not to be taken lightly, but it was a decision easily made.

Alberg is a good man, the Pope reminded himself. *Married for thirty years to his first love, and blessed with three daughters before a son.*

Alberg had even saved the Pontiff's life once, a secret they somehow managed to keep from the rest of the world. A secret that did not compare to the one he must now share with his friend and protector.

For the first time in three centuries, a man who had not taken the cloth would be told a great and terrible truth.

May God have mercy on his soul.

*   *   *

Karl Alberg sighed.

He had just locked himself inside the Papal office with the Holy Father, the Camerlengo and, if he had to guess, two mercenaries disguised as priests.

Wolves in sheep's clothing.

Any of his soldiers would have considered it a great honor to remain in the room for this meeting, but they were young and stupid.

Alberg was not interested in what these men had to say. He was only interested in making damn certain the Pope walked out of the meeting alive, preferably with the Camerlengo in tow. And, if it was all the same to God, Karl would also like to go home to his family tonight.

But that really wasn't up to him.

These two men can take me whenever they want, Karl realized, trusting his proven ability to evaluate soldiers. *On my best day, I may lame one of them before I die.*

On my best day.

"Karl," the Pope said calmly, interrupting his train of thought. It was only the second time the Pope had called him by his given name.

Not good.

"Please describe for these gentlemen the symbols that appear on the Vatican City flag."

Why not? Meetings with mercenaries should always start with papal trivia.

"Crossed keys," Albert replied obediently. "One gold. One silver. Mounted beneath the triple crown, Your Holiness."

The Pontiff nodded and turned his attention to his visitors.

"What did my good friend forget?" the Pope asked.

"Yer red cord."

"He did indeed," the Pontiff agreed with a heavy heart. "Everyone forgets the red cord. It seems so trivial compared to the crossed keys and the papal triregnum."

Where is this going? Karl wondered.

“Forgive me, Karl,” the Pope said, seeing the confusion on his face. “But I must ask you one more question. Why do crossed keys appear on the Vatican City flag?”

Alberg resisted the urge to question the Holy Father, who obviously knew the answer to the question.

“They are the keys of Saint Peter,” he replied. “Symbols of the Church’s power to bind and loose in heaven and on earth, Your Holiness.”

Now the Pope was smiling at him but it was a sad smile, filled with resignation. Alberg’s muscles tensed instinctively.

Something is about to happen.

“Perhaps not so symbolic,” said the Pope.

Pope Simon Peter II slowly reached under the shoulder cape of his white cassock and pulled out a gold key on a red cord.

Merciful Lord!

The Pope looked over at the Camerlengo of the Sacred College of Cardinals and nodded. The Camerlengo nodded back and slowly reached under his own vestments, producing a silver key on a red cord.

Merciful Lord!

*   *   *

Genius does not trust coincidence.

Villere had discovered a rather interesting fact. The last Anti-Pope was Felix V, who was elected in opposition to Nicholas V’s predecessor, Eugene IV.

“What are the odds of that?” Villere wondered, as thunder rattled the window panes of his study. “Not one Anti-Pope after old Nicky V slaps crossed keys on his coat of arms.”

Villere shook his head.

“Crossed keys *and* a cord,” he said, correcting himself.

Villere could not help it. He looked at yet another website purporting to explain the symbolism of the papal insignia and the coat of arms of the Vatican city-state.

“The red cord binds the keys as one?” Villere read aloud, as his grandfather clock softly chimed four times.

"Ridiculous. Cords are made of thread. They're not symbols of strength. If you want to bind keys, you put them on a metal ring, *okay?* Gold. Silver. Whatever."

Villere shook his head and again swore to let the red cord thing go. He wasn't going to solve that riddle tonight. He had a much better chance of solving the other mystery he had stumbled across.

Every article about Pope Nicholas V emphasized the same two facts: the guy was a bibliophile and the first thing he did was reinforce the Vatican City fortifications.

"Why didn't a bibliophile start by building a library?" Villere yawned.

Even more puzzling was Pope Nicholas V's decision to build the Tower of St. John on a hilltop at the westernmost tip of Vatican City. For the life of him, Villere could not figure out the military need to build the tower at that particular time in history or in that location. The expensive tower only protected a portion of the wall.

Villere decided it was time to call it a night. He pulled out a pen and wrote down three questions he still had for Pope Nicholas V.

1 - Why did you put crossed keys on your coat of arms?

2 - What gave you the power to end twelve centuries of Anti-Popes?

3- What did you really build the Tower of St. John to protect?

Suddenly, in his half-exhausted state, Villere realized the answer to all three questions could be the same.

Which could not be a coincidence.

* * *

Brother Liam MacLaren was not a patient man.

But he did feel empathy for the Commander of the Pontifical Swiss Guard. The Steward of the Order remembered how he had felt when he learned the sacred truths.

I'll wait for th' Pope tae finish his story, MacLaren thought to himself. *But this night will end with somebody shovin' those keys into a lock. Time is not on our side.*

"The Order of the Judged was started on May 31, 1431, the day after Joan of Arc burned," Pope Simon Peter II continued. "Started by an angel who hand-picked steadfast men. Men who vowed to protect and police angels serving in the City of Men. Who swore that what happened to Saint Joan would never happen again."

"Joan of Arc was—"

"An angelic spirit sent to earth," the Pope confirmed for Colonel Alberg. "Born into a family like us. An ordinary child until the angel inside her awakened."

The Pope looked at Liam MacLaren.

"Or perhaps I should say until she awakened."

Liam nodded in agreement. It was a more correct statement.

"The Order did not trust Pope Eugene IV, but they trusted his successor," the Pontiff explained. "Pope Nicholas V became the first pope to wear the gold key and Ludovico Trevisan the first Camerlengo to wear the silver key."

The Pope walked over and put his hands on Colonel Alberg's shoulders.

"My dear Karl," the Pope said kindly. "God exists. Angels exist. And in the End of Days, the Commander of the Heavenly Host will rise to fight the Prince of Darkness. When that day comes, the Archistrategos will need something the Order left with Pope Nicholas V."

Karl's eyes widened.

The Pope faced the Elder priest and steadied himself.

"I am the Bishop of Rome, Primate of Italy, Supreme Pontiff of the Universal Church, the Vicar of Christ, and the Successor of Saint Peter."

The Pope paused.

"And now I must ask you one question."

A terrible silence overcame the chamber.

"Who do you come for this night?"

"Who is like God?" Brother Liam MacLaren replied without hesitation.

The Pope nodded, acknowledging the countersign entrusted to him years ago. His heart started racing again. But this time, the Pope made no attempt to control it. Nothing would ever be under his control again, for he was now the Servant of the Servants of God.

The Pope sighed.

"Ask and you shall receive, Brother."

* * *

Practice does not always make perfect. Sometimes, it just makes scar tissue.

Michael walked down the hallway, flanked by Father Finnegan and Coach Will. None of them knew what they were going to find inside the school's large chapel, and only Michael was actually invited to what Finn was calling the first meeting of the Jesuit High School Fencing Club.

Michael paused before opening the door.

"The last time I was trained, I spat up blood for two days," Michael told them. "Are you two really up for this?"

"Boy, open the door," Coach Will told Michael. "I survived Parris Island, and Parris Island is the only reason I survived the war. Way I see it. It's about damn time they got serious about making our lives hell."

"Open the door, Michael," Father Finnegan said. "I need to know what's going on in my school, and I need to know you are safe."

Michael opened the door, but nobody announced his entering this time.

A fierce-looking angel sat on the end of a pew near the middle of the chapel.

"I am called Uriel," he said, standing up and gesturing to an assortment of swords resting on the altar. "You should arm yourselves."

"I'm just here to—" Finn started to say.

"Be cut to ribbons?" Uriel observed matter-of-factly, unsheathing his sword and exiting the pew.

Will immediately grabbed Finn by the collar and jerked him toward the altar. Michael was already three strides ahead of them.

"Jacob predicted your friends would come with you," Uriel noted as he started walking down the center aisle toward them.

"We shall see if they come *next* time."

* * *

Liddy Daigle was tired of making excuses.

"No, I don't know where Father Finnegan is," Liddy assured the caller, which was true. She had already checked the teacher's lounge. "He left about two hours ago, and he hasn't returned."

But I'm going to give him a piece of my mind when he does, Liddy thought. *How dare he go missing in action for an entire afternoon.*

"He could be evaluating teachers," Liddy told the caller, even though she doubted it very seriously. "Yes, I'll give him your message as soon as he returns."

Which, coincidentally, Finn did as she ended the call.

"Daniel!" Liddy yelled hysterically when she saw his condition.

Finn ignored his secretary, walked into his office, and collapsed on his sofa.

"Daniel, are you alright?" Liddy screamed, running into his office.

"No, Liddy. I can't feel my right arm."

"What happened!"

"Fencing practice."

"Your shirt is sliced to shreds!" she declared. "Who were you fencing with?"

"Will."

"Has that man lost what little sense he had?"

"I'd say so," Will replied, walking into the President's office and plopping down on the sofa next to Finn.

"Good heavens!" Liddy screamed when she saw Will's clothes were also ripped to shreds. "Are you bleeding!"

"Not as much as before."

Liddy was beside herself.

"I'm calling an ambulance!"

"No!" they both replied emphatically.

"I...I... I'm going to go grab the first-aid kit from the infirmary. That's what I'm going to do," Liddy announced. "When I get back, I want answers."

Liddy stood there silently waiting for them to volunteer something.

Neither opened their eyes, but together they moaned:

"Fencing."

* * *

Flashlight will never replace torchlight.

Robert Justin McCormick, the Camerlengo of the Holy Roman Church, was five stories below the Tower of St. John and bringing up the rear.

He was feeling the wall with his left hand for balance and aiming the flashlight with his right. The beam was only strong enough to illuminate airborne dust particles and the run of the step below, which made the going painfully slow and treacherous.

We must be getting close, McCormick figured, remembering the last and only time he negotiated the circular stone stairwell. *Maybe three more flights.*

Time passes more slowly in darkness, and the next few minutes lasted an eternity.

"I'm there!" Colonel Alberg called from the darkness below.

McCormick stopped, turned off his flashlight, and stared into the abyss.

One by one, the beams of light below disappeared as the other four members of the expedition reached the foot of the stairs and entered the long tunnel, which led to an ancient door.

McCormick turned on his light and quickened his descent. The temperature had dropped thirty degrees, and he did not relish the idea of his Pope huddled in the tunnel waiting for him. And his silver key.

A few minutes later, the Camerlengo's flashlight illuminated the floor of the great Tower and the entrance to the tunnel. In the distance, he saw the glare of lights held by the men patiently waiting for him.

McCormick moved quickly, swinging the light from the center of his body back and forth before his feet like a cane of light, probing the darkness ahead. When he reached the group, Pope Simon Peter II was running his hand across the symbols on the door, reverently clearing the cobwebs.

"Pope Nicholas V designed this door himself," the Pontiff told the group. "It is his masterpiece. The Chi-Rho Cross appears in the center with two locks at the northwest and southeast tip of the Chi. The distance between the two locks makes it impossible for one man to turn both keys at the same time."

McCormick removed the silver key from around his neck.

"And the locks must be turned at precisely the same time or the door will seal itself and can never be re-opened."

Pope Simon Peter II placed the gold key into the northwest lock and the Camerlengo placed the silver key in the southeast lock.

"On three," the Pontiff told the Camerlengo. "One…"

"Wait!" the American Camerlengo cried. "Do we turn the key on three? Or do we count to three and then turn the key?"

"On three, Robert," the Pontiff said patiently. "We always go on three."

"Very well," the Camerlengo replied as Brother Jackson Reid laughed at something he obviously found very amusing.

"One… two… three!" the Pontiff said as they both turned their keys.

They heard a series of springs and cylinders engage before two locks opened.

The Camerlengo and the Pope sighed with relief. They stepped back and allowed Colonel Alberg and the younger priest to pull open the massive door. Inside, they found a small chamber.

"Karl, please take this," the Pope said, handing him a lighter. "And light the torches that line the wall."

As Colonel Alberg did, flames revealed a circle of magnificent marble angels all facing the center of the room, where an ornately carved altar held upright a sword. The sword reflected the flames and appeared to be afire.

"Behold the flaming sword of Saint Michael," Pope Simon Peter II said solemnly as Colonel Alberg made the sign of the cross.

"We saw an angel with a flaming sword," the Camerlengo practically whispered beside Brothers McLaren and Reid.

"It gave out flames that looked as though they would set the world on fire."

* * *

Chapter 17: Betrayal

For such are false apostles, deceitful workers, transforming themselves into the apostles of Christ.
2 Corinthians 11:13

(2:00 a.m.) Tuesday, November 26

"What time is it?"

Finn poured Will another glass of scotch and topped himself off as well. Only then did he glance at his watch.

"Two in the morning."

"Why am I still here?" Will wondered aloud from the sofa.

"You're hiding from Joy," Finn reminded him while he walked over to the arched window in his office.

"That's right! I forgot."

"You did not," Finn chuckled, vaguely aware he was starting to slur his words but fully aware of the full moon outside. "Now let me ask you somethin'."

"No. Go away."

"Because I'm curious," Finn continued, ignoring him. "I've seen you in a football game go over the middle knowing you were gonna get hit by a slam linebacker."

"Sam linebacker."

"What I said," Finn insisted, suppressing a burp. "And I'm the only guy in this building who knows why you were awarded a Silver Star."

"Where is this going?"

"Well, I'll tell ya!" Finn replied, enthusiastically. "I'm wondering why you're afraid to face Joy. She's ninety pounds soaking wet."

"She has big pointy teeth," Will quipped.

"Be honest with yourself. Why are you here?"

"She doesn't love me."

"Of course she does."

"Not as much as her job."

"Ah!" Finn yelled, declaring some sort of victory.

"You saw her in court," Will reminded him. "You saw her going after one of our boys. Going after a boy who saved my life! Tell me I'm wrong."

No answer.

"No, I'm serious," Will said, resting his eyes. "Please tell me I'm wrong."

No answer.

"Finn, it's not a question," Will clarified. "It's an order. I want to be wrong, and I'm ordering you to tell me that I am."

Still no answer.

"Okay," Will said, opening his eyes. "What are you looking at?"

Finn took another sip of scotch before he answered.

"I'm watching Brother Reid sneak Michael Broussard out of our building," Finn reported. "And I'm watching Unger spy on him from behind your car."

Will bolted out his chair. He got to the window just in time to see Michael reach Brother Reid's car, where an older man dressed exactly like Brother Reid was waiting. It looked like Reid was quickly introducing Michael. Their body language suggested the man was important and their mission was urgent.

Finn and Will stood side by side, watching the scene unfold.

Brother Reid got into the driver seat while the elder priest got in the back seat and Michael hurried around the front of the car. When Michael reached the front passenger door, he stopped and looked up. Directly at their window.

"He's looking at us!" Finn declared.

Michael looked at the car and back up at them again.

"Let's go!" Will ordered, already running out of the office. "Something's wrong!"

Finn knew he was right.

* * *

Ring! Ring!

Detective Cavet opened his eyes and dove for the phone on his nightstand.

Ring! Ring!

"Hello?" Cavet croaked.

"Tommy," the familiar voice said softly. "I apologize for the hour."

Cavet jumped out of bed and scurried out the bedroom in his pajamas.

"Father Hunt," he whispered. "Is everything alright?"

"No," the Archbishop of New Orleans replied. "I'm afraid something may be terribly wrong and everything at stake."

"What is it, Father?"

"Tommy, the Church needs your help."

*   *   *

Trey left the engine running.

He was parked on the side of the Hills' house, directly in front of Derrick's bedroom window. A moment later, he watched the first floor window slowly open and Derrick carefully climb out.

Seconds later, Derrick jumped in the passenger seat.

"Hit it!" Derrick said with such conviction that Trey immediately hit the gas.

"Where are we going?" Trey asked as they pulled away from the curb.

"Saint Louis Cathedral."

Trey nodded. He was not surprised their destination was a church. It was as good a place as any to catch priest-killers.

"Should we call the police?" Trey asked as he ran a stop sign.

"No."

"Why not?"

"He told me not to call anyone."

"Who told you not to call anyone?" Trey inquired, having waited long enough for Derrick to volunteer that information. "Who told you Michael was in trouble and knew exactly where you could find him?"

"He told me not to tell anyone," Derrick said earnestly. "He said there would be consequences if I chose to tell anyone."

"Are you kidding me?" Trey replied incredulously, never taking his eyes off the road. "We're hunting priest killers in the middle of the night! Buddy, check the back seat. If it's empty, tell me who called you!"

Derrick sighed and braced for Trey's reaction.

"Brother Reid."

"That lunatic!" Trey exclaimed. "He thinks the world is about to end! Why would you believe anything that guy said?"

"Something told me to trust him," Derrick explained.

"Well… did Reid say anything else?"

"He said he was following orders," Derrick reported. "And we should too."

*   *   *

Unger was driving like a bat out of hell.

I shouldn't be doing this, Unger thought. *Why am I doing this?*

"Don't lose them, Unger!" Finn yelled from the back seat of Will's car. "Faster!"

"Stop yelling at me, Daniel!" a beleaguered Unger replied.

"Veer right!" Will demanded from the front passenger seat. "Veer right! They went I-10 East toward Slidell."

Unger veered.

"Don't get any closer or Jax will spot you," Will added very seriously.

"What happens if he spots us?"

Will glanced back at Daniel but only for a second.

"We don't know."

"We should call the police!" Unger insisted again as they drove past the Superdome.

"No!"

Unger unconsciously tightened his grip on the steering wheel.

"They're slowing down," Will observed. "They're getting off at Orleans Avenue. They could be headed to the French Quarter."

"Why would they go there?" Unger demanded but Daniel was not in the mood for more questions.

"Less talking, more driving, Unger!"

*   *   *

It was an ambush.

"Break right, Ryan!" Agrippa yelled to his wingman, and they both broke off contact with Derrick and Trey's car.

As they banked right, Agrippa glanced back and saw Trey's car drive unchecked through the intersection, where fifty unseen Fallen were waiting.

Waiting for Agrippa.

"Go for help!" Agrippa ordered Ryan, pointing to a distant steeple as the entire squad of Fallen attacked. Ryan obeyed without hesitation, and none of the Fallen followed the Novice.

Agrippa scanned the neighborhood and realized the largest congregation of Guardians would be at the Orleans Parish Prison, more than two miles away.

I hope Ryan makes it, Agrippa thought.

Because I won't.

* * *

Brother Joshua Jackson Reid was following orders.

As he drove down Chartres Street toward the Saint Louis Cathedral, he did nothing to call attention to his car. But when he reached St. Peter Street, he made a left turn, slammed on the brakes, and shifted the car into park.

"Go!" he yelled.

Jax, Michael and Brother Liam MacLaren jumped out the car and started sprinting toward the entrance to the historic Basilica.

Jax knew they would make it.

Given who was waiting inside the Cathedral, he figured there was an entire Legion of the Heavenly Host securing the Vieux Carre.

He figured wrong.

* * *

Colonel Alberg was wrestling with a guilty conscience.

The Commander of the Swiss Guard was having a hard time accepting the fact that he had secretly smuggled the Holy Father and a priceless artifact out of Vatican City, flown them both on a private jet to New Orleans, and driven them to the Saint Louis Cathedral. In the process, he had ignored Vatican protocol, broken international laws, and endangered the Pope he swore to protect.

Not his finest hour.

Yes, I made a promise, Alberg reminded himself. *But we were several stories beneath the Tower of St. John and the Holy Father was insisting on personally delivering the sword.*

Alberg looked over to the center of the first pew where Pope Simon Peter II was knelt in prayer with the Archbishop of New Orleans. It was a chilly and damp night in the Crescent City, and Alberg was glad the Holy Father decided to wear a black quail jacket over his black turtleneck.

I could have talked him out of it. I should have talked him out of it.

Alberg pushed up the sleeve of his jacket enough to see the local time was 0300 hours. The priests would be arriving soon and, if what they said was true, they would be bringing a very special guest with them.

If anything happens here tonight, the fault is mine. All mine.

Alberg heard the loud knocking on the Cathedral door.

God help us.

He opened the door, and the first to enter was the boy. He was followed by the two priests whose visit to the Vatican had brought them all here.

"Commander," the elder priest said, greeting him with a measure of respect.

Alberg nodded and looked at the young man.

Michael? Is this really the Archangel Michael standing before me?

Alberg did not know whether to shake Michael's hand or kneel. Instead, he nodded respectfully, stepped aside, and gestured for Michael to join the man kneeling in the front pew.

As he watched the boy pass beneath the flags adorning the center aisle of the Basilica, he suddenly realized what he was witnessing.

Karl Alberg made the sign of the cross.

And started to cry.

* * *

The Pope held fast to his rosary.

He heard the doors of the empty church creak open and the echo of Colonel Alberg's baritone. This was the moment of truth for the asthmatic Italian boy who had spent his childhood praying for faith and wisdom.

And somehow got elected Pope.

"My guest is here," the Pope said to Archbishop Hunt. "Would you give us a moment, Your Excellency?"

"Of course, Your Holiness," the Archbishop replied warmly, before making his way out the pew.

The Pope watched as the boy walked up the main aisle and the Archbishop walked down the side aisle, passing like two ships in the night. A moment later, the young man stood at the end of the first pew.

"Will you pray with me?" the Pope asked kindly.

The young man nodded and knelt.

* * *

Knock! Knock!

Jax shook his head, opened the front door of the Saint Louis Cathedral, and found Will, Finn, and Father Unger waiting outside.

"Good morning, Brother Reid," Finn said immediately. "May we please speak with Michael?"

"He's talking with the Pope," Jax told him.

"Such impertinence!" Father Unger gasped. "Do you see now, Daniel? This young man has no respect for anyone!"

"We followed you, Jax," Will explained. "We just want to make certain Michael is alright."

"He's fine, Will," Jax assured him. "But you should leave now."

"The Cathedral should be closed at this hour," Unger snapped. "Who let you inside, Brother Reid?"

"The Commander of the Swiss Guard."

Unger looked like he was going to implode.

"Step aside!" Unger said with surprising conviction.

"Look, Will, this really doesn't concern you all," Jax told them, ignoring Unger and sensing Will was deciding whether to trust or rush him. "I'll see the boy home."

"Brother Reid, I respect you," Finn said. "But you've got one of my boys in there, and I'm not leaving without seeing him."

"That'll do, Brother," an older priest with a Scottish lilt advised. "These are good men. Let them in."

Jax did not agree with the High Steward's decision, but he stepped aside and allowed the three interlopers to enter the Cathedral.

"Your Excellency!" Father Unger gasped as soon as he entered the narthex of the Cathedral and saw Archbishop Hunt.

"Ah, the Jesuits have landed!" Archbishop Hunt proclaimed. "Welcome, Father Finnegan and uh…"

"Father Unger, Your Excellency."

"Yes, Father Unger. Welcome!"

Jax watched as Unger and Finn dropped to a knee and reverently kissed the Archbishop's ring. Will hesitated, but the Archbishop smiled and encouraged him to follow their lead.

"Now, what can I do for the Soldiers of Christ at this unspeakable hour?"

Finn cleared his throat and sobered up.

"We're looking for one of our students, Your Excellency," Finn said. "His name is Michael Broussard."

"Yes, I believe I've seen your Michael, but only in passing," Archbishop Hunt replied with a coy smile.

"I don't understand," Unger said with his usual bluntness. "What does that mean, Your Excellency?"

"It means that Michael is still inside," Archbishop Hunt explained, already a little annoyed with Unger. "Praying with a friend of ours."

Jax cleared his throat to distract Unger from asking his next question.

"Your Excellency, I would be happy to drive Finn and Will home later if Father Unger cannot stay," Jax offered with a portentous look.

"Thank you, Brother Reid," Hunt said, catching Jax's drift. "I would appreciate that. There is a matter I need to discuss in private with these two men."

Jax immediately opened the front door to the Cathedral.

"But--" Unger started to protest.

"Good night, Father Unger," Archbishop Hunt said, making it clear Father Unger was expected to leave.

It took all of Jax's self-control not to laugh as he closed the door.

Fast enough to hit Unger in the butt.

* * *

"What is your name, my son?"

"Will Taylor, Your Excellency."

"Are you a man of faith, Mr. Taylor?"

"I am, Your Excellency."

"Are you a man who can be trusted with a church secret?"

"I am, Your Excellency."

"Good," Hunt continued. "Because I must ask you to take a vow of secrecy that must never be broken."

"I understand," Will said, his posture straightening. "Should I take that vow now, Your Excellency?"

"You may take it after you kiss the Fisherman's Ring."

"You want me to kiss your ring again?"

"No, Will," Finn said with a reverence Will had never heard his friend use before. "The Archbishop doesn't wear the Fisherman's Ring. The man who does--"

"Is talking with your Michael," the Archbishop confirmed. "Or should I say, *our* Michael."

* * *

Pope Simon Peter II finished his prayer and sat down. A moment later, the boy awkwardly made the sign of the cross and joined him on the long wooden pew.

"You hesitated," the Pope noted gently. "Before making the sign of the cross."

"Yes, sir."

"I was told you are Catholic."

"I was raised Catholic, but I am, uh..."

"Having a crisis of faith?"

"Yes, sir."

"As am I," the Pope confessed with a gentle smile. "Perhaps we can weather this storm together."

The young man nodded, his expression uncertain.

The Pope reached over and grabbed a long black leather satchel.

"Forgive me," the Pontiff said. "I know who they think you are, but I need to hear you say it."

Silence filled the Basilica but only for a moment.

"Michael!" Jacob yelled from the back of the church.

The Pope turned around and saw an angel of the Lord standing at the back of the Saint Louis Cathedral. His wings spanned the center aisle and his youthful and handsome face was a testament to God's loving hand. He was the most beautiful thing the Pope had ever seen, and he was overcome with emotion.

"We're surrounded," Jacob reported. "The Fallen have arrived in force. We've been betrayed."

"Two approach!" Jax called from the doorway. His voice was professional but filled with hatred.

The angel strode to the back of the old church before Michael and the Pope could rise from their pew.

"It's Marcellus and Dante!" Jacob reported from the doorway. "They've returned with a Legion of the Fallen. They're standing fifty feet away. And Michael… they have hostages!"

Concerned faces looked down the long center aisle at Michael, and Colonel Alberg was already running toward his Pope.

"Who are the hostages?" Michael called back.

"Michael, get up here!" Jacob replied firmly. "And, Brother, bring the sword!"

The Pontiff felt his chest tighten. He glanced up at the boy standing before him. Michael's face was different. He looked much older than he had only a moment ago.

"I am the Captain of the Army of the Lord," Michael said. "I am the Archistrategos. I am the Archangel Michael. May I have my sword back?"

* * *

Michael Broussard, age eighteen, walked down the center aisle of Saint Louis Cathedral holding the sword of Saint Michael and flanked by the Commander of the Pontifical Swiss Guard and Pope Simon Peter II.

When he reached the front doors, he saw Marcellus and Dante standing at the entrance to Jackson Square.

Damn them both to hell.

To their left, dark angels in ebony clothing stood behind the wrought-iron fence that marked Jackson Square, holding fast to three hostages: Trey, Derrick, and Sheri Stevens.

"Who are th' hostages tae ya?"

"My friends… and, uh, my Homecoming date."

Only the tiny plaza dedicated to Pope John Paul II separated the Cathedral door from Jackson Square. And good from evil.

In a matter of seconds, more of the Fallen appeared. They soon filled an inexplicably-deserted Jackson Square and the balconies of the Upper and Lower Pontalba buildings.

Michael waited.

One by one, the Guardians in Michael's escort, and those assigned to protect the Pope, appeared in the plaza. Unlike the Fallen, their variegated clothing spanned different cultures and centuries.

The Guardians were hopelessly outnumbered.

Michael estimated a hundred of the Fallen for every Guardian outside the Cathedral. But the Guardians stood together, determined to defend the Cathedral.

And the Pope, thought Michael. *And me.*

The two Guardians standing in front of the phalanx turned and headed straight for the Cathedral door. Michael recognized Kadmus and Carson, and he stepped back to allow them to enter. Carson entered first, marched past Michael and disappeared halfway down the center aisle.

Kadmus stopped just inside the door.

"Brother Carson is going to the Seven, but it will take time for reinforcements to arrive," Kadmus reported. "I recommend we pull everyone back inside the church."

"What about the hostages?" Michael asked.

"There's nothing we can do for them," Kadmus said. "We have only two squads of Guardians, and our orders are to protect you and the Pope."

"What about my friends?"

"Your friends become what they are," Kadmus told him sternly. "Casualties of war."

* * *

"Clear the street!"

Dante's order echoed off the bricked promenade and hundreds of the Fallen descended on the Guardians protecting the Cathedral.

It was a massacre.

Michael reacted quickly. He immediately blocked the doorway with his body and issued his first official command.

"You stay with me!" Michael told Jacob and Kadmus with authority. "You can't help them, but you can help me."

Michael watched as both Guardians struggled to obey as their brothers and sisters were vanquished outside. When Michael was certain they were going to stay, he turned around and watched the Fallen dispatch the last of the Guardians.

Each slain body hit the gray slate of the plaza and disappeared, leaving only blood and an abandoned sword. When the last Guardian was gone, the Fallen returned to their posts and Jackson Square grew still again.

Except for two panting police officers.

* * *

"Freeze!"

Detective Thomas Cavet's voice echoed down Jackson Square. Cavet had both hands on his gun, and he was waiving it from one dark figure to the next.

"N-O-P-D!" he yelled. "Put your weapons down! Put 'em down! Now!"

Nothing.

Detective Cavet pointed his gun at Marcellus. His nephew followed his lead and took aim at Dante.

"Let 'em go!" Cavet ordered. "Do it!"

Nothing.

"Now!" Cavet yelled.

Cavet and his nephew had clean shots but they were facing hundreds of men.

Dante glanced at Marcellus, but Marcellus shook his head. The Fallen were not there to kill police officers or to make martyrs.

"Tommy!" Archbishop Hunt called from the doorway of the Cathedral. "Over here!"

Detective Cavet located the Archbishop, nodded to his nephew, sprinted to the Cathedral door, and disappeared inside a second after his nephew. As soon as they crossed the threshold, both immediately turned around. Neither noticed the mortals or the *malachim* in the narthex.

"Code 9! Code 9!" Cavet cried into his shoulder microphone. "Saint Louis Cathedral. Send Swat! Send *everyone!*"

No response.

"Those things have wings!" his terrified nephew exclaimed, oblivious to Kadmus and Jacob standing behind him.

"Code 9!" Cavet repeated. "Respond!"

"You saw them!" Matt continued. "They'll slaughter us like..."

"Secure the rear doors!" Cavet told his nephew as he waited for any response to his transmission.

"Secure the doors... with *what*?" Matt cried. "Those things had wings!"

"Matty—"

"We're dead!" Matt cowed. "We are so dead!"

"Matty—"

"I crapped my pants. I crapped in my—"

"Officer Frosch!" Cavet barked, still not taking his eyes off Marcellus. "Secure the rear doors of this church and report back. That's an order! Do it now!"

Cavet's tone snapped the patrolman out of his panicked state. Matt immediately turned around. And saw Jacob and Kadmus standing behind him.

"Ummh… Uncle Tommy?"

Cavet glanced behind him for the first time and saw the bizarre group assembled in the narthex of the Cathedral.

"Put the gun away, Tommy," Archbishop Hunt said. "It will not protect us against this particular enemy."

Cavet did as he was told.

"What are they?"

"That's hard to explain," said an older man wearing a black jacket.

"Oh my God," Cavet gasped, recognizing his Pope. "Are they here for you?"

"No."

"Who, then?"

*   *   *

"Mikha El!"

"No, Michael!" Jacob insisted. "You're not going out there!"

"Mikha El!" Marcellus called again. "May I have a word, Brother?"

"Agreed," Michael said. "It's what Marcellus wants, and I have no intention of making this easy for him. Check the sacristy for weapons."

"Aye, Michael," Jacob replied as he whirled around and took five strides toward the rear of the church. Then he stopped abruptly and looked back.

As Michael stepped out the front door.

*   *   *

Colonel Karl Alberg watched the dominos fall.

The second after Michael stepped outside the Cathedral, the two angels flew past Karl and out the same door.

A fraction of a second later, the elder priest turned to his comrade.

"Serve well, Brother Reid!"

"Die well, Brother MacLaren!" the young priest replied with a determined grin as they both disappeared out the front door.

"Matty, stay with the Pope!" the detective ordered as he pulled out his asp baton and hurried outside.

"I've got this, Finn," the man named Will said. "You should stay here."

"You're right," Finn replied, but instead of staying, he immediately followed his friend out the door.

Karl watched as the young police officer glanced at the Pope, at the front door, and back at the Pope.

"I'll guard His Holiness," Karl promised. "Your place is with them."

The patrolman nodded his appreciation and practically sprinted out the door toward his uncle.

"Patty!"

Karl wheeled around in time to see Archbishop Patrick Hunt reach the front door.

"Where are you going, my friend?" the Holy Father asked.

"My flock is out there," Hunt replied from the doorway. "I shall face the wolves with them."

When the Archbishop stepped outside, Karl blocked the doorway with his body to make certain the Head of the Roman Catholic Church remained within.

I'm not going home without the Holy Father, Karl swore silently. *No matter what happens outside these doors.*

A strange breeze breached the tall doors of the Cathedral and disturbed the flags down the center aisle. For a moment, all Karl could hear was the snapping of flags and the sound of Pope Simon Peter II praying:

"Let not your hearts faint," the seventy year-old Pope said. "Fear not, and do not tremble, neither be ye terrified because of them. For the Lord your God is he that goeth with you."

Amen.

* * *

Chapter 18: Battle of Jackson Square

... and there was given unto him a great sword.
Revelations 6:4

(2:42 a.m.) Tuesday, November 26

This was Michael's destiny.

Michael walked out the Cathedral to face a thousand dark angels.

"Let them go!" Michael told Marcellus, a moment before Jacob and Kadmus arrived by his side.

"May I ask why, Brother?"

"They were bait to get me out of the building," Michael said, as Brothers Reid and MacLaren joined him. "And here I am."

While Michael waited for a response, Father Finn and Coach Will snatched up abandoned swords and joined his small band of men.

"Mikha El speaks the truth!" Marcellus declared. "Release the hostages!"

Michael watched as Trey, Derrick, and Sheri ran toward him. Trey and Derrick stopped and stood with Michael.

As did Sheri.

* * *

"It has been centuries, Mikha El!"

Marcellus smiled at Michael. *Something* told Michael they were once friends.

Very good friends.

"But we have no time to reminisce," Marcellus said with regret. "As we speak, the Seven are amassing an army to rescue you and your brave friends."

"This does not have to happen," Michael told Marcellus.

"But it does," Marcellus replied. "You are who you are, and we cannot allow you to fulfill the prophecy."

"Michael," Jacob said to his right. "It has been an honor."

"Cut off the head and the body dies!" Dante yelled, and a roar erupted from the ranks of the Fallen.

"Whatever you're going to do," Will told Michael. "Do it now!"

Michael took one deliberate step forward, raised the sword of Saint Michael, and leveled the tip directly at Marcellus.

"Defend yourself!"

* * *

All heaven broke loose.

As Michael's challenge echoed in Jackson Square, Agrippa and three hundred half-crazed Lost Guardians streaked like fighter jets over the spires of the Saint Louis Cathedral and slammed into the center of the Fallen massed in Jackson Square.

At the same time, Ryan and hundreds of angels broke through the Fallen's line at Canal Street and attacked the flank.

But it was the sound directly behind Michael that drew every eye.

Rachel of Judah and hundreds of angels burst out the narrow entrance of the Cathedral like rabid doves freed from a gilded cage.

The battle was joined.

* * *

Jacob reacted first, flying at Dante like a heat-seeking missile, and Kadmus followed on his flank. Liam and Jax drew daggers and attacked the closest pair of Fallen. Will and Finn raised their swords and teamed up on a third. Detective Cavet and his nephew charged a fourth with only their batons. And Trey lunged at a fifth as Marcellus smiled and advanced on Michael.

* * *

"Come!" Dante screamed as Jacob closed in. "Come to me!"

Dante planned on dispatching the Novice quickly and challenging Agrippa the Great. Killing Agrippa would bring him glory.

Jacob landed three strides from him and unleashed a fury of blows. The skill and speed was significantly better than Dante remembered.

He's improved, Dante thought as he parried each attack. *But not enough.*

*   *   *

Marcellus sliced downward with his sword, again and again, at precisely the same angle. Faster and faster. Each time, Michael barely raised his sword in time to block or deflect the blow.

The sound of the beat doubled, and the rest of the battle disappeared for Michael. There was only Marcellus and his deadly blade.

*   *   *

Jax called on the rage.

He thought of his loving father and his sweet mother.

Bound and gagged...

Jax dodged an off-balance lunge and slashed diagonally, left to right, ripping open the chest of the first dark angel.

My father!

MacLaren had trained him never to watch the slain disappear. As the angel fell, Jax was already engaging the next. He deflected an out-of-control thrust and used his momentum to spin around and slice a right wing in half. The angel screamed in pain and swung wildly at Jax, who nimbly leaned back and avoided the blow.

My mother!

Jax lunged forward, driving the sword through the heart of the hysterical angel, spraying blood everywhere. Jax spun the impaled angel around and used the body to shield himself from the thrust of a third. Withdrew his blade and shoved the dying angel at the third attacker, who instinctively caught him. Jax exploited the mistake by charging the third attacker and piercing his exposed larynx with a well-aimed strike. Both fell and disappeared.

"Sky!"

Muscle memory jerked Jax's eyes upward at the sound of MacLaren's warning, but he was too late. A winged-attacker was descending on him, and there was nothing he could do.

A good death, thought Jax a heartbeat before MacLaren shoved him out the way.

Jax instinctively executed a perfect shoulder roll and came-up in a fighting position. He looked back just in time.

To see Brother MacLaren die.

*   *   *

Michael was desperately parrying or blocking all of Marcellus' thrusts, lunges, and cuts, but he was not gaining confidence. Their duel was slower than the duels he witnessed in the Rock 'n' Bowl parking lot.

Much slower. And more predictable.

Marcellus was repeating his sequences and telegraphing each attack. A terrible thought crossed Michael's mind.

He's toying with me.

*   *   *

Beginner's luck, Trey decided as he pulled his sword out of a fourth dead angel. This time, he didn't watch or wait for the body to disappear.

"Sky!" he heard somebody yell.

Trey looked up in time to see two dark angels descending on their position. One was headed at Brother Reid. The other was headed at Trey.

Which Trey found exciting.

*   *   *

Will pulled the sword out of his second kill and wheeled around in time to see a dark angel effortlessly disarm Archbishop Hunt.

"No!" Will yelled, recklessly charging him.

The angel glanced at Will, stabbed the backpedaling Archbishop in the gut, and turned in time to parry Will's first thrust.

As the Archbishop fell.

*   *   *

The Archbishop-Stabber gave ground, allowing Will to swing wildly until he was exhausted.

Rope-a-dope, Will realized too late. *And I'm the dope.*

Suddenly, the angel went on the offensive.

Will somehow managed to block and dodge the first barrage, but his attacker had greater skill and strength.

Just a matter of time.

The angel attacked again, and Will parried his first thrust so weakly that the blade still sliced his side.

Will panicked. Summoning all the strength he had left, he launched a last-ditch flurry of blows. None of them landed, and the dark angel dislodged Will's sword during the final exchange. Will watched helplessly as the angel shifted his weight and lunged forward, aiming for Will's lower torso.

As the blade closed on its target, Finn's sword came crashing down, slamming the tip into the gray slate of the plaza.

Oohrah!

* * *

Michael was overmatched and exhausted.

The next time Michael parried a thrust, Marcellus effortlessly grabbed Michael's arm and pulled him face-to-face.

"Lucifer comes for you!" Marcellus warned barely loud enough for Michael to hear, jerking Michael forward and back to give the appearance Michael was matching his strength. "And you are not ready."

Michael knew he was right.

"Thrust!" Marcellus ordered, breaking contact with Michael and shoving him backward. *Something* told Michael to do exactly what he said, and Michael immediately lunged at Marcellus, who swatted his blade away with disgust.

"At the heart!" he growled.

Michael lunged for the heart, but Marcellus easily parried his blade.

"With hate!" Marcellus insisted.

Michael lunged again, but he was exhausted. This time, when Marcellus grabbed and pulled him closer, Michael did not resist.

"Let me help you," Marcellus whispered in Michael's ear. "An hour ago… I killed your father."

*　　*　　*

"Father!"

Detective Cavet saw Archbishop Hunt lying on the ground, and started running toward him, but a dark angel immediately blocked his path.

Cavet threw his asp baton at the angel's face, tackled him, and wrestled for position. The angel was larger and stronger, but so were most of Cavet's wrestling opponents in high school. He popped the angel's left arm forward, slammed his right arm across the angel's face, and locked the angel in a cross-face cradle.

The dark angel countered by sprouting wings.

The humerus bone instantly broke Cavet's hold, and the scapula slammed into Cavet's face, knocking Cavet unconscious and throwing him off the angel's back.

Cavet's limp body slammed into the ground. The angel wheeled around and reached for a sword.

As Matty's baton cracked the angel's skull.

*　　*　　*

Thunder?

Archbishop Hunt thought he heard thunder as he lay bleeding to death outside the church where, so many decades ago, he had been ordained. The pain was excruciating but Hunt smiled as he realized he was going to die while defending his Cathedral.

Such a good death.

Some part of his cloudy mind was aware of the desperate attempt to save his life.

Such good boys.

Hunt felt his strength failing and decided he wanted—more than anything—one last glimpse of his Cathedral. He turned his head, but his view was blocked by the Commander of the Swiss Guard, who was running toward him with sword drawn.

He closed his eyes.

Not just defending my Cathedral. Defending my Pope.

Hunt felt the cold tip of a sword beneath his chin and opened his eyes. It was exactly what the dark angel wanted, and an evil grin spread across the Fallen's face at precisely the same moment as Colonel Alberg's sword sprang from his chest.

Such violence.

Alberg pushed the slain angel out the way and stooped to speak with Hunt.

"Can you move?"

"Sky!" screamed somebody nearby. A second later, a dark angel slammed into Alberg from above. Hunt heard the horrible sound of bone snapping followed by Alberg's head hitting the pavement.

The Fallen landed, grabbed Colonel Alberg's hair with his left hand, and started to raise his head high enough to cut his throat.

Please. Not him, Lord.

In the midst of a raging battle, the Archbishop's simple prayer was answered, and the dark angel was stabbed in the back.

By a surprisingly quick Pope.

* * *

Derrick deposited Sheri by the Cathedral entrance, spun around, and stopped dead in his tracks.

Jackson Square was unrecognizable. Every inch of the Place d'Armes was consumed with combat, and the sky was filled with angelic dogfights. The angels pouring out the Cathedral were taking flight and splitting into two lines. Both lines angled up like ramps, circled the Pontalba Buildings flanking the Square, and disappeared into the ranks of Fallen.

Michael's band of friends had been overrun, and a dark angel was circling above a very familiar figure.

"Trey!" yelled Derrick, already moving like a freight train.

* * *

Dante was circling his prey.

I must buy Michael more time, thought Jacob, who had been ripped to shreds by Dante's blade. *I must not fall.*

"I smell your fear!" Dante cackled.

Jacob raised his sword and felt the searing pain rip through his body again.

I can't swing it again.

"Yes, it hurts!" Dante chided, enjoying his butchery. "It hurts, Brother!"

Dante slapped away Jacob's feeble thrust and countered by slicing another chunk out of Jacob's left arm. Jacob swung wildly and missed. Before he could recover, Dante slashed the sword out of Jacob's hand and gashed Jacob's side.

Jacob dropped silently to his knees.

Forgive me, Michael.

"Such arrogance," Dante declared with disgust as he rested the edge of his blade against the back of Jacob's neck. "To challenge me."

But, instead of striking a fatal blow, Dante's blade harmlessly dropped to the pavement next to Jacob.

As did Dante's head.

"No!" Jacob screamed, as he looked up and saw Brother Jackson Reid. "I challenged him!"

Jax wiped both sides of his blade on Dante's back before the monster disappeared, and smiled at Jacob.

"Your rule. Not mine."

* * *

Derrick and Trey were fighting back-to-back and inexplicably well.

Trey slammed his sword into the next attacker's blade, punched the dark angel with the hilt of his sword, stabbed him in the gut, shoved his impaled torso into another Fallen, released his blade, wheeled around, grabbed a charging angel, threw him into an iron fence, and immediately collapsed—his heart unable to match his will.

A moment later, Derrick was knocked off his feet by a brutal kick to the chest and landed with a thud near his unconscious friend.

As the dark angel standing over Trey raised his sword to finish the job, out of nowhere, a size-seven high-heel shoe struck him in the face. And, a fraction of a second later, another size seven struck Derrick's assailant.

"No!" an unarmed and barefoot Sheri Stevens shrieked at the top of her lungs while running straight at the enemy and gesticulating wildly.

"Look at me!" Sheri yelled. "Look at me! Look at me!"

Both of the Fallen ignored the hysterical girl, but before either could strike, they were stabbed by Coach Will and Father Finnegan.

"Are you hurt?" Sheri asked as soon as she reached Derrick's side, ignoring the fighting all around her and searching his clothes for wounds.

"Help Trey!" Derrick grunted, clutching his cracked ribs.

Sheri scurried on all fours to Trey's side.

"He's not breathing!"

* * *

Agrippa had lost count of his kills.

He blocked another weak thrust, ran his opponent through, recovered, turned, skewered the dark angel behind him, ducked an ill-advised swing from a passing attacker, and sliced open his back.

A rare respite in the middle of battle ensued, and Agrippa immediately scanned the battlefield for Derrick.

Who was about to die.

* * *

Michael lost it.

He thought only of avenging his father, recklessly slamming his sword into Marcellus' blade with increasing speed and power.

"He suffered!" Marcellus yelled.

No!

Overcome with rage, Michael senselessly combined thrusts and moves, risking everything for the chance to kill Marcellus.

"He bled!"

No!

Michael felt his strength and his resolve double. He had to avenge his father, and he had to rid the world of this evil.

"He cried out!"

No!

"The coward!" Marcellus exclaimed.

Michael let loose a guttural cry and threw himself at Marcellus. Somehow, he knocked Marcellus' blade out the way, grabbed the back of Marcellus' head, and ran him through.

Die! Michael thought, burying his blade to the hilt and finding himself face-to-face with the evil creature.

Marcellus smiled and grunted:

"Promise kept, my Captain."

* * *

Agrippa raced through the battlefield.

Derrick was lying supine on the ground a short distance from where Sheri was caring for Trey. His *protelos* had no idea that a dark angel was circling above and preparing to strike. The boy had seconds to live.

Agrippa was five yards from Derrick and eight yards from Michael, who was also about to be killed from above.

Agrippa did not hesitate. He quickly closed the distance.

And jumped over Derrick's helpless body.

* * *

Michael's head was on a swivel.

He saw Agrippa jump over Derrick, swinging his blade and deflecting the downward strike of the dark angel trying to kill Derrick.

Thank God, thought Michael a micro-second before Coach Will knocked him out of the way of another swooping angel's blade.

Michael regained his balance and attacked the angel who had flattened Coach Will. Almost immediately, Michael realized that his opponent lacked the skill of Marcellus. His attacks were awkward and uncertain.

A Novice?

Suddenly, a conch-sounding horn blew, and the Fallen responded by taking to the sky like flushed game and disappearing into the darkness.

The horn sounded retreat.

Michael immediately scanned the battlefield to see whether Derrick and Trey had survived. He turned just in time to see an angel appear about fifty feet away, directly behind Agrippa.

"Agrippa!" Michael screamed.

Agrippa whipped around as the dark angel impaled his chest. The angel then whispered something in Agrippa's ear and disappeared into the night sky.

But not before Michael recognized him from the bowling alley's parking lot.

Iron Jaw!

* * *

Trey loved good jazz.

He was sitting in a dimly-lit club off Frenchmen Street and enjoying the sound of Dizzy Gillespie. He looked around the bar, but he did not see Adele, who was probably in the bathroom.

Trey picked his trumpet off the table and worked the valves in time with the musicians. He didn't remember learning the song, but he knew every note.

"Are you going to play?" a familiar-looking waitress with beautiful auburn hair asked him.

"I'm not very good."

The waitress placed one drink in front of Trey and another in front of the chair where Adele must be sitting.

"I suspect you're very good," the woman said. "But you should think less and play more."

"Do I know you?"

"Yes," the waitress said calmly, setting a bowl of Trey's favorite assortment of nuts on the table. "I'm Michael's mother."

"Mrs. B!" Trey said with genuine excitement. "I'm sorry I didn't recognize you. I forgot you work here."

"I don't work here, sweet boy," Kathy Broussard admitted. "But I heard you were here for a little while, and I need you to give Michael a message for me."

"Sure, Mrs. B."

"You tell him I love him," Kathy Broussard said with a strange look on her face. "And you tell him to stay away from Scotland."

"Scotland?"

"Scotland," she repeated. "You tell my boy to *stay the hell away* from Scotland, you hear?"

"Yes, ma'am!" Trey replied, shocked to hear Mrs. Broussard curse.

"Thank you, Trey," she said earnestly as the music stopped. "Michael's lucky to have you for a friend. Now get up there and play."

She gave him a pat on the back and pointed toward the abandoned microphone.

Trey obediently got up and walked past a handful of tables toward the alcove where the small stage was located. He sat down on the cracked leather stool, lowered the microphone, and prepared his horn. Just then, somebody must have opened the door to the bar because a breeze surrounded him with the smell of expensive perfume.

"Here goes nothing!" Trey said to a splatter of applause.

Trey placed his lips on the mouthpiece and was surprised to taste strawberry.

That's strange.

Trey pressed his lips to the mouthpiece and again tasted strawberry. Before he could blow, he felt air rush into his mouth and down his lungs.

Now that's really strange.

Trey closed his eyes, started to play a third time, and again felt air rush into his mouth and down his lungs. He felt a stabbing pain in his chest, and it forced him to open his eyes and gulp for air.

What the hell?

Trey found himself lying on the ground outside Saint Louis Cathedral, and the hand under his neck belonged to Sheri Stevens.

Who had just performed CPR.

*　　*　　*

The only virtue of battle is that it ends.

Seconds after the conch sounded, all of the Fallen were gone, and Michael was left surveying the damage, which included a hundred injured Guardians.

A blood-covered Brother Reid was standing over Father Finnegan who was administering last rites to Brother MacLaren.

Pope Simon Peter II was tending to Colonel Alberg's busted shoulder. Sheri Stevens was holding Trey's head in her lap and crying while Derrick rubbed her back.

A battered and bruised Will had shifted into medic mode and was trying to stop the Archbishop's bleeding.

Guardian Kadmus and Rachel of Judah were tending to Jacob, who looked half-dead but was staring at Michael and smiling.

As Jackson Square fell silent, Michael realized all of the angels were looking at him. And, for the second time in his life, Michael knew exactly what to do.

Michael raised his sword high into the night sky and Jackson Square erupted in cheers that quickly became a chant.

"Michael! Michael! Michael!"

* * *

Genius loves company.

It was three o'clock in the morning, and Villere was waiting in his library for Detective Cavet. On the phone, Cavet had said he needed help and would explain in person. Villere was enjoying the anticipation.

And a third glass of forty-year-old port.

"Come in! Come in!" Villere cried when they finally arrived.

"Hello, Doc," Cavet said, wiping his feet and entering the house. He was followed by a familiar-looking man and a tough-looking younger man in a badly-stained black cassock. "Sorry for coming here so late."

"It's not late. It's early, *right?*" Villere joked as he closed the door. "May I offer you a glass of port? I prefer a blonde port, and this is a tawny port. But any port in a storm, *right, right, okay?*"

"No, thanks," a disheveled Cavet said before clearing his throat. "Doc, this is Brother Jackson Reid and this is your… uh, I mean… this is Isaac."

This is my what? Villere wondered as he sized up his guests in a fraction of a second. Then he stepped forward and shook Isaac's hand.

"I've met you before, Isaac," Villere declared with absolute certainty before facing the younger man. "And I've seen your ryassa, Brother Reid."

"Doc, Brother Reid is…" Cavet started to say.

"Covered in bloodstains?" Villere interrupted in his all-business voice. "Yes, I realize that now. Brother Reid, may I see your right wrist?"

The room fell silent.

"Turns out you were right, Doc," Cavet announced with sincerity as Brother Reid pulled up his right sleeve and revealed the symbol seared into his skin.

Same symbol on both victims, Villere noted instantly. *But this branding was very recent. Only a few weeks.*

"The blood on the Broussard car didn't belong," Cavet explained before very deliberately nodding at Isaac.

"Doc, may I introduce you to your guardian angel?"

The one called "Isaac" suddenly sprouted and unfurled magnificent wings, which filled the small library and almost encircled the group.

Villere finished his port with a single swig.

"What can I do for you, gentlemen?"

* * *

Doctor Lagarde was no stranger to late-night calls.

While Kenny Rogers' "The Gambler" blared, he calmly sat up in bed, turned on his lamp, and picked up his cell phone.

"Lagarde."

"Doc, it's Will."

"What's wrong?"

"Finn and I need you to leave right now and go to Jesuit's infirmary without saying anything to anyone," Will replied with a true sense of urgency. "Archbishop Hunt has been seriously injured. We've stopped the bleeding, but we can't take him to a hospital until you've stitched him up."

"Why the hell not?"

"Because nobody can know who stabbed him."

"Stabbed!"

"Doc!" Will interrupted, sounding exhausted. "There's no time to explain."

"Alright. I'll meet you—"

"Negative. A man named Alberg is driving the Archbishop there now. He'll explain everything."

"Why aren't you driving him?"

"Because Finn and I have to be in a fatal car accident."

Doctor Lagarde hung up the phone and grabbed his shoes.

* * *

It also makes a distinctive sound.

Simulated sapphire tapping against a glass window makes a sound unlike any made by branch or bird. It is an unusual sound for an unusual event, and it immediately woke Emma up.

Emma threw back her covers, stumbled over to the window, and pulled apart the curtains. And there he was.

Michael Broussard was standing on her balcony in a drizzling rain. Moonlight shined in his eyes and shimmered on his lips. He looked different.

Determined.

Emma unlocked the window and opened it as quietly as possible.

"Have you lost your mind?" Emma whispered as she stepped onto the balcony. "How did you get up here?"

"I had help."

"But why—"

"I told you I would find you," Michael said. "And this couldn't wait."

Before Emma could say another word, Michael grabbed her face and kissed her like it was the end of the world.

Wow, Emma thought, enjoying the softness of his lips and the way they hungered for hers. Her body soon had a mind of its own. Her fingers desperately explored his hair, and her body practically coiled around his. Overwhelmed by passion and romance, Emma lost herself in the moment. And time stood still.

This is love, Emma realized. *And I never want it to end.*

A post-storm breeze eventually broke the spell, playing with her hair and chilling Michael to the bone. On the first shiver, Emma wrapped her arms around him even tighter. On the second, she buried her head in his neck and covered every inch of exposed skin with warm kisses. On the third, Emma grabbed Michael's shirt with both hands. Pulling him with her, she took one deliberate step back.

Toward her bedroom.

Emma took a second step back, again pulling Michael with her.

Decision time.

And stopped.

Emma lowered her head, sighed, and gently pushed Michael away. It was far-and-away the hardest thing she ever had to do. She looked up, half-expecting to see confusion or disappointment on Michael's face.

Instead, she found the most beautiful smile.

Uh-oh, Emma thought. *I'm in deep.*

* * *

Now, it was Michael's turn.

Michael took one deliberate step back and removed his senior ring. He held it out in front of him at arm's length, showing it to her. Then he pretended to show it to the non-existent family to her left and to the non-existent family to her right before presenting it to her again.

"Emma Rose Landry," Michael said, "Will you wear my ring?"

Emma beamed.

"Yes, Michael Jeremy Broussard," she replied, before gently taking the ring and holding it out in front of her. "I will wear your ring... and you may call on me again."

Emma slid the ring onto her finger, stepped forward, and kissed Michael softly on the lips. Smiling at Michael, she backed into her room, closed the window, locked the sash, and pulled the curtains together.

Alone on the balcony, Michael stared at his reflection in the window.

"Good night, Em."

* * *

Love may be blind, but Rachel of Judah is not.

Rachel was standing below Emma Landry's balcony, and what she saw was breaking her heart.

"He's eighteen," Saraquel gently reminded her.

"He's married," Rachel replied.

Saraquel shook her head.

"That boy was not at your wedding."

"He knows who he is and the vow he took."

"That vow ended when—"

"No!" Rachel growled. "He chose to remember me."

Saraquel stepped in front and faced her jealous friend.

"The fault is mine, Rachel," she declared. "I violated your Vigil, and now you are paying the price."

Rachel shook her head.

"It is the price I will gladly pay to fight alongside my love as I did tonight," Rachel replied. "And, perhaps, to visit with him on occasion."

Thunder rumbled in the distance.

"Let him go, Sister," Saraquel suggested. "Let him live his mortal life. Return to your Vigil and place your trust in God."

"God only helps those who help themselves."

More thunder from the direction of the departing storm.

"What have I done?" Sara wondered aloud, searching Rachel's eyes for an answer. "Have I destroyed your faith?"

"No," Rachel snapped. "You've set me free."

* * *

Chapter 19: Thanksgiving

For every creature of God is good, and nothing to be refused, if it be received with thanksgiving...
1 Timothy 4:4

Thursday, November 28

Russell Landry loved Thanksgiving.

He sat down with his coffee and checked the news. Four photographs caught his eye. The first was an old photograph of Pope Simon Peter II and Archbishop Hunt. The second was an aerial picture of reddish water along the Gulf Coast. The third was a mangled car on Tulane Avenue. And the fourth was a blurry, almost worthless picture of what might be a crowded Jackson Square.

Russell started with the story about the Pope.

Pope Simon Peter II has made a surprise and top secret trip to New Orleans to visit Archbishop Hunt, who was hospitalized early Tuesday morning with acute appendicitis and developed a life-threatening infection. Archbishop Hunt's friendship with the American Camerlengo was well known, but he has apparently become very close to the Pontiff as well. At a press conference last night, Dr. C.J. Lagarde, M.D., announced that the Archbishop is still weak and will have a nasty scar, but is expected to make a full recovery. To widespread disappointment, the Vatican announced that the Pope will not say any public masses and will make no public appearances while in the Crescent City. The Vatican promised the Holy Father will return soon for an extended stay. The Pontiff is staying at the Notre Dame Seminary on Carrollton Avenue and is scheduled to fly home on Friday. This is the Pope's first trip to New Orleans in more than...

Russell stopped reading and took a sip of his coffee.

"Hey Carol," Russell called to his wife who was scrambling eggs in the kitchen. "Pope's in town."

"Really?"

"Yep." Russell said, starting to read the next story.

A rare red tide has appeared off the coast of Louisiana near Port Fouchon. Red tides are harmful algal blooms that can cause seawater to appear red when it reaches a sufficient concentration. The most common red tide organism is Karenia Brevis. Blooms can last months and adversely affect hundreds of square miles. Red tides can kill fish, birds, and even...

"Hey Carol," Russell called. "Did Alabama's nickname come from one of these nasty red tides in the Gulf?"

"No!" the indignant alumna replied. "We're the Crimson Tide, and we earned our nickname beating Auburn in a sea of red mud. Got that, bucko?"

"Yep," Russell said, taking another sip of coffee from his LSU mug and moving to the next story.

Orleans Parish coroner, Dr. Claude Villere, has issued an autopsy report blaming the fatal car accident early Tuesday morning on the deceased driver, Brother Liam MacLaren, a visiting priest from Scotland. Dr. Villere's autopsy revealed that Brother MacLaren experienced sudden cardiac arrest moments before he lost control and crashed into a telephone pole at the corner of Tulane and Jefferson Davis Parkway. No alcohol was found in his system. The President of Jesuit High School, Father Daniel Finnegan, S.J., and Coach Will Taylor were both injured in the accident. A fourth passenger, Brother Jackson Reid, will accompany Brother MacLaren's ashes back to Scotland tomorrow...

"Hey Carol," Russell called. "Turns out the priest who was driving your brother and Will had a heart attack before he ran into that pole."

"That's so sad," Carol said. "How old was he?"

Russell skimmed the rest of the article, but learned nothing more.

"Doesn't say, but I think Finn told me the guy was my age."

"Well, I want you to get checked out," Carol nagged. "It's been years since you had a physical, hasn't it?"

"Yep," Russell said, taking another sip of coffee and continuing to read.

A private funeral will be held for Brother MacLaren this morning at an undisclosed location. In lieu of flowers, please send donations to Boys Hope...

"Hey Carol, it says here to make donations to Boys Hope," Russell announced. "We're going to see your brother and Will this afternoon. Can we make a donation?"

"Of course," Carol said sitting down at the table with two plates of scrambled eggs and bacon. "Will you handle it?"

"Yep," Russell said, eating a couple of bites before moving on to the next story.

Louisiana may be "Hollywood South," but the NOPD is determined to catch the movie crew who illegally filmed an elaborate sword fight in Jackson Square early Tuesday morning. The NOPD issued a statement last night acknowledging it received dozens of complaints and apologizing for their delay in responding to those calls. The delay was the result of serious technical problems that somehow affected phone lines and police scanners at the NOPD Eighth District Sub-Station on Royal Street. By the time officers arrived, the entire film crew was gone. According to the NOPD statement, a torrential downpour prevented detectives from finding anything that could help identify the actors or the movie. Vieux Carre residents are encouraged to come forward with any photographs or information. So far, only one grainy and dark photograph has emerged....

"Who did you invite today?" Carol asked between bites.

"For Turkey Bowl?"

"I refuse to call it that."

"Well, my dad is coming," Russell said. "Ed gets discharged from the hospital today so I invited him and Michael. Emma said some of Michael's friends are coming, and we invited Finn, Will, Joy, and some of our neighbors. Should be smaller than last year."

"Which neighbors did we invite?"

"Now, sweetie, don't get angry...."

* * *

The better the man, the less needs to be said about his life.

Pope Simon Peter II looked at the group assembled in the small chapel at Jesuit High School to say goodbye to Brother Liam MacLaren. He saw Father Finnegan, Coach Taylor, Michael Broussard, and Colonel Alberg.

The rest of the pews were filled with Guardians who had fought at Jackson Square and wanted to pay their respects.

"Here lies Brother Liam MacLaren, High Steward of the Order of the Judged," the Pope said. "I knew nothing of this man two weeks ago, and I knew nothing of the coming storm. Now, I can't imagine facing it without him.

"Today, I give thanks for Liam MacLaren," the Pope continued. "I give thanks for his courage. I give thanks for his service. I give thanks for his sacrifice, and I pray his soul has found eternal peace. I would say more, but there is a man here who knows him far better than I. Brother Reid should say a few words."

Brother Reid reluctantly stood up, walked to the center of the small circular room, and stood at parade rest.

Reid cleared his throat and decided he was ready to begin.

Until Father Unger opened the chapel door.

* * *

Derrick was in heaven.

"Please pass the oyster dressing, Sheri."

Sheri grabbed and passed the silver tray to Derrick, who did his best not to grimace in pain when his cracked ribs objected.

"Hurts, doesn't it?" asked Dr. Alysha Hill, rhetorically. "Serves you right for dropping that bar on your chest."

"It sure does," Sheri agreed, playing along. "Next time you lift weights, bring a helper, Derrick."

"They're called *spotters*," Derrick corrected her, smiling.

"Well, we're *very* glad you and Brandi are joining us for Thanksgiving brunch," Alysha said to Sheri, ignoring her son.

"Me too!" Brandi declared. "The food is good!"

"I'm glad you like it," Lamar Hill said. "I made it myself."

"Really?" Sheri said, with sincere surprise and admiration.

"Please!" Alysha snorted. "The man can't boil water."

"Yes, well, it's time for our Thanksgiving tradition," Lamar announced, pretending to be embarrassed by his wife's rebuke. "Let's go around the table and everybody say what they're thankful for."

On cue, Alysha and Derrick both groaned.

"You first, Luv," Lamar said.

"Alright, I'm thankful for… for these two," Alysha said, glancing at her husband and son. "They drive me crazy, but they're the best men I know."

Lamar and Derrick smiled with a mixture of embarrassment and pride.

They adore her, Sheri realized. *They really do.*

"Your turn, Sheri."

"I'm thankful for… for the Hill family," Sheri said, smiling appreciatively and rubbing Brandi's back. "For giving Boo a real Thanksgiving meal."

Sheri's voice cracked.

"Well, it just means everything to me," she added, tearing up and struggling to finish. "Especially this year."

Sheri's gratitude silenced the table. Mrs. Hill glanced at Derrick and took Sheri's hand in her own.

"You are always welcome here, sweet girl," Alysha said, starting to get emotional as well. "Besides, I like it when the girls outnumber the boys!"

Sheri collected herself and turned to her sister.

"What are you thankful for, Boo?"

"The orange stuff," Brandi replied, swallowing another spoonful of sweet potato soufflé.

"That's my favorite too," Alysha said. "I'll write down the recipe for you, Sheri."

"You'll what!" Lamar exclaimed.

Everyone jumped.

"My sister has begged you for that recipe since we got married," Lamar reminded her. "And you've never given or offered it to her."

"Well, I don't like your sister," Alysha said, winking at Sheri.

"Alright, it's my turn." Derrick announced, putting an end to his parent's good-natured bickering. "I'm thankful for my new school because…"

"Because you don't want to live in this house anymore," Lamar grumbled.

"Hush, L.J.," Alysha said. "Let the boy finish."

"Because it brought me new friends," Derrick said looking right at Sheri. "Friends who have opened my eyes. Friends who bring out the best in me."

"Oh, Derrick!" Dr. Hill sighed using her napkin to wipe her eyes. "I'm so happy for you."

"Hey, this is supposed to be fun," Lamar declared. "That's enough crying. There's no crying during this tradition. No crying!"

"Leave me be," Mrs. Hill said. "It's your turn anyway."

"About time," Lamar replied before pausing long enough to look at each person at the table.

"I'm thankful for the three beautiful young ladies at this table," Lamar said.

How sweet. He meant every word.

"And I'll ask you all to join me in a toast."

Lamar waited while everyone raised their glass.

"To my son, Derrick," Lamar said. "For finally bringing a girl home for supper. Son, it was worth the wait. Cheers!"

"Cheers!" Mrs. Hill and Derrick said as everyone clanged their glasses in the middle of the table.

"I'm the first girl you've brought home?" a rather surprised Sheri asked Derrick.

"Yes. Does that terrify you?"

"It should," Sheri said with a slightly flirtatious look. "But it doesn't."

* * *

"Villere, Claude Villere."

"Happy Thanksgiving, Doctor Villere. It's Joy."

"Happy Gobble Gobble!" Villere practically yelled into the telephone.

"Happy, uh, Gobble Gobble," Joy said, chuckling at the eccentric coroner. "I'm sorry to disturb you."

"That's alright. I was already disturbed, *right, right, okay?*" Villere joked. "How's Will feeling?

"Better, but he's still pretty sore from the car accident," Joy informed him. "We're going bowling this afternoon."

"I'm sorry to hear that, *okay?*"

"Me too."

"What can I do for you?"

"I was hoping I could ask you a few questions about the MacLaren autopsy."

"Of course." Villere replied in a very different tone. "What do you want to know, Ms. Glapion?"

"Did you perform the autopsy?"

"I did."

"Was there any alcohol in his system?"

"No," Villere replied. "I tested his blood and vitreous fluid."

He's telling the truth, thought Joy.

"Did he have a heart attack?"

"That's what my autopsy report says," Villere replied. "And I don't mean to be rude, but I'd like to get back to my family."

That's not an answer, Joy realized, but Villere would not suffer cross-examination on Thanksgiving. She needed to cut to the chase.

No guts, no glory.

"Doctor, did MacLaren have crossed keys and wings on his right wrist?"

"Joy, do you really think I would miss something like that?"

"No, I don't," Joy practically whispered, knowing that falsely accusing the coroner would get her fired. "But I'd like to see the autopsy photos."

"There are no photos," Villere said with unexpected patience and grace. "And the body was cremated."

And here goes my career....

"How can I be sure of that, Doctor Villere?"

Joy heard Villere sigh on the other end.

"Your heart is in the right place, but you're getting lost in the weeds, Joy," Villere said. "Take a look at this from fifty thousand feet. I performed the autopsy. Your boyfriend and the President of Jesuit High School were in the car with Brother MacLaren. Do you really think there's a conspiracy to protect a serial priest killer? Do you really think that conspiracy includes Will, Father Finnegan, me, and the investigating officer, Detctive Cavet?"

Joy sighed deeply.

I do now.

* * *

"It's my dying request."

"You're not dying, Your Excellency," Cavet reminded Archbishop Hunt.

"Well, it will make me happy."

"I think you should, Uncle Tommy," Officer Matthew Frosch agreed. "Do it because it will make your Archbishop and your nephew happy."

Cavet wavered.

"If I do this, do I have your word you will never ask me again?"

"You do," promised Hunt.

"Ring-a-ling-a-ling!" Cavet chimed, trying to sound like an enthusiastic altar boy. "Ring-a-ling-a-ling!"

Hunt laughed so hard he started coughing.

"Ring-a-ling-a-ling!"

"Enough!" Doctor Lagarde ordered as he walked into the room and grabbed Hunt's chart. "You'll rip open your stitches."

That ended the merriment.

"How are you feeling?" Lagarde asked his patient.

"Grateful," Archbishop Hunt panted, exhausted by a few seconds of laughing. "Grateful my friends here got me to you as quickly as they did."

"How's the pain?"

"I feel stronger," Hunt reported. "But the pain is worse."

"That's actually a good sign," Lagarde reported. "Do you want some pain medication?"

"Would that be unusual after removing an appendix?"

"Yes," Lagarde replied. "But I didn't remove your appendix. I operated on your open stab wound."

"Then I shouldn't," Hunt decided. "I don't want to raise any red flags."

"Suit yourself," Lagarde said, lowering his voice. "But I don't think anyone at this hospital suspects you were in a sword fight."

"How are your other patients, C.J.?" Cavet asked.

"Trey's much better," Lagarde said. "I can't say what cardiac arrhythmia he experienced, but he's damn lucky that girl performed CPR. She saved his life."

"Will he ever be—"

"A hundred percent? Absolutely," Lagarde assured him. "I told his parents he probably had mono, and he spent Tuesday and Wednesday in bed. I'm going over there now to tell them the test came back negative, and he must have had a bad virus. I'll do some more testing when he's at full strength."

"How about Jacob?"

"Healing at the Broussard house," Lagarde said, shaking his head. "But it was touch and go there for a while. I thought he was going to die, or whatever angels do when they lose too much blood."

"Thank you, C.J.," Hunt said. "I hope we won't need your services again, but I fear there will be more casualties before this war is over."

"I'll do my part," Lagarde promised as he wrote something in Hunt's chart. "And right now, that means kicking everybody out so you can get some sleep."

Matthew Frosch walked over and put his hand on top of Archbishop Hunt's.

"I hope you feel better, Your Excellency. Happy Thanksgiving."

"Thank you Matty, and Happy Thanksgiving," Hunt replied. "I'll see you in our Cathedral for the Christmas Vigil. I may even let you serve as an altar boy and swing the silver censer."

"I would be honored," Matt said sincerely before walking out the room.

Detective Cavet walked over and took the Archbishop's hand.

"That boy seems different," Hunt observed.

"You're telling me," Cavet chuckled. "He's allergic to incense. Holding the censer might just kill him."

Archbishop Hunt smiled and cupped Cavet's hands in his.

"Thank you, Tommy," Hunt said, holding his hand for an extra moment. "Thank you for saving my life."

"You're welcome," Cavet said, smiling warmly. "I'll visit you tomorrow."

"Will you do something for me first?" Hunt asked.

"Of course."

"Do the bells again."

"You promised!" Cavet objected.

"Forgive me," Hunt chuckled. "I lied."

"You lied?"

"Yes, I lied," Hunt confessed. "Tommy, I'm no angel."

* * *

If you do not feel welcomed at a funeral, rethink your life.

Father Unger looked around the small chapel, slipped into one of the back pews and found himself sitting next to a beautiful, raven-haired woman. When Unger finally stopped moving, Jax cleared his throat again.

He's just trying to call attention to my arrival, thought Unger. *So juvenile.*

"The Order saved my life when I was ten," Jax announced. "But it was Liam MacLaren who gave my life direction and meaning. He believed in me. He showed me what I could become. What all men can become. He was strong. He had faith. He was truly a man of God, and he died saving..."

Jax stopped abruptly and glanced at Unger.

Saving what? wondered Unger. *The man drove into a telephone pole.*

"He died serving God."

Oh, "serving." Yes, well, that makes more sense.

"He died among friends," Jax said, deciding to cut his eulogy short because of Unger. "He died well."

Jax walked over to the casket.

"I'll see you in the City of God, Brother," Jax said as the line of people who wanted to pay their respects formed behind him. That line started with Michael Broussard.

"Thank you for standing with me," Michael said, placing a plastic yellow ring in the casket. "Soldiers win battles, and generals get all the credit."

Why is Michael quoting Napoleon? Unger wondered. *That boy is very strange.*

"I'll never forget you," Michael said. "And I will always be grateful."

Michael was followed by Coach Will Taylor, who said nothing. He simply removed a Silver Star from his pocket and gently placed it inside the casket. Then he made the sign of the cross and moved on.

Will was followed by Father Finnegan, a large man with his left arm in a sling, and a man in a black jacket.

"Oh my God!" Unger gasped.

"Silence!" the lady next to him demanded, never taking her eyes off the front of the chapel. "Do not take His name in vain, priest. I will not stand for it."

"I'm sorry, but I think that's ..." Unger started to say before regaining his composure. "Look here, I don't care for your tone. Who are you, young lady?"

The lady slowly turned her head and batted her beautiful eyes.

"Michael Broussard's wife."

* * *

Father Finnegan decided to take one for the team.

"Father Unger, may I speak with you outside?" Finn asked as he quickly reached Unger's pew.

"Daniel, this woman is delusional. She thinks she is married to—"

"We need to talk outside," Finn said quickly as the woman's face began to contort with rage. "It's important."

"Very well," Unger said, standing up and exiting the pew while staring at the back of the man in the leather jacket. "Daniel, doesn't that man look like the Holy Father?"

"Who?" Finn asked, gently steering Unger toward the chapel door and without looking back into the chapel. "The man with a sling?"

"No, the man in the black jacket!" Unger said indignantly as he stepped outside the chapel.

"A little," Finn said quickly, closing the door behind them.

* * *

Saraquel felt the tension in the Great Chamber.

“We had thousands of volunteers to replace the Guardians lost at Jackson Square and to defend the city perimeter,” Sara reported, even though nobody was listening to her.

“In addition to the Legions that now defend the City, I’ve assembled elite Old Guard units to personally protect Michael and the Pope. I’ve also hand-picked Guardians for Thomas Cavet, Daniel Finnegan, Joshua Jackson Reid, Matthew Frosch, Karl Alberg, Patrick Hunt, William Taylor, and Sheri Stevens.”

“What about Derrick Hill?” Raphael asked. “Who did you select to serve as Derrick’s Guardian?”

“I have decided to resign from the Seven,” Saraquel announced. “And to swear the Guardian’s oath for Derrick Hill.”

“That is a very generous offer,” Raphael informed her diplomatically, well aware Sara was the lone dissenter when the Seven voted to move Derrick to Jesuit High School. “The Seven will consider your request for a sabbatical, but I speak for the Seven when I say we would miss your counsel. This was a great victory, but the war has just started.”

“A great victory?” Raguel repeated, sounding surprised. “Why do you consider it a great victory, Brother?”

“Please do not start with this, Rags!” Uriel begged.

“I am not starting trouble,” Raguel promised, sounding mentally exhausted. “Above all others, I want Raphael to be correct. I just want to hear his reasons.”

“Well, we saved Michael,” Raphael replied. “We saved the Head of the Roman Catholic Church and the Archbishop of New Orleans. And we rid ourselves of Marcellus and Dante. Lucifer’s rage must be terrible.”

“I am not so sure,” Raguel sighed.

“What do you fear, Brother?” Raphael asked.

“I fear we have been deceived.”

“What does not ring true about this battle?” Raphael wondered.

Raguel looked at Uriel.

“Marcellus’ death,” Uriel reluctantly answered.

“Why?”

“Michael was not skilled enough to defeat Marcellus,” Uriel explained. “The boy shows great promise, but I only trained him for a few days.”

Silence filled the Great Chamber.

"Maybe Marcellus *was* loyal to Michael after all," Saraquel proposed. "Maybe he was the double agent Lucifer always suspected him to be."

"Perhaps," Raguel said, his voice filled with resignation. "And perhaps we should assume everything has happened according to Lucifer's plan."

"Agreed," Uriel said, returning to the war table.

"Agreed," Saraquel said, though it obviously pained her.

Raphael was not as quick to agree.

"Let us say your fear is justified," Raphael eventually said, refusing to succumb so easily to paranoia. "What do we do now, Brother?"

"We focus on the questions we can't answer," Raguel suggested. "Like who is the Founder and how did he know Marcellus and Dante were going to ambush Michael in the parking lot?"

"Forget the Founder," Uriel said, resting his hand on the hilt of his sword. "We need to find the angel who protected Michael in the parking lot and killed Agrippa in Jackson Square."

"Aye, Brother," Raphael said. "Let us begin by avenging our friend."

* * *

Brother Reid closed the casket.

"This concludes our celebration of Brother MacLaren's life," Pope Simon Peter II said. "Thank you, my friends, for coming to pay your respect."

Most of the Guardians disappeared down the aisle of the small chapel, while Michael walked over to where Rachel was standing.

"I have something to ask of you, Rachel," Michael said, taking her hand in his.

"Ask me, my love."

"Jacob explained how vigils work," Michael said. "And I want you to return to your Vigil until my, uh…"

"Service in-theatre."

"Until my service in-theatre is over," Michael said. "Will you do that for me?"

Rachel smiled.

“This is the second time you have asked this of me, husband,” Rachel said. “But War has come, and I won’t make the same promise I made last time.”

“A promise you broke,” Michael noted.

“To save you from dying in a parking lot,” Rachel reminded him with a mischievous smile.

“True,” Michael admitted. “But this time, I’m asking you because--”

“But…” Rachel interrupted, determined not to let Michael finish his request. “There is much to be done in the City of God. So I will say goodbye for now, my love.”

Rachel stepped closer, cupped Michael’s face, gently kissed him, and then pressed her perfect lips next to his right ear.

“When the Final Battle is over, and your service ends, your memory will return,” she whispered. “You will remember me, and you *will* choose to forget her.”

Michael did not reply, even though he knew exactly what Rachel wanted him to say. Knew exactly what words would make her happy.

Rachel smiled a sad smile, released him, and took a step back.

“Give ‘em hell,” she said loud enough for the others to hear.

“I’ll try,” Michael promised, returning her smile.

Rachel turned and disappeared down the center aisle, followed by Kadmus and the remaining Guardians. Only mortals remained, and the chapel fell silent.

“What happens now?” Michael asked Brother Reid.

Reid looked confused by the question.

“I take Brother MacLaren back to Scotland and bury him.”

“No, I mean. What happens to me?” Michael asked. “Isn’t this the part where you take me to some gothic castle and train me to kill Lucifer?”

Reid looked at Will and at Pope Simon Peter II before answering Michael.

“Well, we do have a castle.”

* * *

Jacob was standing on the sidelines near mid-field.

The game was still scoreless, but the Saint Augustine Marching One Hundred Band was rocking Tad Gormley Stadium to celebrate a spectacular Keith Hill catch against the stout West Monroe Rebel defense.

Jacob scanned the stadium and located his *protelos*.

Michael and Emma were sitting on the Purple Knights' side of the stadium next to Derrick, Sheri, Trey and Adele. All of them were clapping for Derrick's cousin, who was jogging back to the huddle.

Jacob looked over at the end zone where the Old Guard always gathered and was surprised to see Agrippa the Great waiving him over.

He smiled and quickly joined them.

"Welcome, Brother Jacob!" Agrippa said, warmly embracing him in front of a hundred members of the Old Guard. "You fought well at Jackson Square."

"Thank you, Brother," Jacob replied as many of the Old Guard nodded in agreement with Agrippa. "It's good to see you."

"Where's our boy?"

"Michael's in the stands with Derrick," Jacob reported, glancing over at the stands. As he did, Jacob caught a Novice staring at him from the far sideline. The Novice held Jacob's gaze just long enough to nod respectfully before continuing his scan of the stadium.

"He admires you, Brother!" Agrippa said, slapping Jacob on the back.

"Only because I'm with you," Jacob assured him.

"False modesty!" Agrippa exclaimed. "The Novice admires you because you earned his respect. He'll follow you and fight for you. But remember, Brother, you must lead from the front."

"Aye, Brother."

Agrippa smiled and stole one last look at Derrick in the stands.

"It is time for you and Kadmus to lead," Agrippa told Jacob. "And it is time for me to go."

Suddenly Jacob remembered something he had forgotten about the Battle of Jackson Square. Something he had tried very hard to forget.

Agrippa put both hands on Jacob's shoulders. His eyes burned with an intensity that terrified Jacob.

"My spirit could not depart until I said this unto you," Agrippa said seconds before Jacob awoke inside the Broussard house.

"Kill Jackson Reid or kill Michael Broussard."

* * *

Emma finally found her happy.

She had all of her people with her. Uncle Finn was bowling on Lane One with the two older gentlemen he brought with him. Michael, Trey and Adele were waiting for her to start bowling on Lane Two.

Coach Will and his girlfriend, Joy, were bowling on Lane Three with Judge Landry and the Cavets. Somehow, Michael had forgiven the prosecutor and the detective who threw him in jail.

Well, technically, Paw-Paw threw him in jail.

Emma's parents were supposed to be bowling on Lane Four, but they were sitting and talking with Ed Broussard, who had come straight from the hospital.

Emma was in such a good mood that she decided to stop and deal with Lane Five.

"Hi, Derrick," Emma said. "How are you feeling? Heard you cracked your ribs while lifting weights."

"I'm still hurting," Derrick admitted before reciting his well-rehearsed story. "But it's my own fault. I was trying to bench press too much weight and dropped the bar on my chest."

"Well, no bowling for you," Emma said before addressing Derrick's date. "Happy Thanksgiving, Sheri."

"Happy Thanksgiving, Emma," Sheri replied. "Thank you for inviting us."

"Well, who do we have here?" Emma asked sweetly when she saw the smiling seven-year-old.

"This is my sister, Brandi," Sheri said. "And this is her first time bowling."

"Hello, Brandi," Emma said warmly. "It's nice to meet you."

"You're pretty," Brandi giggled.

"I like you!" Emma exclaimed. "I think you and your sister are very pretty too."

"We are!" Brandi agreed.

"Yes, you are!" Emma chuckled. "Hey, do you want me to put the rails up?"

"That would be great," Sheri said. "And thank you, Emma. Really."

Emma put the rails up and flashed Brandi a thumbs-up. As she moved on to the next lane, Emma was a little less mystified by Trey's recent declaration that he had been "dead wrong" about Sheri.

Maybe there is more to her than meets the eye.

"How are you feeling, Mr. Broussard?" Emma asked as she reached Lane Four.

"The doctors said I'll live," Ed replied.

"Well, you take it easy today," Emma begged.

"Yes ma'am," Ed promised. "You sound like your mother."

"What a terrible thing to say!" Emma joked, already moving to Lane Three.

"Hey, Paw-Paw!" Emma said, giving him a long hug.

"Do you need anything?"

"We're good, pumpkin," Judge Landry assured her while he watched Detective Cavet pick up the spare. "How's your little friend?"

"Be nice, Paw-Paw!" Emma warned before walking toward Lane Two. "I know the owners!"

Emma saw Michael smiling at her as she approached Lane One.

"You're up, Em!" Michael said when she arrived.

Emma gave Michael a quick kiss on the cheek and grabbed her bowling ball. She took a deep breath, exhaled, and started toward the foul line.

"Strike!" Emma yelled as she knocked down all the pins. She raised her right hand in front of Michael. "High five!"

Michael reluctantly returned it.

"Nice high five!" a weakened Trey teased from where he sat. "I haven't seen one of those in years."

"Emma has a problem," Michael announced. "She high-fives people way too much. It's a sickness. She can't help herself."

Emma folded her arms and pretended to be indignant.

"Do they have interventions for high-fiving?" Trey asked Adele.

"No, but they do for rudeness," Adele said, siding with Emma. "We should stage an intervention for you two."

"You tell 'em!" Emma exclaimed, high-fiving Adele, who played along perfectly.

"Hey, don't do that!" Michael begged Adele as he sat down next to her. "Please don't encourage her."

"Why?" Emma asked.

"Because that's my job," Michael replied plainly, before glancing down at Emma's hands and lowering his voice.

"Looks like someone's not wearing my ring."

Emma reached into the pocket of her favorite jeans and pulled out Michael's class ring. The bottom of the band had several layers of athletic tape.

"I've tried everything," Emma promised. "But it's too big for me to wear."

Before Michael could think of a solution, the kind and familiar-looking man who had arrived with Uncle Finn walked over from Lane One.

"Try this, young lady," he said, handing her a length of red cord. "And keep the ring close to your heart."

"Thank you," Emma said. "That's very sweet."

Emma slipped the cord through the ring and allowed the nice man to tie it behind her neck.

"Yes," Michael said. "But the cord should be blue because Jesuit--"

Michael stopped talking abruptly, and Emma followed his eyes toward the main counter, where she spotted Gavin Driscoll walking her way.

Smiling that smile.

* * *

"Happy Thanksgiving!"

"Gavin Driscoll," Emma drawled, noticing that Michael and his friends remained seated. "Why am I not surprised?"

"Because you know how much I love Turkey Bowl!" Gavin said jovially. "And because we need to talk, Babe."

"Gavin, I had this whole big thing prepared," Emma advised. "But I think I'm just going to ask you to leave."

"What are you talking about?" Gavin asked rhetorically before stepping a little closer to Emma. "We always spend Thanksgivings together."

"Spent," Emma corrected him. "We always *spent* Thanksgiving together when we were dating, which we are not."

"But, Babe—"

"Gavin, you know the way out," Emma said, pointing toward the front door. "Please leave."

"Hey, I'm not going anywhere until we talk," Gavin said, gently grabbing and lowering Emma's pointing hand.

Emma looked down at the gigantic paw now gripping her wrist. It was the second chance she had been praying for. But before she could give Gavin a piece of her mind, she heard a voice say:

"Let go of her hand, son."

* * *

"Mind your own business, old man."

Gavin flashed a warning look at the old man in the black leather jacket as a much larger man with a broken right arm moved quickly toward Lane Two.

"Hey, uh, er..." Michael stammered, unable to remember how Father Finnegan had introduced Pope Simon Peter II when they arrived at the alley.

"Rocky," the Pope reminded him.

"Right," Michael said, unable to bring himself to repeat the moniker. "Emma's got this."

"Yeah Rock-O," Gavin barked. "Grab a seat. Emma and I have..."

With catlike quickness, Emma stepped on Gavin's foot, punched Gavin in the stomach, and kneed him in the groin.

Twice.

"Whoa!" Trey exclaimed.

Gavin made an inhuman noise and dropped to the ground.

Father Finnegan and Will walked over, helped Gavin off the ground, and half-carried him out the bowling alley with Emma on their six.

"Yes, I see what you mean, Michael," the Pope said a moment later. "We could have used her in Jackson Square."

"We could have used her in World War II," Colonel Alberg chuckled.

"Michael, if I may ask," the Pope continued. "Is she your girlfriend?"

"Yes, sir."

The Bishop of Rome, Primate of Italy, Supreme Pontiff of the Universal Church, the Vicar of Christ, and the Successor of Saint Peter smiled a grandfatherly smile.

"I shall pray for you."

* * *

Another storm had arrived.

Thunder could somehow be heard above the cacophony of bowling. Michael whispered an excuse in Emma's ear, gently patted his dad on the back, and hurried outside. By the time Michael reached the bottom of the stairwell, the sky was getting dark and a heavy rain was about to fall on the Crescent City.

She's still with us. She never left us, Michael thought, as he always did while watching the arrival of a storm. But this time he knew why.

"You should be in bed, Jacob."

"Enough, Brother," Jacob said, appearing next to him. "You worry too much."

Michael smiled. His very public awakening seemed like a million years ago.

"Where's Brother Reid?" Jacob asked.

"Headed back to Scotland to bury Brother MacLaren," Michael reported. "But he said he would come back for me."

Of that I am certain, thought Jacob.

Together, Michael and Jacob waited in silence, side by side, for Kathy Broussard's favorite moment. They did not have to wait long.

One by one, the street lamps sprang to life.

"Clever storm," Michael said, imitating her voice. "It tricked the lights."

Michael smiled as he remembered her and the way her auburn hair danced in the wind. Almost immediately, he noticed that the closest lamp had not been fooled. But this time, he did not give it a second thought.

To hell with any light that does not stand against the darkness.

*   *   *

"Michael!"

Emma Landry's torso sprang out the entrance like a jack-in-the-box.

"Will popped the question!" Emma squealed. "And Joy said yes!"

"That's great!" Michael responded, genuinely happy for his coach. "Hey, Em, say hello to my very good friend, Jacob."

"Hello, very good friend Jacob!" the deliriously happy Emma said, still leaning out the door.

"Hello, Emma Landry," Jacob replied affectionately.

"Michael, Will says he needs to ask you something and it sounds important," Emma said excitedly. "So get your cute butt back in here!"

Emma disappeared inside and sprinted up the stairs like her hair was on fire.

"Looks like I have to go," Michael said, shaking his head.

"You don't *have* to do anything," Jacob teased. "You're the Supreme Commander of the Armies of God."

"Maybe," Michael chuckled. "But she's Emma Landry."

Thunder rumbled ominously overhead, drawing their eyes upward. The storm did not approve of their banter, and it prompted Michael to ask the question that had been plaguing him.

"How bad is it going to get?"

"The Light-Bringer is coming," Jacob replied grimly. "He will fill the sky with the Fallen and sacrifice everything to defeat you."

"Right. So… not that bad," Michael said sarcastically.

"We have time," Jacob assured him. "Lucifer has waited centuries for the End of Days, and your defeat of Marcellus marked its arrival. He will gather the Fallen to him with the promise of the Final Battle and wait until he has the advantage."

Michael's concerned eyes glanced at Jacob.

"Aye, Brother," Jacob replied, answering his unspoken question. "We *will* be ready, and we *will* prevail."

Cloud-to-ground lightning, the likes of which the world had never seen, struck in the distance. The corresponding thunder arrived sooner, and was far more terrible, than either imagined.

The End.

Epilogue

And the angel answering said unto him, I am Gabriel,
that stand in the presence of God...
Luke 1:19

Saturday, December 14

Tulane-and-Broad favors beat the crap out of other favors.

Attorney Lamar Joseph Hill did a Tulane-and-Broad favor for the owner of the Spotted Cat Music Club on Frenchmen Street. Let's just say the owner's nephew was never prosecuted for stripping naked and climbing a greased pole at the Royal Sonesta Hotel.

Laissez les bon temps rouler!

Lamar called in that favor for Trey and Derrick. Trey had always dreamt of playing jazz in the Marigny, and Derrick wanted to make that dream come true. Naturally, the owner of the Spotted Cat was more than happy to let the boy play one song with the band.

But only one song.

"You've been practicing, right?" Michael asked as they paused to allow Adele and Emma to enter the club.

"Not really," Trey admitted. "But something clicked after Jackson Square."

"Something clicked?"

"Don't worry," Trey assured him with unfamiliar confidence before stepping inside. "I got this."

Michael held the door and his tongue.

"This is going to be epic," Derrick chuckled as he and Sheri walked past Michael.

The Spotted Cat was packed. But, for the first time in Spotted Cat history, someone had written the word "saved" on six pieces of paper taped to six seats. Derrick and his friends knew the seats were reserved for them, but they waited at the bar while the band finished a very respectable rendition of Dizzy Gillespie's "A Night In Tunisia."

"Small stage, huh?" whispered Sheri when she saw the four gentlemen playing in the alcove by the Frenchmen Street window.

"Cool, right?" replied Derrick with a smile so irresistible Sheri found herself nodding in agreement.

"Thank you," the seventy-four-year-old saxophonist breathed into the microphone after the song ended, prompting the six friends to take their seats.

In his peripheral vision, Michael saw the hostess catch the saxophonist's attention and point at Trey.

"Thank you very kindly," he continued. "Well, ladies and gentlemen, we've got a real treat for you tonight. Trey Charbonnet is here."

"Wahooo!" Emma squealed. "Doctor Trey!"

Derrick snorted and Adele clapped.

Michael just shook his head.

"Make her stop," Trey begged while removing his trumpet and sliding the case under his chair.

"Doctor Trey!" Emma fearlessly repeated, inspiring a splattering of applause.

"Yeah you rite! Let's see if we can get Doctor Trey up here," the saxophonist urged while winking at Emma, who winked right back.

Trey stood-up and started walking toward the stage. After two steps, he stopped to let a middle-aged waitress pass. Something about her was familiar.

Something about her auburn hair.

"Come on up! Don't be shy now!" the saxophonist said, trying to coax Trey, who was still standing in the same spot.

"Alright now, let's show him some real love!"

"Doc-tor Trey!" Emma clapped emphatically. The crowd instantly yielded to her will and joined her in the chant.

Suddenly, Trey turned around and looked at Michael.

"Doc-tor Trey!"

"Listen, Michael," Trey demanded. "I just remembered someone... I mean, *something*."

"Doc-tor Trey!

"You have to stay away from Scotland."

"Doc-tor Trey!"

"What?"

"Doc-tor Trey!"

"Listen to me. You have to stay *the hell* away from Scotland!"

"Doc-tor Trey!"

"Why?"

"Promise me," Trey insisted.

"Doc-tor Trey!"

"Just get up there!" Michael exclaimed, pointing at the stage.

Trey relented and took the stage, silencing the crowd.

"Let's play 'Take Five,'" Trey said as he sat down on the cracked leather stool.

The saxophonist quickly covered the microphone.

"Son, wouldn't you rather try something a little easier?"

"No, we're good," Trey assured him.

The band glanced at each other, not sure what to do.

"It's like watching a car wreck," Emma confessed as the confused musician set down his saxophone and moved to the upright piano. "I can't look away."

A moment later, the piano played the first bars of "Take Five" and was quickly joined by experienced drums and a soulful bass guitar.

Trey waited a few bars and then launched into an absolutely brilliant version of the Paul Desmond classic.

Every jaw hit the ground.

Trey's friends watched with joy and disbelief as the Spotted Cat fell in love with Doctor Trey. Outside, people on Frenchmen Street shoved their way into the club and crammed around the window to watch.

When the song ended, the entire neighborhood erupted.

"Well alright!" the bass player said, grabbing the microphone as the other members of the band shook their heads and clapped. "How 'bout dat!"

"Doc-tor Trey!" the hysterical crowd chanted again.

"How 'bout dat!"

"Doc-tor Trey!"

"Can we get him to play one more?" he asked the rabid crowd.

"Doc-tor Trey!"

Trey humbly nodded his agreement and politely gestured for the crowd to stop and for his hysterical friends to sit down.

"Thank you. Yes, I will play one more," Trey promised, unconsciously working the trumpet valves as he spoke.

"This next song was written in 1952," Trey continued after the crowd quieted down. "I want to dedicate it to a special young lady here tonight."

Trey locked eyes with a beaming Adele.

"Her name is Miss Adele Fontenot," Trey said. "And the song is called 'My One and Only Love.'"

Trey started solo this time, and the piano joined a stanza later. It was masterful and moving. The crowd hung on every note. Mesmerized.

And then *something* happened.

At the bridge, Trey abandoned the 32-bar melody and indulged in improvisation. The ecstatic pianist stayed with him, and Trey created brilliant solo melodies over the piano's chord progression.

It was haunting and sweet. It married the best of jazz and blues, effortlessly flirting with big band and ska. It took everyone on an emotional journey. Innocence and happiness, followed by struggle and loss. True sadness and pain.

Tears rolled down Adele's expressionless face. Sheri grabbed Derrick's hand, and Emma placed her head on Michael's shoulder.

The song held them. Something in the music offered hope and promised salvation. And, slowly but surely, Trey led them out of the darkness and into a raucous celebration of light and life that reached a feverish pitch. It was exhausting and liberating. And then it was over.

Nobody in the band or in the crowd moved.

They stared at Trey, and Trey stared at his horn. Eventually, a single clap broke the spell and sparked a wild standing ovation that seemed to last forever.

Michael glanced toward the door and was surprised to see a concerned-looking Jacob standing in the doorway. He quickly made his way out of the club and found all of the Guardians waiting anxiously for him.

"Wasn't that amazing?" Michael said, still shaking his head.

Jacob said nothing, but looked over at Kadmus.

"I know it sounds crazy because he was improvising," Michael continued. "But it sounded so familiar. I swear I've heard him play it before."

"You have," Kadmus replied matter-of-factly. "Many times. In the City of God."

"Wait. What?"

Kadmus abruptly turned to a member of the Old Guard.

"Go to the Seven," Kadmus ordered. "Tell them we found Brother Gabriel."

Right where they said we would.

*   *   *

Acknowledgments

To Mom, for driving me to the Little Professor Book Store.
To Paw-Paw, for beating knots on head.
To Mr. Wehrman, for having the front steps we needed.
To Mr. Torre, for not falling off the carport in a Santa suit.
To the Flying Fontanas, Crows, and the Higgins family for Sunday nights.
To Mrs. Ruddy, for sitting next to me at the 2nd grade Holy Name of Jesus awards assembly.
To Brother Gregory, for Friday Jeopardy and Frisbee golf.
To Mrs. Tarantino, for reading my "short" story and not laughing.
To Mrs. Alexander, for sending me a postcard from Wales.
To Raymond S. Rizzo '32, for playing catch.
To Fr. Harry Tompson, S.J. '54, for the hug.
To Trey, for the extra cup of water at Scout Island.
To the College of the Holy Cross, for putting me in Hanselman One.
To Prof. Joseph Lawrence, for loving his job.
To Dad, for not killing Prof. Lawrence when I changed my major.
To Neil, for making sure I turned 21 in the *waiting room* of the jail.
To Janet, for making a good man better (and for the godson).
To Fr. Phillip Postell, S.J. '56, for the job and the ride to Pensacola.
To Fr. Anthony McGinn, S.J. '66, for con-celebrating our wedding.
To Barrett, for always believing in me.
To Bobbie, for figuring out (eventually) how to dial 9-1-1.
To Dr. Emory, and the team at Ochsner, for the second chance.
To Brad George Theard, for giving us Kelly.
To Kelly, for loving pizza.
To Nanette, who flips ahead until she sees "Emma."
To Eric and Gwen, for Thanksgiving Eve.
To Shannon and Mike, for my sanity. Geaux Outlaws!
To Ed, for introducing me to Deborah, who makes dreams come true.
To Claire, Katie & Molly… for this Wonderful Life.

About the Author

Jerry Glas was born in New Orleans and grew up loving the people that Michael Broussard tries to save in Vigil.

Jerry is a proud graduate of Jesuit High School. He was the 1987 State Champion in Lincoln-Douglas Debate. And, thanks to a rash of injuries at his position, he also started at defensive end for the Jays' 13-12 playoff loss, which was not entirely his fault.

Jerry continued his Jesuit education at the College of the Holy Cross in Worcester, MA, where he earned a bachelor's degree in philosophy and was awarded the Flatley Medal during commencement. The following year, he earned a master's degree in philosophy from the University of Toronto School of Graduate Studies.

After graduate school, Jerry returned home and taught Sacred Scripture and History of Church at Jesuit High School before attending the Paul M. Hebert Law Center at Louisiana State University, where he earned his Juris Doctor.

After law school, Jerry served as a Senior Assistant District Attorney at the Office of the District Attorney for Orleans Parish, trying more than fifty jury trials to verdict at "Tulane and Broad."

Since 1999, Jerry has been a trial lawyer at the law firm of Deutsch Kerrigan, LLP, where he serves as the Vice-Chair of the Civil Litigation Department. You can learn more about him on the firm's website, deutschkerrigan.com.

Jerry and Claire have been married for more than eighteen years. They have two wonderful daughters, a black miniature schnauzer, and a mild addiction to the crabmeat salad at Clancy's.